Advance Praise for *Fast Girls* by Elise Hooper

"*Fast Girls* is a compelling, thrilling look at what it took to be a female Olympian in prewar America. Rich with historical detail and brilliant storytelling, the book follows three athletes on their path to compete—and win—in a man's world. Brava to Elise Hooper for bringing these inspiring heroines to the wide audience they so richly deserve."

—Tara Conklin, *New York Times* bestselling author of
The Last Romantics and *The House Girl*

"*Fast Girls* is a high-speed, heart-pounding romp as ambitious as its trio of track-star heroines. Golden girl Betty, underestimated African American phenom Louise, and awkward farmgirl Helen make three very different heroines, but they are united by fast feet and big dreams. Their fight to compete in the 1936 Berlin Olympics in the face of sexism, racism, and the rising tide of fascism makes for poignant, inspirational reading. A gold medal read from Elise Hooper!"

—Kate Quinn, *New York Times* and
USA Today bestselling author

"In *Fast Girls,* a novel about three remarkable women and their journey to the 1936 Berlin Olympics, Elise Hooper seamlessly interweaves history and fiction, and the results are kinetic, mesmerizing, and terrifically entertaining. Her frank depiction of the obstacles faced by her heroines, all real-life champions, brings to stunning life three women whose stories have been long overlooked but whose courage and groundbreaking achievements have endured. This is a wonderful novel from an accomplished historian and ferociously talented writer, and it will surely appeal to anyone with an interest in the pioneering women who paved the rocky and uphill way for today's female Olympians."

—Jennifer Robson, author of
The Gown: A Novel of the Royal Wedding

"*Fast Girls* will hurl you down the track of American history and have you rooting for some of the toughest underdogs ever to aspire to Olympic gold. Three of the fastest girls in history finally get their day in the sun, and we get to bask in their glory. I couldn't put this one down."

—Kerri Maher, author of
The Kennedy Debutante and *The Girl in White Gloves*

"Based on the real lives of three female Olympians in the 1920s and '30s, *Fast Girls* is a moving novel of strength, courage, and ultimately perseverance. Expertly researched and deftly crafted, this novel is a fascinating portrait of what it took to survive and thrive as a female athlete at this moment in history. I was absolutely captivated by the lives, struggles, and triumphs of Betty, Helen, and Louise."

—Jillian Cantor, *USA Today* bestselling author of
The Lost Letter and *In Another Time*

"An exhilarating journey that begins with the humble beginnings of promising female runners and culminates in their inspiring and obstacle-filled quests for Olympic glory. I fell in love with the characters and their stories of determination, hope, friendship, grit, and the strength of the human spirit. Perfect for readers who want to be motivated by strong women and their pursuit of seemingly impossible dreams."

—Susie Orman Schnall, author of
The Subway Girls and *We Came Here to Shine*

FAST
GIRLS

ALSO BY ELISE HOOPER

Learning to See
The Other Alcott

FAST GIRLS

A Novel of the 1936 Women's Olympic Team

ELISE HOOPER

WILLIAM MORROW
An Imprint of HarperCollins*Publishers*

PS™ is a trademark of HarperCollins Publishers.

FAST GIRLS. Copyright © 2020 by Elise Hooper. All rights reserved. Printed in the United States of America. No part of this book may be used or reproduced in any manner whatsoever without written permission except in the case of brief quotations embodied in critical articles and reviews. For information address Harper-Collins Publishers, 195 Broadway, New York, NY 10007.

HarperCollins books may be purchased for educational, business, or sales promotional use. For information please email the Special Markets Department at SPsales@harpercollins.com.

FIRST EDITION

Designed by Diahann Sturge

Title page image © Sergio Rojo / Shutterstock, Inc.

Library of Congress Cataloging-in-Publication Data has been applied for.

ISBN 978-0-06-293799-5

20 21 22 23 24 LSC 10 9 8 7 6 5 4 3 2 1

For all who support young athletes,
no matter the time of day, weather, location, or score

Historical Note

During the 1920s and '30s, "athletics" referred to track and field events, but given that this word has expanded over the years to include many different types of sporting events, the modern label of "track and field" is used throughout this novel.

All newspaper stories, letters, telegrams, and memos in this book have been created by the author and reflect the language and attitudes used to describe women athletes during their era.

PART 1

July 1928–December 1929

1.

July 1928
New York City

BEFORE THEY LEFT THE PRINCE GEORGE HOTEL, BETTY'S mother warned her to be careful aboard the steamship and avoid the girls from California. Apparently they were a loose set, something to do with year-round sun and mild temperatures softening one's moral fiber. Up until that point Betty had only been half listening, but now she perked to attention. A roommate from some glamorous-sounding location like Santa Monica or Santa Barbara—wouldn't that be a lark? With a series of decisive clicks, Betty fastened the latches closed on her suitcase and started for the door. Maybe if she was lucky, some of those objectionable girls from California would be her cabin-mates aboard the S.S. *President Roosevelt*.

Minutes later, Betty and her mother, Mrs. Robinson, sat in the back of a taxicab on their way to Pier 86. A heat wave had been pressing over New York City for a week, and Betty fanned herself while her mother fussed with their taxicab driver over the best route to take. Traffic clogged the street and newspaperboys hawked their wares, bobbing from one stopped vehicle to the next. Their driver bought one and rested it against the steering wheel, studying the headlines.

"Are you sure this is the fastest way?" Betty's mother huffed.

"Ma'am, if there was a faster one, we'd be taking it, I promise. Now pray to the Virgin Mary that my engine doesn't overheat." He crossed himself.

As if on cue, the automobile shuddered and her mother inhaled sharply. "Pray all you want, but my daughter simply cannot be late. She's on the Olympic team set to depart for Amsterdam at noon."

"That so?" He turned around to inspect Betty.

"Please, sir, keep your eyes on the road," her mother said.

"But we're not moving."

Her mother folded her arms across her chest. "So I noticed."

"I didn't realize there were lady Olympians."

"This is the first year women will be competing in running events," her mother said, and though she still sounded annoyed with the man, the unmistakable pride in her voice made Betty sit straighter.

"Running doesn't seem like a very ladylike business. Aren't you worried she'll become a bit manly if she keeps this up?" he asked, squinting at her from under the rim of his porkpie hat. "I could see encouraging rowing. Builds up the chest, you know." He smirked.

"What an absurd notion, and anyway, she's not running the marathon or undertaking anything too dangerous. She's a sprinter."

"If you say so," said the driver, cracking his knuckles. Clearly, he was enjoying rankling her mother, and Betty hid her glee by turning to gaze at the throngs of people on the sidewalks. Heat rippled in the air above the pavement.

"Here we are," the driver said, nosing his taxicab into a line of vehicles at the edge of the road. Band music floated over the crowd. When he opened the door, Betty paused on the running board, tenting her hand to study the S.S. *President Roosevelt* in the distance.

Red, white, and blue bunting decorated the ship's decks, and its brass railings gleamed to a high shine, but it looked awfully small, its proportions unbalanced, especially when compared with the majestic vessels gracing neighboring piers. It appeared Betty's journey was to begin with a steamship better suited to pleasure cruising in New York Harbor than the far more serious task of transporting America's Olympic team across the Atlantic.

Betty reached for the U.S. Olympic Team pass dangling around her neck and wrapped her fingers around it, taking comfort in the solidity of the thick card stock. *None of this was a dream.* Only several months earlier, the boys' track team coach spotted her sprinting for the train, and now here she was in New York City, a member of the inaugural women's track and field team bound for the Amsterdam Olympics. A flutter of anticipation surged through her.

"Never thought I'd live to see the day when lady runners would compete in the Olympics," the driver muttered, shaking his head as he fetched Betty's suitcase from the trunk of the taxicab. He straightened and searched their surroundings. "Now, where's a porter who can take this?"

Betty reached for the luggage, but the man shook his head. "Aww, miss, you're a wee thing. Let's put a porter to work."

"I can do it."

"Impatient, are you?" He shrugged and placed it in front of her.

Betty leaned into the vehicle where her mother sat. "Well, this is it, Mother. So long. I'll be sure to write." They embraced. When Betty pried herself free from her mother, her voile blouse stuck to her damp back.

"Make us all proud, dear."

"I will. Look for me in the newspapers," she said, winking.

Mother shook her head, but Betty detected a softening in her expression. Mother had always been a staunch believer that a woman's name should appear in the papers only when she married and when she died, but since Betty's success had begun on the track, she seemed to have loosened her position.

Betty turned back to the crowd, lifted her suitcase, and stifled a groan. It was heavier than expected, but there was no way she would ask for help. She gritted her teeth and took a step past the driver.

"Best of luck to you, miss," he said.

She could barely stifle her delight. "I think you'll need it more than me. You're the one staying behind with my mother."

THE TIDAL PULL of the crowd pushed Betty toward the gangway, where she handed her suitcase to a liveried steward, and there was a moment when she glanced back to consider all that she was leaving behind. Her country, her family, everything that was familiar. But the moment was brief, because she hungered for the adventure of something new.

She pushed toward the plank and found General MacArthur

at the top greeting everyone individually. The previous evening, at a meeting in the hotel's ballroom for the athletes and their families, he had been stern, but now when she reached him, he grinned. "Ah, Miss Robinson, the fastest girl in the Midwest. Ready to serve your country?"

His transformation from fearless leader to something akin to more of a garrulous uncle made her uneasy, like the uncomfortable feeling of overfamiliarity that comes from hearing someone use the lavatory or seeing the dark cloud of a man's chest hair through his shirt.

She forced a smile.

"Good, good. You'll find your chaperone in there and she has your cabin assignment. We've got you bunking with two other midwesterners. Chicago and St. Louis, I believe. You'll feel right at home."

St. Louis? What about those Californians? She hid her disappointment by thanking him in a cheerful voice and marched into a dizzying tumult of porters shouting directions and athletes gawking at the rails and calling out to the spectators lining the wharf below. Never before had she seen such a spectacle.

"Betty, dear, is that you?" Mrs. Allen, the track team chaperone, jostled through the crowd, huffing loudly as she fanned at herself with a sheaf of paper. "Do you have your cabin number?"

"Yes," Betty said, raising her pass. "How in the world does General MacArthur manage to remember everyone's room assignments?"

"Follow me," Mrs. Allen called over her shoulder as she waddled along the narrow corridor. "Oh, that General MacArthur, bless his heart. He appears to have a soft spot for the younger athletes. Now, how old are you again?"

"Sixteen."

"Sixteen, my goodness. Well, you're hardly the youngest. There are a few other high-school-age track and field girls and some swimmers and divers too. I believe little Eleanor Holm is fourteen and Olive Hasenfus can't be much more than that. Good heavens, isn't this heat wave dreadful? The *New York Post* is reporting that six people died yesterday, poor souls. I hope it goes away when we get out onto open water." With her silk stockings and tightly fitting lilac-colored serge suit, it was easy to see why the woman had a steady stream of sweat rolling down her temples. She stopped by a door and checked her list. "Let's see . . . yes, here we are. This is your cabin. It will be tight. I'm afraid we were supposed to be on a different ship, but it suffered a recent fire. So now everyone's jammed aboard this one. All three hundred and fifty of us, dear me."

"I'm sure it'll be fine."

"Yes, well, you're going to have to be very careful and alert. We're packed in here like sardines. You could get knocked over by gymnasts flipping on their mats on the C Deck, stabbed by the fencers or punched by the boxers on the Sun Deck, shot by the men competing in the modern pentathlon on the rear back deck, or kicked by the horses galloping on the treadmills set on the D Deck. I make it all sound positively lethal, but keep a lookout and you'll be fine. Just wait until tomorrow when you try the track installed on the Promenade Deck. We've told the athletes doing field events that they are not to throw javelins and discuses while we're out at sea. Too risky. The cyclists are only permitted to ride their bikes during certain times, but I'm sure they'll be whizzing around without any respect for the rest of us." She leaned over and said in a conspiratorial tone, "They can be a bit superior, but if you ask me, they look rather absurd on their little contraptions. And just wait until the boat starts rolling while they're speeding around. Mark my words, it will knock them down a few pegs." She gave a breathy giggle. "Now, General MacArthur plans to have a meeting up on the Promenade Deck once we've pushed offshore, and he will explain the assigned practice times. Just keep a cool head, follow directions, and everything will go smoothly."

Betty's mind reeled. Stabbed? Shot? Kicked? What exactly had she signed up for? But then she looked at the matronly figure of Mrs. Allen buttoned up in her department store ensemble, topped with her carefully constructed beauty-salon coiffure. She didn't appear to be the type who would live too dangerously.

Mrs. Allen cleared her throat. "I can tell you're a good one. Everyone's been so skeptical of the girl runners. You know all of this talk about being morally objectionable? Well, it's ridiculous. And what of those girl swimmers and divers? Now, *they're* the ones who need to be watched closely. Between the two of us, it seems that prancing around in those little bathing costumes gives them airs. Why, they're just counting the days until they land film deals. In the meantime, they think they can get away with murder. Oh goodness, their chaperone"—she clucked—"that poor woman is going to have her hands full." A blast of the ship's horn made them both jump and Mrs. Allen placed her palm on her chest. "Mercy me, I need to get back up to the gangway to find some of the other girls and make sure they know where they're going." She frowned. "You're a quiet thing, but you can introduce yourself to the girls in your cabin, right? Can you do that?"

Betty nodded. "Yes, everything will be grand."

"There you go," Mrs. Allen said over her shoulder as she hustled herself back toward the stairs.

Betty inhaled and gave a little knock on the cabin door before entering. Two young women lounged on a pair of bunks; one had her head hidden behind a copy of *Photoplay*. A third empty bunk hung above the other two, its height clearly designating it as the least desirable of the set.

"Sorry, kid. This isn't the nursery. Keep moving down the hall," one of the women said, folding an arm behind her neck and stretching her lanky legs out on the thin wool blanket beneath her.

From the narrow space between the bunks, Betty looked back and forth at her cabinmates. She had a sister in her late twenties back at home, Jean, and Betty had always been relegated to being the baby of the family. No more. She dropped her suitcase. "I'm Betty Robinson, your other roommate."

The second woman put down her magazine as she pushed herself into a sitting position and extended a hand toward Betty. "Don't pay any attention to Dee. She's deluded into thinking she's a riot, poor thing. Hey, don't I know you from home? You're from Chicago, isn't that right?"

Betty studied the woman. She appeared forthright and plain, her smile genuine.

"Yes, I've been training with the Illinois Women's Athletic Club."

"I'm on the South Side of the city and getting to the IWAC is a pain in the neck for me, so my boyfriend trains me. My name's Caroline Hale and"—she pointed to the other woman—"that's Dee Boeckmann. You're another sprinter, right?"

"Yes, I'm running the hundred."

"Trying to be the fastest women in the world, huh?" Dee asked with an air of self-importance. "I heard that Elta Cartwright is a real speed devil. Didn't she win the trials? And then there are those Canadians—what are they calling them? The Matchless Six? Sounds like you two have your work cut out for you."

Caroline flashed her palm at Dee to stop her. "Cripes, quit giving us such a hard time and loosen up. This is supposed to be fun, remember?" And with that, she raised a lipstick and traced it carefully around her mouth before plucking a battered pack of Lucky Strikes from her pocketbook lying on the edge of her bunk. "Want one?" she asked, holding it out.

Betty had never smoked before, but she was on the adventure of a lifetime, so why not? She slid one from the packet and leaned in for Caroline to light it. The smoke burned her throat as she inhaled and she coughed, but it felt sophisticated to hold a cigarette aloft. She took another drag. Thankfully, the second try went down smoothly.

Dee frowned. "Couldn't you two do that outside? I'm feeling a little seasick."

"Already? We haven't even shoved off from the dock yet.

Don't be such a killjoy." Caroline swung her legs to the floor and balanced her cigarette between two long fingers as she stood, grinning. "But that's not such a bad idea. What do you say, Betty, want to go out to the deck and see what kind of trouble we can get into? If we're lucky, maybe Johnny Weiss-muller will be out there in his swim trunks. Did you see the pool? It's barely bigger than a piss pot."

"There's a pool?" Betty asked.

"Sure, how do you think the swimmers keep up their train-ing?" Caroline said.

"Say, why are you so interested in Johnny Weissmuller? Don't you have a boyfriend?" Dee asked.

"Sure, but that doesn't mean I can't look. There's no ring on my finger yet." She winked at Betty, exhaled a long plume of smoke, and held the door open. "All right, well, that settles it. Put down your bag, Betty. Let's take a tour of this place. If we're lucky, the fellas will already be training with their shirts off. Let's have some laughs. We've earned them! For God's sake, you know what I did to raise a little spending cash for this trip?"

"What?" Betty asked.

"I jumped out of a plane."

"On purpose?"

"Yep, I was paid twenty-five dollars to parachute out of a plane."

Dee snorted. "What on earth were you thinking?"

Caroline rolled her eyes. "I was thinking about making an easy twenty-five dollars, what do you think? I needed it. I'm the youngest of eleven kids, so it's not as if I could ask my parents for money. They're strapped."

"What did your fella think?" Betty asked.

"Oh, he thought it was nuts, but he's figured out that discouraging me is the best way to encourage me to do something, so he stayed quiet."

Betty laughed.

Caroline ran her fingers through her messy bob of dark hair. She seemed to offer fun even if she wasn't from California. Betty pinched some color into her cheeks before sashaying toward the door. "So, Dee, you're staying behind to memorize the Olympic oath?"

Caroline giggled.

"No, wait," Dee said, scrambling to her feet. "I'm coming too. The fresh air will do me some good."

There would be plenty of time to unpack later.

2.

A few months earlier

Thornton Township High School
15001 S. Broadway
Harvey, Illinois

February 27, 1928

Mr. and Mrs. Harold Robinson
3 East 138th Street
Riverdale, Illinois

Dear Mr. and Mrs. Harold Robinson,

This communication is intended to clear up a misunderstanding. Coach Price has brought it to my attention that he believes your daughter possesses exceptional athletic abilities. After seeing Betty run for the train last week, her speed impressed him and he invited her to train with the boys' track team. While I applaud Coach Price's initiative and enthusiasm, I must set the record straight on school policy: Betty cannot train with the boys' track team. In fact, the Illinois State Athletic Association prohibits interscholastic competition for girls in track and field events for good reason; it is well documented that women cannot be subjected to the same mental and physical strains that men can withstand.

Upon reviewing Betty's academic record, I daresay she appears to have stellar grades and commendations from all of her teachers, which leads me to believe that her future lies in the direction of more wholesome and virtuous pursuits. Thornton Township High School offers many wonderful opportunities to develop the intellect and extracurricular interests of its female students. As John Locke once said, "Education begins the gentleman, but reading, good company and reflection must finish him." Here at Thornton Township High School we are certainly not narrow-minded enough to believe this sentiment extends only to gentlemen, but also gentle*women*. Betty is off to a fine start in life. She is a conscientious student and keeps good company, but she must have time for reflection to ready herself for her future role as wife, mother, and citizen. It is important not to overburden this developing young feminine mind with the distractions of sport and competition.

Sincerely,
Principal Umbaugh

From the Legal Offices of Lee, Maginnis & Finnell

MEMORANDUM

March 5, 1928

Dear Mr. Harold Robinson,

   After your meeting with Principal Umbaugh yesterday in which you insisted upon indulging your daughter's interest in training with the boys' track team, Thornton Public School District disavows any responsibility for Elizabeth "Betty" Robinson's participation in activities not befitting a female student. Enclosed is a waiver for you to sign that declares Elizabeth is competing independently and entirely at her own risk.

Sincerely,

Mr. V. L. Maginnis, Esq.

THE CHICAGO EVENING STANDARD

June 3, 1928

Sporting Corner News

Soldier Field—In only her second sanctioned race, Elizabeth "Betty" Robinson of Riverdale finished first place, beating national champion Helen Filkey at the Central American Athletic Union meet by running the 100-meter sprint in 12 seconds flat, an unofficial new world record. Due to high winds above acceptable levels, the new time will not stand, but it was enough to earn the emerging track star an all-expenses-paid invitation to compete in the Olympic trials in Newark, New Jersey, next month. For the first time in history, women will be competing in several track and field events at the Ninth Olympiad in Amsterdam, and we wish young Betty all the luck in the world as she competes to win a spot to represent the U.S. of A.!

The Western Union Telegraph Company

Received at Newark, NJ   1928 Jul 6   1:26 PM

CONGRATULATIONS ON QUALIFYING FOR OLYMPIC TEAM.
YOUR FRIENDS AT THORNTON HIGH ALWAYS BELIEVED IN
YOU. GOOD LUCK IN AMSTERDAM! PRINCIPAL UMBAUGH.

3.

July 1928
Fulton, Missouri

HELEN PLINKED OUT A FEW NOTES ON THE FAMILY'S UP-right Wurlitzer. The woolly needlepointed piano seat scratched at the backs of her thighs. Her mind was supposed to be on Chopin, but instead she glanced out the window long-ingly before placing her fingers on the yellowed keys of the piano and wiggling herself into sitting straight. The sooner she was done practicing, the sooner she could get outside to play. She hit a C note and listened to it reverberate off the walls of the faded parlor. If only she could play a melody that swelled dramatically, fanned the still air, moved things around a bit—wouldn't that be grand?

She tried a chord. Nothing changed. If anything, the twang of the slightly out-of-tune piano just made everything feel flatter, hotter, more oppressive.

Every minute Ma made her sit in front of the piano reaf-firmed the futility of harboring dreams of her musical talents. Even at ten years old, Helen understood the likelihood that she would ever become a virtuoso musician felt as far-fetched to her as owning an elephant as a pet. It simply wasn't going to happen.

Helen stopped playing and tilted her head, straining to listen for sounds of Ma working in the kitchen. Nothing. The only sound came from the parlor's window, where Doogie's nails were clicking against the wooden planks of the porch. Helen crept to the screen door without making a sound and peeked outside. Sure enough, the dog lay in her usual spot next to the wooden rocker, paws jerking as she ran in her sleep. Helen opened the door and tiptoed across the porch. Doogie's bloodshot eyes flickered open, and without raising her head, she watched Helen from under half-opened lids.

Helen's gaze swept the area, looking for action, a game, something of interest. A lone shingle lay near the stairs. She reached for it and, without thinking—it was too hot for thinking—stuck it into her mouth, clenching it between her teeth. Though she kept her tongue away from the splintery surface, the taste of dust and the powdery grit of dried-out wood filled the insides of her mouth. She shook her head back and forth and barked, trying to get a reaction from Doogie.

Nothing.

The creature only furrowed her furry brow in puzzlement. It wasn't until Helen bent over and clapped her hands and stamped her feet that Doogie's tail started to wag. The dog rose and stretched from her haunches, extending her back legs one at a time. As she watched Helen's antics, the rhythm of her wagging tail increased.

Helen turned and ran down the stairs, hoping Doogie would

chase her. With each step, the creases behind her knees felt slippery with sweat, but she wanted to run, feel the air move around her, no matter how hot it was. She wanted escape, action, and freedom from tedium.

She aimed for the front gate. When she was running as fast as she could, she turned and found Doogie loping along beside her. At that moment, Helen's foot caught on something. Maybe it was one of Bobbie Lee's toy trucks, or a gardening trowel of Ma's, or maybe just one of her big feet got in the way—she never figured it out.

But she flew.

She sailed over the flat ground and marveled at the surrounding stillness. The dusty brown yard. The fields stretching beyond the fence. The silent barn. And then she landed with a *whoomph!*

Pain screamed through her chin, lips, and neck. Everything burned. With the wind knocked out of her, she simply lay in the cloud of dust, lungs straining, eyes tearing from the pain, mind reeling. Doogie's snout poked her cheek, her breath snuffling hot against Helen's face. A gurgling sound came from her own throat. She tasted copper in her mouth. She wanted to cough, but something blocked her throat and a bib of blood appeared to be blooming over her pale yellow cotton work shirt. Doogie barked, quick staccato sounds that made the hair on Helen's arms stand at attention. She tried to pull the shingle from her mouth, but it hurt too much and, defeated, she dropped her hands back to the ground.

From behind her, the screen door banged open. Ma screamed.

Bobbie Lee's high voice whimpered. A stampede of feet. The toes of Pa's scuffed work boots appeared and a towel was pressed into her neck. Voices rose and fell, but what were they saying? She stopped trying to understand. Her throat burned as if consumed by flames. She closed her eyes and faded from her surroundings.

From far away, Doogie continued to bark.

WHITE SHEETS, WHITE walls. An unnatural, sterile sense of blankness surrounded Helen. She couldn't move her head.

"Helen," Ma's voice said gently from somewhere beside her. "We're at the hospital. You've had an accident. Don't try to talk."

She tried to swallow but it felt like trying to jam a boulder down her throat. She gagged, unable to breathe. Her eyes watered.

"There, there," Ma murmured, but Helen couldn't see her. She wanted to move, adjust herself from the overwhelming sense of stiffness, but she couldn't. She wanted to look around, but she couldn't. Her eyes now watered from frustration, not just pain.

"Bertie, is she awake?"

"Yes," Ma answered.

"Aha, here she is." A man's voice hovered farther away, low and calm, and then a round face with glasses and gray hair bobbed into her vision. Dr. McCubbin. "Helen, we need to stop meeting like this." Cold hands cupped her cheeks, lifted up her eyelids, prodded her chest. "Your broken wrist mended a lot more easily than this will, but sit tight. I've performed a small procedure that will leave you feeling tired for a spell. In fact, you're going to need a quiet summer. Lots of rest and no talking. You've punctured an important part of your throat and it's going to need time to heal properly."

The doctor disappeared from Helen's line of vision. The white wall returned. Her mother's voice drifted past her, along with the doctor's. She closed her eyes and slid into a heavy, dreamless sleep.

4.

July 1928
Malden, Massachusetts

LOUISE'S HEART HAMMERED. THE GROUND SPED PAST and gravel pinged off her shins, but she didn't let up.

When her basketball teammates had led her to the railroad tracks and pointed down the long straightaway, she almost hadn't believed them. *This* was where the track club trained? She had been running along these tracks for as long as she could remember and knew this section like the palm of her hand. With a shrug, Louise set off in a pack with the others, not wanting to shoot to the front right away, especially since she was one of the youngest girls out there. She'd be fifteen in the fall and attend the high school. At this point, it was best to fit in, get a read on the different girls. Only after they were done warming up and Coach Quain had explained the interval workout did she allow her gait to lengthen. She rocketed to the front, savoring the feeling of letting loose. When she ran, her thoughts faded and the burn of exertion took over. It hurt, but that was part of running's draw, hitting the delicate balance between pain and release. It was a relief, a reprieve from thinking too much. From remembering.

When she reached the railroad tie with a splash of red paint on its end, she slowed, turned, and dashed back to where Coach Quain waited, stopwatch in hand. The other girls trailed behind her, their faces splotchy and strained with exertion.

Louise was fast.

For as long as she could remember she had run everywhere. When most people walked, she ran.

But then there was the accident with her sister and running changed. It became less about having fun and more about testing herself. She *needed* to be fast. She had memories, painful ones, that reminded her she would never be fast enough to save what was important.

When her basketball teammates encouraged her to go to Coach Quain, the man who sponsored the Onteora Track Club, she wasn't sure she could do it, yet a curious longing in her wouldn't let up. Could a stopwatch tell her something she didn't already know?

Suddenly, the earth seemed to quake. The five o'clock train from the city roared past. She blinked her eyes to keep from getting dizzy as it clattered along beside her, a streak of glistening metal, smoke, and moving parts. Pale faces pressed to the windows, a few grinning and waving. Not until it rounded the bend and disappeared did its import sink in.

Five o'clock.

She needed to get home. Emily could be left in charge only for so long. Louise summoned a final burst of effort and Coach Quain blurred as she sprinted past him and then slowed.

He whistled, looking at his stopwatch. "Now, look at that. You're the speediest girl I've ever seen."

Pride stirred in her chest.

"You don't even look winded," he marveled, appraising her up and down.

In truth, she felt exhausted but had no intention of revealing how hard she had been working. The other girls ran past, their eyes glassy with fatigue, sweaty hair plastered to their foreheads. The exposed skin on their bare legs and arms looked pale, mottled, and vulnerable to the blazing-hot sun, but the darkness of Louise's skin hid the sizzle of blood coursing through her veins. In a town full of fair-skinned Irish, Louise was from one of the few black families, but Coach Quain didn't appear to give the color of her skin a second thought.

"I hope you'll join us. With your natural ability, think how fast you'll get with a little training and coaching. What do you say?"

"Thank you, sir, but I need to talk to my parents."

"You do that. We'll be back out here tomorrow. Same time, same place. You're young, and I wouldn't put you in any big meets until next year, although some time trials later this summer season might be useful. Could be good training for a girl with so much potential like you." He held *The Boston Globe* out in front of him and pointed to a page. "Did you know girls are running in the Olympics this year? All the way over in Europe? Who knows? Maybe one day this could be you."

Louise nodded as she jogged away, but she had no idea what he was talking about. Girls racing in Europe? She veered off the railroad tracks and loped along the sidewalk past modest brick houses lining the streets. Figures visible in the windows went about their evening routines. Dinner dishes clattered.

Cooking smells wafted along the evening air. Fried onions. Roasted chicken. Freshly baked bread. Her stomach rumbled in response. When Louise reached her family's dark shingled house, she cut across the lawn, took the porch steps two at a time, pushed the front door open.

"Louise, that you?" Emily's voice called from the back of the house.

Louise glided down the hallway, past closed doors, and entered the kitchen to find her sisters—Emily, Julia, and Agnes—and brother standing around the kitchen table. Emily and Julia both held books in their hands while grass stains covered Junior's trousers.

"I'm here, I'm here. Sorry, it went later than I expected. Let me wash up and I'll be in to start dinner. Junior, go clean up. Girls, set the table, please."

"Did you make the team?" Junior asked, his wide dark eyes shining in anticipation.

"Yes." She paused in the door of the washroom. "But now don't you go saying anything about it to Mama yet. Understand?"

"When you gonna ask 'em?" Julia asked.

"Not sure." A sense of guilt eclipsed the triumph that had fueled her run home. How could she fit running on a track team into all of her responsibilities?

Moments later, she was back in the kitchen assembling plates of cold roasted chicken from the icebox and making a potato salad. The sound of the front door wheezing open caused all of their heads to swivel toward the hallway entrance. Mama and Papa were home.

"How are you all?" Mama asked, working her way around the table, kissing the tops of everyone's heads. Louise breathed in her mother's smell of laundry soap. It was Tuesday, washing day over at Mrs. Grandaway's house, where Mama worked as a domestic. She would be extra tired from wrestling with the wringer all afternoon.

After Mama and Papa retired to their room to change out of their uniforms, homework was set aside, Julia set the table for dinner, and then they all sat and clasped hands, heads bowed.

"Thank you, Lord, for this fine meal and for granting us another day to live in your good grace." Papa looked around the table. "Anyone want to add anything?"

"Lord, thank you for making me the best pitcher in Malden." From under his long fringe of dark eyelashes, lashes that Mama always lamented were wasted on a boy, Junior looked at everyone with an impish smile. "I struck out a bunch of the boys at the park today."

"Please, Lord, grant Junior humility," Mama said with a sigh, though the wrinkles around her eyes crinkled in amusement.

"I been thinking about Baby Grace today and hope God's found her some kind angels who take care of her and play with her so she doesn't get bored and whiny," Agnes said, her lisp making the seriousness of what she was saying take a moment to sink in.

Mama let out a whimper that was halfway between a gasp and a sob.

"No one gets bored and whiny in heaven," Emily corrected. "It's perfect there."

"Well, I hope those angels are nice and give her some of those peppermints she loved," Agnes said, her little sharp chin jutting out in indignation.

The kitchen stilled for a moment. Thinking about Grace caused a pain to shoot straight through Louise's heart. How could she have been so foolish as to leave her brother and sisters alone for a couple of hours? How could she risk something like what had happened to Grace happening again? Right there, she decided she would not return to practice with the Onteora Track Club. Not the next day or any day after that. How could she have been so selfish? She had failed to look after her siblings properly once and she would never make that mistake again.

Papa cleared his throat. "I hope he's keeping our baby close and giving her everything she wants too, sweetheart. Now let's enjoy some of this wonderful meal that Louise put out for us."

The tenor in the room shifted, loosened a little, and without looking at each other, everyone raised their forks to begin eating, but Louise's appetite had vanished. A hollowed-out sense of grief and failure weighed upon her, heavy and suffocating.

AFTER DINNER, LOUISE scrubbed the dishes as Mama settled the younger children in bed. The house's creaks quieted and the sound of crickets floated over her as Papa opened the kitchen door to have his evening smoke on the back stoop. Louise sat at the table, awaiting her allotment of evening mending work. When Mama joined her, she took a few items from her basket, angled herself toward the light, pulled out one of Junior's shirts, and handed it to Louise, pointing to the spot where a button needed to be sewn on. Mama bowed her head, placed her needle at one end of a tear in Papa's gardener's uniform, and began stitching. Moments later, Papa came back into the house, rested a hand on Mama's shoulder, and looked at Louise.

"When Dr. Conway arrived home this evening, he mentioned seeing you today. Said you were running along the train tracks like a bear was chasing you."

Louise's hand with the needle froze midair. The last time she had seen Dr. Conway was seven years ago, when she had raced over to the man's house, frantic to find Papa. Dr. Conway had been working in his home office, and when Louise spluttered out the story of what had gone wrong, he insisted the three of them ride back to the Stokes home in his automobile, but their speedy return was not enough to save little Grace. The tiny girl had spent four days unconscious, burns covering her small body, before she succumbed to her injuries.

In a flash, Louise could be back in that moment when she entered the kitchen to find flames licking at little Grace's pretty blue striped pinafore. That awful smell of burning fabric, hair, and skin could return to Louise all too easily and unexpectedly—when she brushed her hair in the morning; when she sat in English class contemplating an assignment; when she set the table for dinner. Each time, grief could still descend upon her with startling intensity that, even seven years later, left her reeling.

Every night before Louise fell asleep, she replayed the memory of when she had found her sister, matches strewn around her, flames lighting the kitchen floor like fallen stars. She couldn't help herself. Reliving that afternoon had become part of a sickening ritual for sleep and she couldn't stop it. If she replayed the afternoon step by step, she slept deeply and dreamlessly, but if she tried to push the memory away, it prowled around the corners of her mind, rearing up and clawing throughout the night as she tried to sleep. Each time, she fixated on the moment when she froze, watching her sister scream. She had been slow to throw the tablecloth over Grace and beat at the flames, and even slower to run for help. Her legs had felt spongy and her feet ungainly as she made her way to Dr. Conway's house. The panic binding her chest had left her unable to breathe, and she felt sick to her stomach. Why had she been so slow? Would Grace still be alive if Louise had run faster?

Louise stared at the pale pink puckered burn scar along her left hand, the visible reminder of all that had gone wrong that horrible afternoon. In a flat voice, she said, "I was invited to try out for the Onteora Track Club. Dr. Conway must have seen me running with them earlier today."

Mama glanced up from her sewing.

Her father took a seat at the table. "Did you make the team?"

"Doesn't matter because I'm not going to do it. There's too much to do here."

"It's true, you have responsibilities, but you've always loved to run. Is this something you want to do?" Mama asked.

"No, ma'am."

Mama placed her mending on the table and shook out her hands, exchanging a look with Papa. "It strikes me that your sisters and brother are getting old enough to handle themselves a bit . . ." Her voice trailed off. The ticking of the kitchen clock filled the room. "Listen, Louise, what happened with Grace was an accident. It's too big a burden for a girl your age to carry."

"It's too big a burden for anyone to carry," Papa said in a low tone.

Mama bowed her head a moment. When she raised it, her eyes were shiny and she reached for Louise's hand.

"Dr. Conway said your running was a sight to behold. What you've got is a God-given gift, it is," Papa said. An unmistakable glow of pride showed on his face.

Mama's hands, dry and calloused, gripped Louise's tightly. "As long as you keep up on your schoolwork, you have our blessing to try this, see what happens. You'll be going to the high school this fall. Seems like a good time to let your brother and sisters take on more responsibility."

"But they—"

"I'll handle them. It'll be fine."

Louise considered how she had felt leading the pack as she raced past Coach Quain. For those few minutes, the pit of sorrow and guilt she carried had dulled. The self-consciousness she felt about her dark skin had eased. Her mind quieted and she existed only as a body in motion, powerful and free. She wanted to feel that way again.

She nodded. "I'll try it."

THE CHICAGO EVENING STANDARD

July 30, 1928

"Dispatch from the IX Olympiad: What's the Matter with the Americans?"

Amsterdam—American athletes have always run roughshod over the rest of the world in track and field events, but in the most stunning reversal in Olympic history, the men from the United States are experiencing one setback after another. Before shoving off from New York, Major Gen. MacArthur insisted his American team had nine gold medals "all sewn up," but that prediction appears to be unraveling as three of those nine events have already been won by other countries. At this rate, the American flag won't be waved from the winner's podium once. Team managers and coaches are quick to point out that Amsterdam does not have its facilities ready, and the team is stuck living aboard the S.S. *President Roosevelt* and contending with everything from a leaky pool to tennis courts of differing sizes to a swampy track. Dutch engineers are busy at work fixing the venues.

When Olympic officials advised the women's swim and dive teams to train in the harbor, they headed to Paris on a shopping excursion. "If they think I'm dipping a toe into that icky water," said perky fourteen-year-old swimming champion Miss Eleanor Holm of California, "they have another think coming!"

The dreary weather is also being blamed as less than ideal for peak performances, but all nations are training under the same sky, and rain clouds do not appear to be targeting only the American athletes.

Team managers have been grumbling about the lack of recovery time for the athletes. "With the Olympic trials a mere couple of days before departing for Europe, our fellows had to work too hard to qualify and now they're out of steam," explains one coach. And it is not just the men. Uncle Sam's fleetest sprinter, Miss Elta Cartwright of California, is sick, leaving the door open for one of Canada's speedy lady runners to win gold.

But aside from unfinished facilities, bad weather, and illness, reports are surfacing that the main problem for American athletes might be that they are spending too much time in the buffet line aboard the S.S. *President Roosevelt.* It seems our athletes have been under the false impression that pie eating has been added as an Olympic event! In fact, the ship's supply of ice cream ran out midway across the Atlantic. At last check with the team's coaching staff, eating dessert does not count as training.

When asked if he wanted to revise his initial prediction about the team's success, Major Gen. MacArthur responded, "We have not come three thousand miles to lose gracefully, but rather to win, and win decisively. Just wait and see."

Well, we're waiting.

5.

July 1928
Fulton, Missouri

Dr. McCubbin hadn't been joking when he told Helen that her summer would be quiet. She felt like she had been stuck in bed forever. Through the languid days of July, Helen read *The Boxcar Children*. She read it so many times, she started creating her own stories about Henry, Jessie, Violet, and Benny in her head, but one morning Ma left *The Missouri Daily Observer* next to Helen's bed, and she picked it up. The paper was a couple weeks old, but it was something different.

Helen thumbed through the sections until she noticed an article titled "Chicago's Betty Robinson to Sail for the Olympics," and read about a sixteen-year-old girl from Chicago who could run so fast that she was being sent to Amsterdam, a small city in the Netherlands, to compete against athletes from every far-flung country on earth. Argentina, Estonia, Egypt, India, Japan, New Zealand, Rhodesia, South Africa—yes, *everywhere*, it seemed.

Helen reached to her dresser and pulled her beloved globe onto her lap. Mama often quizzed her on the locations of various countries and cities and Helen had won a school geography bee the previous year. She spun the globe so the United States faced her and then she leaned in. She found *Chicago* and traced the letters of its name crawling across the blue of Lake Michigan. Slowly, she rotated the globe, sliding her index finger across the wide expanse of the Atlantic until she reached the coast of Europe and the huge green expanse of *France*. Just north lay a tiny blob of yellow marked *Belgium* and, above that, there was a splotch of pink labeled *Netherlands*. Quite a distance separated Chicago from the Netherlands. What would it be like to get on a ship and travel so far from home?

Helen placed the globe on the bedspread next to her and clutched the newspaper closer, scanning the article to find where it described how athletes from countries all over the world would convene to participate in a series of competitions. All thoughts of *The Boxcar Children* paled next to the cast of characters described in the newspaper article. Boxers. Cyclists. Gymnasts. Equestrians. Soccer and field hockey players. Most of the athletes would be men, but a small group of women would also be competing, including Betty. This would be the first time women could compete in track and field events.

A grainy photograph of the girl from Chicago caught Helen's eye. A man stood next to her. Even in the black-and-white image, anyone could plainly see how tightly his arm wrapped around the girl's shoulders, how wide his smile stretched. According to the article, the man was the girl's father and it quoted him saying, "Without any sons, I never imagined I'd have a girl competing in athletics. I couldn't be prouder of her."

Helen read his quote over and over. She couldn't imagine her stern-eyed father ever saying something similar. Frank Stephens didn't believe in spending time on doling out compliments. His life was one of singular focus: farming. He believed in operating his 140-acre farm the old-fashioned way: with guts and muscle. No newfangled John Deere machines for him, thank you very much. Even at ten years old, Helen understood that part of Pa's disdain for tractors and threshers stemmed from his inability to pay for the equipment. He farmed his land with a horse and plow and dismissed what he called "the easy way to a dollar."

In the photo of Betty, her short blond hair curled to frame her face. Her grin glimmered off the page as if she hadn't a care in the world. Helen smiled back at the image. She tried to forget the birthmark staining her forehead, her unruly hair, enormous feet, and clumsy limbs, but her smile slackened thinking of how her classmates taunted her with *Helen the Huge* and *Smelly Hellie*.

She sighed, folding the article so the picture of Betty disappeared from view. Helen could run fast—none of the boys at school would dispute *that*—but being someone like Betty Robinson felt about as achievable as becoming Queen of England. Still, she opened the newspaper again to view the article once more.

Could Betty really win?

Helen pulled the page with Betty's story from the newspaper and tucked it under her bed, vowing to keep her eyes out for more updates. She needed to see what would happen next to this girl.

6.

August 1928
Amsterdam

ABOARD THE FERRY ON HER WAY TO CENTRAL STATION, Betty drummed her fingers along the window's railing. Clouds scudded low overhead, the morning's downpour having done little to rid the air of humidity. It was the day of the 100-meter finals and she was the only American woman left competing. She wrapped her arms around her belly to stop the flip-flopping sensation inside her. Deep inhalations would help, but who wanted to breathe in the putrid stench of the canal's brackish water?

When Betty and her teammates arrived at the stadium, they exited the bus and stood on the sidewalk, shifting their weight from foot to foot, awed by the throngs of spectators bustling past and the honking from snarled traffic.

Caroline reached out and squeezed Betty's hand. "Good luck. Knock 'em dead."

Betty thanked her as the rest of the girls crowded round, rubbing her shoulders and slapping her back. Mrs. Allen brushed Betty's hair off her forehead. "Go get changed and I'll meet you in the locker room after settling the girls in some seats."

Betty said goodbye to her friends. They strolled away giggling about something and Betty watched them, twisting the edge of her Peter Pan collar between her fingers. She squared her shoulders and entered the long corridor to the locker room. The thud of her heels striking the ground echoed with each step she took. A metallic-smelling mixture of rainwater and newly poured cement wafted over her.

She entered the locker room and found three Canadians gathered between a row of lockers, talking and laughing. In the next row, two Germans sat on the bench between the lockers, their expressions serious as they cleaned dirt from their running spikes. Betty passed them, found an empty row, dropped her bag on a bench, and slumped down next to it, gnawing on the cuticle of her index finger.

Never had she felt so alone.

If only Caroline or Elta was there with her. Even Dee would have been better than being alone. Her heel jiggled up and down, but she pressed on it to stop. *I cannot be nervous anymore. I've got a job to do.* She repeated these two sentences over and over. Each time she recited them, her mind cleared a little from the anxiety swirling inside it. She stood, shook out her legs, and hopped up and down a few times. Her shoulders dropped, the jitters in her belly settled. She closed her eyes, raised her hands above her head, and pictured herself leaning into the finish tape. *Yes!* Opening her eyes, she smiled, bent over her bag, and pulled out her white shorts and top, along with her navy-blue sweat suit.

Once she'd changed, she sat down to put on her track shoes. First, she slid her foot into her left shoe and laced it, listening to the guttural sound of the German athletes talking.

She started to slide her right foot into her other shoe, but her toe jammed inside.

Perplexed, she lifted the shoe for closer inspection. Her breath caught.

It was a second left shoe.

Two left shoes! How had this happened? Panic rose inside her. She spun toward her bag, rummaging through it to find a shoe for her right foot. Nothing. She blinked. Could she run barefoot? Even if officials allowed it, which she doubted, the sharp surface of the track would ruin her feet. Clutching the shoe to her chest, she ran, limping unevenly on one shoe, toward the door of the stadium. With each step, the roar of the crowd became louder and louder. As she lunged for the doorknob, it opened toward her. Mrs. Allen stepped into the locker room, squinting as her eyes adjusted to the dim lighting.

"Heavens, Betty, you nearly gave me a fright." She raised a hand to her chest. "Are you ready, dear?"

"I have two left shoes. I . . ." Betty stammered. "I own two pairs of track shoes and somehow I grabbed only the left ones this morning." Saying the words out loud made her predicament real and she blinked back tears. "What am I going to do?"

"All right, all right, don't panic. You stay here. I'll hurry down and speak with Coach Sheppard to see what he thinks. You go back and sit down."

"But what about my race? Doesn't it start soon?"

Mrs. Allen inspected her wristwatch. "Yes, dear, it does. Sit tight. I'll be back in a jiffy."

Betty's hands dropped to her sides and she returned to her

bench and sat, her head falling into her hands. The Canadians passed by on their way to the doorway, looking curiously at her. Betty's face burned. Somewhere nearby, a leaky faucet dripped, each drop echoing through the otherwise silent room. Her throat tightened and tears burned at the corners of her eyes, but she blinked them away. This was not the time to fall apart.

From a distant corner of the locker room, a door slammed. Footsteps slapped along the floor, getting louder and louder. "Betty? Betty? Where are you?" Caroline rounded the corner and stopped, panting. "Whew, that was close. Here's your shoe, but there's no time to put it on now. Officials are checking racers into your event. Come *on!*" She thrust Betty's right shoe at her.

Betty grabbed it and chased after Caroline. "How in the world did you get this so quickly?"

"You better forgive Dee for all her snoring. You know how she was planning to catch a later ferry?" Caroline pushed out of the locker room door and studied the track below. "It looks like the judges are taking a quick break—put on your shoes now, but hurry. Before she left our cabin, Dee noticed two right shoes and had the presence of mind to figure out what you had done and take one for you. She found us in the stadium and gave it to me. What a lucky break, huh?"

Crouched down, lacing up her shoes, Betty sucked in her breath, amazed. Around her, colorful flags waved and cigarette smoke clouded over the crowd. People sang and called out to the athletes in languages she couldn't understand. The noise was deafening, so loud that it became meaningless. A background roar. She peered through the thicket of people surrounding her, knowing the track lay somewhere below. Within minutes, she would be racing and the outcome would be decided. She just needed to push forward.

"Let's go," urged Caroline, turning toward Betty, her eyes wide with worry.

An odd sense of calm descended over her. "I'm ready."

BETTY TOOK HER position at the start, bent over, and dug into the cinder with a trowel the way Coach Price had shown her, to create two small indentations that would hold her feet in place when she assumed her crouched starting position. When the divots were in place, she sat back to survey her work; the spacing between the two appeared acceptable. She laid down her trowel, eyeing her competitors. The two German girls bobbed up and down in place to warm up. The three Canadians stretched their quads. All the women wore serious, grim expressions.

Next to her, Canada's Bobbie Rosenfeld lowered herself into a lunge and Betty copied the move, focusing on the stretch of her hamstrings and hips. Her gaze wandered over the swarm of faces in the stadium surrounding her, but they faded into a blur. All she felt was the beating of her own heart. The steady cadence of her breath. The easy stretch of her legs, first one side and then the other. *She had made it. This was the Olympics.* With these realizations, her shoulders loosened away from her ears. What did she have to lose? A flush of glee filled her. She needed to run like she was trying to catch the train—that was all.

One of the officials gestured for the girls to get ready. Each racer stood in her lane above her starting divots.

"On your marks," said the official in a thick French accent. The next few minutes were a confusing blur of false starts and the elimination of two racers, but through it all Betty gazed straight ahead to where the finish line lay, determined not to get distracted. She felt ready to spring, her mind clear, her body loose. Out of the corner of her eye, she watched the starting official raise the gun into the air.

BANG!

Quick off the start, Ethel Smith of Canada surged ahead, but Betty easily overcame her. Only Bobbie Rosenfeld lay ahead, but Betty punched her arms up and down. Step by step, she came alongside Bobbie, and the two ran together, stride for stride, but Betty pumped her legs faster and faster to increase the turnover of each step. She inched ahead.

She could have been racing alone because everyone dropped away. The crowd. Bobbie. Ethel. Everyone. She may have been flying. Not once did she feel the surface of the track under her whirring feet. Her mind was quiet. Every gear in her body turned easily. Nothing else mattered. The white finish tape got closer and closer. She threw out her chest and reached her arms upward, hurling herself into the tape with everything she had. As it caught on her chest and she crossed the finish line, she closed her eyes and lifted her face upward toward the sky. She had done it!

But wait . . . had she?

Bobbie Rosenfeld's left shoulder nudged Betty as both women slowed their pace to a jog. They turned to each other, their expressions clouding with uncertainty. A horde of officials and judges descended upon them, gesticulating and shaking their heads. Who had crossed the line first?

Betty's breath caught as she looked around the stadium for answers. What had happened? Several feet away, Coach Sheppard, Dee, Caroline, and Elta climbed over the railing of the track and raced toward her, their expressions exuberant, mouths wide open as they yelled with glee. They enveloped Betty, hugging and kissing her. She fell into them but kept watching the judges, who remained huddled, immune to the celebration on the track. Beside them, Bobbie waited for the official judgment with her Canadian teammates, their faces grim as they watched the judges too.

Even as congratulations showered upon her, Betty's stomach tightened. Had she crossed the line first? She tried to think back, but she didn't trust her memory. Certainly, it had been close. The Canadian coach jogged over to his racers and stood with them, staring at the judges, a wary glint in his eyes.

Finally, an official broke from the cluster and marched toward the racers.

"We're declaring Mademoiselle Robinson the winner with a new world record of 12.2 seconds. Mademoiselle Rosenfeld wins the silver with a time of 12.3, and Mademoiselle Smith will be awarded the bronze."

"Say now," said the Canadian coach. "We think Bobbie took first place."

The judge raised his eyebrows. "It's five dollars to file a contest to our verdict."

The coach glowered at the judge and stalked away as the

Dutch band broke into "The Star-Spangled Banner" and Betty's teammates lifted her onto their shoulders. "You did it!" they shrieked. She beamed as a light breeze blew her hair from her forehead and she gazed up toward the sky. One day she was a schoolgirl, now she was an Olympian. In only twelve seconds her life had changed forever.

THE CHICAGO EVENING STANDARD
August 23, 1928

"Olympic Champ Heading Home Sweet Home"
By Ralph Martins

After being feted in New York City for her athletic accomplishments in Amsterdam, Chicago's very own Elizabeth Robinson is heading home tomorrow. Clad in an all-white ensemble, pert and plucky "Betty" appeared to be Artemis herself as she stood in front of the boisterous crowd of well-wishers at Pier 84 in New York City, beaming from ear to ear. But maybe it wasn't just her accomplishments that pleased her; after all, it's her birthday and next to her on the small stage stood the victorious University of California's eight-man crew that rowed for gold to defeat the heavily favored Brits. Miss Robinson still has one more year of high school to complete, but the college men appeared all too eager to help the pint-size lass celebrate.

Along with winning silver in the 100-meter women's relay, the diminutive teenager restored American prestige with her surprising gold medal victory in the 100-meter dash, an event certain to go down as one of the most entertaining races in Olympic history. In a display of feminine histrionics never before seen in an Olympic stadium, Canada's comely Myrtle

Cook sobbed lustily for half an hour after being disqualified for several false starts. But Cook's act was just a warm-up for the next round of thrills delivered by blond and buxom Fraulein Schmidt of Germany, who shook her fist furiously under the nose of the official after being the second racer to be disqualified for two false starts. Everyone in the stands held their breath, wondering if a face-scratching, hair-pulling act would follow. Instead Schmidt threatened vengeance upon the official the next time they meet. This reporter isn't alone in hoping to snag a front row seat at their next face-to-face encounter!

Women's track and field is under provisional status for these Olympic Games, and officials have given some indication that the ladies will not be asked to return because these feats of endurance can be too strenuous for the fairer sex. Pierre de Coubertin, founder of the International Olympic Committee (IOC) and its second president, always a staunch advocate of banning women from athletic participation, has made his vision of feminine participation clear by saying, "At the Olympic Games, a woman's role should only be to crown the victors." But after seeing firsthand the entertainment value that these ladies provided, this reporter hopes the IOC will continue to include feminine athletic participation.

On her way home, Miss Robinson's new luggage carried not only gold and silver medals, but also a beautiful golden globe charm given to all the lady athletes by Major Gen. Mac-Arthur and a medal from the City of New York. But what about athletes who returned home without Olympic prizes packed into their suitcases? Don't worry, they've been having a grand time. Several reporters peeked into their luggage and glimpsed enough bottles of gin, champagne, and whiskey to keep the city's speakeasies soused for weeks. Government officials looked the other way and did not press charges. Apparently being back on dry land won't be so dry after all!

CHICAGO LADIES SOCIAL CLUB NEWSLETTER

August 29, 1928

"Girl About Town: Olympic Gold Medalist Betty Robinson"

Chicago's newest celebrity, Olympian Betty Robinson, arrived home earlier this week to great fanfare. Bedecked in wreaths of red roses and pink carnations, Betty beamed at the crowd that included classmates from Thornton Township High School, teammates from the Illinois Women's Athletic Club, and officials from Harvey, Riverdale, and Chicago. After signing autographs and dispersing souvenirs to her friends and fans, she settled between her parents in a black convertible for a victory lap around the Loop, ending at city hall, where Chicago rolled out the red carpet for its new hometown hero. So overwhelmed by emotion, our dear, modest girl could barely speak, but with tears shining in her eyes, she thanked everyone for their support and encouragement.

Praise wasn't the only thing heaped upon our golden girl. She received a diamond-studded wristwatch from the City of Harvey, a golden track shoe charm from the IWAC, a silver tea set from the Edgewater Beach Club, a gold bracelet from the Central Amateur Athletic Union, and a princess-set diamond ring from admirers in Riverdale. We don't know how she will pull off breaking more world records weighed down with all of this loot, but if there's anyone who can do it, Betty's our girl.

Perhaps the biggest prize came from her parents: a shiny brand-new cherry-red roadster has been parked outside the Robinson family home in Riverdale awaiting its new driver. Be sure to wave if you see her spinning around downtown enjoying her new set of wheels.

The Chicago Ladies Social Club welcomes Miss Robinson to be its guest of honor at its Annual Fundraising Luncheon on September 15. Please contact Mrs. Dudley Armison, Club Secretary, for tickets.

7.

September 1928
Malden, Massachusetts

LOUISE LOPED ALONG MALDEN'S SIDEWALKS, HER MUScles loose, her stride confident, her breathing rhythmic, as she and her teammates ran to the park where they would be competing in an unofficial time trial against a few local running clubs. For weeks she had been looking forward to today, this first opportunity to try racing and see what she could do. Coach Quain had shown them a newspaper article about Olive Hasenfus, a girl from the neighboring town of Needham who had gone to the Olympics earlier in the summer as a reserve member of the women's 4-x-100-meter relay team. Olive hadn't ended up racing, but Louise was eager to see how she stacked up against this girl.

Leaning against his automobile, Coach Quain waited for his girls at one of the entrances into the park. When Louise and her teammates reached him, they stopped and spread out to stretch on the grass. Dahlias as large as dinner plates bloomed by a park bench, and Louise held on to the trunk of an oak tree as she balanced to stretch her quadriceps. Well-maintained houses, bigger than what she'd find in her neighborhood, tidy landscaping, and tall, established elms fringed the park. Within minutes a group of the Medford girls appeared. Louise searched the other team for any black girls, but they were all white, setting off a familiar tinge of disappointment deep within her.

The girls called out greetings and approached the Malden runners to mingle, stretch, and chat. A small stringy girl with a broad face, nondescript lank blond hair, and freckles took a spot on the grass next to Louise and bent into a lunge. She couldn't have weighed over a hundred pounds. Her shorts inched up slightly on the backs of her thighs, revealing a lattice of faded white scars. Louise lowered her gaze to the grass. This was the type of thing you minded your own business about.

A few minutes later, a station wagon chugged to the curb. Runners from Needham poured from it and found places to stretch in the grass around the other girls. Louise recognized Olive from the newspapers and watched as she flopped onto the grass and lifted her leg into the air to lengthen her hamstring. Apparently the Olympic experience hadn't imbued Olive with a special glow or left any outward marks upon her. She looked like a regular fifteen-year-old, much to Louise's disappointment.

When the Medford team's coach arrived and parked behind Coach Quain, the men got to work explaining the order of racing. Within minutes the girls were running sprints up and down the grassy section of the park. Each time, Louise, Olive, and the stringy girl from Medford tried to edge ahead of each other for the lead, but they remained within a couple of inches of one another as if connected by a short string, none of them able to get a consistent, decisive lead. Between each interval, the three girls eyed one another while catching their breath. Louise tried to remain calm, but she couldn't believe she was maintaining the same pace as Olive.

In each race, a dark-haired girl trailed them in fourth place. She was never a contender for one of the top three spots, but she kept trying to catch them. Between races, she sauntered among the group, tossing her inky black curls, her pale blue eyes taking in the crowd as she spoke in a loud voice clearly vying for attention. Louise knew the type: pretty girls who had everything yet still believed they were coming up short somehow and put on a big show to cover up their own shortcomings.

After several minutes the coaches separated Louise, Olive, and the blonde from Medford from the rest of their teammates. As if as an afterthought, the coach from Medford waved the fourth girl, the one with dark ringlets, to join them.

"You four have been the fastest. Let's try a longer course around nearby Craddock Park," said Coach Quain. "I've chalked the route with arrows so you'll know exactly where to go. It's an out-and-back course so watch for the tree with a white ribbon around it as your turnaround point. Touch it and come back." He turned to the two girls from Medford. "Now, I know Louise and Olive, but what are your names?"

"Mary," the freckled blonde answered.

"Rosie," said the one with dark, shiny curls and full lips.

"Right," Coach Quain said. "Now let's do one more."

Louise, Mary, and Olive appeared serious as they took their places on the chalked starting line, now blurry from all the other starts, while Rosie pranced around them impatiently.

And then they were off.

Once again, Louise, Mary, and Olive vied for the lead, racing side by side. Several yards behind them, Rosie's heels pounded the packed dirt path.

Craddock Park came into view. The tree with the white ribbon neared and Louise reached it first, gave its bark a good smack, and turned. Olive trailed by only a second, but suddenly, from several paces behind, Rosie pivoted and turned without touching the tree. Now in the lead because of her early turn, Rosie darted ahead toward the finish.

What was Rosie doing? Louise faltered and the delay cost her. Olive took advantage of Louise's confusion and moved in front as Mary pulled alongside Louise and the two girls exchanged wide-eyed glances.

Louise and Mary managed to catch Olive and they all dashed toward the final stretch into the park with Rosie still leading by several long strides. *How dare Rosie take a shortcut!* Indignation fueled a final burst of effort from Louise. Though it felt like her heart might explode from the effort, she bore down, trying to turn her stride over faster and faster to catch the girl. But it wasn't enough. A roar of cheering erupted from their teammates as the racers barreled across the finish line. The Medford girls surrounded Rosie, heaping praise upon her, but Mary, her teammate, stood alone.

Their coach beamed in surprise. "Rosie Lawton, that was your best time yet. Guess you were saving a little something for the end, eh?"

She flushed. "I think I'm better with longer distances."

Louise opened her mouth to say something about Rosie not

touching the tree but then closed it, overcome by caution. She was the only black girl out there. How would it look if she accused Rosie of cheating? If there was one thing she had learned over the years of being one of the few black girls in Malden, it was to stay quiet. She glanced at Mary standing alone, hovering on the fringe of the group, her eyes downcast, arms wrapped around her narrow frame. Silent.

Why wasn't *she* saying something about her teammate's shortcut?

A few steps away from her, Rosie laughed at something before her gaze searched the group and found Louise. The two stared at each other, Rosie's pale blue eyes flashing with smug satisfaction. Louise's hands balled into fists. Her muscles still twitched from running. With the energy from the race still pumping through her, she wanted nothing more than to march over and smack the self-satisfied grin off the girl's face, but she knew this was a terrible idea.

She turned away and bent over, resting her palms on her thighs, and tried to catch her breath, cool down. What else could she do?

Olive stepped forward from her cluster of Needham teammates. "That girl cheated," she announced, raising her index finger to point at Rosie.

Coach Quain and the other two coaches looked back and forth at the girls in surprise.

Rosie huffed, "I did no such thing."

The coach from Medford frowned. "Mary, is this true?"

All heads rounded in her direction, and she appeared to shrink once she was the center of attention. Rosie placed both hands on her hips and glared at her teammate. Mary blanched. "I . . ."

"Oh, come *on*," said Olive, and she turned to Louise. "You saw her, didn't you? She didn't run all the way to the tree like the three of us did."

Louise froze a moment before nodding her head.

Rosie's eyes blazed. "Don't be sore losers. I touched that tree."

"She did not. She cheated," Olive repeated. She lowered her chin as if preparing to pounce on Rosie.

"All right now, let's not get ourselves worked up," Coach Quain said, stepping between the girls.

"This is just a time trial," the coach from Medford said. "You all ran well. I'm sorry you ladies got confused at the turn-around, but again, this was just for practice. No hard feelings." He faced his team. "I suppose it's time to get my crew home. You girls ready to run back?"

At the Medford coach's urging, his runners jogged toward the sidewalk with Rosie in the lead and Mary disappearing into the middle of the pack.

Louise remained rooted to her spot in the grass. Her heart still pounded, both from exertion and the confrontation. The cavalier way the coaches had dismissed the injustice infuriated her.

Olive stepped next to Louise and watched the Medford girls disappear from view. "You know she cheated, right?"

"It all happened so fast. I couldn't really believe it," Louise said. And it was true. With every minute that passed, Louise became less and less sure of what had actually occurred, but at the same time, her stomach soured with the knowledge that Rosie had cheated.

"But why didn't you say something?"

"I have to be careful . . ." Louise's voice trailed off. How was she supposed to explain to this girl that accusations could be dangerous? How Olive's white skin made it safer for her to say something? "I . . . I didn't know what to say."

Olive gave her a long look. "How about the truth? Next time, be ready to defend yourself. No one else is going to do it."

Louise gritted her teeth together and walked away, not looking back, but she could feel the girl watching her. Sometimes standing up for the truth could be complicated. Louise seethed with resentment toward Olive, but also felt a wave of shame for how she envied the simplicity of the girl's opinions and the confidence with which she defended them.

The other girls called goodbyes and dispersed while the team from Needham returned to their coach's car and drove away. Coach Quain remained standing next to his car and waved Louise over. Louise looked around, but couldn't pretend she hadn't seen him. She walked over to where he waited.

"What happened during that race?"

A knot formed in her throat.

"Was Olive telling the truth?"

Louise nodded.

Coach Quain let out a gusty sigh and leaned against the door of his car. "Today's runs were nothing to get upset about."

"Yes, sir." She kept her gaze on the buttons of his jacket.

"Next time, I'll keep an eye out for any funny business, you hear me? I know that kind of thing is frustrating. Unsports-manlike conduct will not be tolerated in the future. Got it?"

"You mean cheating."

He looked taken aback, but Louise wanted to say the word aloud, feel the weight of it lift from her chest.

He adjusted the brim of his cap, but looked her straight in the eye. "Yes, no more cheating."

"Thank you, sir." She turned toward home and set off running. The knot inside her chest loosened with each step. When she cut through Craddock Park, she slowed and headed toward a monument in the corner of the park. She neared the marker and stopped to read the plaque.

Eight years earlier, her uncle Freddie had brought Emily and her to this very spot, swept along by the throngs of Fourth of July parade-goers, jubilant marching-band music swelling around them. Red, white, and blue bunting decorated a make-shift raised stage where the town's officials prepared to speak. Louise could still taste the achingly sweet cherry sucker Uncle Freddie had handed her as they waited for the ceremony to honor the town's veterans from the Great War to begin. Even as their neighbors wilted in the July heat, Uncle Freddie looked so handsome in his khaki uniform with its sharp pleats running along the trousers and badge with a red fist glowing on his chest. Louise looked around, expecting to see others admiring her handsome uncle, but the eyes of the parade-goers passed right over him and settled on the white veterans. From what she could see, they were the only black people in the crowd.

Finally the mayor had cleared his throat into the micro-phone. After he led the crowd through the Pledge of Allegiance, he spoke about the sacrifice Malden's men had made and read a list of men who had been killed during the war. With each name, Uncle Freddie's proud grin lost its vigor. Emily fidgeted and tugged at her knee socks. Louise's head began to ache from too much sugar and she wished she hadn't drunk the tall glass of lemonade back at the house. Her bladder felt fixing to burst, but she kept quiet, knowing Uncle Freddie was waiting for something.

After the speeches ended, the crowd began to break apart as everyone headed back to their respective homes and holiday celebrations. Uncle Freddie took Louise and Emily by their hands and led them from the park, making no complaint of how sticky they were. In fact, he said nothing at all. Halfway down the block, as the crowd thinned and they were no longer in danger of disappearing into its jostling mass, Emily slipped from his grip and skipped ahead, her pigtails bobbing up and down. After a minute or so, she stopped and turned. "Hey, Uncle Freddie, did you know some of those men who died during the war?"

"I did."

"Which ones?"

A vein pulsed in his neck. "Their names aren't on that memorial."

Emily wrinkled her nose in confusion. "But didn't the mayor read the names of the men who died? Aren't all of the names on that old rock?"

"It's a memorial plaque," Louise corrected.

Emily rolled her eyes and then refocused her attention back on Uncle Freddie. "Why didn't the mayor read all the names?"

He plucked a handkerchief from his back pocket. As he mopped his face, it seemed that a flash of anger crossed his expression, but it happened so quickly that Louise couldn't be sure. He lowered his handkerchief and looked around, and with no one close enough to overhear them, he said, "Girls, when you got dark skin, your sacrifices aren't counted in the same way they would be if you had white skin."

"So the names of your friends aren't on that plaque?"

Uncle Freddie shook his head. "No, they're not."

Emily considered this and made a tutting sound before spinning around to recommence her skipping.

Uncle Freddie still held Louise's hand and his grip had tightened to the point where it felt like the bones in her fingers might crack under the pressure, but she figured he needed something to hold on to so she stayed steady and held her breath. After a minute, his grip slackened. Louise exhaled and asked, "Why did you go to the war? Couldn't you have died?"

"Yes, I could have." He tented his hand over his eyes to watch Emily's antics. Just when Louise thought the conversation was over, he said, "Sometimes you have to do things because they're the right things. If we Negroes continue to participate in this country, someday our white countrymen will have to start seeing us as people who deserve every bit of respect that they expect for themselves."

"But what if you had died?"

"I would have died in hopes that my sacrifice would help others, like you and your sisters, Junior, all of you."

"How would it have helped us?"

Uncle Freddie fished his wallet from his back pocket and

thumbed through its contents until he extracted a photograph and handed it to Louise. In it, Uncle Freddie and another black man sat at a café with a bottle and two fancy glasses set in front of them. Their legs were crossed and they appeared relaxed, yet they sat with the dignified bearing of military posture.

Louise studied the photo. "*This* was the war? It doesn't look too bad."

"It was plenty bad, but this picture was taken after it had ended. We had a weekend in Paris. My friend and I went to cafés, to the theater. No matter where we went, we were treated with respect. The French were grateful for our service no matter the color of our skin."

"Huh. Did you consider staying there?"

Uncle Freddie laughed. "Your grandma wouldn't have stood for that. This is my home. I needed to come back, but going there made me realize that we've got to do risky things because they remind us that we're worth more than we're led to believe."

Louise pondered this, but she couldn't shake the way the white people had seemed to dismiss Uncle Freddie when they were in the park. It didn't seem right that he had gone and risked his life but no one seemed to pay him any respect. "Are you going to do something about those names being left off the plaque?"

"No," he said, looking straight ahead. His tone indicated the discussion was over.

Eight years later, the memorial was unchanged except for a bright green scrim of pollen that covered it. Louise brushed it off the plaque and traced the engraved names with her index finger. Since that afternoon, they had never again discussed the fact that the names of the black veterans were missing from the plaque. Still, every morning Uncle Freddie hung an American flag outside the main window of his garage apartment and every evening, he took it inside; and every Fourth of July, he donned his uniform and joined the town's festivities. It never appeared to occur to him to not honor his country, even though that honor wasn't reciprocated by his countrymen, and that was that.

Now Louise had a faint understanding of what Uncle Freddie had been thinking that afternoon. Maybe sometimes you had to keep your head down and know that what you were doing was important even if no one seemed to acknowledge it. Just like Uncle Freddie's patriotism remained unshaken, she had to keep running and doing her best, no matter what happened. Despite the coaches saying that the results of the day meant nothing, they meant something to her. She would remember today and hold her coach to his word. Everyone needed to follow the rules.

And as for Mary and her silence? That was still confusing to her. But then she thought about those striped scars on the backs of the girl's freckled legs. A cold pit hardened in Louise's stomach. Once she had caught a glimpse of the lower half of her grandmother's back and seen a similar pattern. Grandma never said anything about her youth in Mississippi and Louise knew better than to ask. Sometimes silence meant survival.

Often it seemed as though the color of Louise's skin provided code for how she needed to act, what she needed to say. Or not say. Back in the park, all kinds of forces pressed upon her to prevent her from being as decisive as Olive. But what kept Mary from speaking her mind? Maybe Mary's silence indicated more than weakness. Maybe it had something to do with survival. Sadness overcame Louise, and she drifted away from the plaque a few steps before starting to run again. Her earlier energy had faded and she was left with a headache and legs that weighed enough to be made of concrete.

Rosie got away with winning that day, but cheating would take her only so far. But Mary? Olive? They were fast and followed the rules. The stopwatch would tell the truth.

Louise couldn't wait to race them again.

8.

October 1928
Fulton, Missouri

B Y FALL, HELEN WAS BACK AT SCHOOL. DESPITE DR. Mc-
Cubbin's assurances that her throat had healed, her voice
was different. Deeper, huskier. Sometimes it was more of a
rasp. It certainly did not sound feminine, and it gave the other
girls in her fifth-grade class one more reason to avoid her. As a
result, she played with the boys during recesses and before and
after school.

"Hey, bet you can't hurdle that fence," Tom Egglethorpe
said to Helen, pointing toward the edge of the schoolyard. The
group of boys surrounding them crowed in delight at the challenge. Tom was the only boy in school who even came close to
Helen's athleticism. Like her, he was a head taller than everyone else.

"Bet I can," she said, rolling her eyes to get a rise out of him.
She needed to get home to muck out the henhouse, but there
was no chance she'd leave a dare unmet. Helen never said no
to a challenge.

"Fine, you go first." Tom stuck one hand on his hip in a defi-
ant gesture.

"Why? Need me to show you the way? You a sissy?"

Tom's face, already pink from perpetual sunburn, flushed a darker shade of crimson. Even his scalp flushed through the thin layer of the almost-white blond hair of his buzz cut. Everyone could see it. "Nah, I ain't a sissy. Take that back."

At this rate, their parlaying would take all day. Helen snorted in disgust, turned, and took off in a sprint toward the split-rail fence. She balled her hands and punched up at the sky with each stride. Faster and faster. She neared the fence. It was higher than she'd expected, but there was no turning back. She sucked in a breath and held it, launching herself into the air. Up, up, and over. Her heel caught the top plank of the fence and she wobbled, straining to keep her feet underneath her, to keep her balance. She landed with a *thump,* stumbling slightly on her landing, but kept upright and exhaled before gulping down some desperate breaths, glad to be facing away from the boys so they couldn't see the relief she knew to be stamped all over her face. She slowed to a stop, turned, and raised her arms over her head. "Ha! See if you can do that!"

At that moment, Miss Thurston emerged from the school-house. From where Helen stood, she couldn't hear exactly what her teacher said to the boys, but from the way their chins dropped to their chests, there was little doubt it was a good tongue-lashing.

Miss Thurston turned to scan the schoolyard, but stopped when she caught sight of Helen. "Miss Stephens, you come here right now."

With heavy legs, Helen headed back toward the school, slipping between the middle portion of the split-rail fence. By the time she sidled in front of her teacher, Tom and the other boys had edged away, eyes averted and sniggering, but they dawdled, anticipating the scolding everyone knew was coming.

"You're far too old for these shenanigans, Miss Stephens. Start acting like a lady. Tomorrow I expect to see you walk home with the girls."

The girls? Helen almost choked. The girls wanted nothing to do with her. The boys didn't care much for her company either, but at least they valued her abilities. Racing, ditch jumping, and games of ball had won her a good dose of respect from them, respect that she sorely missed from the girls. Helen looked up to Miss Thurston's face in time to see a flash of pity in the woman's dark eyes.

"I mean it, Helen," Miss Thurston murmured. "If you keep up with the boys, you're going to find yourself in trouble. Nothing good will come from this. You hear me?"

"Yes, ma'am." Helen angled her head down, but annoyance surged through her ten-year-old brain. What did Miss Thurston know anyway? She had straight teeth, wore pretty dresses, knew how to wear her hair in a fashionable style. How was it that someone purported to be smart about books could be so ignorant about people? Did adults forget the battlefield that was childhood when they left it behind?

THE NEXT AFTERNOON, while everyone else dawdled, gathering their things and gossiping, Helen took off out the front door at a sprint and cleared out of the schoolyard, eager to avoid Miss Thurston's wrath. It wasn't until she passed the school's outbuilding by the front gate that she slowed, her lunch pail banging into her thigh with the change of pace.

"Hey, Hellie!" a voice called.

She turned to search the shadows of the outbuilding, her vision spotty with the sudden shift toward the afternoon's brightness. There, standing in the doorway, her sixteen-year-old cousin Jimmy shifted his weight from one foot to the other. She glanced over her shoulder to see if anyone had come out of the schoolhouse but no one appeared to have left. Silently, she congratulated herself on getting out of school without any trouble.

"C'mere," he said. "I want to show you something."

Helen had seen him doing odd jobs around the school, but they never spoke. Like many of the kids from the surrounding farms, his attendance at the local high school had become more and more infrequent with every passing year. Curious, she picked her way through the scrubby grass toward him. He waved his hand at her to follow him and disappeared into the building.

Helen entered the outbuilding and blinked a few times for her eyes to readjust in the low light. Streaks of sunshine edged through the cracks of the building walls, creating veils of dust motes in the air. Jimmy stood at the far wall and pointed at a pile of hay bales next to him. She neared him, wondering what he had found. Perhaps a dead snake? One neighboring farmer had even found an unbroken bottle of moonshine in one of his hay bales. When she reached Jimmy's side, she examined the bales but saw nothing out of place. She glanced at him. His narrow, tanned face studied her. Grubby hands held on to the snaps of his overalls, revealing bare arms, ropy with lean muscle. He wore no shirt under his overalls.

"Wanna see my pecker?"

Helen considered this. Farm life necessitated a certain familiarity with all things pertaining to reproduction. The animals on their farm revealed their various anatomical features without shame and even engaged in the business, often violent, of procreation in public spaces, but aside from the little worm on her younger brother, visible when he bathed and dressed, she hadn't seen anyone else's. A small pulse of warning began at the base of her neck, but before she could say a word, he had unfastened his dungarees and the dirty clothes fell to the floor with a sigh. She took a long look, unimpressed.

That was it?

She had seen the thing on her neighbor's stallion Nero. Now *that* gave her pause. But Jimmy's pecker was exactly that—a strange, chicken-necked thing poking out from his dirty fist. She moved her gaze up his body to his narrow chest, usually covered by the bib of his overalls. There, his tanned skin paled into a milky white. Blue veins ran underneath his chest in a crackle pattern that reminded her of her grandma's china tea set.

"Now let's see what you got," he said, and without waiting for her reaction, he tugged at the snap on her overalls and, like his, the straps gave way. He then bobbed his chin at her once-white underpants, now more of a gray color from frequent laundering. "Pull those down." She did as instructed and when she straightened back to standing, he frowned at the unremarkable cleft between her legs. Without any warning, he stepped toward her, pushed her into the rough-hewn wall, and thrust himself into her. The back of her skull banged into the wooden board behind her with such force that stars danced across her vision. She gasped.

Her chin was held in place by pressure from his shoulder, and the earthy combination of his sweat, grass cuttings, and wood shavings pressed upon her with sickening intensity. Rendered silent with shock, she hung limp as he pumped himself against her and a white flash of pain shot through her. Good God, how could that measly pecker create such a godawful feeling? It felt like time had stopped, but then, he grunted and stepped away, reaching down to pull his overalls up over his narrow hips. The skin along her spine burned from being pressed against the splintery surface behind her. Dazed, she shifted her hips from side to side in search of some way to ease the raw ache pulsing deep inside her. He reached forward and brushed some dust off her temple in a way that struck her as both awkward and tender at the same time.

"Let's do that again tomorrow," he said, looking pleased.

She stared at him, trying to make sense of what had just happened.

He took her silence as agreement. "Go on, better get dressed 'fore you leave."

She looked down at her clothes on the floor and pulled them up slowly, wincing against the pain between her legs. He slapped the hay off her overalls and pointed at the door for her to leave ahead of him. She turned to him, searching for something to say, but he was whistling a tune, a piece of hay stuck between his lips like a cigarette, and he gave her a wink. She hurried out, eager to push what had just happened from her mind.

OVER THE NEXT few days, a dull headache plagued Helen. She struggled to focus on her lessons. When classes ended each day, she considered leaving the schoolhouse in a knot of students. Nothing would happen with Jimmy if her classmates surrounded her, but then she pictured the condescension of the other girls. The way they would eye her overalls, uncombed hair, and dirty fingernails and then whisper about her, cruelty glimmering in their viper eyes. *No, thank you.* But she didn't dare risk falling in with the boys and riling Miss Thurston again either.

So she was stuck. She continued to meet Jimmy in the barn after school and knew these meetings were wrong, but the other options felt bad too. At least Jimmy seemed pleased with her.

Each time she saw him standing in the doorway, she looked backward, hoping a classmate would be near enough so that she couldn't go to the outbuilding unnoticed. But each time there was no one. It always felt like she was being pulled on a rope, a fishing line of sorts, as she moved over the clumps of grass to enter the outbuilding. At the door, he always patted her shoulder and she wanted to pull away, but for reasons she couldn't explain, she followed him.

One afternoon, with her back up against the wall of the barn, Helen watched with a strange detachment over Jimmy's shoulder as Miss Thurston appeared, marching up behind Jimmy and yanking him off her by his ear. For some inexplicable reason, she could hear nothing, but watched Miss Thurston's red-lipsticked mouth contort into a slash while Jimmy's turned into a large O, and then her ears worked again, although everything sounded far away, as if she were underwater.

"Jimmy, I never want to catch you around this school again," her teacher was saying, giving him the stink eye. He slunk away. With a frustrated-sounding sigh, Miss Thurston turned to Helen. "Well? Pull up your clothes. I'm walking you home."

Helen knew she should have felt embarrassment standing there practically naked, but all she felt was like the wind had been knocked out of her. She dressed and then trailed her teacher out of the barn in silence. What should she say? Was she supposed to apologize? It had been Jimmy's idea. But was it her fault somehow? How had she let this happen? And why on earth had she let it happen several times? She wanted to ask Miss Thurston these questions, but didn't know where to begin.

And also, silence felt easier. If they didn't speak, maybe all the bad feelings would go away. But they didn't. Those bad feelings wormed their way deep inside her gut and stayed there, hurting.

By the time they reached the gate to the Stephenses' yard, Helen felt awful. Miss Thurston paused and took Helen's chin in her hand, turning it this way and that as she studied the girl. "Why couldn't you've done what I said and stayed away from the boys?" she murmured, her hand lingering on Helen's face for an extra beat before she turned and sighed, unlatching the gate. Helen remained frozen outside the yard. So, it *had* all been her fault. She wished she could turn and flee from what she knew was coming, but she followed reluctantly, drooping as her teacher rapped at the Stephenses' front door. When it opened, Helen kept her gaze to the ground, even as Ma urged them into the kitchen and they stood around the table.

A window across from Helen was half-open, its Swiss dot curtains limp in the still afternoon. In the distance, she could hear Bobbie Lee's laughter and Doogie's barking. Helen rubbed her sweaty palms up and down the sides of her overalls and then alternated between clasping and unclasping them in front of her. Pa appeared in the doorway, a suspicious look creasing his features into a scowl.

Miss Thurston waved away an offer of a cup of tea. "I won't stay long but wanted you both to know I've just discovered Helen in the barn behind the school with Jimmy Leary."

Silence yawned among the four of them, broken only by the occasional *pop* coming from a pot of baked beans simmering on the stovetop behind Ma.

"Jimmy? Her cousin?" Ma looked confused.

"That's the one. He's been doing some repair work around the school for me, but not anymore. They were up to *no good*." Miss Thurston emphasized the last two words with a raise of her eyebrows to stress that she was talking about a very specific type of *no good*.

Helen wished that a gust of wind would blow into the kitchen and push her right outside the window, far away from the stunned consternation filling Ma's and Pa's eyes as the full implication of what Miss Thurston was telling them sank in.

Pa vanished from the doorway. Moments later, a clicking sound rang through the kitchen as he reappeared cocking his shotgun. Miss Thurston gave a small nod, but Ma's face blanched as she looked from Pa back to Helen.

"Helen, you best go upstairs. Clean yourself up," Ma said.

Helen didn't need to be told twice. From her bedroom window, she watched Miss Thurston stomp from the house, straight-backed and grim-faced. Helen crawled out of her overalls and underpants and put on pajamas and climbed into bed, wishing that if she fell asleep, everything that had happened in that darned outbuilding could disappear. She couldn't tell how long she lay there, but the shadows in her room elongated, the lighting dimmed. Her stomach moaned from hunger.

"Hellie?" Bobbie Lee's voice squeaked from the hallway outside her room. She crawled out from her bed and cracked the door open to peer back at him. From over his gray eyes, blond lashes blinked in confusion. "What's happened? What did you do? I just ate supper all on my own. Ma's saying nothing and Pa just came back from somewhere cussin' a blue streak. He's in the barn now, smashing things around and making a racket. What happened?"

"Nothing."

"I don't believe you."

"Believe whatever you want." Her stomach grumbled again. "Will you go down and nick me something to eat?"

Bobbie Lee's eyes narrowed, no doubt considering if he could strike a deal for information in exchange for grub, but Helen gave him a severe expression so he thought better of it, nodded, and retreated downstairs. Several minutes later he was back, with a biscuit wrapped in a muslin dish towel that he pushed through the crack in the door before disappearing. Helen wolfed down the flaky biscuit and then climbed back into bed, hunger gnawing at her as if the biscuit had awakened all that she was missing. She stared out the window into the velvety darkness, pushing thoughts of her parents, Miss Thurston, and Jimmy from her mind.

The next morning, Ma served up Helen's usual two strips of bacon and hard-boiled egg with no mention of what had happened the day before. Pa was already working in the field, so Helen didn't have to face him. At school, Miss Thurston only remarked that Helen's spelling needed improvement. When she got home that afternoon, she went straight to her room and sat on the edge of her bed, staring at the newspaper photo of Betty and her father that Helen had cut out and taped to her wall. She would never have that. After a minute, she turned and curled into a fetal position, facing the wall.

No one ever mentioned anything more about what had happened, but they didn't have to. In the space of one week, Helen felt like she had lost everything and was alone.

9.

October 1928
Riverdale, Illinois

BETTY RETURNED TO HIGH SCHOOL FOR HER FINAL year. One of the first things she did was fill out a form for her senior page in the yearbook. In the section for "plans for the future," she wrote: *Go to the 1932 Olympics and win another gold medal.* She spent the rest of the year busy with the Girls' Glee Club, serving as president for the Girls' Club and secretary of her class, and performing in several school shows, all while managing to take the forty-five-minute train ride into Chicago almost every day after school to train with her running club, the IWAC.

One afternoon when IWAC practice ended, Betty found Coach Sheppard, her head coach from the Olympics, sitting on a park bench gazing at the lake.

"You're looking faster than ever," he said as she jogged to where he sat.

"I'm working at it. What brings you here, Coach?"

"I've just come from a meeting over at the IWAC. Are you heading back? I need to talk with you. Let's walk."

She raised her eyebrows and followed him. "This sounds serious."

They headed across the park to Chicago Avenue, and out of the corner of her eye, Betty studied how his weak chin bobbled as he appeared to unclench his jaw and clear his throat. "I have it on good authority that the International Olympic Committee will be voting to bar women from competing in track and field events at future Olympics."

Betty gasped and stopped walking. "What?"

"It's true."

All that Betty had been focusing on for the future was wrapped around the premise that she would be able to keep running competitively. "But why?"

"It's no secret that many on the committee don't want women competing in the Olympics at all, but track and field is the focus of their ire. The old guys are saying that it's too strenuous and they want women to compete in only what are being called 'aesthetic-only' events. Sports like gymnastics, swimming, tennis, and skating."

Betty shook her head in disbelief. Too strenuous? She had seen her older sister, Jean, wan and exhausted but triumphant, after giving birth to her daughter, Laura. Now *that* had looked strenuous, and it was considered the utmost accomplishment for a woman. But running? By comparison, running was easy. This news made no sense. "I won a gold medal and haven't suffered from any problems. Where's all this fuss coming from?"

"Remember what happened with the women's eight-hundred-meter race?"

"Sure, those women ran hard and the ending was a real nail biter."

Coach Sheppard jammed his hands into his pockets. "But that's not why it made it into the papers."

A quick, furious heat spread through Betty's chest. Back in Amsterdam, she had attended the 800-meter finals. Betty and Caroline had sat next to Dee, who hadn't made it out of earlier preliminary rounds and scowled at the track, her arms crossed. At the starting line on the track, nine women lined up, and when the starter's gun exploded, they took off at a furious clip. Betty and Dee both cheered the lone American in the field, Florence MacDonald, who was in the middle of the group, racing neck and neck with Canada's Bobbie Rosenfeld. Though they weren't among the top three finishers, as Florence and Bobbie neared the finish, Bobbie lunged forward and fell over the line to stay ahead of Florence. She lay for a moment before rising slowly and staggering to the side where the other finishers stood, hands on their hips, panting, their faces slack with weariness. It had been a tough race, hot and fast, and the announcer came over the loudspeaker and proclaimed, "The top three finishers have all set new world records—" but the crowd's excitement drowned out the rest of his message.

"What a race!" Caroline shouted over the cheering, clapping.

Dee leapt to her feet, applauding. "I sure wish I had been out there, but those girls did us proud."

The following day, the sense of excitement evaporated when reporters appeared at the practice track as Betty and her teammates arrived to train.

One man called out, "Girls, *The New York Times* is reporting that Miss MacDonald fainted and all of the finishers collapsed at the finish line of the eight-hundred-meter yesterday and needed medical care. Renowned football coach Rockne was in the stands and he said"—the reporter glanced down at his notebook—"'It was not an edifying spectacle to see a fine group of girls run themselves into a state of exhaustion.' So, whaddya say about that?" The fellow cocked his pencil, the delight on his face unmistakable.

Betty and Caroline looked at each other in confusion. There had been no fainting, no medical care on the field.

Another reporter shoved his way in front of Betty. "The *New York Evening Post* describes the women looking 'wretched' and said that five of the racers couldn't even finish the course."

"That's not what happened," Betty said. "Are we talking about the same race? Yesterday's women's eight-hundred-meter?"

The reporter scratched his forehead and scanned his notes. "That's what I've got, but wait, have the lady runners collapsed in other races too?"

"No, no, they haven't," Caroline said, tugging Betty away from the reporters and into the entrance to the locker room. Once inside, the women put their track shoes on in silence.

"Why do those reporters say such horrid things?" Dee asked.

"Because they don't want us out here," Caroline said.

"But we've been doing well. Better than the men, that's for sure. We're winning medals for our country. The satisfaction these reporters take in making us all sound like a bunch of ninnies sickens me."

The memory of that race made Betty grimace at Coach Sheppard. "I don't care what made it into the papers. None of those reports were right. I've been running my heart out and now I'm just supposed to quit? I can't do that."

Coach Sheppard's expression slid into something approaching wariness. "What do you mean?"

"I mean that this debate isn't over. I'm going to write to General MacArthur as soon as I get home and tell him this isn't fair. And then I'm going to write to all of the women who were my teammates and tell them not to quit either just because we make a bunch of old men feel uncomfortable. Amsterdam was just the beginning."

Coach Sheppard scratched his forehead. "Sure, go ahead and try to enlist as much support as you can. The AAU has been working for years to find and cultivate talent—talented runners like you—and we don't want to see women dropped from the Games in Los Angeles either, got it? You gals have been costing us money, time, and a lot of effort. I hate to see it all go to waste. We'll fight it with you, tooth and nail." They had reached the entrance to the IWAC's stone building and paused in front of the main entrance. "But here's another thing: you've got to continue to have good races. Great races, in fact. You need to set records at the next AAU Championships. You need to show that you've got more to offer, that you're not going to fade away before Los Angeles."

"Are you worried I'll get married and retire?"

"It's been known to happen."

"I have no plans to marry. But even if I did, who says that would be the end of my running?"

"Listen, just keep getting better and better," Coach Sheppard said, squeezing her shoulder before turning and waving goodbye. Betty watched him saunter toward Michigan Avenue and tried to shake the sense she was treading on shaky ground.

WHEN SHE RETURNED home that evening, she flopped across her bed, jotted a quick letter to General MacArthur, and then dropped her head onto her forearms. She'd write to everyone else tomorrow. She couldn't believe she had gone to Amsterdam and won gold right under the noses of all those Olympic officials and now they were telling her to quit. What exactly did she and the other women need to do to be considered good enough? She pictured the intensity of Coach Sheppard's expression as he told her she needed to win at the next National AAU Championships and shuddered. And what would happen when she lost a race? Would it undermine everything she had accomplished?

FROM THE OFFICE OF COUNT HENRI DE BAILLET-LATOUR
PRESIDENT, INTERNATIONAL OLYMPIC COMMITTEE
LAUSANNE, SWITZERLAND
January 6, 1929

Dear Mademoiselle Robinson,

Thank you for your recent correspondence regarding the participation of women in future Olympiads. The passion you show for your cause is admirable. The IOC strives to provide an event that demonstrates goodwill, athletic greatness, and peace between the advanced nations of the world. While your recent athletic successes are commendable, there are a number of reasons for why the IOC plans to bar women from future competition. Promoting good health is the foremost concern of the IOC and many notable physicians have stated unequivocally that engaging in strenuous physical activity has many adverse effects on women, both physically and mentally. Athletic competition makes a woman overly assertive and bold and ruins the beauty of the feminine physique by eliminating her soft curves through strengthening her arms, broadening her shoulders, narrowing her waist, adding bulk to her legs, and developing power in the trunk, all characteristics that could render a woman overly masculine and unattractive.

Our founding member, the visionary Baron Pierre de Coubertin, has always believed that the primary measure of a woman is the number and quality of offspring she produces, not the number of athletic records she achieves. A woman is best suited to encourage her sons to excel rather than focus on her own ambitions. It has become fashionable for women to claim attention in physical and mental endeavors outside of the domestic sphere, but the IOC supports the timeless ideal of maintaining traditional roles for women as wives and mothers and does not bother itself with fads.

We urge you to look ahead and focus on the most important feminine job: shaping the young minds and bodies of the next generation. Best of luck.

Cordially,
Johann Clieg
Undersecretary, Public Affairs of the IOC

Dear Miss Robinson,

Thank you for writing to us to share your frustration that women may be banned from future Olympic competition. We appreciate your proposed editorial on the subject of encouraging women's participation in sports, but after discussing it with our editorial team, we concluded a "Day in the Life" piece with a focus on your fashion choices would be far more popular with both our readers and sponsors. In fact, one of our leading cosmetic advertisers would be willing to name a shade of lipstick in your honor if you are interested in developing some compelling business opportunities that capitalize on your recent accomplishments.

We must handle the topic of lady athletes delicately with our subscribers and sponsors. During last summer's Olympic coverage, we received many complaints about photos that showed lady athletes appearing overtaxed and unattractive. According to one of our readers, "There are few things more depressing than opening the evening paper after a long day at work only to find a photo of a tired girl dragging herself across a finish line." It's fortunate that you smiled happily as you won your race so that we could publish the photo of your victory!

I've included the business card for Betsy Miller, our senior fashion and lifestyle editor. She will be following up with you to schedule an interview and discuss possibilities for us to work together that I believe fitting for an attractive and talented young woman like yourself.

Respectfully,
John Lynch
Editor-in-Chief
The Chicago Evening Standard

10.

CHICKEN STEW, FRIED SQUASH, GREENS, AND SOUTH-ern spoon bread. Louise's great-aunt Vera could always be counted on to cook a meal that left them all near-catatonic, but still, even after too many courses to count, no one could resist her aunt Lucy's desserts. Louise slid a slice of apple pie onto her plate and took a seat on the steps to watch Junior, Julia, Agnes, and her cousins play baseball in her great-aunt's backyard. She bit into a forkful of Macintosh apples, cinnamon, and sugar and let out a low moan as its buttery sweetness hit her tongue. Shadows stretched across the golden light of the yard, and the sounds of her mama and aunts gossiping provided a steady hum under the shouts of the younger children as they played. A feeling of contentment spread through her.

"Pretty good stuff, huh?" Uncle Freddie said, dropping to sit beside her and nodding at the pie before sitting back to watch the kids play. "Junior's been bragging about his pitching for a while, but now I see he's not full of hot air. The boy's got a fine arm."

"He's still full of hot air, though," Louise said.

"I suppose that's probably true." Uncle Freddie laughed and

they continued to watch the game in companionable silence. Eventually twilight descended and it became harder and harder to see the boys in the "outfield," but no one stopped playing, even as the whiteness of the ball dimmed in the backyard's violet-hued low light. The fall days had been unusually warm, but as soon as the sun set, a sharp coolness pierced the evening air. Already the leaves on the trees were brightening into vibrant shades of gold and crimson.

"You gonna lick that plate clean?" Uncle Freddie asked as Louise scraped her fork over the plate to get the last bit of apple chunks.

"I might."

"Reckon you earned it. Your mama was saying you ran a good race yesterday."

Louise took a final bite of the pie and placed her plate on the ground. "I sure tried."

"That kind of effort counts for a lot," said Uncle Freddie, nodding. Julia, who was playing third base, missed a wild throw from Junior. The ball rolled across the grass toward where they sat on the porch steps.

Julia trotted after it, snorting as she scooped up the ball. "Junior, you really think you're going to play for the Tigers someday? That was a crazy throw."

"Take that back!" he shrieked.

"Oh yeah? You take *that*," Julia said as she wound her arm and threw the ball back straight at him, before sticking her tongue out to make the insult complete.

The ball smacked into his glove and he glared at it for a second before howling and turning to hurl the ball into the outfield.

"Junior, what's your problem?"

"Why'd you go doing that?"

Disgruntled voices rose from the far edges of the yard, and Junior stormed from the game.

Uncle Freddie shook his head. "Junior? Come on back here and pull yourself together," he called, but a moment later, the back door slammed and Junior's wail rose from inside the house. Uncle Freddie chuckled. "Julia, you'll be the one playing in Playstead Park if you keep throwing like that."

Louise could see the whiteness of Julia's teeth as she grinned, and then her younger sister turned and wandered into the outfield in search of the baseball.

"You looking forward to moving to California?" Louise asked.

"It'll be a good adventure. I'm going to miss being close to all of you, but I'm restless. I figure it's time to try something new, find new work. I've stayed in touch with one of my friends from the army, and he finished his engineering degree when he returned home to Chicago. Now he's in flight school in Los Angeles and believes there are opportunities for more coloreds in aviation. Says he can get me some work."

"You going to be the next Lindbergh?"

"No, but my friend writes about promising opportunities. I'm ready to take my chances and join him."

Big, bold headlines in Friday's newspaper had reported a crash in the stock market, and despite President Hoover's assurances, people were jittery. Uncle Freddie's plans for California had been in the works for over a month, but a new urgency seemed to underlie all his talk of the future.

"California sounds grand. All that sunshine."

"I won't miss our winters, that's for sure." He paused and lifted a fallen elm leaf from the step of the porch and studied the swirl of vivid colors bleeding along its surface. "I'll miss fall, though. Not much can beat the beauty of these colors."

"It's not going to be the same around here with you gone," said Louise. As the bachelor of the family, Uncle Freddie could be counted on to pay attention to his nieces and nephews. He'd help with geometry homework, debate the merits of chewing Chiclets versus Juicy Fruit gum, and provide exercises to strengthen pitching arms—these were the important things the kids could entrust to Uncle Freddie.

"Don't worry, this isn't the last you've seen of me, but I wanted to give you something before I go." He reached into his pocket and pulled out his wallet. When he saw Louise's face brighten, he laughed. "Don't get too excited, I'm not giving you money." He pulled out a photo and handed it to her. "Maybe you don't remember because you were pretty young, but I showed you this photo after I took you to a Fourth of July parade, the one where they unveiled the Great War memorial in 1920. Remember?"

Louise looked at the photo's younger version of Uncle Freddie, sitting in a café with a friend. Both wore their army uniforms, and they looked handsome and confident, content. "I remember this. After I saw it, I thought the war didn't look so bad."

"True, if you only saw this photo, no one could blame you for thinking that. Do you remember what I told you about why I served in the war?"

Louise nodded, though her uncertainty must have shown because Uncle Freddie continued. "I told you I served because

I felt it was important to show my respect and pride for my country, even if the same type of respect and pride wasn't necessarily returned to me by my countrymen?"

"I remember."

"You've been racing awfully well, and this whole running business could lead you to something bigger. I saw some of those newspaper stories in the *Globe* about women competing in the Olympics. Maybe you could be one of them. You're strong, fast, and have a good head on your shoulders."

"I didn't see anything about girls like me competing in such important races."

"You mean colored girls? It'll happen someday."

"Really?"

"Sure, change may be slow, but it's coming."

It sounded like a long shot, but if her uncle wanted her to try, she could do that. Since she'd started practicing with the team, she felt stronger and her mind was quieter, freer of the worries that had nagged her. She was tired at the end of each day, but tired in a good way that helped keep her bad memories at bay. She no longer climbed into bed and replayed that awful afternoon of Grace's accident in her mind. Now she fell asleep quickly and slept hard. "All right, I'll stick with it."

"Good girl. If you ever end up heading to California for races, I'll come and cheer you on." He put out his hand to shake hers. "Deal?"

Louise nudged his hand aside and embraced him. "Deal."

11.

October 1929
Fulton, Missouri

ONE SATURDAY AFTERNOON, HELEN SHAMBLED TO-
ward the barn. The air felt warm on her bare forearms,
but there was a crispness in the wind, a feeling that the weather
would turn soon. An eerie silence hung over the farm. Pa was
off working in a distant field. Ma had taken to her bed the day
before, complaining of a headache, and one of Pa's sisters had
taken Bobbie Lee to her house for a few days. Helen couldn't
remember the last time Ma had taken to bed. Even after Bobbie
Lee's early morning arrival several years earlier, Ma had been
back in the kitchen by lunchtime making Pa his midday meal.

Her thoughts were interrupted by a red-tailed hawk's scream
cutting through the whisper of the surrounding cornstalks. She
glanced at the sky and saw the creature gliding on updrafts, circling, focused on an unfortunate victim below. Helen stopped
for a moment, admiring how it moved with effortless speed.

For the last year Helen had been reading and rereading the
Missouri Daily Observer's Amsterdam Olympic coverage. The
newsprint smudged, the paper turned brittle and yellowed, but
she continued to pore over the articles, memorizing the results.

Since Miss Thurston had found her in the outbuilding with Jimmy, Helen had been spending more time alone, thinking. She couldn't change the past, but moving ahead, she could do things that would make everyone proud of her. Reading about the Olympics had given her some ideas.

She proceeded to the barn, went inside, and rummaged around Pa's worktable for a moment, looking for a hammer. Once she found one, she walked to the barn's wide entryway, drove a couple of tacks into the dry wooden doorframe, and strung a line of twine across the opening. She then paced a couple of hundred feet down the driveway away from the yard, turned, and raced back toward the barn with everything she had. Her bare feet thundered along the packed-dirt road. Her lungs burned with the sudden exertion. She reached the doorway and pulled through the twine, imagining it was finish tape. Truth be told, she hadn't made it loose enough and it stung a little across her chest, but she didn't mind. She welcomed the pain. It told her she had been running fast. Really fast.

When her breathing settled, she reached for the pitchfork leaning against the wall next to her and got to work mucking out the horse's stall. After she finished her chores in the barn, she headed for the house. Dr. McCubbin's Model A was parked next to the picket fence by the farmhouse. Helen slowed. What brought him out here? At the fence gate, she paused, peeling a few chips of white paint off the wood with her grubby fingers. Tense voices floated toward her from the open windows of the parlor. She edged toward the house, stopping upon the first step of the porch, listening, and hunching her shoulders, making herself small so no one would see her.

Dr. McCubbin said, "Now, Frank, you must take this seriously. Your wife is to have no more children. All things considered, it's fortunate this pregnancy ended as it did. Bertie needs some rest, but everything will be fine."

"Fine?" Pa huffed. "Doc, don't you see where I live? What farmer doesn't have a bunch of kids to pull their own weight around the homestead? I need help."

"You have a mighty strong daughter. Sure, she's a bit accident-prone, but she's stronger than most boys her age."

"A girl." A derisive snort. "I never wanted her."

Dr. McCubbin spoke again, assuring Pa that Bobbie Lee would be helpful, but the words dropped away. Helen suddenly felt light-headed and she dropped to the first step of the porch. She rested her skinned elbows on the knees of her overalls, staring into the distance.

I never wanted her.

Her vision blurred with tears.

There were so many ways she had disappointed her parents over the years. She knew Ma wished she could muster enthusiasm for playing an instrument. She knew Pa wished she were a boy. She knew both Ma and Pa were shamed by what she had done with Jimmy. Why, she had shamed *herself* with that too. She gave an involuntary shudder at that memory and glanced back at the door.

From the sounds of it, Dr. McCubbin would be leaving soon. Desperate to avoid detection, she dashed from the porch steps, out the gate, into the cornfield adjacent to the yard. She galloped along a path where the cornstalks stood tall, blocking her from view. When she reached the far end of the field, near a bare patch of ground, she stopped at the salt lick. No one could see her here. She could be by herself, do some thinking. To keep her lower lip from trembling, she tore a foxtail from next to a cornstalk and placed it in her mouth, the bitter taste of it a welcome distraction from what nagged at her.

I never wanted her.

She lay down on the warm, hard-packed earth. The cornstalks fanned around her, cutting her off from the rest of the world. Above, cumulus clouds swept across the sky. She studied them, playing her favorite game, looking for shapes. A lamb. A pail. A feather. She tried to push Pa's words from her mind.

I never wanted—no, *stop.*

She closed her eyes, tried to banish the sick feeling that slithered around her stomach as she thought about Ma's troubles. At least Dr. McCubbin made it sound like she would be fine after a few days with her feet up. In the distance the rumble of the doc's automobile revved, but she stayed, savoring the feeling of the sun warming her. Her breath slowed. Her toes splayed out as the cords of her legs loosened. It felt as though she were drifting on one of the clouds overhead.

And then she was running again, surrounded by people smiling and cheering. Hands waved in the air, applauding. She ran and burst through a finish ribbon; a sensation of silk slipped across her chest and arms, almost like walking through a spider-web. Someone handed her a silver winner's cup and she held it aloft. It glimmered in the sunlight, blinding her as she turned in a circle so everyone could see. She basked in the crowd's joy. Hands patted her shoulder. The warmth of victory suffused every inch of her.

Everyone wanted her.

Her eyes cracked open to see blue sky but she closed them again, eager to hold on to the sense that everyone loved her. A line from one of the newspapers about the Olympics came back to her, the typed words drifting across her mind's eye the same way clouds floated across the sky. *When notified by phone, Mr. Robinson said of his daughter reaching the finals, "She's the greatest girl in the world. I'm the happiest man alive."*

A searing pinch scorched the soft inside of Helen's forearm and she smacked it reflexively with her other hand. A horsefly lay on its back next to where her arm had been resting, its legs still twitching slightly. Helen pulled her knees into her chest. The race, the crowds—it all felt so real. Her finger pads still tingled with the feeling of the smooth silver of the winner's cup.

Surrounded as she was by parched fields and cornstalks, Amsterdam felt mighty far away, but still. The vision of the race was trying to tell her something. Though the papers had made such a fuss about Betty being young, Helen was even younger. She had time. Maybe she could overcome all the ways she had disappointed everyone. What could she do to make people proud of her? How would it feel to make Pa the happiest man alive? She clambered to her feet. The first thing she could do was go back to the house and make Ma a cup of tea.

PART 2

July 1931–December 1932

THE CHICAGO EVENING STANDARD
July 5, 1931

"Betty Robinson Defeated by Stella Walsh"
Lady Athletes Look Forward to
Olympics in Los Angeles

Dallas—After a history-making series of recent victories, the tide has turned for Chicago's hometown sprinting champion, Betty Robinson. She returned home today disappointed after running into stiff competition in the form of Cleveland's Stella Walsh at the National AAU Championships held in Dallas yesterday at Southern Methodist University Stadium. The two girls raced the sprint as if their lives depended on it, but in the last few yards, Walsh pulled ahead to take top billing. After setting world records in both the 50-yard and 100-yard dashes, Miss Robinson of the Illinois Women's Athletic Club (IWAC) had set a high bar for the rest of the world's lady runners.

Miss Walsh, who competes for New York Central Railway, enjoyed a banner day and set records in the 100-yard, 220-yard, and broad jump. When Miss Robinson was asked how it felt to come home empty-handed of her usual haul of medals and trophies, she conceded, "Miss Walsh competed admirably. If I'm to recapture my top ranking, I need to get more serious about my training and make some changes." Pressed about what kind of changes she is considering, Robinson refused to provide any clues to her plans.

With last spring's International Olympic Committee's confirmation that women will be permitted to compete in future Olympics, Americans can look forward to all the drama that lady athletes bring to the sporting arena. More than 150 of the nation's top racers turned out to compete in the National AAU Championships, no doubt inspired by the possibility of traveling to the next Olympics in sunny Los Angeles to compete, sightsee, and socialize with other top-notch athletes from all over the world.

Up-and-coming all-around girl athlete Miss Babe Didrikson of Dallas made her debut on the national stage by setting new records in the javelin and baseball throw and placing second to Walsh in the broad jump. Keep an eye on the outgoing blond girl from the Lone Star State—we think she's going places!

12.

August 1931
Fulton, Missouri

AFTER HELEN FINISHED HER STUDIES AT MIDDLE RIVER School, no one in the Stephens family spoke about what she would be doing in the fall. She was thirteen years old. A few of her classmates would travel to the other side of town to attend Fulton High School, but many would stay home to work or be hired out at other nearby farms, while a few would go on to work in the shoe factory near the rail yard. Pa often said he wanted her to earn wages at the shoe factory, but she didn't know how quickly he hoped to see that plan materialize. Helen wanted to go to high school, but didn't dare ask about her future because not knowing kept the less desirable options at bay for as long as possible.

Times had gotten tough around the Stephens farm. Ma cobbled together more and more one-pot dinners, and as meat became an increasingly scarce menu item, chipped beef on toast, a meal not often viewed as a delicacy in most quarters, was greeted by Bobbie Lee and Helen as a treat. Letters with the bank's return address arrived in the mail drop with increasing frequency. Pa would read them with a scowl etched across his face, and then he'd mutter darkly and thrust the latest missive into a cupboard where Helen could see a stack of similar letters yellowing out of sight.

Pa's presence at meals that spring and summer was a rarity as he wrung out every last minute of daylight to work, but he could always be counted upon to join them for Sunday supper. It was during one of these evenings in early August that Ma chewed her lip as she spooned out macaroni and cheese to each of them. Before she sat, she folded her scarecrow-thin arms across the bib of her apron and announced, "Helen should get her high school diploma. She needs to start classes at Fulton High next month."

Helen and Bobbie Lee froze. The moment Helen had been dreading had arrived.

Pa appeared to ignore what she had said and raised his fork over his plate as if to dig in, but paused. "This is what happens when girls like you go to college. You start thinking everyone needs educating, but look at Helen."

Bobbie Lee and Ma swiveled their heads in Helen's direction.

"See? Look at her." Pa glowered. "All she wears is work shirts and overalls. She's no student."

Helen lifted her fork with as much dignity as she could muster and surveyed her plate. She wasn't hankering to get all dolled up each day like she imagined the other girls at school did, but that didn't mean she didn't want to go. "I like history and reading and writing," she said.

Pa snorted. "None of that's useful."

Ma batted a hand in the air as if brushing away her husband's skepticism. "She's going," she said, her face stony. From her pocket, she pulled out a letter and pen and placed both items by Pa's left arm. "I've secured her a room in the home of Miss Humphries, one of the English teachers. Her house is three blocks from the school. Helen will stay there during the week and come home on Friday evenings in time for supper." She pointed to the document. "You'll need to sign that."

Pa's fork fell to his plate with a clatter and he pushed the paper and pen away. "She ain't staying somewhere in town. I need her here to help in the evenings."

"You think she's going to spend half her day marching to and from school? No. She needs time to study. Or are you planning to hitch up the wagon and take her back and forth?" Again, Ma pushed the letter in front of Pa, but now she hovered over the table, hands on her hips, glaring at her husband.

Pa shoved his chair away from the table, crossing one leg over the other. "How you think we're going to pay for this?"

"The state's making some money available for boarding rural students this year. I secured an allowance for us."

"You been thinking about this for a while now, huh?"

"I have."

Helen sucked in her breath and gawked, dumbstruck. This was a whole new Ma. Helen had never seen her stick to her guns like this. Ma's jaw clenched and her face paled, but her resolute expression never wavered.

No one said a word.

"It figures Uncle Sam's gonna waste his money on something like this. How about a little more help for us fellas working our knuckles bloody each day?" Pa's eyes darted back and forth along the letter and then he scraped his chair toward the table and commenced eating again. "Fine," he said, through a full mouth. "I'll sign it, but I ain't driving her back and forth from town on the weekends."

"She won't need any rides. She can walk."

Pa kept his gaze on his plate and used his fork to spear his food with such force, Helen wondered if he was leaving gouge marks on the plate, but Ma slid into her seat, her head held high, and started eating. Helen exchanged a wide-eyed glance with Bobbie Lee.

Silence.

After several long minutes, Pa grabbed the pen to scrawl his signature at the bottom of the page, leapt to his feet, and stormed out the kitchen door to the backyard. With the gust of wind from the slammed door, the paper blew off the table and fluttered to the ground. Unfazed, Ma bent to lift the document and smoothed it against her apron, not looking at either child as she tucked it back into her pocket and then took a long drink of water from her glass. She turned to Bobbie Lee. "Now tell me about what Miss Cross taught you in Sunday school earlier."

Helen only half listened as Bobbie Lee nattered on about his morning. Often, in the evenings before bed, if she poked her head out of her doorway and looked down the hallway into her parents' room, she could catch a glimpse of Ma in the midst of her nighttime routine. Before Ma climbed into bed, she always paused in front of the diploma from William Woods College that hung on the peeling wallpaper above the lamp on her bedside table. She would stare at it, slowly wringing her hands together as she rubbed lanolin into her fingers, roughened from vegetable gardening, laundry, and washing endless dishes. Helen watched Ma's faraway expression as she took in that piece of paper on the wall, and sometimes she'd adjust its black wooden frame, even though it always hung perfectly straight. Though the paper curled at the edges within its frame, the cursive lettering had faded, and the gold foil stamp looked dim, Ma appeared to take comfort in it.

Now, sitting at the kitchen table, she saw the faint glow of pink in Ma's cheeks and the way her hand kept ghosting over her pocket, touching it to reassure herself the document was still there. Helen started to think. She glanced at the few pieces of macaroni remaining on her plate. For once, her appetite had left her. In its place was a hunger for something else. An education.

13.

B Y THE END OF THAT SUMMER, BLUE RIBBONS AND medals filled the Stokeses' front room from all of Louise's running successes, but the most important award, the one that made her the proudest, was the Mayor Curley trophy. Louise had won this gleaming silver cup after clinching first place in Boston's largest track and field meet, and it now held a place of honor, perched front and center on the mantel. It was Louise's final year of high school and the outdoor racing season would be ending soon.

One evening Louise and Emily were preparing dinner in the kitchen when Mama appeared in the doorway. Julia and Junior were working on homework at the table and Papa was replacing a latch on the girls' bedroom door that had become loose. Until Mama cleared her throat, no one noticed her arrival.

"Oh, you're home early," Julia said.

Louise turned and couldn't miss the ashy pallor to Mama's complexion. "What happened?"

Mama sighed and moved to the table, where she dropped

onto an open chair and massaged her temples. "Mrs. Grand-away passed this morning."

The children gaped, all thoughts of dinner forgotten.

"How?" Junior asked, his dark eyes wide.

Mama rubbed her palm across her forehead. "When I went into her room this morning to help her rise, I found her."

"So you saw her . . . dead?" Julia asked.

"She looked peaceful."

"Were you scared?" Junior asked with a noticeable gulp.

Mama shook her head with a weary heaviness. "No. She led a long, commendable life."

"But what did you do?" Agnes said.

"I went about the business of making calls and alerting her family. My day's been filled with preparations for her service and readying the place for guests. Her children descended upon the house, so I helped them find important documents, fed them, and made up the guest rooms for them to stay."

"Is her body still there?" Junior asked.

Mama shook her head.

Papa moved to put his hands on Mama's shoulders and rub them. "Mrs. Grandaway was an admirable lady. Always treated you well. What does this mean for your job?" he asked, his expression solemn as he comforted her. With colder weather approaching, his hours would be reduced, as they were each winter when there was less to do in the Conways' yard and garden.

"I don't know. We knew the old lady was becoming frail, and she had her health issues to be sure, but this comes as a surprise. I've been so busy all day, I've scarcely had time to realize what's happened." Mama accepted a glass of water from Louise and drank it all in one gulp. "It's the only place I've ever worked. Mrs. Grandaway hired me to work when I was about your age, Louise. Since then, the house has grown quieter as her children moved on to start lives of their own. Charlie and I are the only ones left."

Louise felt a pang of sorrow when she pictured Charlie, Mrs. Grandaway's driver and groundskeeper. He was older than Mama and always had butterscotch candies in his pocket. What would he do now?

"Are you sad she's dead?" Junior asked.

"I'm sorry to see her go. Papa's right, she's taken good care of our family over the years in many ways."

Louise remembered the last time she had gone over to Mrs. Grandaway's to bring Mama a message. Of course, Louise never went anywhere in the house, just stayed in the kitchen, but even there, she got a sense of the old lady. Lists lay on the counter or were tacked around the room, all covered in a spidery but graceful script. These lists contained exacting directions for how Mrs. Grandaway wanted tasks completed. On the second Wednesday of each month, all windowpanes needed to be scrubbed with newspaper and a mixture of warm water and vinegar. The silver was to be polished every Thursday, and the china in the corner cabinet needed to be taken out every Friday, dusted, and placed with dinner plates along the back, salad plates stacked on the right, dessert plates to the left, and all other pieces in between in rows from largest to smallest.

"Where will you go next?" Emily asked.

"I don't know. Jobs are not easy to come by these days."

"Everyone knows Mrs. Grandaway was fond of you in her own special way," Papa said.

"True, but you know as well as I do that no one's hiring help, and certainly no one will pay me the wage that she did."

Emily brushed some dust off the apron she wore and said, "I've been getting lots of compliments lately on my stitching at church. Mrs. Brown always tells me I could take in mending work, probably land myself some sort of sewing job too if I wanted."

Mama nodded. "Your handiwork is lovely. Everyone's been talking about that altarpiece you made. I don't doubt that Mrs. Brown is right, but I don't want anything taking away from your schoolwork."

"I can sew during the afternoons and complete my schoolwork in the evenings. It will be fine."

Mama cocked her head to gaze at Papa, and the two exchanged a glance. "That's a good idea, but don't get carried away with taking on too much. It should only be a little piecework. Nothing that keeps you too busy, nothing that detracts from your academics."

Emily agreed and, without saying anything more, she and Louise went back to preparing dinner while Julia rose and set the table. Mama and Papa disappeared into their room, but their voices could be heard through the wall, low and tense. Louise envied the way Emily could help and it troubled her that she had nothing similar to offer. Running certainly didn't pay anything. She would be done with school in the spring, but what would happen then? With no means and her dark skin, none of the nearby women's colleges were realistic possibilities. She needed to start thinking about what would come next.

THE FOLLOWING DAY at practice after school, Louise lingered a couple of minutes to speak with Coach Quain. "Excuse me, sir, but are there any jobs that would use my running skills? Or could I win any money or something like that?"

Coach Quain tucked his clipboard under his arm. "I don't know. What do you mean?"

"Well, what's going to happen with me after I graduate in the spring?"

"I guess that depends. How's your family doing, Louise?"

A cool breeze blew down the straightaway on the railroad tracks and dried leaves scraped along the ties. Louise wrapped her arms around her chest in an attempt to stay warm. "We're fine. I've started thinking about getting a job."

"Yes, I see. When I'm out on my postal route, I talk to a lot of folks. Would you like me to keep an eye out for you?"

"Thank you, sir. Is there any way I can make some money out of doing this? I've put a lot of time into training."

He shook his head. "In fact, the AAU rules are pretty strict. In order for you to maintain your amateur status, you can't accept any paying jobs pertaining to running, no cash prizes, nothing. You've been racing awfully well, though, and if you keep it up through the indoor season this winter, you could get an invitation to the Olympic trials in the spring."

"Will the Olympics pay me?"

"No, I'm afraid not."

"So what's the point of competing in them?"

"I suppose it's just an honor and could give you a unique experience. You could see more of the country and meet new people." He scratched at his chin. "I'll tell you what, though. Not many colored athletes have competed in the Olympics, and certainly no colored women, but there are no rules banning anyone. I believe you have what it takes. You just need to hang in there and stick with it."

Uncle Freddie and her promise to keep racing flashed through Louise's mind, and pride bloomed in her chest. "Thank you, Coach."

"Of course. And while I'm on my route, I'll keep an ear out for any work that may suit you. See you tomorrow."

Louise nodded and turned away to run home. While Coach's words sent a thrill through her, unique experiences and seeing more of the country weren't going to pay the bills. Her family needed more money and she needed a way to find it.

14.

September 1931
Evanston, Illinois

BETTY HESITATED BEFORE PASSING THE STATUES LOOMing over the entrance to Northwestern University's Patten Gymnasium. To her right, a sculpted woman in an empire-waist gown gazed toward Sheridan Road. It seemed promising that the athletic facility had a woman guarding over it.

"You getting to know Pat?"

A tall young man with bright blue eyes and a shock of blond hair combed back from his face stood beside Betty, pointing at the statue.

"Excuse me?" Betty asked.

"This is Pat. And that's Jim." He pointed to a statue of a man on the opposite side of the entrance's steps. "Jim's all right, but I'm with you, Pat's much more captivating. And I'm Bill." He put out his hand for her to take.

"I'm Betty Robinson, a new transfer." Betty took his extended hand into her own. His palm had a sharp callus that scraped across her fingers, sending a tingle along her arm. He had big hands. Big but graceful. Long-fingered and wide-palmed, they connoted confidence, resourcefulness, and strength—they implied that he could be relied upon. Betty felt her face redden as she admired them, then pulled her hands behind her back as if that would clear her mind of thinking about Bill that way. "So why do you like Pat more?"

"She looks smart and her serious expression tells us she's not suffering any fools. Look at the little guy crouched at her side. She's the boss, you can tell."

"She's got a big job to do." A steady stream of male students passed, coming in and out of the building. Betty bit her lip. "Looks like a lot is happening around here."

"If I can be of service, just say the word."

"I'm looking for Coach Hill's office."

"Sure, I'm heading into Patten and can take you there. He's on the main floor." Bill gestured for her to lead the way. "Where'd you transfer from?"

"I've spent the last two years at Thornton Community College, but I wanted a few more options than they offer. This could be a good fit for me."

"Sounds like it's Northwestern's lucky day. I'd say you've come to the right place," he said, stepping ahead to open the door for her. "What are you planning to study?"

"Physical education. I'm a runner, actually, and hoping to coach someday," she said quickly before she could change her mind. It felt like a test, telling this man that she was a runner. Maybe he'd raise his eyebrows and make an excuse to escape, uncomfortable with the idea of a girl who liked competition.

But he didn't. If anything, he looked delighted.

"You don't say. I'm on a few teams around here and, well, Coach Hill's just the fellow for you."

"I'm actually hoping he'll take me on and coach me."

"No kidding, that would be terrific. Here, his office is this way." Bill ushered her to a warren of doors with frosted windows. When he faced her, his bright blue eyes seemed to look straight through her, and suddenly she felt nervous. Would Coach Hill be as open to her plan as this young man seemed to be? Bill seemed to sense her uncertainty and he straightened his tie as if girding himself to get down to business. "Would you like me to take you in there?"

Betty shook her head. "You're kind, but no, I can do it. Thanks, though."

"You bet. I sure hope to see you again soon. If you ask me, you're just what this place needs. Best of luck to you, Betty."

She waved goodbye and watched him saunter away with a confidence that she figured came from the ease of his athletic nature, but also from the fact that he had never had to worry that a team wouldn't accept him on account of something as arbitrary as his sex. Did he have any idea of all the perks that being a man afforded him? Of course not. She hadn't thought about it either until she started trying to figure out this complicated world of competition.

The sweet scent of floor polish and the itchy smell of chalk dust hovered in the air around her. Surrounding her was the low tone of men's voices and shadowy figures visible through the frosted-glass windows. She slowed to read the name placards outside of each door. She found Coach Hill's office, took a deep breath to quell the nerves roiling her stomach, and knocked.

"Come in," a gruff voice called.

She pushed the door open and found a man with rumpled graying hair sitting back in his chair reviewing a pile of type-written pages set on the desk in front of him. "Yes?" he asked without looking up.

"Coach Hill, I'm Elizabeth Robinson, a new student."

He glanced at her sharply and then pointed at the empty chair facing his desk. "I know who you are."

"You do?"

"You think I don't read the papers?"

"No, that's not what I meant." This was not how she wanted this conversation to go. She took the seat he offered, taking a moment to settle her purse on her lap and gather herself. "I just transferred here."

"I see." He sounded bored. "I'm sure this isn't merely a social call. What can I do for you, Miss Robinson?"

"I'm interested in continuing my training and want to de-fend my title at the Los Angeles Olympic Games."

"You've been running for the IWAC, isn't that right?"

She nodded.

"Then why are you here talking with me? That club has a good coaching staff."

"Yes, they do." Betty spun her diamond ring around her finger. "It's just that I want to work harder."

She expected him to laugh at her, but he remained expres-sionless. "Harder, huh? Didn't you set a world record in the hundred? You've got a gold medal already. A silver in the relay too, right?"

Betty's mouth felt dry. Her tongue seemed to stick to the roof of her mouth. "I recently lost a race. I came in second at the National AAU Championships back in July."

"If I recall the newspaper reports, it was a close finish. Could have gone either way. I'm sure you'll be just fine for the Olympic team when the time comes." He dropped his gaze back to his papers as if dismissing her, but she didn't budge.

"It's just that I felt like something was missing in Dallas. Some motivation." She paused. Coach Hill raised his gaze and squinted at her as if refocusing. She had his attention now. "After Amsterdam the IOC announced it was planning to ban women from future Olympics, and I worked like the devil with my teammates to have us reinstated, but the refusal disappointed me more than I was willing to admit. If I'm honest, my motivation suffered. I slacked off on my training."

"That's understandable."

"Well, the IOC met last spring and reinstated us, so now I want to be ready to race in Los Angeles. You have a record of getting terrific results from your racers. Let me train with you. I really want this. Please."

He sat back. "I'm sure a girl like you has options for all kinds of pursuits."

A girl like you. She hated having her ambitions dismissed by people who thought they knew everything about her. She gritted her teeth, but kept her face earnest. "I want to show everyone that I'm better than ever."

"You'd be the only lady here. What do you think about that?"

"I can handle it."

"I don't doubt it. But I don't want you to distract my fellas either. They're serious about racing and my job is to coach them. There's nothing in my contract about coaching women."

"I understand. I won't do anything to get in the way of your job."

"And I don't want you flitting about looking for a husband on my team."

"Sir, with all due respect, do you really think if I was in the market for a husband I'd spend my time running? I can't think of a better way to scare most men off."

Coach Hill barked with laughter. "Fine. Based on everything I've read, you're a talented runner. Now it's time to add some discipline to your routines and start some healthy habits, like eating correctly and sleeping enough every night. If I decide to work with you, I'd put you on a diet of specific foods and give you a sleep log. And no smoking. If I take you on, you'll have to follow my directions. Are you ready to give up some fun in exchange for running better?"

Betty squared her shoulders. This was the opportunity she wanted, and though she hated begging, she would do it. "I'll do whatever it takes."

"Fine, you can start training with my team, but if it's not working out, I reserve the right to stop our arrangement at any time."

"Yes, sir."

"And another thing. No dating my boys. Do you understand? Look elsewhere for that kind of entertainment."

"No dating your athletes. Got it."

"You say that now, but this deal includes my welcoming committee out there, Bill Riel. No dating Bill or any of them."

Bill was on the track team? She glanced to the door, flustered, but quickly straightened. How had Coach Hill known about their conversation?

"Of course, sir, none of them. I'm here to run."

One of Coach Hill's nostrils flared as if he caught a whiff of uncertainty in the air, but he nodded. "If you want to start with the indoor season, be here on Monday. There's no women's locker room, but there are a couple of changing rooms on the ground floor. You can use those."

BETTY SPENT FALL training with the men's track team and racing during the indoor season. Under Coach Hill's rigorous coaching, her times improved, and she built confidence. He urged her to try longer distances, so she added the 220-yard dash to her repertoire and experienced promising results. Through it all, she found the men on the track team to be friendly and supportive. And competitive.

One afternoon as she worked on starts, she stumbled as she rose and Ned Martin, a sophomore on the team, called out, "Hey, Robinson, don't trip and break your ankle. You won't beat Stella Walsh hobbling around on one foot."

She laughed and put her hand on her hip. "Thanks for the vote of confidence, Ned. Now don't trip over that ego of yours when you head home tonight for an exciting evening of backgammon with your mother."

They all chuckled at the ribbing, and even Coach Hill

cracked a smile as he headed over to the high-jump area. Betty ran a couple more laps around the indoor track, dividing the distances into varying levels of effort as Coach Hill had advised. When she began her cool-down, Bill caught up with her and ran at her side. Outside the gymnasium's windows, the light faded into a deep, velvety blue.

"I hear you're planning to race at the next Olympics," he said.

"I hope to, yes."

"So that'll mean you're a two-time Olympian."

"First I need to qualify again, remember?"

"I'm pretty sure you'll be heading to California and going to fancy Hollywood parties next summer while all of us chumps are trying to cool off in Lake Michigan."

She laughed. The two ran the straightaway, their breathing the only sound between them. Since she'd met Bill on her first day, he always offered compliments on her races and made small talk while they practiced.

"Say, I've worked up an appetite," he said. "Would you have any interest in going out for dinner after this?"

"I can't. When I joined this team, I promised Coach I wouldn't socialize with any of his runners, and I intend to stick to my word."

"Socialize? Who said anything about that? We don't have to talk. We can just eat."

"Sorry, I can't. I'm lucky to be here at all. The last thing I want to do is rock the boat."

"Lucky to be here? You're the one with an Olympic medal. You're the most accomplished runner out here! What's Coach thinking?"

"His job is to coach the men, not me. There's no women's track team, so he's just taken me on to be helpful."

"But how about if we don't tell anyone? After all, it's just one meal."

They had stopped running and were stretching a short distance from the rest of the group. Betty spotted Coach Hill in the entryway of the gymnasium talking to a staff member.

"I'm sorry," she whispered, "but I can't. I don't dare risk it."

Bill's gaze followed Betty's and he too watched Coach Hill, exasperation furrowing his brow. "What a ridiculous deal. Well, I'll tell you what, I'm not giving up easily. Coach Hill always says I'm single-minded in my pursuit of victory, and now the challenge is on."

"Is that so?"

"Yep, mark my words."

"I'm pretty stubborn too, and I refuse to lose my spot here, so I don't know what to tell you. Good luck," she said. And she strode out of the gym, trying to keep from looking pleased.

15.

January 1932
Fulton, Missouri

HELEN SLIPPED THROUGH THE CLASSROOM DOOR AND took her seat for algebra. Instead of Principal Newbolt's dour face at the front of the room, Miss Schultz, the music teacher, stood behind his desk. "Good afternoon, everyone," she said. "Principal Newbolt has an important meeting so I'm here today. We'll start off with returning your recent tests and then work on corrections."

Helen fidgeted in her seat as Miss Schultz's heels clicked up and down the aisles between the desks while she handed back quizzes. The most recent one had been a disaster. When Helen had looked at the quiz's long column of equations, the numbers had appeared to swim. Her palms had sweated. She had abandoned several problems and guessed the answers on many others. When her test slid across her desk, Helen lifted it with trembling hands. Sure enough, a red *F* and *See me* were emblazoned on the top in Principal Newbolt's angry scrawl. Her heart sank. Grimacing, she pushed the test into her notebook and sank into her seat, regretting that Miss Schultz had seen her lousy grade.

"Sit up straight," Miss Schultz whispered to Helen, but apparently it was loud enough for nearby classmates to hear.

"Hey, Stephens, ya falling asleep?" a reedy voice called out. Isham Holland. Every day brought a fresh insult from the scrawny boy who sat two rows behind her. Name calling, taunts, spitballs, water on her seat. Math had become insufferable. Usually Ish hid his harassment from the strict rule of Principal Newbolt, but with their usual teacher gone, a current of insubordination eddied through the room.

Grinding her teeth together, Helen unfolded from her slouch and let her head rise, spine straighten.

"Whoa, now none of us can see from back here. You're too big. It's like you're Popeye." Sniggering. "Yeah, that's it. Popeye!"

Giggles erupted. Whispers of *Popeye, Popeye, Popeye* surrounded her.

"Dry up, Ish," she said through gritted teeth.

"From now on, everyone should call you Popeye," he crowed. "It's perfect!"

Before she had time to think, Helen reached across Maxine Dulcey's desk and grabbed the pink eraser next to her pencil, whipped around, and threw it at Ish. The eraser hit him square on the forehead and bounced away, landing somewhere on the floor nearby.

"Owww." He rubbed at the angry red welt already rising on his pale freckled face. Laughter drowned the room. He scowled. Now everyone was laughing at *him*.

Miss Schultz spun around. "What's going on?"

"Popeye's distracting us from working on our corrections," Ish said with a smirk.

"Mr. Holland, that's not how you speak about a lady," Miss Schultz said.

"Popeye ain't no lady," Ish said loudly enough for everyone to hear. Helen winced.

"You're treading on thin ice, young man." Miss Schultz glared at him. "In this classroom, we call students by their given names."

Ish raised his eyebrows in defiance. "Bet she doesn't mind."

Helen could feel her classmates studying her. Underneath the faded cotton of her shirt, sweat dripped down her sides, but she plastered a grin across her face and forced out a laugh.

"I yam what I yam," Helen said, imitating the cartoon sailor character's distinctive voice. She felt the tone of the laughter shift from jeering to amusement, the tension slacken. She savored the sense of leading the entertainment, not being on the wrong side of it.

Miss Schultz rested her hands on her hips. "Enough. Gladys, Martha, Martie, and George, please head to the board and demonstrate the corrections for questions one through four. Now."

The room filled with the rustling of paper and several students moved from their desks to the blackboard. The moment had passed and Helen had survived. She sighed and brushed her hair from her face as she opened her notebook and glared at her test. She had no idea where to begin fixing her mistakes.

WHEN THE BELL rang to signal the end of class, everyone jumped to their feet to push through the scrum and move toward the hallway for their next class, but Miss Schultz signaled for Helen to remain behind. While waiting for the room to clear, Helen closed her notebook slowly and rubbed her clammy hands down her denim-clad legs. Once everyone else was gone, Miss Schultz approached Helen and leaned against the desk next to her, crossing one silk-stockinged leg over the other.

"Why on earth did you play along with Ish?"

"Maybe if everyone thinks I'm funny, it will all go away," Helen answered in a small voice.

"Boys like Ish Holland do not go away."

Helen stared at scuff marks on the floor.

"In the staff room yesterday, Miss Morris was saying you're one of the top students in her English class. You're bright. You have a great deal of potential if you can stay focused on your schoolwork."

Helen's shoulders sagged. This was the best advice Miss Schultz could give? Didn't she know that the importance of school had nothing to do with the books they read, the algebra equations they solved, or the dates they memorized? Helen was sick to death of falling asleep imagining the funny things she could have said in class to make her classmates laugh. She was sick of pretending she didn't notice the way girls wrinkled their noses when they saw what she was wearing. School was about fitting in, plain and simple, and she was sorely lacking whatever was needed to accomplish this very skill that most of her classmates appeared to take for granted. She gestured at her worn brown work boots and dungarees. "I've got size twelve feet and am roughly a foot taller than all of the other girls. And then there's this godawful mark over my eye. I fit in like a cow in a henhouse."

Miss Schultz's expression softened in sympathy. She reached

out and smoothed Helen's hair. "You have a lovely complexion and enviably high cheekbones. Your hair is thick and it's a pretty color." She examined Helen a moment longer before dropping her hands. "Move to the back of the room where no one will see us if they pass in the hallway."

She then hurried toward the door and closed it before moving to Principal Newbolt's desk, where she pulled open the top drawer, bent over, and rummaged through it. Without looking up, she called out, "Why are you still sitting there? Go on, hurry up."

Helen tucked her notebook against her chest and scurried to a seat in the back row. Miss Schultz straightened, a pair of scissors held aloft, and grabbed at her pocketbook resting on Principal Newbolt's desk chair.

"Wait—" Helen shrank as her teacher headed toward her.

"Trust me," Miss Schultz said, pressing her hand on Helen's shoulder to hold her in place. "Now don't move an inch."

Helen closed her eyes and grimaced. *Snip, snip, snap.* Whispers of hair tickled Helen's face. She held her breath. *What was going on?*

After a couple more clips of the shears, Helen sensed a pause and cracked an eye open. Miss Schultz stood back, her head cocked, assessing her handiwork. From her pocketbook, she pulled out a compact and clicked it open. Helen leaned in and flicked her finger across the mirror, dusting the thin layer of powder from its surface to see her reflection better. A fringe of hair ran along the side of her forehead, covering her birthmark.

"Bangs?"

"Yes, they soften things a little. Give a sense of style, don't you think?"

Amazed, Helen nodded. Finally the purple splotch marring her forehead no longer resembled an ugly target, front and center on her face.

"See? You don't have to do anything fancy that will cost money. Just put a little effort into yourself each morning."

"Thank you. But how do you know to do this kind of stuff? I feel like there's a world out there filled with"—she paused—"information, like what to wear, how to do your hair, and all of that kind of stuff, but I don't know how to figure it out."

Miss Schultz studied her. "Sometimes mothers can help with this, sometimes friends share advice, and lots of girls study magazines like *Photoplay* or *Cosmopolitan* to see what's fashionable and get ideas. But really, you need to just pay attention, experiment."

"The girls at my boardinghouse spend all evening looking at those magazines while I'm usually doing homework."

"Maybe you could ask one of the girls to borrow one of their magazines." Miss Schultz gave her a mischievous smile. "Make sure you're still keeping up with homework, but I think a little leisure time wouldn't kill you."

Helen smiled back at her teacher. Already she felt lighter, freer. Even hopeful.

16.

February 1932
Malden, Massachusetts

LOUISE PEERED IN THE WINDOW OF HER CHEMISTRY
teacher's door, and when she saw Mr. Callahan sitting
at his desk, she knocked. Annoyance crossed his face, yet he
waved her in as he studied the papers in front of him and said,
"I moved my waste bin from its usual spot."

She slowed as he pushed the bin toward her, her face heating with humiliation, but she moved around it. "Sir, I need to speak with you about my latest test."

"Huh, so you're not one of the custodians? It's hard to tell you all apart," he grumbled, moving his wastebasket to the other side of his desk. He then pushed his wire-rimmed glasses up his long beak of a nose, before focusing on her anew. "And you are?"

"I'm Louise Stokes. From your chemistry class." She held back from adding that she had been in his physics class the previous year and biology the year before that. During her first year in his class, he had once stopped in front of her desk as she took notes and mused, "Left-handed, eh? They used to burn women like you at the stake for being witches." Louise's mouth had gone dry as she felt everyone staring at her, but she held her pencil even tighter in her left hand.

She cleared her throat and continued. "I failed the last chemistry test and am concerned about my overall grade."

He made no move toward the leather-bound grade book on the corner of his desk, but drummed his fingers on his desk as he considered her. His shoulders hunched, giving him the posture of a vulture. "This is your final year?"

"Yes, sir."

"You've done well to make it this far."

"Thank you, sir." She kept her eyes lowered to the ground so he couldn't see the anger she knew to be written all over her face. For her first three years of high school, Louise had been an exemplary student, and it was only recently that her grades had begun to suffer. In December, she set a national record in the broad jump, and everyone had been talking about it. Even *The Boston Globe* had written an article about it that Louise had clipped out and sent to her uncle Freddie in California. Despite all of these successes, every new accomplishment in track and field seemed to lead to less time for her to study. And since more paid sewing work was coming Emily's way, Louise had been taking on more work around the house. Ever since Mrs. Grandaway's death in the fall, Mama continued helping the family ready the house for sale, but no one had said a word to her about how much longer she would have a job. The uncertainty was stressful and wearying Mama and Papa.

Mr. Callahan picked at his ear. "Tell me, what do your parents do?"

"My father's a gardener and my mother's a housekeeper."

He opened the top drawer of his desk to retrieve a cigarette and lit it, placing it between his thin, chapped lips and letting it dangle out of the corner of his mouth. "Chemistry is a difficult subject. Perhaps this isn't the class for you."

"But, sir, I need it to graduate."

"Ahh, graduation." He rubbed his thin lips together. "A high school diploma isn't meant for everyone."

Hot shame filled Louise. At that moment, the sound of throat clearing interrupted their conversation and they turned to see Norm Northam, one of her classmates, lean into the room and grin as he ran a hand along the part of his chestnut-colored hair, held perfectly in place by a shiny pomade. He entered with the easy confidence of a boy whose yearbook page listed a lengthy column of clubs, office positions, and sports teams. "Mr. Callahan, may I have a word?"

"Of course, of course, Mr. Northam. We're just finishing up." He beckoned Norm to come in and then reversed the motion as if nudging Louise away from him. "All right, then, Miss . . ."

But Louise didn't answer. She bolted for the door and hurried out into the hallway. Only once she could no longer hear the teacher and Norm talking did she stop to lean against the wall of lockers and collect herself.

Directly across the hall from her were some large framed class photos. In the photos, it was clear the number of black students diminished each year that the class progressed, but in the last couple of years, fewer students, white and black, had returned to classes at Malden High. More young people were looking for work, even though jobs were harder to come by.

She let out a shuddering sigh. Cutting back on expenses seemed to be the goal of every household in Malden, both among the well-off and the less so, but this last year had been exceptionally lean and the results were trickling down to the families teetering on the fine line between "scraping by" and "flat-out broke" with calamitous results.

Mama always said to keep her head down and keep focused on the end result: a high school diploma. But now Louise wasn't so sure. What would come next? What was the point of enduring all of these daily humiliations? She dropped her chin to her chest and inspected the toes of her scuffed brown shoes. Small, careful repair seams were visible on her gray knee socks upon close inspection. Her family needed more money and if she stopped going to school, she could do something to help.

Her parents had been insistent that she stay in school, saying they didn't want Louise to take a job away from someone who really needed it, but Louise was getting impatient. A loose sheet of paper covered in quadratic equations lay on the ground by her toe and she kicked it away.

AFTER WASHING AND drying the dinner dishes that evening, Louise and Emily settled in at the kitchen table to work on their homework. Mama sat alongside them, mending in hand. When Louise looked at the long line of computations to be calculated, she took a deep breath. "I'm not going to school anymore."

Mama continued slipping her needle in and out of the skirt she was hemming, but Emily's pencil stopped moving across her composition book as she stole a look at her sister. "What do you mean?" she asked.

Louise's heart hitched in her chest as she forced herself to look at Mama. "I'm failing chemistry and possibly a couple of other classes, all because of my teachers. They don't want me to graduate."

Without lifting her gaze from her needle, Mama said, "Since when does what *they* want dictate what *you* want?"

"It's just starting to feel like I'm wasting time in school. Ever since I set that new national record in the broad jump in December, Coach Quain says my Olympic prospects are looking better and better. I could end up going to Los Angeles to compete. Why do I need to know how to solve equations or analyze Shakespeare?" She spoke quickly, pointing at her battered copy of *Hamlet*. "I don't want to do this anymore."

Papa had come back inside now, the sweet smell of his pipe trailing behind him. He leaned against the door, his face lost in the shadows. "You think your mama has wanted to clean other people's houses for the last twenty years?" His voice sounded tired but firm. "You think I want to tend to other people's lawns, weed their flowerbeds? You've been going to school all this time so you can do better than us."

Louise shuddered and licked her lips, steeling herself for what she needed to say. "The best thing I can do for myself is compete in the Olympics."

Sorrow flashed across Mama's face and she sighed. "But what makes you so sure you'll qualify?"

"I can do it. I know I can."

Papa shook his head. "That's an awful big bet. Stick with school. Get that diploma and you can go on to become a teacher, a nurse. You're almost done. Why quit now?"

Exasperation ballooned inside Louise's chest. There were no options for a black girl like her in nearby colleges, and she had no desire to leave her family and move away to attend a farther one. "I've been thinking about this a lot, and I'm not going to be able to go to college. We simply can't afford it."

At that, her parents quieted and shame filled Louise. "I can make it to Los Angeles," she whispered. "I'll make you all proud of me."

Mama rubbed her eyes in exhaustion. "We've *been* proud of you. Being a good daughter and sister is enough."

"Well, it's not enough for me." Louise pushed her chair back and headed for her bedroom, leaving a silent kitchen in her wake.

THE NEXT MORNING Louise rose and dressed in a clean navy-blue skirt and matching knee socks, a cream-colored midi blouse, and a light gray wool cardigan that her grandmother had knitted for her. While her brother and sisters scrambled around the house, washing themselves, dressing, and eating, she made a pot of oatmeal and doled out bowls of it for each of them. After Mama and Papa left for work, she called good-bye to her siblings, cleaned the breakfast dishes, straightened the kitchen, and then made her way over to Dr. Conway's house late enough that the household would be up and running, but early enough so that she could catch Mrs. Conway before she left the house on any errands or social calls. When she reached their house she paused, checking to see if Papa was anywhere nearby, but there was no sign of him so she circled around to the kitchen door at the back of the house and knocked.

Miss June, the housekeeper, opened the door. "Why aren't you at school?"

"I need a job."

Miss June harrumphed. "Your parents know about this?"

"Mama's job could go away any day now. I need to line something up."

"Louise Stokes, you've always been a stubborn girl. Why, I remember you in Sunday school when you drew that picture of the nativity scene. You remember what I'm talking about?" Miss June chuckled. "You drew that little round man in the corner of your nativity scene picture and when Miss Hayes asked you who it was, you said, 'Round John Virgin, ma'am.' She tried to correct you and sang you the correct lyrics of 'Silent Night,' but you refused to budge. Not until the reverend came down and showed you the lines in the hymnbook and explained to you what 'Round yon virgin mother and child' meant did you back down." She laughed and shook her head, repeating, "Round John Virgin."

Louise gave a grudging nod. "I still think it's strange that everyone cared so much about what was in my nativity scene."

Miss June's chest stopped heaving with silent laughter and she became serious. "Miss Hayes wanted to make sure you understood that scene. She didn't want you going about your life with such a mistake and embarrassing yourself in school. She knew every opportunity to teach a colored student the correct way to say something was important for when you would be out in the real world someday. She didn't want you to look ignorant when you went off to school with white students."

"But I was just a little kid."

Miss June shook her head. "Still stubborn as always, I see. Well, c'mon, let me take you in to see Mrs. Conway, but don't you go telling either of your parents that I had anything to do with this scheme of yours."

They found Mrs. Conway perched at her walnut desk, several letters fanned in front of her. If she thought it odd that Louise wasn't at school, her kind face gave away nothing. "Why, Louise, what a treat to see you this morning. What can I do for you?"

After Louise explained that she was looking for work, Mrs. Conway tapped her perfectly rounded fingernails on her address book for a moment as she thought. "You could try Mrs. Clark, over on Fairview Avenue. I believe she mentioned needing a girl when I saw her at a Women's Club meeting last Tuesday. Her young daughters will keep you busy. Tell her I sent you."

"Thank you, ma'am."

"If Mrs. Clark has found a new situation, try Mrs. Mason over on Stone Street."

"Yes, ma'am. Thank you." As Miss June led Louise through the kitchen to the back door, the older woman said, "Mrs. Clark could be good, but don't even think about Mrs. Mason. She's mean and her husband's even worse. If Mrs. Clark don't work out, come back here, I got more suggestions, though the pay won't be so good. It's tough out there."

"Thank you, Miss June."

"Now hold up a moment. All that running has you looking

too thin." She reached to a cutting board on the counter, cut a slice of cinnamon raisin bread, then handed it to Louise. "See you at church on Sunday."

"You won't say anything to my father, will you?"

"Do you plan to tell him about this tonight?" When Louise nodded, Miss June said, "Good, because I've got no plans to lie for you."

Louise bobbed her chin in gratitude and closed the door behind her. Cupping the still-warm fresh bread in her hand, she slunk around the side of the house to be sure Papa wouldn't catch a glimpse of her. She made it to the sidewalk and took off at a run to escape any notice. Only when she was a few blocks away did she stop and eat the bread.

By lunchtime, she had a job with Mrs. Clark tending to her two young daughters and helping the main housekeeper. Mrs. Clark, a small-waisted woman with a precisely marcel-waved coiffure, had presented Louise with a long, detailed list of her daily tasks, but her young daughter and baby seemed sweet and the house bright and clean. After work, Louise would still be able to attend track practice in the late afternoon. Louise had no illusions about the work. She had seen Mama's exhaustion every night. The days would be long and tiring, but she would be helping her family, and her parents wouldn't be able to object to her working once she announced she had a job.

17.

February 1932
Fulton, Missouri

W HEN HELEN PINNED THE LAST SECTION OF HAIR into place against her scalp, Mildred, one of the other girls who boarded at Miss Humphries's, took a step away and studied her. "Good, you've got the hang of it. Your hair will look pretty in the morning when you take the pins out." She sat back down and huddled toward Helen. "Now listen, we never get much homework on Thursday nights. What do you say about coming to the movies with us? *Mata Hari*'s playing and Garbo's supposed to be sensational."

Helen placed the remaining hairpins in a tin and glanced at Mildred to see if she was serious. Since her talk with Miss Schultz, she had become friendly with the three other girls who boarded with her. She often helped them with their homework by editing their writing assignments and they had reciprocated by helping her with styling her hair and selecting what clothes to wear, but this invitation from Mildred marked the first invitation to do something social. As the other two boarders leaned in the doorway and joined in with Mildred's urging, Helen beamed, not quite believing her good fortune.

"I like the idea of a story about a lady spy. I just read a letter to the editor in the newspaper complaining that the cinema has hit a new low by showing a film featuring such skimpy costumes and a racy plot. Do your parents know you're seeing films like this?"

Mildred giggled. "If my parents knew I was even thinking about it, they'd probably lock me up."

"Well then, let's go before the cinema stops showing it!"

The date was sealed and when the following Thursday evening arrived, all the girls traipsed along the brick sidewalks to the cinema to take their seats in the crowded theater. Helen inhaled the smells of soap, powder, damp wool, and cigarettes and absorbed the sighs and breathless giggling of the other girls as she settled into the dark, delighted to be in such proximity to the group. When the film began, Helen could hardly focus on the screen. Instead, she watched the girls around her, the way the light flickered across the smooth skin of their faces, but then Greta Garbo appeared and everything else was forgotten. Each time Mata Hari danced, Helen could barely breathe. The slinkiness of her sparkly gown, her bare back . . . Helen was transfixed. She'd never seen anything like it.

That evening as she lay in the dark in her narrow twin bed, images of Mata Hari returned to her, setting off a contraction deep inside her core, a fluttering in her chest—sensations she'd never felt before. With visions of Greta Garbo filling her mind, she allowed her fingers to travel down to between her legs and lost herself in the sensation of pleasure that she was able to summon all by herself. This was nothing like what had happened with Jimmy in the outbuilding. He had been rough and smelly and everything he had done had hurt. But this feeling she could conjure herself? *This* was something entirely different. After several minutes of being lost in her arousal, she jolted as if an electrical current had zapped through her and gasped. *What was she doing?* Even in the dark by herself, she felt her cheeks flush with mortification. She was not supposed to be doing anything like this, especially as a girl. Thinking about— much less touching—*that* part of her body was wrong—she had gotten that message loud and clear. From school, from church, from home—everywhere. What was wrong with her?

But . . .

Why was it wrong? What was so wrong about pleasure? She was by herself, not hurting anyone. Was she hurting herself somehow? The shame that suffused her felt confusing.

Did any of the other girls feel this way too? Did Mildred? Did they ever do this to themselves? She straightened in her bed, stared at the ceiling, and wished she could stop her mind from spinning with questions. But even more, she wished she didn't always feel so different from everyone else.

THURSDAYS AT THE cinema became a regular pastime for Helen and her roommates, and *Frankenstein* became a favorite. No matter how many times they watched it, when the thunder clapped and the monster's hand first moved, they never failed to shriek and reach for each other. Every time one of the girls buried her head in Helen's shoulder, she held her breath. Every time one of them squeezed her hand, she studied her face for any sign of attraction, but as far as she could tell, there was nothing but camaraderie in anyone's gestures. And while these new friendships felt wonderful—she realized she'd been hungering for this laughter, the easy conversations, and even the simple pleasure of sharing silly jokes—what would it be like to discover something more? Something like what she saw happening between Marlene Dietrich and Clive Brook when she watched *Shanghai Express*. The problem was that she couldn't really picture exactly what she wanted to discover. The lead actors never excited her the way they did everyone else.

When the other girls sighed over men like Charles Farrell and Clark Gable, Helen nodded and agreed that the movie stars were dreamy and handsome, but she didn't really feel the collective excitement that engulfed the other girls. How she wished she did! The palpable longing in the girls' voices when they described how they imagined their future husbands elicited something akin to pain in Helen. Getting married, having babies, tending to her future house? She couldn't picture herself doing any of these things. She'd contemplate her future, her mind straining to come up with a picture of what it looked like, but nothing materialized and this left her in a cold sweat.

After all, what could be more terrifying and lonelier than a blank future?

As SPRING APPROACHED, boys began meeting Helen and her roommates in the lobby, and when it came time to file into the theater, all the girls jockeyed for position to pair with the boys. All except for Helen. Each of the scenes that—before the boys had started joining them—had caused the girls to link arms with each other and scream now prompted them to quiver with glee-filled terror and nestle closer to the boys. All except Helen.

No boy ever leapt for a seat next to her, and she didn't want them to. Their chapped lips, square jaws, dungarees—none of it appealed to her. She missed the warmth of her friends' whispers in her ears and the tight grasp of their soft hands. Now, the girls leaned into the shoulders of the boys at their sides.

And Helen was left with no one.

THE CHICAGO EVENING STANDARD
February 14, 1932

"Betty's Back on Top"

Chicago—Three of North America's most outstanding athletes lined up for a spectacular speedfest on Friday night. Hometown heroine Miss Betty Robinson, Cleveland's Miss Stella Walsh, and Canada's Miss Myrtle Cook faced off at an indoor meet at 24th Field Artillery Armory.

From the outset, the race promised plenty of excitement. A small but fervent contingent of Canadian fans, bedecked in red and white and brandishing flags, went wild when Miss Cook entered the arena. Miss Walsh's entrance received a cooler reception, but it didn't appear to faze her and the dark-haired girl quietly took her position. Miss Robinson was the last athlete to be announced, and from the roar of the crowd, it was clear that the stands were filled with spectators supporting the city's native daughter. The third-year coed from Northwestern University arrived at the starting line, waving and calling greetings to her many fans. If the wattage of her smile was any indicator of her speed, her competitors must have been shaking in their track shoes. Once the starting gun went off, the girls rocketed down the straightaway, but by the last fifteen yards, it was clear that Miss Robinson would take first place, with about a yard separating her from Miss Walsh as they crossed over the finish line. The winning time was 11.2 seconds.

As the Wildcats fight song rang out across the track from the stands, Miss Robinson, sporting a Northwestern tracksuit, took a bow and accepted a diamond-studded track shoe pendant from her friends at the IWAC. When asked about her win, Betty gushed, "I couldn't have done it without my friends at Northwestern and Coach Hill. He's whipped me into the best shape of my life and I'm ready for the next Olympics."

In her typical no-frills manner, Miss Walsh says she's focusing on the future. "I will win gold in Los Angeles and, once again, I'll be the fastest woman in the world."

18.

February 1932
Evanston, Illinois

"YOU LOOKED GOOD OUT THERE ON FRIDAY NIGHT, Robinson," Bill said, passing Betty in the hall of the gymnasium.

Even several days after her victory in the IWAC meet, Betty still brimmed with excitement, not to mention a measure of relief. Her success validated all of her hard work with Coach Hill. "Thanks for coming to cheer me on."

"I wouldn't have missed it. You planning on coming to see my basketball game this Saturday night?"

Betty tried to look serious and feigned nonchalance. "Hmm, not sure. I'm planning to wash my hair and do some laundry. I'm getting tired of being here all the time."

"Wear a hat and save the hair-washing extravaganza for Sunday morning, though now that I think on it, you may be busy all day at church."

"All day?"

"Yep, you're going to be busy praying for mercy because you'll be so impressed with my playing on Saturday night that you'll be throwing yourself at me by the end of the game. Just you wait."

Betty threw back her head and let out the loudest laugh of her life. When she steadied herself and looked back at Bill, he affected a wounded expression. "I'm sorry we can't all be Olympians around here. Do you really have to go killing all of my dreams?"

"You're too much. You win, I'll come to your game. I owe you." The truth was that Betty owed Bill more than merely coming to one of his games. As her showdown with Stella Walsh had approached, Betty found herself becoming increasingly nervous, and each time he saw her, Bill took the time to give her pep talks about how well she was running. He could be counted upon for a steady stream of support. No matter how many times she avoided him or brushed him off, he kept finding her.

"Great, I'll see you there," Bill said. "A bunch of us will be going to White Castle afterward. Maybe you'll want to come and bring some of your friends?" He raised his hands in surrender. "I swear, it won't be a date. There will be tons of people there. Don't worry, Coach Hill will have nothing to hold against you."

"We'll see. Good luck, Bill. I hope you have a great game."

He thanked her, and they went their own ways, but Betty found herself unable to stop smiling. Bill was such a card, but he also always appeared genuinely interested in her running, her classes, and her family. Though he attracted a swarm of admirers, both male and female, whenever they spoke, everyone else seemed to fall away. He possessed the ability to make her feel like the most fascinating woman on earth.

BETTY INVITED CAROLINE Hale and her longtime boyfriend, Howard, to join her for the game. The two women had remained in touch since the Olympics in Amsterdam, and Howard, always a good sport, frequently accompanied them on their adventures. He owned a rattletrap of a Model T and never balked at chauffeuring them around the city.

As they approached Patten Gymnasium, the noise of the crowd swelled. The Wildcats had been enjoying a winning season, and this was the final game of the regular season. A steady stream of fans wound along the sidewalks heading in the direction of the game.

Once inside the gymnasium, they wedged themselves into the crowded bleachers. Betty looked around at the rows and rows of jubilant fans, waving Northwestern flags and cheering on the Wildcats. The entire seating structure seemed to be shaking with the energy of the crowd. Though it was a close game, the Wildcats were ahead and Bill caught a pass, coiled into shooting position, and sank a shot. Everyone went wild, and Betty joined in the cheering. The opposing team inbounded the ball and dashed across the court, passing it back and forth. Their star player got his hands on the ball and went for a shot, but it careened off the rim.

"Get the rebound!" shouted Howard.

At that moment, three players tumbled to the ground as they battled for the ball, Bill among them. Two of the players righted themselves and stood, but when they reached down to help Bill to his feet, he hunched his shoulders and remained on the ground, curling over his legs. Betty leapt to her feet to see down the court better.

"What's going on?" Caroline asked, but no one answered. They all craned their heads toward the far end of the court, anxious to know what had happened to Bill.

AFTER THE FINAL buzzer, everyone streamed toward the exits, excited about the Northwestern win, but Betty found herself dragging her feet. Where was Bill? Since being carted off the court by a trainer, he hadn't reappeared for the rest of the game. She tried not to worry. If there was one person who was invincible, it was Bill. He seemed powered by the rare engine that never seemed to need fuel. She allowed herself to be swept along with the fans, but couldn't stop herself from searching the area by the locker room's doors where a cluster of his teammates lingered. When she was almost at the door, Ned Mason appeared next to her. "Hey, Bill's asking about you, and he's about to head to the hospital. Come down to the trainer's with me?"

She signaled to Caroline that she'd be back soon and hurried after Ned. "What's happened to him?"

"I don't think they really know yet."

They arrived at the trainer's office and passed a huddle of basketball players and the team's coach and assistants. Sitting on an exam table with a wool blanket around his shoulders and his foot elevated on some pillows, Bill beckoned. His face looked pale and waxy, but his gaze brightened at the sight of her. The antiseptic smell of Mercurochrome in the room made Betty shudder, and she glanced away from his bare foot, already swelling and darkening with shades of violet and green.

"Looks like I may have broken it. Rotten luck, huh?" He closed his eyes for a moment as his features tightened in pain.

"The worst," Betty agreed. "I'm so sorry."

"At least we won." He became distracted as a cadre of the trainers swarmed him, and Betty stepped back to let them examine him. After a few minutes, they peeled away, so she stepped closer again. He grimaced as he propped himself on his elbow. "Looks like I'm off to the hospital for the docs to check it out."

Before she could say anything, two trainers bustled forward, and Bill groaned as they hoisted him onto a stretcher and headed for the door.

"Take care of yourself," she called to him. "Have someone get word to me on how you're doing."

He twisted and his gaze locked with hers as he was carried off. Betty waved, but could only see the top of his blond head before he disappeared into the crowd outside the trainer's room.

A WEEK LATER, Mrs. Riel, elegant in a riding costume, led Betty into the family's house, a large stucco Tudor on a quiet street not far from Lake Michigan. Bill had once mentioned that his father owned a clothing manufacturing company, and judging from the thick carpet runner in the hallway and oil paintings in gilt frames, business was going well. They headed to a solarium where Bill sat ensconced on a chintz sofa. A pretty dark-haired girl resembling Clara Bow sat on a matching ottoman next to Bill, a stack of papers and textbooks perched on her lap. Betty eyed her and tried to smile.

"You have another visitor, Bill," his mother announced.

"Thanks, Ma. Hey, Betty, do you know Millie Billram?"

Millie removed the stack of schoolwork from her lap and leapt to her feet, pushing out her hand. "Hi, aren't you a Kappa Kappa Gamma?"

"I am." Betty shook her hand. "Of course I recognize you. Are you a second-year?"

"Yes. I just came by to bring Bill some of the work he's been missing from our accounting class. I guess I should be going." She looked back and forth between Betty and Bill as if hoping for an invitation to stay longer.

"Millie, you're a peach for bringing me all this," Bill said. "Thanks. I should be back at school sometime in the next couple of weeks."

"Swell. If you need someone to help you around campus, carry your books or anything, just let me know. I'd be happy to help." She placed the books on a corner of the card table next to Bill and began sifting through the sections of the *Chicago Tribune*, also on the table, organizing pages and stacking them into a single pile.

"You don't need to worry about the newspaper. I'm still going through it."

"Millie dear, I'm heading upstairs to change, shall I walk you out?" Mrs. Riel asked, stepping forward, and Betty understood where Bill's smooth congeniality came from.

Millie allowed Mrs. Riel to guide her out, leaving Bill and Betty alone. His foot, covered in a thick white plaster cast, sat high on a mountain of pillows. A plate with a turkey sandwich and a glass of iced tea rested on the card table beside the newspaper and the schoolwork that Millie had delivered.

"It looks like you've got plenty of company coming through."

"Yeah, I wish the fellas would stop by, but it's you I'm most happy to see."

Betty gave him a skeptical look. "Really? Even with all of these pretty girls visiting?"

Bill gave a mischievous smile and folded his arms behind his head as he stretched out. "I can't fall behind on my studies, can I? I'm grateful for all of the help that's being offered to me."

"I'll bet you are." Betty laughed and sank down on a matching chair.

"I know you're too busy to ferry my classwork back and forth. How's training going?"

"It's fine."

"You miss me?"

She affected a dramatic expression and tone of anguish. "I do. So much, in fact, that I can barely run. I'm afraid Stella Walsh is going to cream me the next time I see her."

"Is that so?" He propped himself up on his elbow. "You know, I'm out for spring track."

"The whole season?"

"Yeah, I'm disappointed. Apparently, this foot break is a real bugger, with tendon damage, the works, but you know what I realized?"

"What?"

"Because of this injury, I won't be an official member of the track team this spring."

"Does Coach Hill know you're out for the season?"

"He does. He came by the other day to check on me, and I broke the bad news to him. I also told him that I plan to ask you out."

At this, Betty straightened in surprise. "You did?"

"Yep. So, what do you say? Give an injured fella some mercy and go out for dinner with me?"

"You don't look like you're going anywhere any time soon."

"I don't intend to wait until my cast comes off and risk you falling for some other guy. How about you come over tomorrow night and join me for dinner? Just the two of us."

"As you said earlier, I'm very busy. I don't think I can fit anything else into my schedule."

"Too busy for a poor fella who can't walk? Now, that's just cruel."

"Well, I don't want you to ruin my reputation as a nice person, so I suppose I'll come after all."

Bill raised his brows. "I make no promises I won't ruin your reputation."

Betty threw a cushion at Bill as she stood to go. "Fine, you don't scare me. See you tomorrow night."

19.

Spring 1932
Malden, Massachusetts

WHEN LOUISE RETURNED HOME TO TELL HER PAR-
ents she had taken a job with Mrs. Clark, they met the
news with stoic resignation. Louise had steeled herself for an
argument, but it never arrived. Instead, Mama folded herself
onto a kitchen chair and rested one of her hands, cracked and
worn, on the table. "Mrs. Grandaway's children tell me I've
done all that's been needed. Friday will be my last day. The
house is being sold this weekend. Time for me to go."

Louise checked Papa for his reaction. Gray lightened his
hairline, gray that hadn't been there the last time Louise had
taken a good look at him. His brown eyes, usually sparkling
and teasing, appeared weary. Louise bit her lip. "Maybe my
job with Mrs. Clark would be better for you."

"No, it wouldn't. You were hired to be an assistant to Miss
Mabel. They can't have Miss Mabel and me, that'd be too
much. You go on and take that work. I'm not sure if anyone in
town needs someone. If they don't, some of the ladies in church
have spoken of the laundry."

"Oh, Mama, you don't want the laundry."

"Of course I don't, but it's reliable work, and in some ways, it might be easier. The idea of just doing a job and not getting mixed up in family affairs offers some advantages. I spent years with the Grandaways and it's been exhausting."

Working in the laundry was steady, as Mama said, but brutal, filled with harsh cleaners and backbreaking labor. The pay wouldn't be as good as Mrs. Grandaway's, but now Louise understood why her parents hadn't argued when she had announced she didn't plan to return to school. They needed her wages. The family needed her. Knowing that brought a heavy sense of responsibility, but also pride.

"I can give everything I earn to you," Louise said.

Papa shook his head. "No, if you're earning wages, keep some of it. You're an adult now and it's only right."

"But I'll give you most of it."

"Let's give this new arrangement a few weeks and see what happens." Papa stroked Mama's back. "You're going to be able to keep training?"

"Yes, Coach Quain's told me that I should hear from the Olympic committee this spring about being invited to the National AAU Championships in Chicago in July. The Olympic team will be decided at that meet."

"You'll need to keep some of your earnings from Mrs. Clark to pay for that trip."

"But Coach Quain says the AAU and the club will pay for it."

"You should have some of your own money too. Just in case. Sometimes things change and you don't want to get stranded somewhere far from home. And you'll need some spending money. Start thinking about how much you'll need and be sure to save for it."

"Have you discussed time off to travel to Chicago?" Mama asked.

"No, I figured I had plenty of time to bring that up."

"Mrs. Clark won't like any surprises," Mama said. "Make sure you tell her immediately."

When Louise had accepted Mrs. Clark's offer of working for five dollars a week, it seemed like a windfall, but now she wasn't so sure. Her glowing sense of contribution faded. And what if Mrs. Clark didn't accept her plan to travel to Chicago?

The next morning she awoke in the dark and pulled on a navy-blue work dress that Mama had given her. She wrapped a scarf around her hair and set off for the Clarks' house. The day passed briskly under Miss Mabel's tutelage as she moved from one task to the next, learning the ins and outs of how the family operated. The older woman seemed pleased to focus on her work in the kitchen while Louise took on entertaining Mrs. Clark's daughter Beatrice. When the little girl rested, Louise dusted, polished, and put away toys.

One afternoon Louise was watering a large pot of maidenhead fern in the living room when Mrs. Clark passed through. "Excuse me, ma'am, I need to ask you about my summer schedule. I need to leave town in July and won't be able to work for several weeks."

Mrs. Clark checked her lipstick in the mirror above the fireplace. "We'll be going to the Isles of Shoals for August like we always do. I'd thought I might bring you to care for the children, but if you can't come, I'm sure there will be a girl up there who can work instead, but I won't be paying you while we're gone. Miss Mabel works reduced hours to care for the house when we leave. She's all I need."

"Yes, ma'am, but I'll need to leave work on July fourteenth to go to Chicago."

"Chicago?" Mrs. Clark tilted a pillow on the emerald-green damask couch and stood back to check the effect.

"Yes, ma'am. I'll be running in the national track championships."

"You'll run in a competition? Do your parents know about this?"

"Yes, they come and watch me when I run locally on weekends. We're all keeping our fingers crossed that I qualify for the Olympic team."

"My, my. Isn't that singular?" Mrs. Clark had a way of making a compliment sound far from complimentary. "I had no idea girls did such things. Well, let's see how things are working out with this situation here. No need to get too far ahead of ourselves."

Louise was relieved Mrs. Clark hadn't dismissed the idea out of hand, but also worried about the uncertain nature of her response. When she returned home that evening, she told Mama what Mrs. Clark had said. Mama sighed, saying, "I'm afraid that's as much commitment as you'll ever get from her, even if you had been working there for years."

Louise's days assumed a sameness, and she liked the predictability of her schedule and enjoyed playing with Beatrice while the baby, Ann, slept. She always cleaned their rooms so the white eyelet bedspreads looked smooth; toys lined the shelves with precision as if measured with a ruler; the windows gleamed, free of smudgy fingerprints; and colored pencils and crayons remained in drawers when not being used. She did everything with diligence in hopes of keeping her job secure. When Louise wasn't working at the Clarks', she continued to train during the week and race on weekends. During the winter's indoor season and the spring's meets, she raced well enough for Coach Quain to become increasingly optimistic about her chances for qualifying for the Olympics.

One evening in late May, she sat at the kitchen table at her home. Emily entered the room with her mending basket and a roll of powder-blue silk tucked under her arm. "What do you have there? Is there space for me to sit down and work with you?"

Louise didn't answer immediately because she was busy signing her name. When she finished, she looked up at her sister, standing in front of her. "I just finished filling out my application for the National AAU Championships in Chicago. Coach Quain has acquired the funds for the Onteora Track Club to sponsor me to travel to race in them. I'm all done so the table is yours. Now I just need to focus on running."

"This is your big chance, huh?" Emily brushed some crumbs off the table and reverently placed the blue silk on it, next to her basket. "You've been working so hard. I'm sure you'll knock 'em dead."

"Thanks, I hope so." Louise looked at the fabric. "My, that's pretty. What are you making?"

Delight dawned over Emily's face, and dimples appeared on her cheeks. "I've got my mending work for Mrs. Jackson, but she sold me this fabric at a discount." She held out a pattern envelope. "I'm going to make a dress for the spring dance at school. There will be a few changes to it, but I think this will be perfect." Louise looked at the sketch of the dress and fingered the cool, slippery silk. The dress featured a sophisticated yoke above its flared skirt, a wrapped bodice, and shawl sleeves. It would be beautiful. Louise hadn't ever gone to any dances, but Emily was a different creature. Outgoing and confident, she always had a busy social calendar.

"It will be lovely on you," Louise said. "When's the dance?"

"First Friday of June. I've got plenty of time to make it. I'm going with Doris and Mavis, but I've got my eye on Jackie Newton. I'll bet you've seen him at church."

"Doesn't he have those pretty golden eyes?"

"That's him. Did you ever go to the Spring Fling?"

"No."

"You're always so serious."

"Well, I'm busy." Running, working for Mrs. Clark, helping around the house—there was no time for dances. Louise edged away from her sister and began drying the dinner plates, placing them back on the shelves, and searching for the cutlery to put away, anything to hide the wistfulness she knew to be on her face. Was she giving up too much? It would be nice to go to a dance with a boy who had kind eyes.

20.

May 1932
Fulton, Missouri

EVER SINCE THE STOCK MARKET CRASH IN 1929, TIMES had gotten tough on the Stephens farm. When Helen was home on weekends, Pa often flung the newspaper down after reading it and stalked off to the backyard to smoke. Ma rarely played her harp anymore. The atmosphere in the house felt tense.

For as long as Helen could remember, the Stephenses had been boarding young women who came to town to interview for teaching positions with the district, and as the economy worsened, these boarding arrangements took on a new significance since every penny added to the household was appreciated. When they had taken in boarders while Helen attended Middle River School, she would sleep on the trundle bed in her room while the teachers slept in her bed. Helen always loved the arrangement. It was with great pride that she would escort the women back to her house to spend the night after a day at school. It gave her a special sense of ownership to host the visitors, a sense of claim and importance. It also made her a figure of interest with the other students, especially the girls.

They wanted to know all sorts of things about these visiting teachers. Did the women tell Helen of any beaus? (Never.) Did they wear curlers at night? (Often, yes.) Did they snore? (Sometimes.) Did they smoke? (Rarely.) One evening after supper, a certain Miss Fecklemore had pushed open the curtains in Helen's room and gestured her to follow her outside to sit on the shingled roof and join her in smoking a pipe. Truth be told, Helen had thought the pipe to be horrid, but she enjoyed the illicit thrill of smoking outside with an adult. Miss Fecklemore was never heard from again, which was probably just as well.

Since Helen had moved to town, she was rarely around when one of the boarders came to stay, but late that spring, Ma asked Helen to stop by Middle River School to walk one of these visiting teachers home with her. The following Friday, Helen trudged up the stairs to the schoolhouse, and the sharp scrape of a desk being moved across the floor's rough planks made her cringe. Voices just out of range rose and fell. She paused and tilted her head to listen.

"No, Mr. Waddington, you don't need to sit so close to me," a woman's voice said.

"But I wanted to show you something in this book," Superintendent Waddington's deep voice pleaded.

"No," the woman said loudly, and then the sound of something crashing to the floor punctuated her protest.

Helen took the final step and entered the schoolhouse to find a woman hunched behind a desk as if using it as a blockade and Superintendent Waddington hovering across from her, red-faced, expectant, and out of breath. A globe rolled in lazy circles around the floor between them.

"Ah yes, Helen, here you are." He cleared his throat. "Our visiting teacher, Miss Albright, had an idea for how to rearrange the desks." A parenthesis of graying hair had fallen across his forehead and he pushed it back before straightening and smoothing the lapels of his jacket.

Miss Albright turned, an expression of relief crossing her face. She stepped back from the desk, away from Superintendent Waddington, and Helen gaped. Green eyes the color of pine needles, a slender figure, wavy honey-colored hair. Her skin, eyes, hair—everything seemed to glow.

"So, Miss Albright, as I was saying: I'd be more than happy to spend time with you this evening to explain more aspects of the job to you. Let me take you to dinner and give you more information about what to expect here."

"Oh, you've given a very clear idea of what to expect. No, thank you," the woman said, glancing at Helen.

Helen had never particularly liked Mr. Waddington. It had always struck her as odd that he ran the school district though he never showed much interest in its children. Whenever he visited Middle River School, he inspected the desks, the supply closet, and the building itself, but his gaze traveled over the students as if they were obscuring his view of the furniture. She rarely saw him at the high school and when she did, he was always counting the number of students in each room and tallying them on a clipboard the way a grocer would take inventory of the goods on his shelves. "Oh, Mr. Waddington, my ma has made a special supper in honor of our guest. I'm sure she'd be disappointed to not have Miss Albright join us."

"Is that so, Helen? Thanks for piping in," he said in an irritated voice. "That being the case, Miss Albright, I'd be happy to drive you to the Stephens farm. I'm sure you don't want to carry your suitcase all that way."

"I'd be happy to carry it," Helen said, smiling sweetly while enjoying the murderous look that darkened the superintendent's face.

"I'll bet. You could probably carry her on your back and heft the suitcase as well," he grumbled.

"Now, now. I'm sure we'll manage just fine." Miss Albright lifted her suitcase and beckoned Helen to join her.

"I'll be in touch about when you can start," Superintendent Waddington said.

"*If* I decide to take the job. I already have another offer," Miss Albright called over her shoulder.

"If?" he echoed, taken aback. "Well, I just assumed—"

But Miss Albright didn't linger to continue the conversation. She yanked Helen out the door, and as they hurried from the building, Helen stole a glimpse of Miss Albright out of the corner of her eye; the woman appeared to be weeping. "Are you going to make it? Our house is about a mile away. Want me to carry that for you?" She pointed at the teacher's valise.

"No need." Miss Albright wiped her eyes, and when she turned to Helen, she was laughing. "Oh my goodness, I thought he was going to throw a fit back there. I would carry this all the way to New York City if I needed to. Anything to get away from that man. His views on educating young people struck me as very outdated and showed a real lack of imagination. I also didn't appreciate how rudely he treated you—or me, for that matter."

Helen liked how the woman seemed to stick up for her. "So, you don't plan to teach here?"

"No."

"Where's the other school that already offered you a job?"

"There is no other school." When she saw Helen's confusion, she chuckled. "I just said that because I can't work for him."

"Yeah, Waddington's a real drip. All of the kids have been making fun of him for years. He comes and gives an opening address to the school every year and rambles on forever. I think some of the speech is in Latin. None of us can quite figure it out. Back when I first started at that school, there was an older teacher and she fell asleep in the back row and we could all hear her snoring. That's the only year that I can remember when he kept his speech relatively short."

Miss Albright laughed. "He certainly does seem like the type who enjoys the sound of his own voice."

Helen nodded. "But isn't it hard to find jobs these days?"

"It is, but something will come along. I like to think I'm the kind of gal who can land on her feet. I'm from somewhere like here, and *this* is exactly what I'm trying to get away from."

Helen's gaze swept the farmland surrounding them before turning back to Miss Albright. "You're from Missouri?"

"No, South Dakota. But trust me, small-mindedness can be found everywhere."

AFTER DINNER THAT evening Helen led the way to her small room at the end of the hall and stood back to let Miss Albright go in first and settle her suitcase on the ground under the window. Before Helen followed her, she went to the washroom and wriggled out of her skirt and blouse before pulling on her plain light blue cotton pajama pants and top. All the girls at Miss Humphries's teased her for wearing men's pajamas, but she didn't like how nightgowns bunched around her waist when she was in bed so she insisted on getting her sleepwear from the men's section of the Sears catalog. As she finished buttoning the pajama top, she paused and peered into the tiny mirror over the sink. She frowned at a couple of the pimples scattered across her forehead. Miss Albright's complexion was perfect. Helen imagined running her hand across the woman's smooth cheek, and even in the gray light of the washroom, she could see her face flush a dark red.

She balled up her clothes and returned to her room, sank to her knees, and pulled the trundle out from under her bed. With her knees practically knocking into her ears, she sat on the low-lying trundle and brushed her hair to distract her from thinking about Miss Albright. She lowered her hairbrush and breathed in the mixture of something floral emanating from the teacher, perhaps rosewater, and though she longed to lean in closer to inhale deeper, she kept focused on the plain white sheets of her trundle bed.

But then she snuck a peek at the woman. She couldn't resist. With her back to Helen, Miss Albright unbuttoned her poplin dress and hung it on a peg on the back of the door, slipped off her brassiere from under her slip, and rubbed a damp washcloth over her face and neck, then dabbed it at her underarms. Helen flushed at the intimacy of the gesture and pretended to check the buttons on her pajama top, but out of the corner of her eye, she kept studying the woman. Tendrils of blond curls had fallen from Miss Albright's French twist and clung to the soft white skin of her neck. The graceful ridges of the musculature of her shoulders rose and fell beneath the ivory-colored straps of her slip as she continued her grooming. Helen found her gaze traveling downward along the curve of the woman's back. She swallowed and looked down at her own feet. Thin lines of dirt clung to the wrinkles around her toes as if sketched in black ink. From where her chest leaned against her thigh, she felt her heart racing.

"Want me to brush your hair?"

Helen startled. "What?"

Miss Albright gestured at the hairbrush lying on the floor beside Helen. "Your hair. Want me to brush it?"

"It's not very long. All of the other girls I know have longer hair, but mine seems to work best short."

"Short or long, it will still be good to have it brushed."

"Um, yes, ma'am. Thank you."

"You're welcome. And since we're sharing a bedroom, you might as well call me Polly."

Polly. Turning away from her, Helen mouthed the name, but couldn't actually bring herself to say it aloud. "All right."

Miss Albright—or Polly—bent over to pick up the hairbrush and lowered herself to sit on the trundle bed. Helen caught a glimpse of the pale swell of her breasts through the thin slip she wore and quickly turned away. The woman placed the hairbrush on Helen's scalp and began to brush downward, slowly and smoothly. Helen felt the woman's breath on the back of her neck and sat straighter, as if this could bring her closer.

"You have lovely hair."

Lovely. Helen's heart felt as though it expanded by several inches. A compliment such as this felt extravagant and she fumbled over how to respond. "I've started pinning it into curls at night during the week." Her voice sounded deep and gravelly, more so than usual, but she continued. "But since I help Pa with chores on the weekend, it seems like a waste of time to get it all dolled up while I'm here."

"Why wasn't your pa at dinner with us?"

"He's working. He's doing everything himself. Well, mostly. I help too. When I can."

"He's lucky to have you."

Helen pondered the way Pa always wanted her help, but never appeared satisfied by her efforts. "He doesn't really see it that way."

The brushing paused. "How come?"

Helen thought back to that time she'd overheard Pa talking with Dr. McCubbin. *I never wanted her.* She shook her head as if the memory could be knocked away. "He just doesn't."

"Hmm. I see." Miss Albright sounded wistful. "Fathers can be like that."

The brushing started again. Determined not to let thoughts of Pa ruin the moment, Helen closed her eyes and let her head roll with the steady pace of it.

After several minutes of silence, Miss Albright lowered the hairbrush to the blanket. "Perfect, my dear. Your hair looks wonderful."

Again, Helen savored the compliment, and the feeling of goodwill emboldened her. "Polly, shall I brush your hair too?"

It felt daring to use the woman's first name, a little risky and wild, but the woman appeared unfazed.

"My, what a treat. How can I say no to that?"

The two shifted on the trundle to switch places and Polly ran a hand along Helen's hip to guide her past. Helen slowed, relishing the touch before settling into position. With the first downstroke of the hairbrush, a small sigh escaped from Polly. Helen reached forward to smooth Polly's hair back toward her and allowed her palm to linger along the teacher's cheek. It was smooth and warm, just as Helen had imagined.

After several minutes of quiet brushing, Polly gave a long yawn. "I suppose it's time for bed." The trundle shifted as she slid off to stand and switched off the light.

Helen slid down under her covers into the space warmed by where they had been sitting. "Good night."

"Good night, my dear."

Helen gazed upward at the woman's standing figure, slatted with silver streaks of moonlight sifting through the window. Polly stretched her arms upward and—to Helen's amazement—lifted her slip and held it overhead like she was using it as a kite awaiting a breeze. She dropped it to the foot of the bed and stooped to shimmy out of her underpants, then straightened—stark naked. Helen watched, mesmerized, as the woman crawled onto the bed and disappeared under the bedspread.

Helen's face burned as if on fire. She never had been so grateful for the cover of darkness.

How much time passed? Later, when she tried to recall exactly what happened next, she could never be sure. All she could remember was that she startled at the touch of fingers grazing her forearms as they crept along her skin to her shoulders. Helen cracked her eyes open to find Polly leaning over her, a tender expression playing across the woman's face.

Helen inhaled sharply and pushed herself up onto her elbow to be closer, to see how Polly's skin glowed luminous in the moonlight. "You're beautiful," Helen murmured.

It was at that point Polly leaned in and brought her lips to Helen's. Astonished, Helen squeezed her eyes closed and concentrated on the gentle pressure coming from the woman's soft lips, the flicker of her tongue. Helen leaned in to deepen the kiss. This was nothing like what had happened with Jimmy years before in the school's outbuilding. This was tender and soft. Every part of her tingled. Her eyes shot open. *How can people close their eyes during this?* She wanted to see exactly what was happening, to make sense of what was happening.

This felt both entirely unexpected, yet also somehow exactly like what she had been waiting for. At first she didn't know what to do, and she watched how Polly's face transformed into delight, so she settled into feeling what was happening instead of thinking about it.

The two became breathless as they merged into a tangle, hands everywhere, sighs of delight. An urgency overcame Helen and she pressed her body harder against Polly's. It felt as if her insides were reconfiguring into a million sparks. And then an explosion blossomed deep inside Helen—at some point her eyes had closed, but now they popped open in both shock and thrilled excitement. She tried to catch her breath. How had she gotten carried away and let all caution evaporate?

Gently, Polly began to extract herself from the bed and Helen's heart stalled, but when she pushed her hair from her face to get a better look at Polly, a sated smile stretched across the other woman's face. Helen exhaled. Polly had seen Helen stripped of all pretending and not only was she not disgusted—she looked pleased.

Tears came to Helen's eyes, and she felt weak with relief. Under the sheets, she stretched, enjoying a languorous sensation of fulfillment, drifting off to sleep. She was no longer alone.

HELEN AWOKE THE next morning feeling as though she was trying to cling to the outline of a memory that was just out of reach. The harder she tried to remember it, the further it retreated. She blinked from the heaviness of sleep and turned toward the whisper of her bedroom door closing in time to see the disappearing figure of Miss Albright. Helen's breath caught in her throat.

Miss Albright. Or Polly?

In the glowing light of morning, Helen flinched. Visions of the two of them tangled together swept through her. Was it a dream? Surely what had happened—*if* it had happened— couldn't have been right. Miss Albright had to be older, but how much older? Helen's mind spun. Whatever *might* have happened last night—*that* was not what girls were supposed to do with each other.

She pried herself from the bed. The hands on the clock were already nearing seven o'clock. She washed and dressed in work clothes and descended the stairs.

Helen entered the kitchen and avoided looking at Ma and

Miss Albright, focusing her attention on Bobbie Lee instead. His damp blond hair still revealed the tines of the comb that Ma must have dragged through it before starting breakfast. As she took her seat, Miss Albright said, "Good morning. Your hair still looks shiny and smooth." She then turned to Ma and said, "Helen let me brush her hair last night and look at how marvelous she looks."

Ma approached Helen with a freshly topped-off tureen of oatmeal that she placed in the middle of the table. "I can't even remember the last time Helen let me near her with a hairbrush."

Pa entered the kitchen from the yard and reached for an empty coffee cup from a cupboard, appraising his daughter. "Just like a horse, she looks better with a little grooming."

Miss Albright's jaw appeared to tighten. "Good morning, Mr. Stephens."

"Don't mind me," he said, his voice gruff as he poured himself a cup of coffee. "Just here for a refill before I head to the back fourth of the fields."

Helen reached for the coffeepot.

Ma, not missing a thing, put her hands on her hips. "So now that you're living in town, you're drinking coffee? Better put milk in there. You're only fourteen. Too much of that stuff at your age will stunt your growth."

Pa chuckled. "Maybe stunting her growth wouldn't be the worst thing. Make her look a little more like a girl."

Helen pretended she hadn't heard and instead turned to look at Miss Albright, but the woman's face appeared ashen. She stared at Helen, her brow furrowed. "You're only fourteen?"

"Huge, isn't she?" Pa drawled.

It was at that moment that Helen sensed a shift in the air, as if a cloud had obscured the sun. A cooling. A settling. She had not dreamed up the night before. She knew it with startling clarity, and any sense of thrill that she felt vanished when she took in the stricken look on Miss Albright's face. Helen's fingers trembled and the coffee cup that was almost to her lips slipped and spilled down the front of her and onto the floor.

"Mercy me." Ma sighed, surveying the mess.

"Girl, you sure make a hash of everything," Pa muttered as he stalked to the back door and let it slam behind him.

Relieved to hide her stinging tears, Helen dropped to the floor to retrieve the broken shards of her cup. She took the dish towel Ma extended to her and swabbed at the pool of spilled coffee.

Miss Albright cleared her throat and rose. "Well, I'm ready to catch the next train to St. Louis. Mrs. Stephens, thank you so much for everything you've done to make my stay a comfortable one. Before I left town yesterday, I arranged for a ride and I believe he'll be meeting me in front in a few minutes."

"Of course. Helen, please help Miss Albright with her valise and walk her to the gate."

Helen took a final swipe at the floor and stood and followed Miss Albright to the parlor. When they reached the front door, Helen pushed it open to allow their guest to walk out first. In the distance, waves of heat blurred the fields. The hot sky appeared to be the color of bone. A plume of dust appeared, indicating a vehicle was on its way.

At the gate, Miss Albright paused and turned to Helen. "I'm sorry for last night."

Now it was Helen's turn to feel stunned. The previous night had been one of the most exciting things that had happened to her, but now she was left with a sick feeling in her stomach. She felt mortified that she had acted on the feelings that had been swirling through her for years. And at the same time, how on earth had she possibly believed someone like Miss Albright could be interested in someone like her? Shame and sorrow engulfed her. "You're sorry that it happened? Or you're sorry it was with me?"

Behind Miss Albright, the station wagon slid to the gate. She glanced back at it and shook her head. "You're a dear girl, but it's hard to explain. Someday you'll leave here and find all kinds of possibilities."

"Someday?"

But Miss Albright appeared not to have heard her. She hurried to the car, opened one of the doors, tossed her valise inside and slid in after it, then slammed the door shut. As the car drove away, she looked forward, never once turning to see Helen.

From where Helen stood, the fields stretched as far as she could see in every direction. It felt hard to imagine the possibilities beyond the confines of Fulton.

21.

June 1932
Chicago

WITH EVERY PASSING DAY OF JUNE, CHICAGO'S HEAT increased and the sky paled as if the sun were baking the blue right out of it. Summer parties and outings filled Betty's days. Sometimes her cousin Wilson took her up in the air in his little jaunty red Waco biplane. They'd sweep through the skies over Lake Michigan, admiring the views and taking in the cooler air high above the streets and buildings of the city.

And of course, there was Bill.

Back in February, when Betty had shown up for her dinner date with Bill at his house, she'd had no idea what to expect, but he turned out to be the kind of man for whom grand gestures came easily. She arrived to find him sitting at a table in the solarium next to a bay window, dressed in a suit with one leg tailored in a mystifying way that allowed for his cast. In the distance, the night sky glimmered off the surface of Lake Michigan.

After dinner, he directed her to look out the window. Four small orbs of light appeared as if floating. The sound of singing drifted in with the cold winter's night air and she cracked the window open to hear better.

> *Let me call you sweetheart*
> *I'm in love with you*
> *Let me hear you whisper*
> *That you love me too.*

"What is this?" Betty breathed in amazement.

"I have some friends who sing in a barbershop quartet, and when I told them you were coming over and my entertainment options were limited, they offered their services."

> *Keep the love light glowing,*
> *In your eyes so true . . .*

"They're marvelous. This is a wonderful surprise."

Bill looked pleased, but he gazed at her sideways as he spoke. "You know, Betty, you're not the easiest girl to impress. You're very accomplished, and I've had no idea what to do."

"You seem to have done just fine. And really, I don't need impressing."

"Easy to say, and yet—" He paused and the expression of genuine befuddlement on his face made him look so boyish and sweet that Betty felt herself weakening.

That evening had been the beginning and the end all at once. It surprised Betty how easy it had been to fall for Bill. He was confident and that made him appreciative of others. She never sensed he was trying to compete with her and they had an easy compatibility, the kind of friendship that felt like it had been cultivated over years balanced with an electrical current between them that made the discovery of each other seem brand new. They became a steady item. At first, they spent afternoons and evenings alone, talking and laughing, developing silly jokes and stories, but as Bill regained his mobility, they socialized and headed to the cinema and then dances and parties. And he was good for her. When she worried about the news headlines touting the talents of Babe Didrikson, the rising track star from Texas, Bill reminded Betty how good she was and told her not to worry.

"You should try something different. Give yourself a change from athletics," Bill mused, reading the newspaper one afternoon at Betty's house. "Look here, the Miss Chicago Pageant is next weekend. You should do it. Wouldn't that be a lark?"

Betty giggled. "When I was in high school, I did all of my school shows. I could sing and dance for the talent segment."

"So why not try this? It will keep your mind off Babe."

"You're right, why not?" Betty said, nodding and leaning over Bill to jot down the pageant entry information. Several days later, she surprised herself by winning a spot as a finalist.

A WEEK LATER Caroline visited Betty at her house, and the two sat on Betty's pale pink eiderdown comforter with two color harmony charts spread in front of them.

"See? With your blond hair, you're supposed to wear delicate colors like pink." Caroline pointed to the chart with the picture of a brunette. "I'm supposed to wear deeper shades and dark red lipstick."

There was a knock on the door and Betty's father leaned in.

"You're home!" said Betty.

Caroline pulled at Betty's arm to see the time on her wristwatch and then hopped off the bed. "How's it almost three o'clock already? Howard's picking me up outside in a few minutes. I've gotta go." She scooped her sandals off the floor and headed toward the door.

"I don't care what these charts say, I'm not giving up bright colors," Betty called after her.

"Suit yourself. Bye!" Caroline said, laughing.

Betty's smile vanished as she took a good look at her father and realized his face appeared ghostly. "Goodness, what's wrong?"

Mr. Robinson grimaced. "I need to talk with you."

Betty knocked the color charts aside. *What was this all about?* She walked to the parlor and found her father pouring himself a brandy from the sideboard. Odd. He never drank at this time of the afternoon. She sat on the love seat and he took a seat in the wing chair across from her, swirling his brandy, his gaze lost somewhere on a spot on the Persian carpet underfoot.

Without preamble, he said, "I lost my job today."

She gasped. "How?"

"All winter my supervisor's been urging me to let some of the staff go, but I kept refusing and even offered to have my salary reduced to cover some of the budget shortages. My negotiations have been in vain because now we've all been fired."

Betty struggled to make sense of it all. "Should I look for a job?" she asked, half expecting the offer to be dismissed, but her father's silence revealed his uncertainty. Her heart sank.

Everything had been going so well lately. Bill. Her training. School. Sure, the Robinsons had been tightening their belts over the last couple of years, everyone had, but life had felt steady. Jean, her sister, and her husband, Jim, weren't going to get rich off his job as a professor at the University of Chicago, but he was tenured, worked consistent hours, and enjoyed his students. Over the last year, Mr. Robinson's job had become precarious, but he had been with his company for as long as Betty could remember. How was it all gone?

"I'm going to try to find something new, of course. You should still plan to race in the Olympic trials next month, and hopefully you'll qualify for Los Angeles. Beyond that, I don't know what will happen."

Betty felt as if the air had been knocked out of her chest. This was serious. "What about school? There's only one more year."

Mr. Robinson's shoulders sagged. He raised his glass slowly as if it weighed a hundred pounds and slugged back its contents. "I'm not sure we'll be able to afford it."

THE NEXT MORNING, Betty awoke to another sweltering day. Outside the window of her second-floor bedroom, the leaves hung on the oak trees, limp and faded as butcher paper. The dull drone of motorcars hummed in the distance, and the usual clamor of early morning bird chatter was subdued. Her sheet lay in a tangled mess at the foot of her bed, pushed down sometime while she slept, so she tugged it up and spread her coverlet over the mattress. All night, worries had circled her mind and kept her from sleeping well.

She groaned as she swung her legs off the bed, but was brought up short by a postcard from Amsterdam pinned to her wall. Only a couple of weeks to go until the championships. She needed to focus on that. She had been waiting almost four years for another trip to the Olympics, and it was almost here. The first time around almost seemed like a dream. This time, she'd be able to enjoy it, knew more what to expect. And now she knew she was good, not just a fluke. Maybe Olympic success would lead to new opportunities, chances to help support herself. Some of the Olympic swimmers had gotten film contracts. Who knew what could happen?

She pulled a seersucker shift from the closet and dressed. The mirror reflected her lean legs and tanned, toned arms, and she ran a brush through her sun-lightened short hair.

Betty headed to the kitchen and found a plate of sliced melon waiting on the counter. She slid a cool piece of the fruit into her mouth with her fingers, savoring the sweetness as it hit her tongue.

Out of the corner of Betty's eye, she noticed a Marshall Field's shopping bag resting on the floor by the kitchen door. A tuft of fur poked out of the top. Betty leaned over to inspect the tan-colored cashmere coat with its soft rabbit-fur collar and pale pink satin lining as her mother appeared in the doorway.

"What on earth is your favorite winter coat doing out here in this heat?" Betty asked.

"I never really wear that old thing anymore, and it can fetch a good price. A little bit of money to stash away, just in case." Her mother placed the shopping bag into the pantry and turned back to Betty. "Is Bill coming around today?" she asked, her voice unnaturally chipper.

Betty wanted to embrace her, say something about how they would be fine, they'd figure out a way to get through this hardship, but the words wouldn't come. Instead it was easier to nod and feign cheeriness. "Yes, we're going to have a picnic by the lake later, but first I'm going to ring Wilson and see if he'll take me up in his plane. It's the only place I imagine where I'll find any break from this heat."

"You and Bill should go for a swim in the lake."

"Maybe." Betty took a final bite of melon. She hadn't yet told Bill about her father's unemployment and how her future at Northwestern looked uncertain. She wanted to focus on the National AAU Championships. Bill had been following the news about Babe Didrikson and Stella Walsh in the newspapers, even stopping by the library to read papers from their hometowns, Dallas and Cleveland.

When he had stopped by to pick her up last night, Bill had pulled a piece of paper from his back pocket and reported that Babe's times in the 100-yard sprint didn't come close to Betty's. "You've got nothing to worry about. You've beaten Stella twice now, and Babe's strengths, while impressive, do not lie in sprinting. She's good at everything else, but she's not a threat to you."

"You sure? I've been worrying."

He winked. "I've got some ideas about how we can help you relax."

"I'll bet you do."

"Let me take you to this new little spot I've found to park by the lake." He tugged at the neckline of her dress as he spoke and nestled close to kiss her earlobe.

As Betty thought back to what they had done to entertain themselves the night before, her face heated, but her mother didn't seem to notice. It had been almost five months now and everything had been going smoothly with Bill, but if she wasn't returning to Northwestern in the fall, what did that mean for the two of them?

Betty decided she needed a distraction and telephoned her cousin Wilson to ask if he'd take her for a ride in his plane. After he agreed and told her to meet him at the airfield at one o'clock, she telephoned Bill. As the hour neared, she powdered her face, fetched her flying cap and goggles, and sat outside on the front stoop in the shade waiting for Bill to appear. His Chevrolet coupe rounded the corner and Betty trotted down the front walk and pulled open the passenger door to hop inside.

From behind the wheel, he grinned at her. His only concession to the day's heat was the fact that his crisp light blue broadcloth shirtsleeves were rolled up around his elbows. "Hiya, kiddo. Aren't you a cool sight for a hot day?"

"Hardly. I'm practically melting. Thanks for taking me to see Wilson. Sure you don't want a ride too?"

"If there's time I'll go for a spin, but some of Wilson's tricks can leave me feeling a little green around the gills. I don't have your stomach of steel," Bill said.

Betty peeked in the back seat and spotted a straw basket and red-checked tablecloth. "Your favorite? Chicken salad?"

"The one and only. Don't get mad if I start on some while you're up in the air."

"Just don't eat it all." Betty ran her fingers through her hair, relishing the air as it rushed by them through the open windows of the car, but then they turned at an intersection. Betty glimpsed a handwritten sign that said *Evacuation Sale* tacked to a dented mailbox, and the perilousness of her own family's situation came roaring back to her. All her gaiety evaporated.

Over the purr of the car's motor, she cleared her throat. "I have some bad news. My father lost his job."

"Aww, Betty, I'm awful sorry. How's he taking it?"

"He's not missing a beat and is already out looking for a new one. It's distracting him from all of the bad news about Al Smith so I suppose that's an upshot." Nominating conventions for both the Republican and Democratic Parties were being held in the city that month, and all anyone could talk about was the candidates.

"At this rate, it sure looks like Governor Roosevelt's going to steamroll his way into the nomination," Bill said.

"Father wants nothing to do with Hoover anymore, so we'll see what happens." A vision of her mother's coat about to be hocked flashed before her eyes and her mouth went dry. "But here's the real stinger: I'm not sure I'll be returning to Northwestern in the fall. I may have to start looking for a job."

Bill kept his gaze on the road, and only his fingers tightening on the steering wheel gave her any indication that he had heard her. He turned the car off the main street and onto the bumpy dirt road that led to the airfield. When the vehicle rolled to a stop, he turned to her. "Betty, I was planning on waiting until next year for this, but why not talk about it now? What would you say to marrying me? I'm going to take over my father's company after graduation, and while business has been shaky, I can keep it together, and keep *us* together."

Betty inhaled sharply. "Bill, I didn't expect this."

"I know, this is hardly the way I pictured asking you, but maybe this is fate's way of telling us something. Let's get married this summer, and my parents can put us up in a place for one more year. It won't be fancy, but it's only until graduation. You could finish school, but you won't need it anymore if we're married."

He was right. Her degree in physical education wouldn't do much for her if she accepted his proposal, since a school district would be unlikely to hire her if she was married. "And what about the Olympics this summer?"

"Go and compete. We can marry at the end of August. You could still coach if you want to. You don't need a college degree for that." He laced her fingers through his own, and his hands were cool and dry. How did he always manage to stay so calm and collected? A lifetime with Bill would be safe and happy. How could it not be?

And I won't be a burden on my family anymore. The temptation to alleviate her father's worries pulled at her.

"Yes, of course." She wrapped her arms around his shoulders and pulled close to him. He tilted her head back and kissed her.

"You're shaking," he said.

"I can't help it. I'm so excited." She pulled back and looked around the airfield like she'd forgotten where they were and then started to pull on her leather flying cap. "My stomach is already flipping before I've even gone up into the air."

"Forget the plane. Let's go celebrate now."

"No, this'll just take a minute, and I'm so hot. I'll yell the news from the plane to everyone below."

"Well, in that case." He laughed and kissed her on the nose. "Be sure to wave at me from up there."

She opened the car door and stepped onto the grass not far from where her cousin's sporty little red Waco biplane waited. Wilson and his friend Harold were inspecting the control panels in the pilot's cockpit.

"Hey, Betty," called Wilson. "I had some trouble getting her started a few minutes ago, but it looks like we're back in business."

Bill stepped from the car and cupped his hand around his mouth to shout, "Take care of this girl. She's going to be my bride."

"No kidding." Wilson looked at Betty, eyebrows raised. "Wow, congratulations! You still want to go up? Don't you two have something better to do now?"

"We'll have all summer to celebrate, but I've been dreaming of cool air over the lake all morning," she said. "Want me in front here?" She gestured toward the front seat and Wilson nodded.

Harold dropped to the ground and backed away, waving. "Yeah, it'll be perfect up there. You two kids have fun."

From his seat behind Betty, Wilson saluted Harold and Bill and then flipped the switch to start the plane's engine. The roar of the propeller filled the air. Betty arranged her goggles over her eyes before blowing a kiss to Bill as the little plane sped down the runway and then lurched upward. There was a blur of parched grass and the field dropped away. Betty's stomach flipped as the small plane rose. The miracle of flying never failed to leave her breathless. She allowed her gaze to leave Bill and she watched the houses and buildings of Harvey and Riverdale shrink to something resembling a child's doll village. From above, the missing sections of roofs on abandoned factory buildings gaped; dusty yards littered with abandoned tires, broken appliances, and other garbage became visible. Acme Steel's smokestacks belched out wisps of black smoke. Automobiles crept along the ribbons of roads like ants. Ahead, Lake Michigan glittered across the horizon, tiny white sailboats dotting its surface like pieces of confetti. The air cooled and the tiny blond hairs on Betty's forearms rose in goose pimples in the sudden coolness of the altitude. She was on top of the world and let out a loud cheer.

Wilson hooted in response and put the plane into a dive to show off his latest maneuvers. Betty grabbed on to the edges of her seat as the plane began a steep decline. For several minutes he wowed her with a series of steep ascents and descents, and she laughed and laughed, loving the exhilaration that filled her with each new trick.

They had just reached the top of an ascent when a jolt shuddered through the plane. The propeller in front of Betty stuttered and then appeared motionless. An eerie silence surrounded them.

Betty sat straighter in surprise at this latest stunt.

Behind her, Wilson mumbled to himself. Everything felt suspended. Aware that she had stopped breathing, Betty exhaled and marveled at the stillness. Blue sky surrounded them, not a single cloud in sight. A perfect day to be in the air.

And then the plane tilted downward.

Sharply.

Before she could register what was happening, they were plunging toward the earth. Where was Bill? Could he see what was happening? The tops of trees, mere pinpricks moments ago, now swelled like opening umbrellas as they hurtled toward them. A riot of sounds filled Betty's ears, but it wasn't from the propeller—it was the roar of rushing air, Wilson shouting, and her own screaming.

THE CHICAGO EVENING STANDARD

July 1, 1932

"Girl Olympian Mistaken for Dead"

Harvey—When Mr. Fisher, the undertaker at Oak Forest Funeral Home, received the lifeless body of a young girl taken from the wreckage of a plane, he paused before preparing her for the Great Beyond. Even in her grievous state, she looked familiar. It was at that moment that he noticed her chest rising and falling and called for emergency services, thereby narrowly averting a tragic mistake!

So who was this hapless victim?

None other than Miss Betty Robinson, whose infectious smile and fleet feet captured the nation's heart after she won a gold medal in the 1928 Olympics in Amsterdam.

On Sunday, June 28, Miss Robinson, 20, had joined her cousin Wilson Palmer, 18, in his plane for a short ride to escape the heat. After several minutes in the air, the engine stalled at a height of 400 feet before plummeting into a nearby marshy field. A witness found Palmer alive and took him to Ingalls Memorial Hospital, where he is in serious but stable condition with a fractured jaw and broken legs.

Miss Robinson, currently a coed at Northwestern University, remains in a coma at Oak Forest Infirmary. Doctors are not yet commenting on the extent of her injuries, but her accident has shaken her former Olympic teammates and coaches. Major Gen. Douglas MacArthur, head of the 1928 Olympic team, expressed his shock and sorrow, saying, "This tragedy is a great loss for our nation." Since winning her gold medal in Amsterdam, Miss Robinson had been training for the Olympics taking place in Los Angeles later this month and was favored to win gold again in the 100-meter sprint.

LOS ANGELES MORNING SUN

July 10, 1932

"Stella Walsh for Sale!"

Cleveland—With the Olympic trials less than a week away, Stanislawa Walasiewicz (better known by her Americanized name, Stella Walsh), speediest of the nation's sprinters, declined American naturalization papers and announced she plans to run for her native country of Poland. Her statement comes as a stunning blow to America's chances for gold in the upcoming Olympics.

Her trainer and coach begged her to decline the invitation to join the Polish Olympic team, but Walsh remained firm, citing financial concerns. She explained that after being given a furlough of indeterminate duration by her employer, New York Central Railroad, economic hardship is motivating her decision to race for Poland, a country that has offered to pay training and travel expenses for its Olympic athletes, along with offering an academic scholarship to attend university.

Despite criticism that she is being disloyal to the country that raised her, Miss Walsh insisted she had no choice but to accept Poland's offer. Mr. Walsh, a father of five and a part-time steel-mill worker, tearfully claimed he had no additional means to support his daughter. Cleveland's mayor, Mr. Raymond T. Miller, offered her a position in the city's recreation department, but the American Athletic Union stated that taking any recreation-related job would compromise her amateur athlete status and make her ineligible to compete as a member of the United States Olympic team.

Her announcement has raised eyebrows and confirmed the feminine prerogative to change her mind, not to mention the untrustworthy nature of non-American people. "This is a brazen case of professionalism winning over patriotism," lamented famed basketball coach Mr. R. Baker. Bob Leahy of Cleveland's city council also expressed his disgust with her decision, saying, "Walsh clearly has no loyalty to her adopted country, so this unemployed Slavic immigrant should go back to where she came from. Good riddance."

In the last three years, the young woman has set ten records in a variety of different distances and is widely considered a top contender for being the fastest woman in the world.

BOSTON UNION LEADER

July 15, 1932

"Boston-Area Girls Depart for Olympic Trials"

Malden—Three of the state's top sprinters boarded the train
this morning for Chicago, where they hope to secure spots on
the Olympic team heading to Los Angeles later this month.
Miss Louise Stokes of the Onteora Track Club, Miss Mary
Carew of the Medford Athletic Club, and Miss Olive Hasenfus of the Boston Swimming Association have been invited to
compete in the women's 100-meter dash, one of six Olympic
events open to the fairer sex. For the last two years, these
three women have been thrilling New Englanders with their
nail-biting races, during both the indoor and outdoor track
seasons. Miss Stokes, the Negro phenom, achieved a national
broad jump record in 1931, and Miss Carew holds a national
title for the fastest 40-yard-dash time. Miss Hasenfus traveled
to the 1928 Olympics in Amsterdam as a reserve member of
the American women's relay team and has held several national titles in various distances since she was fifteen years
old, but she's endured a challenging year as she recovers
from a surgery last winter.

Of the fifty hopefuls who will be competing in the 100-
meter race, only the top six women sprinters will be selected
to travel to Los Angeles as official members of the women's

team under the expertise of Manager Fred Steers and Coach George Vreeland. In the last two weeks, the women's sprinting field has broken wide open for American racers with Stella Walsh's announcement that she'll be racing for Poland and former Olympic gold medalist Betty Robinson's horrific plane crash. Perhaps one of our Boston girls will find herself leading the charge to gold.

22.

July 1932
Evanston, Illinois

LOUISE HAD RUN IN SOME HOT RACES, BUT THE National AAU Championships in 1932 made all the challenging conditions that had come before seem mild by comparison. That morning, she stayed in the shade of the bleachers whenever she could. After she finished first in her preliminary heat of the 100-yard dash, she returned to the shade and discovered that race officials had decided the high temperatures merited blocks of ice to be brought in to keep the athletes cool. She'd never seen anything like this and was delighted, but even more exciting was who was sitting on one of the blocks of ice, fanning herself with a race program: another black woman. Since Louise had started racing several years earlier, her competitors had been almost all white women.

"Aren't your shorts getting wet?" Louise asked, hiding her surprise by pointing at the puddle of water pooling by the woman's feet.

"In this heat, I don't mind," the woman answered, running her hand along the side of the ice before placing it on her forehead and smiling. "My name's Tidye."

Tidye was small and her skin was the color of coffee with a good dollop of cream stirred in.

Louise introduced herself and sat on a neighboring block. "Where you from?"

"Not far, just south of here. How about you?"

"Massachusetts."

"Never been, but I'd like to visit someday. I hear it's pretty, lots of history. Is it hot there too?"

"It can be, but I've never felt anything like this," Louise said, savoring the way her entire body relaxed as it cooled.

At that moment, a tall girl arrived, pushing her short dark hair off her sweaty beet-red forehead. "Hey, Tidye, can you make room for me? Whew, I'm dying."

"Can't you find your own?"

"No, they're all claimed by other girls. Come on, scoot."

Tidye inched over to make room for her friend and introduced her to Louise as Caroline Hale, another runner from Chicago.

"So, how did the hurdles go?" Tidye asked Caroline.

"I've made it into the final heat with that dreadful Babe Didrikson. She's competing in too many events and it's slowing everything down while we wait for her to finish one thing before she moves to the next. Every extra second in this sun is making all the girls pretty grouchy."

"I thought we were limited to three events," Louise said.

"We're supposed to be and clearly all the delays prove there's good reason for that, but apparently the rules are flexible if you have a coach who's willing to argue loudly enough on your behalf." Caroline grimaced.

Tidye giggled. "What? Howard's not doing his job?"

Caroline flushed even redder than she already was from the heat. "My fiancé is my coach," she explained to Louise. "But I wouldn't want him to be a squeaky wheel. I want to earn my spot on the team fair and square. That Babe Didrikson's already got the press eating out of the palm of her hand and can't stop bragging she's going to win all the gold medals in Los Angeles."

"Why do you keep calling her *that* Babe Didrikson?" Tidye asked.

"Because I don't like her and this heat is driving me plumb crazy. Is that a good enough reason for you?"

Both Tidye and Louise burst into laughter, and Caroline cracked them a grudging smile.

When the announcer instructed the women in the first semifinal heat to approach their lanes, Louise's legs felt like they'd turned into liquid. This was her group. Tidye and Mary would be running in the next one.

Since leaving Boston, she and Mary had been inseparable, but not necessarily by choice. They were sharing a room at the AAU-sponsored boardinghouse so it seemed there was never a moment in the day when the two weren't together, yet if someone had asked if they were friends, Louise would have been hard put to know how to answer. (Fortunately no one asked.) More than anything, they were bound together by knowing each other from home, but both women were reserved by nature, and there was the discomfiting fact that they were in competition with one another. The Olympic team would only take six of the fifty-something women who were entered in the 100-meter sprint. How likely was it that both women would make it? Whenever the thought that Mary would be the one to go to Los Angeles entered Louise's mind, she pushed it away, not able to bear thinking about it.

Everything hinged on this race.

If she finished in the top three, she was guaranteed a spot in the finals of the sprint and a place on the Olympic team.

The officials prompted the racers and the usual starting routine commenced. Louise fell to a crouch, relieved to allow her legs to buckle. She took a moment to steady herself, quiet her mind, just like Coach Quain had instructed her to do. *Feel the ground under your two feet, breathe in and out deeply.* In her mind's eye, she sprang from her crouch and raced down the track with the feeling of the wind at her back, sweeping her along.

When the gun fired, Louise leapt from her start smoothly, her arms and legs moving with precision and purpose. She ran as if her life depended on it, and at that moment, it felt as if it did. The other racers fell behind, but one woman charged ahead in first place, her shoulders just a couple of inches out of reach. Louise put forth a final surge and felt like she was leaving her body, melting into the heat, taxing every cog in the machinery of her body. Just one more beat faster, that was all she needed. *One more beat . . .*

When she crossed the finish line, she was still in second place, but that was wonderful! Never had she been so thrilled to be in second place. She raised her arms in victory, tears blurring her vision. After years of hard work, she was going to the Olympics.

Tidye jogged out to Louise to clap her on the shoulder.

"I can't believe it," Louise said, almost limp with relief, but her euphoria was dampened by a rabble of voices coming from the judges' area. There, a coach stood with one of the women who had been ejected earlier for falling before the finish of her semifinal heat. The man's hands gripped the judges' table and he leaned in, his face flushed and furious, yelling at the semicircle of race officials in front of him. "You must include her!"

Tidye blew out her breath. "Good grief. What's all of that about?"

Louise shook her head in dismay, unsure what the commotion was about, but certain that it didn't bode well for what was to come next.

When it came time for the finals, Mary and Tidye were also advancing from their heat and Louise fell into place beside them on the way to the track. What a relief that they had all qualified for the Olympic team and would be heading to Los Angeles! It was almost too good to be true and Louise couldn't believe their good fortune. The purpose of this final heat was simply to determine their Olympic events: the first two finishers would race in the individual 100-meter sprint and the remaining four would constitute the 4-x-100-meter relay team.

But when they arrived at the lanes designated for their race, there were seven women, not six, awaiting the start.

Confused, Louise looked to the officials for clarification, but the man directed them to their assigned lanes without any explanation. The athlete whose coach had been yelling at the judges' table earlier stood on the starting line with them.

Louise knew she had not seen the runner race in either of the semifinal heats, but the official began his starting routine, no time for questions.

The seven women dropped into crouches, the gun fired, and they were off.

Louise's toe failed to gain purchase in the cinder, causing her to stumble, but she regained her footing and burst ahead. Everyone was fast. Legs whirred, lungs heaved. Two women were a step or two ahead, and Louise found herself in third place with Mary at her side. A spark took hold inside Louise. She would beat Mary—after all, she usually did. Louise pushed her legs to go that much faster. *Just a little farther, push, push, push!* Her heart thundered, her lungs were on fire. Each step came faster and faster as she bolted along the straightaway, yet Mary clung to her side, undeterred.

Louise crossed the finish line in a clump of racers. Had she beaten Mary?

Immediately the judges huddled to argue over the finishing order.

In the late afternoon heat, Louise's thighs burned and her vision seemed to swim. She bent over, resting her hands on her kneecaps as she tried to steady her breathing while awaiting a verdict on the results. She couldn't bring herself to look at any of the other racers.

Finally a judge stepped from the crowd, a clipboard in his hand. "Congratulations to our Olympic qualifiers. Please let me remind our spectators that since we only measure finishes to the tenth of a second, we can end up with some real close calls, but often judges can detect who crossed the finish line first even when the clocked time is the same. So in first place, Ethel Harrington won with a time of 12.3 seconds; in second, Billie von Bremen at 12.4 seconds; a close third, Elizabeth Wilde, also with a time of 12.4 seconds; and because judges just couldn't make a firm ruling with this one, we have a rare tie for fourth with Louise Stokes and Mary Carew at 12.5 seconds . . ."

A tie! Even through her joy of advancing to the Olympics, she couldn't believe she hadn't been able to beat Mary. She knew she needed to congratulate her, but she just wanted a minute to process her irritation, to put the prickly edge of competition away so she could move on with the excitement of traveling to California. But then she heard a gasp and turned.

Tidye's face blanched as the judge called her name out last in seventh place.

"But I'm going to Los Angeles, right?" Tidye asked, her voice thin with anguish. "Why are there seven women here? There were only supposed to be six! I earned my spot in this final."

The man with the clipboard studied his notes again. "There was some confusion in an earlier heat with Ethel Harrington. She stopped running before the finish, but based on her past performances, it was decided to include her. Only the top six will be going to Los Angeles. Sorry, you didn't make the team."

In the silence that followed the judge's announcement, another official stepped forward. "Now see here," he said, looking at the judge but pointing at Tidye. "This girl made it to the final six, fair and square. Under the rules, she's earned a spot in the Olympics too."

Surprised, the sprinters studied one another, then cast a wary look at Tidye.

Again, the judges conferenced, and after a brief conversation, the man with the clipboard stepped forward. "This year we will send seven girls to the Olympics to be eligible for the hundred-meter and relay. Congratulations to all."

The women applauded, and the onlookers in the stands, listless and tired in this late hour of the afternoon, roused themselves into cheering. Louise wrapped her arms around Mary and Tidye, happy to celebrate the exciting news about qualifying, but she still didn't understand how the Olympic officials planned to resolve the problem. Why send seven women to Los Angeles for only six racing spots?

THE CHICAGO EVENING STANDARD
July 17, 1932

"A Big Day for Babe Didrikson!"
Lady's Olympic Track and Field
Trial Mired in Controversy

Evanston—In sweltering heat that could have knocked a heavyweight boxer to his back in a split second, a swarm of tenacious lady athletes competed in a range of physical challenges to determine who will continue to Los Angeles to compete in the Olympics. Yesterday's National AAU Championships served up thrills and chaos in equal measure. Unexpected accidents and injuries and questionable judgments from officials made it a fascinating day from start to finish.

Miss Mildred "Babe" Didrikson delivered on the hype that has surrounded her ever since she began competing in her home state of Texas. She nabbed first-place finishes in the shot, javelin, high jump, and 80-meter hurdles, and fourth place for the discus. A close finish in the 80-meter hurdles also set off sniping when officials initially awarded first place to Caroline Hale of the IWAC and then changed their minds and gave it to Didrikson. When asked about how the day went, Miss Didrikson shrugged off any criticism. "I won this whole thing. Of course, these gals aren't happy, but I proved that I'm the best."

With almost 50 entrants, the real drama lay in the 100-meter sprint. Normally six women would have been selected from the top finishers of the qualifying heats and these athletes would advance to the Olympics, but several disputes in preliminary rounds allowed the judges to loosen their rules so seven women sprinters will be traveling to Los Angeles, all hoping for a spot to compete in the individual 100-meter and the four-woman relay team. You don't need to be a mathematician to count that there are too many runners heading to California so get out your hankies, because some disappointed lady sprinters will be sitting on the sidelines of the Olympics, tugging at your heartstrings, in a couple of weeks.

THE CHICAGO EVENING STANDARD
July 18, 1932

"Girl Olympic Champ Clinging to Life"

Chicago—Betty Robinson, the 19-year-old Northwestern coed and 1928 Olympian who narrowly survived a plane crash on June 28, has regained consciousness and battles to survive. She remains in critical condition at Oak Forest Infirmary with a shattered left thigh, a right leg broken in several places, and a fractured left arm.

After examining her most recent X-ray, Miss Robinson's doctor reports that once her left leg heals, it will be shorter than her right leg because of the extensive damage incurred by the crash. He says, "A return to running is unlikely, given the severity of her injuries."

Despite the prognosis, the girl's father, Harold Robinson, promises his daughter's spirit is not crushed. "She's a very determined young lady, and we're hoping she'll be up and walking again within the year."

Miss Robinson's absence at the Olympics will leave a gap in the competition for new stars to emerge. Her primary competitor, Miss Stella Walsh of Cleveland, who recently announced she'll be racing for Poland, remarked, "My prayers are with the Robinson family, and I hope for a speedy recovery for Betty." With everyone's favorite American lady sprinter fighting to live, Miss Walsh is now favored to win gold in the women's Olympic 100-meter sprint.

23.

July 1932
En route to Los Angeles

LOUISE AND HER TEAMMATES HAD A BUSY FINAL FEW days in Chicago, filled with preparations for the trip to California. Telegrams. Training. Dinners and luncheons with oyster-colored table linens and silver cutlery. Even though the nation was slogging its way through the worsening Depression, people appeared eager for good news and fervor for the Olympics grew. When the women gathered in the parlor of the boardinghouse where the AAU was paying for them to stay, Tidye untucked a newspaper from under her arm to show her teammates as they lined up for a team photograph.

"I'm a student reporter for *The Chicago Defender* and wrote an article about the Olympic trials. See?" Tidye pointed to a long column in the middle of the page.

Babe leaned in closer to look. "Never heard of it, and, I swear, every reporter in town has introduced himself to me at this point. I would've given you a special quote if you'd asked."

"*The Chicago Defender*'s the most widely distributed Negro paper in the city," Tidye said, the pride unmistakable in her voice.

Without saying anything more, Babe wrinkled her nose and handed the paper to Louise without taking a look at the article.

Caroline crowded over Louise's shoulder to read it. "This is really good, Tidye. You bring the race to life so well that I almost feel my heatstroke coming on again."

The other girls drifted away, uninterested, and Louise watched Tidye's expression fall.

"Can I keep this for my scrapbook?" Louise asked. "I can't wait to tell everyone at home that I became friends with the reporter who wrote this. Want to sign your name underneath it?"

"Of course," Tidye said, autographing the article before handing it back to Louise with a grateful smile.

THE NEXT DAY, the women were chauffeured to the train station and boarded a Pullman passenger car decorated with red, white, and blue bunting and a banner that said *U.S. Women's Olympic Athletics Team* on its side. At each train stop, the women pressed their noses to the glass of their railcar windows, eager to see the crowds awaiting their arrival. Each dusty town appeared to awaken from its summer stupor, hungry for a reason to celebrate good news, and the crowds formed on the station platforms, waving flags, as bands played. Hope and excitement spread across the faces of the spectators, most of whom appeared to be people of modest means, and fueled the delight of the women aboard the train.

When the train stopped in Denver, motorcars awaited the athletes, and they were driven to the top of Pikes Peak. For Tidye, Louise, Mary, and Caroline, women who had never crossed the Continental Divide, the dramatic view of the craggy peaks of the Rockies spreading far in every direction left them speechless. Eventually the women climbed back into the motorcars and were driven to the Brown Palace Hotel in Denver to spend the night.

With her valise tucked under her arm, Louise headed for the elegant main entrance of the red granite hotel, already relishing the prospect of spending the night in a real bed instead of being jostled and quaking in a Pullman sleeper.

"Excuse me, miss," the hotel manager called, smoothing his suit as he marched toward her. "This entrance is for whites only. Please use the servants' door in the back."

Louise froze. Someone took her hand and Tidye nudged in beside her, her lips pressed together in a thin line. Ahead, Babe Didrikson and a few of their teammates disappeared into the hotel's lobby, but Mary remained beside Tidye, looking bewildered. "What did that man say?"

"Apparently Louise and I have to use the entrance in the back," Tidye whispered, her face screwing into a scowl.

Mary's mouth opened in indignation, but before she could say anything, Caroline pulled her bag to her chest and linked her arm through Louise's. "Come on, we're going with you."

Instead of liveried porters waiting to greet them at the back door, the only things marking the nondescript service entrance were several large overflowing garbage bins and a cracked flower-pot filled with cigarette butts. Louise held her breath against the putrid smell of rotting fruit filling the air. Silently, the women entered a narrow, dim corridor and squeezed past a large cart filled with freshly laundered white towels waiting to be folded. The manager conferred with a woman before turning to Caroline and Mary. "Ladies, please head toward that door, where you'll find the main lobby and receive your room assignments. You two"—he pointed at Louise and Tidye—"follow Miss Martin. She'll take you to your room."

Caroline started to protest, but Tidye shushed her. "Just go. We'll find you in a bit."

Caroline and Mary plodded away while Louise and Tidye watched them wistfully before turning to follow the maid up a flight of stairs. One set of stairs became two, and then three, and by the ninth floor, the women were perspiring and huffing in the heat of the tight passageways. The maid opened a door, revealing a pair of twin beds and a washbasin atop a small shared bedside table underneath a tiny window. One bare lightbulb hung from the ceiling. "There's a washroom on the floor below with the other women's staff rooms," she said in a flat voice that brokered no further discussion.

"Where are our teammates?" Louise asked.

"They're staying in guest rooms on the lower floors. We're not accustomed to accommodating colored guests. You must remain in your room here because your kind isn't allowed in the dining room downstairs. Meals will be brought up to you." Miss Martin gave her instructions as if reciting a weather report. No inflection, no change in demeanor.

Tidye stepped inside the room and knocked on the strange-looking unpainted tan-colored walls. "What in the world is this?"

"Terra-cotta. This is only the second building in the country to be constructed of fireproof materials."

"Huh, finally some good news for us, given that we're stuck all the way up here. I'd hate to think of our deaths weighing on your conscience if a fire broke out," Tidye said, keeping her features expressionless.

Without another word, the maid huffed past them and headed for the stairs.

Louise gave a weary shake of her head and placed her valise on the ground before leaning over the washbasin to peer out the window. Thankfully, it opened with a groan, and a gasp of air stirred through the room. It was a small victory, but not enough to take the shame out of their circumstances. In silence, both women peeled off their travel clothes and lay atop the beds' thin pale cotton spreads in their slips.

As promised, a maid delivered a tray with two plates of roasted chicken and baked beans, no dessert, and nothing to drink except for a small pitcher of lukewarm water.

"If I thought they'd care, I wouldn't even eat their dried-out chicken and soggy beans," Louise muttered.

"I thought the same thing, but I refuse to give them the satisfaction of us going hungry. Let's not make ourselves any more uncomfortable than we already are," Tidye said with a sniff.

When the light in their room started to fade, a knock at the door roused them.

Louise answered the door and found Caroline, wearing a mint-colored georgette dress, her hair in glossy waves. She held on to the doorframe, looking around their meager quarters, and wrinkled her nose. "This is it? After all of those stairs, this is all you get? When I received my room assignment, the manager said that this is the tallest building in Denver. He wasn't kidding, huh?" Caroline shook her head in apology. "I'm sorry. This is terrible."

"Never thought I'd look forward to sleeping on the train," Louise said.

"Oh dear, I know. This isn't much, but I nicked a few slices of lemon chiffon pie from the dining room. Figured you both enjoy sweets."

Louise accepted the pie wrapped in a napkin edged in scalloped trim and thanked her.

"If only Howard was stopping in Denver, we could just get off the darned train and ride with him," Caroline said.

"You miss him, huh?" Tidye asked.

"I just wish he had qualified for the men's team."

"He's a good one, Caroline. He's really proud of you."

"I know. I can't wait to see him when we get to Los Angeles. Poor guy, he's going to be sleeping in his car most nights unless I can sneak him into our hotel. I can count on you girls not to rat me out, can't I?"

They all laughed, and Caroline stayed for a couple more minutes before saying good night and heading downstairs. After she left, Louise took the napkin filled with pie and dropped it into the hallway wastebasket before shutting the door behind her.

Tidye nodded with satisfaction. "They can keep their darned pie."

After Louise switched off the light, they lay in their beds staring into the darkness.

"I'm getting worried Coach is going to change the relay team and we're going to be dropped," Tidye said.

Louise rolled to her side, trying to make out Tidye's outline in the darkness. "Why? What makes you say that?"

"Well, why are we stuck up here when everyone else is downstairs?"

THE NEXT DAY, aboard the train, Louise and Tidye lay in their berths, subdued, but relieved to be leaving the humiliation of the Brown Palace Hotel behind. From her upper bunk, Louise flipped the pages of a *Photoplay*. The experience at the hotel had left her with a tense stomachache, but the constant swaying of their train eventually lulled her into a sense of lethargy until a screech from Tidye's bunk pierced the quiet. Startled, Louise shimmied to the side of her own bed and peered over the edge, where she came almost eye-to-eye with Babe. A smug grin split across the blond woman's angular features. Tidye sprang from her bunk, her clothes dripping with water as Babe tucked a silver pitcher, the kind the waiters in the dining car carried, under her arm.

"Why on earth did you do that?" Tidye shrieked.

Babe guffawed and leaned over and smacked her thighs. "Lordy, I wish you could see your face right now."

Outraged, Tidye pulled her soaked dress from her chest and stared at the drips of water pooling underneath her feet. "Have you lost your mind?"

Drawn to the commotion, Mary and a couple of other

women appeared in the berth, circling around Babe and Tidye with grim expressions.

"What?" Babe surveyed the group. "It was a joke. Y'all have no sense of fun. I was just trying to liven things up."

"I suppose it's no accident that I'm the one you picked for your stupid joke." Tidye was practically spitting in fury.

"What's that supposed to mean?"

"I'm pretty sure you know *exactly* what I mean." Tidye poked a finger straight at Babe and the Texan took a step backward.

"Sheesh, I thought I was doing you a favor. It's blazing hot. Figured you'd appreciate cooling down."

"Yeah? Well, I don't appreciate it at all. Keep away from me, you hear? I don't want any more of your jokes or favors. Nothing, got it?"

"Spoilsport. Can't we have a little fun around here?" Babe huffed.

The other women averted their gazes and shuffled from the compartment. Only Mary stayed behind and helped Tidye step out of her wet dress.

"How can you stand to room with her?" Tidye fumed.

Mary bit her lip. "No one else would, and I felt bad for her."

"You think I should feel sorry for her too?"

"No, of course not." Mary lowered her gaze and shifted her weight from side to side. "Sorry," she mumbled before handing the dress to Louise and hurrying from their berth.

With hands trembling in outrage, Louise snapped the wet dress to shake out the water. She would have hoped, even expected, her teammates to scold Babe or at least say *something*, but the girls who had convened to see what had happened seemed cowed by the Texan. She sighed. In her annoyance, Louise thrust the dress onto a hook with such force that she heard a small ripping sound come from its waistband.

Sheepish, she turned to Tidye, who stood in her slip, her arms folded across her chest. "Oh, that dress is the least of my concerns. But it sure is starting to feel like you and I are on a different team from the rest of 'em, huh?"

24.

July 1932
Oak Forest Infirmary, Illinois

BETTY AWOKE TO FIND A NURSE HOVERING OVER HER, A woman she didn't recognize. The nurse raised a thermometer and Betty opened her mouth reflexively to receive it. After a minute or so, the nurse plucked the thermometer from Betty's mouth and inspected it, smiling. "No fever. No sign of infection. Today's going to be a good day. I can feel it."

Mrs. Robinson leaned forward from where she sat by Betty's side. "I agree," she said, cocking her head at Betty to check for her reaction.

Betty coughed. What made today any different from the other days? Her hours of wakefulness stretched into a long tunnel of uncertainty. Her mother read books to her, but Betty couldn't remember what they were. Her father updated her on the newspapers, but none of it stuck with her. Both of her legs were encased in plaster casts from the tips of her toes to the tops of her thighs, while her left arm, also in a plaster cast from her hand to her shoulder, dangled from the ceiling in an elaborate traction system of pulleys and cords. Her life had gone from one of promise to one of pain and doubt. She'd been trying to ignore her worries, lose herself in the haze of medicine that had kept her in a fog, but she knew she needed some answers. "What's the date? How long have I been here?"

The nurse and her mother looked at each other for a moment before the nurse looked back at Betty and said, "You've been here for almost a month."

It was like a blow to the chest. *That long?* Minutes, hours, days, daytime, nighttime—everything had become a blur, impossible to measure.

Her mother clasped Betty's hand. "The nurse told me that she can help you with a bath and then we could do your hair. You know who would like to come and see you?"

Betty shook her head.

Her mother glanced at the lines of cards filling the two windowsills and swallowed. "Bill calls every day to ask about you." Betty's stomach gave a sickening lurch, and she turned to look at the vase of daisies on the bedside table; her mother followed her gaze. "He sent those. Aren't they lovely? Just think, we can get you all fixed up and you can see him."

The white petals glowed in the indigo shadows of the morning light.

Bill.

Kind, funny, smart, and talented Bill.

Betty scratched at one of the plaster casts entombing her leg. She didn't remember much from the day of the plane crash, but she did remember Bill proposing. It was the last memory she had. Now that she was injured, what would he make of her? Her mother had not called him Betty's fiancé. Had he not told anyone about the proposal? Did he still want to marry her?

"You're looking so much better. Do you feel better? Don't you want to see Bill?"

Did she? From within her cast, Betty's knee began to itch. Everything ached and ached, but she felt the weight of her mother's hopefulness more than anything. "Yes, of course, I can't wait to see him."

LATER THAT AFTERNOON, she settled into the crisp, fresh sheets on her hospital bed, wearing a pink cotton nightgown instead of her flimsy striped hospital gown. No matter how many lavender sachets her mother sprinkled in the room, the smell of laundry bleach lingered, even over the lily-of-the-valley-scented-shampoo smell of her hair. Her hospital room was finally quiet and empty. After weeks of constantly being surrounded by nurses and her parents, solitude came as a relief. It was like she was a marionette and someone had let go of the strings. She could finally relax.

Her vision swam with tears and she let out a sob. Until that moment, she hadn't realized how hard she had been working to appear cheerful and patient. Not only was her body immobilized, but she could scarcely allow her true feelings to stretch out and reveal themselves for fear of upsetting her parents or disappointing the staff working so hard to make her comfortable. *What in the world was going to happen to her?* She felt ruined. She wept with a ferocity that frightened her, but gradually her sobs subsided, leaving her raw but relieved and emptied of a weight that had been jammed deep in her throat and chest for weeks.

There was a knock at the door and her mother pushed her head inside the room. "Betty, Bill's here. Are you ready?"

Betty inhaled deeply and hoped her face didn't look blotchy from crying.

"Betty!" Bill called as he entered the room. Her mother withdrew to leave the two of them alone, and Betty felt a surprising shyness and almost wished her mother would stay. Bill's skin shined with good health and summer color, and when he reached the side of her bed and leaned over to embrace her, she could smell the outdoors on him. A tinge of perspiration and the sun-warmed cotton of his shirt. Here in the bland sterility of the hospital, he felt like a strange outlier with his broad chest and glowing health. "Geez, Betty, you're a sight for sore eyes." He grabbed her hand and squeezed it tightly.

She gasped.

"Oh no, did I hurt you?"

"No, actually you didn't. Your strong grip just surprised me. Everyone handles me like I'm fragile and might break."

He dropped into the chair and leaned forward, elbows set gamely on his knees. "I've missed you."

"I've missed you too." As she said the words aloud, she meant them. She searched his face and he glanced away.

"Say, this place isn't too bad. The staff seem mighty proud to be taking care of you. How are you feeling?"

She didn't know how to answer that. Should she tell him how she dreamed of hurtling through the air every night? How she awoke sometimes in a cold sweat, only to find herself trapped in these wretched plaster casts? Should she tell him about the moans that emanated from the other rooms at night and how they scared her? Should she ask if he still wanted to marry her? Had anyone told Bill that she might not walk properly again?

All these questions stretched between them like a gaping chasm that she didn't know how to cross.

"Everything feels different."

Bill frowned. "I know."

Betty decided there was no more postponing the inevitable. "One of the last things I remember from before the crash is that you proposed to me, and I want you to know that I'll understand if you've changed your mind."

"Betty, my feelings for you haven't changed at all."

"But everything's changed. My recovery's going to be slow. They don't know if I'll walk again."

"The wedding can wait. Sure, you're a little dinged up, but you're the same girl. I'll wait for you."

Betty winced. She would never be the same girl who had gone up in that plane. She had changed in ways she didn't fully understand and couldn't explain. It was just like Bill to want to be a hero, but did he understand what he was committing to? Did either of them?

"Your doctor said I could only stay for a couple of minutes." He squeezed her hand. "I hate to leave you."

"I understand. Thank you for coming."

"Should I come back tomorrow after work?"

"I'm not going anywhere."

He smiled tenderly, bending over to take her free hand. "May I kiss you?"

She nodded, feeling her throat tighten. He bent deeper, and when he kissed her, no amount of morphine could dull the surge of awakening she felt within the plaster covering her body. She longed to be free of her confinement, free to reach around his shoulders with both hands and feel his chest against hers. He pulled back. "You're so brave. I'm proud that you're my girl."

She suddenly felt exhausted. How could she tell him that she didn't feel a single ounce of bravery?

25.

BLUE SKIES. ORANGE TREE GROVES. ENDLESS SUNSHINE. Louise had never seen anything like Los Angeles. It felt magical with its elegant lines of palm trees edging the wide boulevards and the air's sweet and salty mixture of hibiscus and ocean. The men were ferried out to the Olympic Village in an area called Baldwin Hills, where bungalows had been hastily thrown up to accommodate them. The women were given rooms at the Chapman Park Hotel on Wilshire Boulevard, a busy spot central to all the excitement.

"Miss Stokes, I've got some mail for you," the hotel's front desk clerk said, rummaging around under the check-in counter.

Louise grinned and took the small stack of envelopes from the young woman and held them to her chest with delight. Everything about California was wonderful, including the lovely welcome they were receiving at the hotel. It was a far cry from the disappointing accommodations and poor treatment they'd encountered in Denver.

Around her, the other girls clutched their mail, shrieking with joy, but Mary walked away from the front desk empty-handed.

As much as Louise had felt annoyed by her ever since the incident with Babe on the train, Mary's forlorn expression now made Louise feel a pang of sympathy.

"After you've settled in, do you want to join Caroline, Tidye, and me to visit the salon around the corner? It's offering free haircuts for Olympians," she asked Mary as she headed to the elevator.

"Sure, that would be fun. Thanks." She eyed Louise's letters hungrily. "You got something from your folks?"

Louise nodded, unsure what to say, but Mary, brightened with the invitation to the salon, didn't seem to notice.

"That's nice. I live with my aunt and uncle and they have a bunch of their own kids and probably don't have time to write. They're always busy."

"Well, maybe you'll get something in the next few days."

"Maybe," Mary said, trying to look like she believed it. "Find me when you're ready to go?"

"Of course."

The busy hive of the Chapman Park Hotel and the nearby salon kept the Olympians occupied when they weren't training. All the girls had their hair done, and Caroline even had her eyebrows plucked. Howard finally rumbled into Los Angeles in his dusty jalopy, and Caroline, Louise, and Tidye had dinner with him each night, eager to tell him about the beautiful training facilities over at the stately campus of the University of Southern California, where they spent their mornings.

The morning of the Opening Ceremonies dawned with

more perfect weather, and the women were abuzz with excitement, but the energy shifted when they received their uniforms in the team captain's room. When Mary held hers up, the top almost hung midway down her thighs.

"How are you supposed to compete in that?" Caroline cried. She lifted the shorts in her bundle. "Why, look at the width on this waistband! Three of us could fit into this."

Their chaperone took one look at Caroline and Mary and raised her eyes to the ceiling. "Oh heavens, they've given you the same uniforms the men are getting. Sit tight while I call the hotel's seamstress."

"It's almost like they don't even want us girls here," Caroline fumed. "Couldn't they prepare proper uniforms for us?"

After a few minutes, the seamstress arrived and the women swarmed her, asking for waistbands to be taken in, armholes cinched, and tops hemmed. After an hour most of the women had left to prepare for practice with their tailored uniforms in hand, but Louise and Tidye noticed their shorts and tops kept being put aside even though they had been among the first to speak with the seamstress.

"We're running out of time," Louise whispered to Tidye, pointing to a clock hanging on the wall. "Do you think she's forgotten about us?"

Tidye frowned and shot Louise an impatient look. "No, I think we're the lowest on her priority list, and I think I know why."

Louise felt the same wave of stomachache that she had experienced in the Brown Palace Hotel. "Let's leave. I'm not great with sewing, but if we take our uniforms now, I can make the adjustments in our room. My mother made sure I brought a sewing kit with me for emergencies."

Tidye nodded and grabbed their uniforms, shooting the seamstress a dirty look on her way out the door.

Louise pressed down her frustration and got to work. She hemmed their shorts by cutting them and stitched the shoulder seams to make the armholes smaller, but still, the uniforms didn't fit properly. When she ran a warm-up lap around the track later that morning, she slowed to roll up the waistband of her shorts to make them a bit shorter.

Tidye slowed alongside her. "Look! Who's she?" she whispered, pointing to a young woman in track clothes approaching Coach Vreeland. They completed their warm-up lap and returned to where their coach awaited them with the new woman by his side.

"Ladies, remember Eve Furtsch from Chicago?" Coach Vreeland asked. Eve beamed at the group, adjusting the red bow in her hair. "She's joining the pool of sprinters available for the relay. So, now that you've all warmed up, we're going to work on starts. Line up into groups of four over on that line." When he finished speaking, the women headed toward where he'd toed positioning marks into the cinder.

Tidye whispered, "Isn't she the girl who fell at the finish of my semifinal heat back in Chicago? She was eliminated and didn't even race in the finals."

"What's she doing here?" Louise shot back. "Why do they keep adding more and more women to the relay reserve?"

Tidye's brows knitted together. "Apparently she must know someone important. I don't like this at all."

Louise took her spot in one of the lines of women and then crouched into starting position when it was her turn, but her mind was spinning. What exactly were the coaches doing?

IN THE EVENING, when Louise returned from dinner with her teammates, exhausted from the thrill of parading into the Coliseum and watching the fanfare of the Opening Ceremonies, she perked up to find a surprise waiting for her in the hotel's lobby. Uncle Freddie. Louise ran to him and he enveloped her in a tight embrace. Something had changed in him since he'd arrived in California. Louise tilted her head, taking in the glow of his skin. "Life in the West agrees with you."

"It sure does. Your mama sent me a letter telling me you were on your way to Chicago, so I started following the newspapers, trying to figure out if you had made it onto the team. Sure enough, the *Los Angeles Times* ran an article listing you as a member of the relay team, and I started making plans to see you. How were the Opening Ceremonies?"

"Thrilling! When we marched into the stadium surrounded by cheering fans, I got goose pimples. I've never felt anything like it. To be here representing our country is amazing. It's an honor that words can't even begin to describe. A few unfortunate things have happened, but today's ceremony made all of that fade away."

"Unfortunate? What do you mean?"

The troubled expression on Uncle Freddie's face made Louise wish she hadn't brought the subject up, and she didn't even know where to start with an explanation. The constant adding of girls to the relay pool? The Brown Palace Hotel? The uniforms? No, she didn't want to focus on any of that—the important thing was to look ahead. "Oh, nothing worth dwelling on. I need to focus on running my best now. I'm so happy you encouraged me to pursue this, and I'm even happier to see you here," she said as they walked into the garden and took one of the paths to lead them through the white stucco bungalows surrounding the hotel. "So what are you doing in Los Angeles now?"

"I'm working for my friend from the war. He's started an aviation company, Bessie Coleman Aero, and I work in the factory."

"Building airplanes?"

"I have a hand in them, yeah. Say, I saw that you'll be running the relay. Anything else? Didn't you hold the national broad jump title at one point?"

"Good memory."

"It's not everyone who has a niece with a national title."

"The broad jump isn't an Olympic event, so I'm only sprinting."

He let out a low whistle. "I'll have to tell everyone at work, see who can come with me to watch you. I'll bet your parents wish they could be here. Can you believe that you made it?"

But had she? Louise thought about the eight women vying for four relay spots and suddenly wasn't sure how to answer that, but she fixed a grin on her face again. "It's a dream come true."

LOS ANGELES MORNING SUN

August 3, 1932

"Walsh Wins Gold"

Los Angeles—Stella Walsh, the Cleveland girl who now races for Poland, set a new world record and won the 100-meter dash in a mere 11.9 seconds. Her manlike stride was enough to beat Canada's fresh-faced Hilda Strike, who finished a close second. San Francisco's Wilhelmina "Billie" von Bremen represented the United States honorably by coming in third.

With the individual sprint settled, competition is heating up for the women's relay. The United States has a veritable treasure trove of fast and feisty lady sprinters, and rumors about who to expect on the relay roster are flying around the Coliseum. Canada possesses four formidable racers so Coach Vreeland must pick wisely.

So, who will he choose?

When asked if he is worried about competition from our gentle neighbors to the north, he chuckled and shook his head confidently. "We have a strong field of sprinters. In Chicago, their times were bunched close together, so I have a lot of options. I plan to announce a shake-up in our relay team within the next few days."

With all of this confidence in the air, we can't help but wonder if turncoat Stella Walsh regrets her decision to abandon her adopted country. After all, what girl doesn't want to wear as much gold as she possibly can?

When Louise read what Coach Vreeland said in the newspaper, she felt like she had taken a punch to the gut. *A shake-up?*

Overnight, the tenor of the team shifted.

The next morning, she was on her way to the front desk to check for mail when a group of her teammates filed through the lobby, all in uniform.

Louise stopped Caroline, "What's happening? Did I miss something?"

Caroline's eyes widened. "We just took a team photo in the garden. I asked where you and Tidye were, but someone said you both weren't feeling well."

"That's not true at all. We were in our room. No one told us anything about a team photo."

"I'm so sorry. I should have known that something wasn't right. Don't worry, I'm sure there will be more photos."

Louise felt tears welling up. Who had said they weren't feeling well? Babe? One of the other girls? How had this been allowed to happen? She reached for the nearby wall, determined not to cry in front of her teammates, not that anyone was watching except for Caroline. All the other women walked by them without a backward glance. Caroline watched Louise struggle to retain her composure, her expression softening in sympathy. "I'm really sorry."

"I know you are," Louise said, her throat thick. "It's fine."

But it wasn't fine. Not one bit.

The next day the women gathered around Coach Vreeland at the track, ready to start practice, but he frowned as he studied a piece of paper on his clipboard. Babe leaned in close to see.

"Hey, Coach, is that a telegram? My publicist said I might be getting one from the president wishing me congratulations on my win in the javelin."

Louise kept her face still, but she sensed a ripple of impatience among her teammates. Beside her Tidye huffed, but disguised it in a cough. At every turn, Babe made certain no one forgot her successes.

"No," Coach Vreeland answered. "It's actually from the NAACP urging me to ensure that all runners who qualified in Chicago should get a chance to compete here."

Though he didn't look at Louise or Tidye when he said this, everyone else did. Mortified, Louise dropped her gaze to her track shoes.

"Let's try some hand-off practice today," he said, stuffing the telegram into his back pocket and holding out two wooden batons. "We don't have much time to prepare."

While he explained how the transitions worked, Louise clasped her shaking hands together. The last thing she needed was to be so nervous that she dropped the baton during practice.

"Make sure that you hold the baton firmly in your hand before you reach the final line in your zone." He pointed at a mark on the track. "Your team will be disqualified if you don't have it by that mark, and all of our hopes for a medal will be gone. Everyone clear? We're *not* going to lose this race."

The women nodded and avoided looking at each other.

Coach Vreeland placed them in pairs and they started practicing hand-offs. Almost every time it was Louise's turn and she thrust her hand back to receive the baton, it was not a steady transition. Often the girls weren't giving her the command to be ready as they approached so she was caught off guard and would bobble it. Or they pushed the baton at her too hard so she'd stumble and drop it. Or the other girl would let go too soon and thc baton would fall to the ground. The girls would gather around and look at her with dismay and annoyance. Coach Vreeland would frown and make a note on his clipboard, but he never came over to help her the way he did with a couple of the others. What was she doing wrong? She had done relays before and never had the same trouble. Why was it suddenly so difficult?

When Tidye was paired with her, the two of them sailed through the hand-off with no trouble. In fact, they were faster than any of the other pairings. "Finally," Louise whispered. "I've barely gotten one hand-off right so far."

Tidye pressed her lips together before saying, "The same thing is happening to me. I don't think it's by accident."

"Tidye, Louise, why are you two just standing there talking? It's like you two don't even want to run this relay! Get back to work," Coach Vreeland brayed.

Shaken, Louise turned away to run back to her starting line. Was it possible that some of the other girls were trying to sabotage Louise's and Tidye's chances for being selected to run in the relay? Or was everyone jittery and making mistakes?

BACK IN THEIR room, Louise dropped her workout bag and fell into a nearby chair, limp with exhaustion. She watched Tidye remove her track shoes from her bag and wipe the cinder off them. "Did you have anything to do with that telegram?" Louise asked.

Tidye shrugged. "The *Defender* and the NAACP are follow-ing this Olympics closely. Between the two of us and the men, there's potential for a lot of Negro success. All of those girls seem to have a coach or someone looking out for them, ready to fight to get their girl a racing spot, but we don't have anyone. I'm glad the NAACP is paying attention."

"But the girls are looking at us like we're troublemakers. Like we're not team players."

Tidye gave Louise a long stare. "Those girls want to be in that relay and will use any excuse to cut someone else's chances. You see that, don't you?"

"But Coach said we were going to race in that relay. We earned our spots on our own merits."

"We did, but I'm not sure merit will have anything to do with his selection."

Louise just wanted the opportunity to race. Why had this gotten so complicated?

SINCE COACH VREELAND'S announcement about relay selec-tion, a constant current of anxiety pulsed in the air around the sprinters. They pretended not to scrutinize one another during practice, but they each searched for weakness, a sign of injury, illness, fatigue. Anything that would push the bal-ance one way or another toward who would be running on the relay team.

For the next few days, the sprinters practiced baton hand-offs and ran 100-meter timed sprints. With the exception of if she was running against Billie von Bremen, each time Louise ran, she came in first. She'd glance at Coach Vreeland to check his reaction, but he always was looking away or talking to someone. She was putting all of herself into practices, yet he barely registered her. When Coach Vreeland experimented with placing the women in different orders and groups of four, he often appeared to forget Louise and Tidye and placed them into the rotations as afterthoughts. With each slight, Louise dug even deeper into her determination to show him her capabilities. Her times got better and better, yet they had no bearing on his treatment of her. Louise began to grow resentful, but there was nothing she could do. Whom could she complain to? Who cared?

One afternoon, Louise and Tidye lay on their beds, depleted from the morning's practice.

"My quads feel like I've torn them to shreds," Louise moaned.

"Coach is making it pretty clear we aren't his first choices," Tidye grumbled.

Louise had felt the same doubts, but by not saying them out loud, she had been trying to ignore them. "But we're both running so well. If he really wants to win gold, there's no way he can't consider us for the relay."

"Honestly, I'm starting to lose hope, aren't you?" Tidye's voice sounded so dejected that Louise rolled to her side to look at her.

"We can't give up on this now. We're good. *Really* good. I think when he sits down and takes the time to go over his notes, he'll see that we're good picks. I keep reminding myself that we're getting a chance to race for our country and we have to give it everything we've got." But even as she said this, she felt a downward tug in her chest.

THE NIGHT BEFORE the relay, Coach Vreeland called for a meeting of the runners in the hotel's dining room and he added Annette Rogers, who had qualified to compete in the high jump, so nine women arrived, Louise, Tidye, and Mary among them. They settled in a corner of the large room. Small flags from nations participating in the Olympics hung from the ceiling. The tables were set for the following morning's breakfast, and when Louise took her seat, she tried to keep from fiddling with the silverware in front of her. Next to her, Tidye sat on her hands. There was the sound of chairs being shifted, but no one spoke.

Five of the women at this meeting were going to leave unhappy, and no one wanted to be one of them.

Coach Vreeland entered the room, checked his pocket watch, and then started talking while looking at a vague spot over the heads of the athletes seated in front of him. "Ladies, I'm making some changes to the relay team. Billie, again, congratulations on winning that bronze medal in the individual hundred-meter." He paused as the women applauded Billie von Bremen and then he continued, his voice fast and terse. "The Canadians have a strong team, so I've made some changes. Billie, Annette, and Eve, the three of you will be racing tomorrow. As for the fourth, Mary and Louise tied back at the finals in Chicago so I'm still considering both of you. You two should be ready to race tomorrow, but I'll make my decision in the morning."

Murmurs of disappointment traveled through the group as Coach Vreeland tipped his fedora to the group and left. Louise could not make sense of his selection. She glanced to

Tidye to see tears streaking her friend's face. Her last-place finish during the finals had come back to count against her. Louise whispered, "Let's get out of here."

"I knew something like this was going to happen." Tidye sobbed as they left the dining room. They crossed the lobby, exited through a back door, and found a nearby spot outside in the garden. By this point, Tidye had wiped the tears off her face, and though she looked sad, her shoulders had a resolute set as she faced Louise. "You've still got a shot," she said, before glancing at the windows overhead and lowering her voice to make sure they weren't being overheard. "I understand why Billie's in the foursome. She's run well. But Annette? She's a high jumper. And Eve? She just got here and didn't even qualify. This is rotten."

"It *is* rotten," Louise agreed. "If Coach looks at our records, he'll see that my times are consistently faster than Mary's," she whispered back. It was true. She almost always beat Mary when they raced. Their times were close, but Louise was faster.

"*If* he looks at your records, but you know he might just go with what's easiest: the white girl. I don't trust him at all."

A nearby light on the side of the building flickered and made a dull buzzing sound as if something had extinguished.

And then, even in the balmy warmth of the Los Angeles evening, Louise felt cold.

26.

August 1932
Chicago

AFTER MORE THAN SIX WEEKS IN THE HOSPITAL, BETTY returned home. When Mr. Robinson eased the car to the curb in front of their home, Bill turned from the front seat to look at Betty, who lay flat across the back seat. "Home sweet home," he said, pushing back a blond curl that had flopped onto his forehead. Before she could say anything, he was out of the car and opening her door. "Ready?"

Bill scooped her into his arms.

Under her hands, she felt the broadness of his back, the way his muscles stretched and contracted as he hefted her. She had once moved effortlessly too. She used to rise and cross the kitchen to fill a glass of water at the tap. Walk to the window to check the weather. Dance at happy news. A few steps here, a few there. None of it had required any effort or exertion. She had done it easily, without thinking, not once stopping to appreciate all the things her body could do. She had taken so much for granted. Now the slightest movement required concentration and exertion and resulted in pain. She was supposed to feel lucky and grateful for surviving—she understood this—but she mourned all that she had lost.

At the door, her mother appeared. "Darling!" she said, her arms outstretched in welcome, but her gaze darted over the three of them with apprehension. She led the way up the stairs, cautioning Bill to watch the step here, the step there. Moments later, Betty was perched on the sofa in the front room, a plaid blanket draped over her legs. From the kitchen, the sounds of cabinet doors opening and closing, drawers squeaking, and footsteps reached her. Her father dropped into his favorite chair near the radio and snapped open his newspaper while Bill settled next to her, lifting her legs so they would lie across his lap.

"Cubs won," her father said glumly, riffling through the paper and stopping on the sports section. It was a relief he had taken a job as a security guard and no longer combed the newspaper for employment notices.

"They got a huge turnout at Wrigley to see 'em whip the Phillies," Bill said.

"Now they're pennant-bound for sure." Her father's gaze remained on the paper. "Sounds like it was a rowdy game."

"I'm hoping to go to one next week. Did you see the Sox lost to the Athletics?"

"Lefty Grove had quite a game."

Both men shook their heads.

Her mother entered the room carrying a tray with a pot of steaming tea and a plate of molasses cookies and set the spread on the coffee table in front of Betty. Bill leaned over and plucked a cookie from the tray. "Thank you, Mrs. Robinson, these look terrific."

She smiled in relief. "Darling? Want a cookie?"

"No, thank you," Betty said.

"Shall I make you a cup of tea the way you like it?"

Though she had no interest in tea, it was easier to let her mother fuss over her than to say no. "Sure."

"Did you read how Roosevelt's come out swinging against Prohibition?" her father asked Bill.

"It's all everyone was talking about at school," Bill said.

Betty slumped back against the sofa, staring at the steaming cup of tea her mother placed in front of her. This would be her future. She would sit on the sofa, useless and dependent on the help of others while everyone else moved through their days productively.

Bill nudged her legs off his lap, and she watched him stand and follow her mother to the kitchen as they discussed the latest news on the city's World's Fair planning. Betty pushed the blanket off her lap, and before she could talk herself out of it, she swung her legs off the sofa and gripped the edge of her seat tightly to push herself up. She gasped at the burn of pain that shot through her arms and shoulders, but fought to raise herself off the cushions. Her eyes filled with tears. *Good Lord.* Every muscle in her body screamed with the sudden exertion, but she pulled in her stomach, trying to straighten her back to stand. She could do this. She lifted her head as high as she could and for one moment, she was standing—she felt it!

It was dizzying and precarious and felt like she was standing on the edge of a cliff.

But then she wobbled and threw her hands out from her sides, grasping for something to cling to, but there was nothing, and before she knew it, she was falling and crying out before hitting the floor.

A thunder of footsteps shook the floorboards under her cheek. Her mother's brown pumps appeared next to her face.

"What happened?" Her mother crouched beside her and the lemony smell of Bill's aftershave enveloped her. He lifted her off the floor. "What on earth happened?" her mother repeated as Bill lowered Betty onto the couch.

It was the tremble in her mother's voice that prompted Betty to say something. "I tried to stand."

"But Dr. Minke said you should still be resting. Remember how the doctor warned you to be careful?" Frown lines scored the space between her mother's pale blue eyes. When had her dark hair turned gray? Back at the hospital, Betty had told herself it was the poor lighting of the place, but now back in the family parlor, there was no disputing that her mother had aged.

"I know, I know. But I need to start trying to walk again."

Without saying a word, her father left the room only to return a moment later, a page of doctor-prescribed exercises in his hands. He handed it to Betty. "Start on these today if you want, but no more attempts at sudden miracles. The last thing we need is for you to fall and break your leg again. Or worse." His face, usually genial, hardened.

She thought back to the stack of bills she had spied on the hospital receptionist's desk. "I'll be more careful."

"Seems like we've had enough excitement for one day. Let's try these later," Bill said, studying the list over Betty's shoulder.

Impatience made Betty's hands knot into fists. She didn't

want to wait. She didn't have the luxury of waiting. This was going to be hard—the throbbing in her knees and lower back would make sure of it—but she didn't want to waste another minute.

"Let's try today. If I'm ever to have a chance of running again, the nurses said I need to start walking as soon as possible while my muscles still contain some memory of the movement."

Bill shrugged. "Why are you so hung up on running? What's the point? Come on, you and I have grown up. We can't play sports forever. Let's be realistic and focus on walking. It's time for us to move on."

Betty stared at Bill. She was supposed to give up on running? She hadn't been "playing" at running; competition had opened up a whole new world for her. Without it, she felt lost.

27.

August 1932
Los Angeles

THE NIGHT BEFORE THE RELAY WAS A QUIET EVENING at the Chapman Park Hotel. When Louise slid between the sheets and rolled onto her side to face the wall, she curled her legs toward her chest and tried to count backward. *Useless.* Sleep would be impossible. The sounds of the hotel felt too loud and jarring. Water whooshing through the pipes. The opening and closing of doors. The low hum of voices. It was too much. Eventually she drifted into sleep, but when she woke in the morning, she felt woolly headed and sick to her stomach.

The women dressed in their team navy skirts, blazers, and straw boaters, and filed downstairs for a subdued breakfast before climbing into the motorcars idling outside the hotel's front doors to take them to the stadium. Once there, Louise followed her teammates into the locker room to change into their white satin tanks and shorts. There was little conversation; a nervous energy hung over the group as if a storm were settling over them. The concrete walls made the room cold and damp, almost subterranean, and goose pimples prickled over Louise's arms and legs. When they filed out toward the track, Louise was the last woman out the door. In front of her, hands waved, flags fluttered, and faces turned toward the racers, shrieking with excitement. The din felt overwhelming and Louise grabbed on to the railing to guide her through the throngs of people. Uncle Freddie's face appeared in the crowd and relief at his familiarity washed over her. *She could do this.*

She reached the edge of the track and stepped onto the cinder, squinting ahead into the sun. Where was she supposed to go? Where was Coach Vreeland?

Eve, Annette, and Billie were taking their places in the team's lane.

And then Louise froze.

Mary was walking to the lane and taking the first spot.

A hand clapped onto her shoulder, pulling her back. She turned to see Tidye looking at her with concern. Tidye cupped her hand around her mouth and, over the clamor of the crowd, she yelled, "Coach Vreeland just told Mary she's racing. I'm sorry."

Louise stumbled into place on the sidelines beside Tidye.

Coach Vreeland wasn't going to say anything to her?

The racers took their places and Louise watched numbly as the starting gun fired. As the first racer, Mary dashed toward Eve. It happened so quickly. The sprinters blurred as they ran by Louise, and she could barely register what was happening. All the cheering, the jostling, the energy of the crowd, it swept past her as if she were a rock in a stream, unmoving and unable to feel the cold of the rushing water. She couldn't believe that Coach Vreeland had said nothing to her. What a coward! Her insides roiled. She tried to breathe through the fury engulfing her. She had arrived at the Olympic trials focused and had run with everything she had to earn one of those six coveted spots. She didn't have a coach who intimidated everyone into giving her a spot in the finals; she came to her spot fair and square. She had followed the rules, bitten back her shame when treated poorly in Denver, ignored Babe's boorish behavior, and focused during practices—but none of it had been enough. Coach Vreeland had betrayed her.

And then she flinched. *Why had she allowed herself to dream that she was going to have a spot on the relay?* After all of Coach's questionable additions to the team, excluding her from the team photo, ignoring her during practices, she should have known. She and Tidye never had a chance.

When the announcer called out that the American women had won and set a world record, Louise stared at the track but didn't see a thing. She didn't see her teammates celebrating. Didn't see officials handing them laurel wreaths and gold medals. Didn't see them singing the national anthem. As everything inside her thrummed with anger, everything outside of her body was a blur.

She felt like a fool for believing that she'd had a chance. She had arrived in Los Angeles a hopeful and excited girl, but within the space of two or three minutes, she had become disillusioned and furious.

WHEN THE TEAM made it back to the Chapman Park Hotel later in the afternoon, Louise peeled off from the group and stalked into the garden behind the hotel. She found a bench next to a fountain and dropped onto it, her forehead falling into her palm. She didn't cry; she felt too wrung out. Though the sweet smell of hibiscus hung over her, she wished she were back home in Massachusetts, away from all of this disappointment. Of course, once she got home, she'd have to face everyone's pity and disappointment on her behalf, and that might even feel worse. She had been such an innocent when she'd arrived, prepared to believe that Babe was the worst of her and Tidye's problems. At least Babe had been plainspoken about her poor treatment of them. Now Louise could finally see what had been obvious all along: she never had a chance. She had just wanted to ignore it.

"Louise?"

She raised her head. In the golden light of early evening, Uncle Freddie was walking toward her.

"Caroline thought she saw you heading back here." Uncle Freddie sighed as he sat next to Louise and extended his arm along the back of the bench. "I'm sorry about what happened back there. Wish I could say I'm surprised."

"That's what makes me feel the worst. I *am* surprised. I believed I was going to race. Ever since we left Chicago, Tidye's been worried that Coach Vreeland wasn't going to race us, but I didn't let myself believe her. I feel so stupid."

"Don't be so hard on yourself. You won big races, got important awards, set records; they made you feel like you had a shot. It's not your fault your coach didn't have the vision to offer you more of an opportunity."

"Us girls? We're invisible." The unfairness of it all felt like an ache that stuck like a rock under Louise's ribs. "It's worse for Tidye and me because of our color, but I think no one ever considers any of us girls to be real contenders at all."

"You did everything right. You've made all of us so proud."

"Really?"

Uncle Freddie patted her arm. "Of course. Things happen that are beyond your control. You gave it everything you had and that's all you can do. You've just got to keep going. That's what we do. So what's next?"

Louise had been avoiding thinking about this. It hurt too much to consider. "I don't know. Mama will probably want me to finish school." But even as she said the words, she knew she wouldn't return to the halls of Malden High School. To go back, not ever having gotten a chance at her shot in the Olympics? It was too maddening to consider. How was she supposed to have any hope for the future when she had experienced such a betrayal?

"I understand your anger, I've been there too many times to count, but don't stop because you're angry. You've got to take that anger and use its energy and power to accomplish something good. Stop when you feel you've accomplished what you set out to do and you're ready to try something new. I think you've still got more running in you, more great finishes. You've got to keep trying and hoping and applying pressure on people to do the right thing."

Louise stared into the fountain, mesmerized by the falling water. "I'm too mad to think about the future so I'm going to allow myself to be good and angry tonight. No one can take that from me. For the next twelve hours, I'm going to allow myself to feel all of it—my hurt, anger, and disappointment. Then, in the morning, I'll rise and spend the day smiling and enjoying parties and events that celebrate this team. I'll be a good girl, a good teammate, but tonight, I get to be angry."

Uncle Freddie nodded. "Being angry doesn't make you bad. It shows you've got heart."

Later, after she and Uncle Freddie had said their goodbyes, she passed by the elevator, choosing instead to climb the stairs to her room. Sometimes it felt best to think while she was moving. With each step upward, she turned over what Uncle Freddie had said in the garden. It was easy to believe that the stopwatch was the ultimate decider of who would win the race, but results could be skewed because of things that had nothing to do with running. Rules could be broken. Judges could be wrong. People did not always do the fair thing. Final results were only as reliable as the system that produced them. Louise understood this now.

She reached her floor and paused. Leaning against the railing to let her heart slow and breathing settle, she made a decision. Even though the system was flawed, she refused to give up on it.

CAROLINE AND HOWARD gave Louise and Tidye a ride back to Chicago from California, and from there, Louise took the train home to Massachusetts. She arrived at the platform in Malden on an afternoon thick with humidity and spotted Papa in the crowd, his gaze roving the disembarking passengers for her. In the six weeks that she had been gone, he had changed. He looked like a parched houseplant. Brittle, drooping, and leached of color. She hurried off the train and was swept into his arms.

She hoped to keep her voice upbeat. "I've missed you. How are you?"

"It's good to have our champion back. Welcome home." He ran his hand along her cheek, as if he couldn't believe she was there. "How was California?"

Louise bit the inside of her mouth. She had known she would be asked this question, and during the long trip across the country, she'd thought of a thousand different ways to answer it. In the end she had settled on an answer that told the truth without dredging up all the pain she still carried. "I learned a lot."

Papa's eyes narrowed. He knew her too well to accept that answer at face value, but before he could prod for more, she asked, "Where's Mama? Junior didn't come?"

Papa reached for Louise's valise. "Come now, Dr. Conway let me borrow his car as a special occasion."

Something was wrong. Where was everyone? She wanted to ask more questions, but Papa had moved ahead, his chin down as if pushing into a headwind. She followed.

Once they were settled into the car, Papa rested his hands on the wheel, but didn't start the motor. "Louise, I'm afraid I have some bad news. We received a telegram from California four days ago. Uncle Freddie was in an accident."

"What? I don't understand. I just saw him in California."

"He was in an automobile accident. There was a storm and the roads were slick and—" He shook his head. "He didn't survive. Your mother is devastated."

Louise couldn't bring herself to imagine Mama's reaction to the loss of her brother. Why had she wasted her last few minutes with Uncle Freddie feeling sorry for herself? Why hadn't they gone to the beach and marveled at the Pacific? Why hadn't she seen the airplanes he was helping to build? She should have asked him more questions about his life. She could still feel the pressure of his leg against hers on the bench behind the Chapman Park Hotel, the way he had looked into her eyes and told her to keep running.

Breathless, she snapped open her purse on her lap, rummaging through it to find the photo, the picture of him in Europe. She held it up and studied the two men gazing into the camera, their expressions solemn yet expectant, youthful. Everything about their posture told her what she needed to know. Their straight backs, their air of sophistication. The handsomeness of their uniforms. They had served their country regardless of how they were treated. They had persevered, and they had done it with pride, not to mention a sense of style.

Louise hid her tears by turning to look out the window. Houses, storefronts, and elm trees blurred past. She would make Uncle Freddie's sacrifice mean something. She would persevere in her own way. She would keep running. In four more years, there would be another Olympics.

28.

November 1932
Chicago

BETTY SLOGGED AWAY AT HER EXERCISES THROUGH-out the fall. Her world had shrunk to the front parlor, the kitchen, the bathroom, and her bedroom. She wanted to get out, but leaving the house in her wheelchair? Demoralizing. She missed school with a sadness that would have been inconceivable to her before the plane crash. Why had she complained about homework? About her training schedule? Since returning home from the hospital, she considered a good day to be one she could make it through without crying.

One November weekend, Bill visited and she smelled the dampness of fall's wet leaves and cool weather on his wool jacket as he bent over to kiss her. "It's a beautiful afternoon outside and the sun feels marvelous," he said. "Want me to take you out for a spin around the block?"

Betty had been knitting and she placed her skein of yarn and needles down on the couch next to her. "Doesn't it embarrass you to go out with me in that dreadful thing?" She pointed to the wheelchair. The caning on the backrest appeared worn, and nicks and scuffs marred its wooden frame.

"No, not at all. When I was in church last weekend, our minister spoke about how sometimes obstacles can be blessings because they teach us humility and gratitude. Do you ever wonder if this happened to teach you something?"

Betty stared at Bill. This wasn't the first time someone had said something similarly well intentioned to her. "I don't think I was particularly egotistical or ungrateful before," she said.

"Of course you weren't. But you survived that crash for a reason. Do you ever wonder why?"

With all of her newfound idle time, she had concocted all kinds of elaborate reasons to explain the crash, but after making herself crazy with fear and guilt, she had concluded that sometimes bad things just happened with no rhyme or reason to them. To attach too much meaning to accidents felt exhausting and unnecessarily punishing. She needed to focus on improving, not overanalyzing the reasons behind the crash. It had been an accident—that was all there was to it.

He removed his coat and straightened his tie. "This might sound nuts, but I envy how much stronger you will be as a result of this."

Betty sighed. "Are you crazy? I wouldn't wish this upon anyone." She looked away from the perfect whiteness of his straight teeth, his unshakable smile. He didn't understand pain, loss, and grief. How could he? He had never lost anything. Life came easily to him. Before the crash, it had come easily to her too, but now she knew how quickly life could change. It would be easy to feel angry with Bill for his naïveté, but the truth was she was glad for his optimism. She needed it because doubt and fear plagued her all the time. She understood she would never be the same girl from before the crash, but who was she now? What would her future bring?

Dr. Minke visited Betty once a week to assess her progress and examine the muscles of her legs and arms and test their flexibility and range of motion. At the end of one of these appointments, he called her parents in to speak with them.

"Betty's progress has exceeded anything I anticipated. She's said she wants to walk again, and I think that home visits with a nurse could really make a difference toward getting her to that goal quickly." He consulted the notes he kept in his appointment book. "I'd recommend two appointments a week."

Betty didn't miss the grave look that passed between her parents. Though no one spoke of it, hospital bills had been flooding her parents since the plane crash. Before checking out of Oak Forest Infirmary, Betty had gotten her first glimpse of the financial toll her injuries were taking on her parents. It happened when Caroline had visited only a day or so after returning from Los Angeles.

"Looks like California agreed with you," Betty had said, admiring her friend's tanned glow.

"It's hard to find fault with Los Angeles." Caroline crossed her long legs. "But ugh, that Babe Didrikson. She was the worst. We tied in the hurdles, but the judges gave her the gold medal and me the silver and said they'd send me a gold one, but I'm not holding my breath." Caroline pointed at a vase of carnations on the windowsill, clearly eager to change the subject. "Those are pretty. Did Bill bring them?"

Betty gazed at the flowers and rubbed at her temples. "He's very sweet. He still wants to marry me, but—"

"Of course he still wants to marry you. He loves you."

Betty's stomach tightened. When Bill had met her, she had been vivacious and attractive, a promising student, an Olympic hopeful. She'd had so much potential. But now?

"Caroline, I'm so sorry to miss your wedding next month."

"You have a good reason. Just send me an amazing present to make up for it." She winked. "Now, what do you say I take you out for a walk? Let's go see the nursery and admire all of those wriggling newborns."

Caroline pushed Betty's wheelchair through the hallways until they reached the window overlooking the nursery. Cocooned in their swaddles, little puckered pink faces contorted in squalls. From a bassinet in the corner, an arm escaped from its pink blanket, and a tiny fist rose and waved in the air in persistent protest.

They continued to watch the babies for a few more minutes before beginning the route back to Betty's room. When they reached the lobby, from the main desk came the sound of raised voices. Betty's father stood in front of the receptionist, his face tense, arms crossed, clearly in the midst of a standoff with her.

Caroline stopped Betty's wheelchair and no one noticed them.

"Sir, I'm afraid we need a payment. This balance has exceeded the amount we normally let carry over," the receptionist said.

"But I don't *have* the money," he said, in a voice so raw, so despondent, that it was unrecognizable. Betty would never have believed this was her father if she hadn't seen and heard him say the words herself.

He let out a chuff of air and thrust his hands into his pockets, hunched his shoulders, and followed the woman to a frosted door labeled *Business Office*. It wasn't until her father was out of sight that Caroline wheeled Betty forward and they returned to her room in silence.

Now a headache blazed through her skull with the blinding intensity of a searchlight moving through the darkness, and she inhaled sharply, glancing at her father. He loosened his tie as if his shirt collar was too tight. "Of course, let's hire a nurse. Anything for our girl."

Desperation made her almost light-headed, but she blinked and tried to look happy. "I know this will be worth it. Thank you." Betty grasped his arm with both hands.

He raised her right hand to his lips, but was there a shadow of doubt in his eyes?

She looked at the doctor's notes, trying to read them, to memorize his instructions. *I will make all of these sacrifices worth it.*

In the weeks leading up to Christmas, with the nurse holding on to her, Betty worked on her weight transfer and balance with more focus than ever. On the last day before Nurse Reddy would leave town to spend the holidays with her family, Betty took five steps on her own across the living room floor. She reached the doorway and clung to it for balance. Exhilaration coursed through her.

Finally, she had walked on her own.

Nurse Reddy clapped her hands and then escorted Betty

back to the couch. Though the house was colder than usual to keep their coal bill down, Betty wiped sweat from her brow.

"Now I don't want you doing this on your own and falling while I'm gone. Do you promise me you'll get someone to help you?" Nurse Reddy asked.

"I promise, but let's do a couple more laps around the room before you leave. I'm going to surprise my family by walking on Christmas."

"You better get your Prince Charming over here to help. I'm serious. I know you're awfully set on this idea but you need to be smart about it. No falls."

"I'll ask my friend Caroline to help. Bill's been busy."

The nurse agreed, and Betty was relieved to let the subject of Bill drop. When he had come to her apologetically to explain that he would be visiting some relatives in Springfield for the holidays, she had assured him she would be fine. The truth was she wanted some distance and time to think.

CHRISTMAS MORNING BROUGHT several inches of snow, and while her mother and her sister, Jean, bustled around the kitchen preparing cinnamon rolls, coffee, and fried eggs, Betty gazed out the window from her usual spot on the sofa, nuzzling the downy head of her ten-month-old niece, Frances. Outside, her older niece, Laura, and the neighborhood children threw snowballs and constructed a lopsided snowman.

"Come on into the kitchen to get your breakfasts," called Jean. "We'll eat in the front room."

Jim looked at Betty. "You still fine with the baby?"

She nodded.

"Sit tight and I'll bring you a plate of food."

"Where exactly do you think I'll be running off to?" she asked.

"Knowing you, anything is possible," he said.

Betty smiled to herself. *He had no idea.*

Within minutes, everyone was sitting in the front room, breathing in the sweet and bitter aromas of cinnamon rolls and coffee. Betty handed off the baby to Jean and accepted her plate from Jim, but she placed it on the coffee table and said, "Mother? Father? I haven't been able to go shopping this year for gifts, but I think I have something that will make you very happy."

Her mother laughed, no doubt expecting a package filled with a scarf or socks, or something else that Betty had been knitting, but instead Betty rose from her usual spot on the couch. As she focused on her balance point, the framed wedding photo of her parents on an end table across the room, she heard her mother and Jean gasp. She straightened and put one foot in front of the other. One step at a time, she crossed the room. When she reached for the doorjamb to steady herself, applause thundered through the room.

"Oh, Betty!" her mother cried, rushing to her and wrapping her in an embrace. "You never cease to amaze me."

Betty leaned into her father's shoulder and allowed herself to be steered back to her seat on the couch. A hot cup of coffee was handed to her. All talk subsided into easy silence as everyone broke apart the cinnamon rolls and ate them.

Betty's father looked around the room, a pleased expression on his face. "Well, the last couple of years have been a challenge, both with the worsening economy and"—he faltered as he looked at Betty, tears filling his eyes—"and all that our

Betty has endured, but let's hope that 1933 brings us some better luck. Certainly this morning's Christmas miracle is giving me some faith in the future."

"Huzzah!" Jim called out.

"Yes, I'll be running again by the time the snow's gone," Betty said, lifting Frances onto her lap again and breathing in her sweet smell of powder and zinc oxide. The thought of the two of them—one big, one small—staggering around the house, lurching into furniture and holding on to anything immobile, made Betty feel lighter. She looked up and found her family staring at her.

"But why on earth are you so focused on running again?" her mother asked.

"Because I know I can do it."

"Won't it be enough to regain your mobility and walk again? Think about your future. Soon you'll be married and starting your own family. Focus on that."

Betty looked to her father, but he was staring into his coffee. Little Frances wriggled, pedaling the air, eager to move, and Betty ran her fingers along the tips of the baby's toes. Was she being unreasonable? Maybe her mother and Bill were right and it was time to move on.

PART 3

March 1933–June 1936

29.

March 1933
Fulton, Missouri

BURTON MOORE, THE COACH OF THE BOYS' TRACK team at Fulton High School, couldn't take his eyes off the tall girl dashing up and down the basketball court. She bounced the ball with ease, zigging and zagging around her opponents. Compared with her, the other girls appeared to be standing still. When she coiled into position to shoot, her shoulders dropped and her arms appeared loose and ropy, yet her expression was one of pure focus. She played with impressive speed, aggression, and dexterity, but more than anything, she showed a rare mix of focus and relaxation. It was a unique blend of qualities that few athletes possessed. In all of his years of running and coaching track teams, he had caught glimpses of talent but had never seen anyone like her. And boy, did she score points! He held his breath as another one of her shots circled the net's rim a few times before dropping downward. The score ticked up to forty-two Methodist versus twenty-eight for Baptist, making the final game of the church league season a blowout. Burton's palms began to sting from clapping so much with each point that Helen earned.

The buzzer rang to mark the end of the game and the hometown crowd went wild. Mary Lou stood and spun to face the band assembled in front of her. She cued the final song, and her students started playing "The Stars and Stripes Forever." The air in the auditorium, hot and sour with the smell of exertion, felt festive. Burton tapped his foot to the tune but found himself searching the crowd for that girl. Grinning broadly, she was in the center of her team, clapping and slapping backs with the others while being swept toward the locker room.

When the song finished and the students were placing their instruments in their cases, Burton leaned toward Mary Lou and asked, "Who was that tall girl? The one who scored all the points?"

"Helen Stephens? She sure runs circles around everyone, doesn't she?"

"She's really something," he said, helping Mary Lou into her coat.

"Yes, that was a good game. Next year I won't wait until the final one of the season to get the band out here. This is good practice for school events."

Burton arched his neck for a better view of the crowd pushing its way to the exit. There was no sign of Helen. He lifted Mary Lou's satchel of sheet music. "Guess so."

ON MONDAY, AFTER the final bell of the day rang, he found the girl alone at her locker, amid the clamor of students packing their belongings. "Helen?"

She turned to him and her face flushed a deep crimson. A frizzy mess of short blondish hair fuzzed around her face. She had an unfortunate birthmark above her brow, but her nose was straight and narrow, cheekbones high, dark eyes bright. She smiled and her whole face lit up. Though not pretty in the conventional sense, and certainly not in the way that teenage boys would judge her, she possessed an appealing charm.

"I caught your game over the weekend against Baptist," he said. "You had quite a night."

"Thanks. It was a good way to end the season, that's for sure."

The huskiness of her voice took him aback, but he stuck out his hand and pressed on. "Sorry, I should have introduced myself. I'm Coach Moore. I run the boys' track team and am trying to gauge if there's any interest among the girls in running."

She shook his hand. Her grip fastened around it with startling strength. He smiled.

"The track team, huh? I followed the news about Babe Didrikson all summer."

"She sure cleaned everyone's clocks in Los Angeles. When I saw you playing basketball I figured you looked pretty fast too. I'd like to see what you can do on the track. With a little training, maybe you'll be faster than Didrikson, you never know."

Helen laughed, clearly pleased by Coach Moore's attention. "How about one of those black-and-gold letter *F*'s?"

"A varsity letter?"

"Yeah, I've been wanting one but figured us girls can't get 'em. We're stuck in PE doing silly calisthenics while the boys are out there actually winning things."

"You've got to run a fifty-yard dash in seven seconds to qualify for a varsity letter."

She snorted. "I can do that easy."

Coach Moore liked the girl's gumption. She was going to

need it. In truth, he had no idea if he could get a girls' track team together, but Helen's athleticism intrigued him. "How about we do a time trial tomorrow after school and let's see what you and some of the other girls can do? Bring out a group of your teammates and anyone else who would be interested. I'll meet you all on the track behind the school twenty minutes after classes let out. Sound good?"

"I'll be there."

"And don't forget to bring some friends, got it?"

A flash of doubt crossed over her face for an instant before she settled into an easy grin and hefted a thick book close to her chest. "Sure, I'll ask around."

He glanced at the book. "What are you reading?"

"*The Road Back*."

"Is it for class?"

"No, but I liked *All Quiet on the Western Front* and the library just got this one in. It's the sequel."

He raised his eyebrows. "Not exactly light reading."

"No, it's not," she conceded, looking sheepish. "But it's literally heavy so if I carry it around enough, it'll make me stronger, right?" She flexed the biceps of her arm that was holding the book and laughed. She sounded loud and nervous, like she was trying too hard to amuse him.

"Huh. Maybe I'll have to try it. I could use something interesting to read."

She closed her metal locker. "See you tomorrow."

"You bet." He watched her make her way through the crowded hallway. Judging from the way she towered over the other students, he guessed her to be about six feet tall. Though she greeted a few kids, she walked alone. A girl like that—tall, athletic, tomboyish—she probably wasn't one of the popular kids. And clearly if she spent her time outside of school reading stuff by authors like Remarque, her social calendar couldn't be too full. Maybe joining a school team could be just the thing to help her fit in.

THE FOLLOWING AFTERNOON, a gaggle of girls led by Helen approached Burton where he stood by the track. He hadn't been sure she would show. Since girls didn't run track at Fulton High School, it felt like a good idea to keep this experiment quiet so he had sent the boys off on a three-mile run. That would keep them busy for a bit. Patches of muddy puddles filled the inside of the track and a sharp wind blew from the north. His nose dripped from the cold, and he rubbed at it absentmindedly, amused by the sense of anticipation filling him. All this for a 50-yard time trial.

Once the girls reached him, he greeted them and explained what he wanted them to do. They listened, blowing on their hands and hopping up and down to stay warm. When he had spoken to her the day before, Helen had been outgoing, but now, surrounded by the other girls, she acted quieter. She kept her shoulders hunched around her ears and slouched as if making herself less noticeable.

Burton showed them how to start by crouching low and springing forward and then pointed to the line he had dug by dragging his heel along the cinder farther down the track. "Don't stop at the finish line," he said. "Run all the way through and wait to slow down until after you've crossed it."

He lined them up and then walked to the finish. On his command, the pack dashed forward and sprinted toward him.

Helen flew past first. He clicked his stopwatch: 5.8 seconds. He stared at the time, scratching his head. *That couldn't be right.* Helen was fast, but there was no chance she could be *that* fast. The girls, panting hard, all gathered around him.

"So?" asked a dark-haired girl. "How did we do?"

"Not sure this darned thing is working." He shook the stopwatch. "What do you say we try it one more time? I'll head to the start, and we'll just reverse direction. Take a minute to recover." Without another word, he turned and paced the 50-yard distance again, hoping none of them noticed him checking his watch, but the girls were giggling with excitement as they resumed starting positions and not paying any attention to him. He clicked his stopwatch on and off several times, watching the hand tick along smoothly, and then held it to his ear, listening to the smooth grind of its interior mechanisms. The darned thing appeared to be working just fine.

He took his spot and called out, "On your marks. Set. Go!"

Off they went, legs and arms pumping with exertion.

Again, Helen cruised over the finish line. *Click.* He took a deep breath before looking at his stopwatch. Again, the timer was frozen at 5.8. He felt his jaw drop, and he gasped. It felt like he had taken a wallop to the chest. The girls crowded around him expectantly, but he continued to stare at the stopwatch in disbelief. *Jesus, she had just run that in the same time as Betty Robinson, the world record holder.*

"Did I earn a varsity letter?" asked Helen in a nervous-sounding voice.

Dazed, he shook his head, still staring at his timer. "In fact, Helen, yes, you did."

One of the girls cheered.

He raised his gaze to meet Helen's. "I mean, this run wasn't sanctioned or anything and my timer may not be fully accurate, but there's no doubt that you're really fast. All of you were fast." His mind was racing. *Holy buckets, what does this mean? What do you do with a find like this?*

"I can't wait to tell my parents about this," said a thin blonde, the second girl to pass over the finish both times. Her time was nowhere near Helen's, but still, under normal circumstances he would have been impressed by her pace too.

"Wait a minute, ladies. Let's keep today's results to ourselves for a bit. I'll follow up in a couple of days to see if we can get some practice times set up."

The girls called out goodbyes, walking off in pairs, already preoccupied with discussing homework and babysitting schedules. Only Helen hung back.

"So, my time was really good?"

"Yeah, it really was." He showed her the stopwatch, still frozen on 5.8 seconds. "I'll be totally honest with you. I don't know what happens next. Let me figure out the AAU's spring meets that are open to girls. Think your folks will approve of you taking up track?"

Helen scratched her shoulder. "I don't know. Money's pretty tight. Will it cost much?"

"Let me see what I can do." He looked out over the field to check that the boys were nowhere in sight.

"Coach?"

His gaze returned to her.

"That felt good. I think I might be able to get pretty fast if I practice more." She grinned, and a surprising shyness lingered in the way she tried to cover her birthmark with her hand.

"Bet you're right. You're a good kid, and you've easily qualified for a varsity letter already. How about you come back on Monday and try practicing with the boys?"

"Really?" Her eyes widened with excitement and her shoulders dropped as she stood straighter. "They're not going to know what hit them."

Coach Moore laughed. Once she had a little training and started running in earnest, he had a feeling *no one* would know what hit them. She said goodbye and headed back to the school building, kicking her cracked leather boots at the occasional pebble in her path, her hands in the pockets of the baggy pantaloons she must have thought constituted a gym suit. *How on earth did she run a world record time in that getup?*

A few minutes later, on Burton's way out of the school, he stuck his head into the music room. A familiar song trilled from a flute being played by a redheaded girl, but there was no sign of Mary Lou. He entered the classroom and headed toward a door on the far side of the room, passing two boys writing music on the chalkboard. Sure enough, in the classroom's office behind a desk covered with several stacks of sheet music, there she sat.

He grinned and leaned against the doorframe. "Good, you're still here."

"Look, I've finally organized the music for the spring concert. Voilà!" She spread her hands. "Percussion, woodwinds, and brass. Everything is ready to hand out tomorrow."

"Great, how about we go out dancing tonight to celebrate?"

"Celebrate? What? That I'm organized?" She flipped back her auburn curls. "What do you have up your sleeve, mister? You never take me out dancing unless you're trying to butter me up for something."

He looked around to make sure no students were within earshot and closed the door behind him. "Remember how I asked you about Helen Stephens at the basketball game last weekend?"

She nodded.

"You wouldn't believe what just happened. I had some of the girls from the basketball team do a fifty-yard dash on the track and Helen tied the world record."

She leaned back in her chair, looking pleased. "No kidding."

"It was amazing. I suspected she was fast, but she ran that time untrained, without proper form, without knowing what she was doing. She wasn't even wearing track shoes!" Describing it, he became breathless all over again. "If she starts training with the boys, I can try to get her ready for some bigger events. Who knows where all of this could lead?"

Mary Lou's enthusiasm faded. "Before you get too far ahead of yourself, you'd better figure out where it *will* lead. Have you gotten a good look at the girl? She's an outcast already. I covered Principal Newbolt's math class a year or two ago, and the kids were merciless with their teasing. Do you want to make it all worse for her?"

"Worse? I figured being on a team might help."

"Maybe, but you better talk with her parents. Make sure they're willing to let her run with the boys." Mary Lou chewed her lip. "Think the district will go for this? Girls don't run track around here."

Burton ran his fingers through his hair. He hadn't thought of any of this.

"And didn't you say she wasn't even wearing track shoes? How will she get the money to pay for a pair? Why, she's poor as a church mouse." She reached out and took his hand. "Look, I'm not trying to rain on your parade, but think this all through before you get the girl's hopes up."

"I'll go see her folks tomorrow evening. But what do you say? Still want to go dancing tonight?"

"Hmm, this girl must really be something to have put you in such a good mood." She swept her hands over her hair to smooth it. "Sure, count me in. Now scoot so I can get everyone out of here and go home to doll myself up."

"You're perfect already."

She pouted. "I know how the other girls will be looking at you tonight. They want to eat you up with a spoon."

"No, ma'am, I only have eyes for you. I'll pick you up at seven o'clock," he said on his way out the door. He pictured Mary Lou and her green eyes looking up at him as he held her in his arms and the way she'd throw back her head to laugh, revealing the pale skin of her neck. Maybe she'd wear that jade-colored dress, the one she knew he liked, the one that twirled and showed off her gorgeous long legs.

Whistling, he ambled through the school lobby and passed the trophy case full of athletic awards, pausing for a moment to look at the rows of medals and trophies his boys had won in past seasons. Forget state champs, Helen could go further than that. She was special. It wasn't just her speed. She had spirit and was smart, but she needed help, and it didn't look like she had anyone in her corner. Right then and there, he decided he'd do whatever it took to take her as far as he possibly could. If he needed to pay for Helen's track shoes himself, by golly, he would. He hated the idea of dipping into the secret stash of money he had been squirreling away for an engagement ring for Mary Lou, but how many times do you discover a world-class athlete smack dab under your nose?

THE NEXT AFTERNOON, Burton drove across town to the Stephens farm, Mary Lou on the seat next to him. He watched her idly wrap a curl around her index finger as she gazed out the window and hummed. It hadn't been hard to convince her to join him to meet the Stephenses. He had waited until after the dance hall closed and he was walking her home to bring up the subject of Helen again.

"Why do you need me?" she asked, shivering and pulling her camel-colored wool coat close. "I don't know anything about running."

By this point, they had reached her boardinghouse. The front porch light glowed. Inside the window of the front parlor, he could see Mrs. Eldridge, the sharp-eyed widow who owned the place, sitting in a chair, her eyes focused on the embroidery hoop clutched in front of her.

"I think you're right. The Stephenses are going to be dubious about this whole idea of their daughter running with the boys. But if you're with me, they'll be dazzled by your beauty and won't be able to say no." He reached for one of her hands and pulled her close. Overhead, stars glittered like hard specks of frost in the clear, cold night air.

She rolled her eyes, but allowed herself to fold into his chest. The heat of her body against his made him want to keep her there forever. He breathed in how good she smelled, something flowery and sweet.

"I'm serious. You'll add a healthy dose of respectability to this whole venture."

"So I'm respectable, am I?" Her eyes gleamed in that beguiling way that made him forget everything except for how much he loved wrapping his arms around her.

"You're always a model of respectability when parents and students are around." He nuzzled her jawbone. "Of course, I like it that you're not *always* so respectable when it's just the two of us."

"Oh, you!" She punched his arm playfully.

"Shh," he whispered, hoping the old widow wouldn't look out her window and see the two of them. He wanted every last minute alone with Mary Lou. "So, will you come with me?"

"I suppose if you can find something that girl is good at, maybe it will help her."

Instead of saying thank you, he pulled her to him and kissed her. She relaxed in his arms and made a small sound of contentment.

On the road to the Stephens farm, his motorcar groaned over the potholes and ruts. When the house came into view, he scanned the place. Empty fields surrounded it in every direction. He parked next to the picket fence and straightened his tie. Then he took a deep breath, opened the door, and emerged, careful to avoid muddy puddles. As he went around the back fender to open the door for Mary Lou, the quiet of the place struck him. They were in the final gasp of winter and the days were lengthening, but it was still too early for planting. All farms were lonely places at this time of year, but he couldn't shake the feeling that this one felt particularly desolate.

The fence's gate squeaked in protest as he held it open for Mary Lou and they stepped inside the yard. Ahead of them on the porch, a shaggy, gray-muzzled shepherd mix raised its head to watch them approach before dropping its chin to rest on its front paws.

Burton rapped on the door and squinted through the window beside it to detect any movement inside the house. Mary Lou reached for her hat to make sure it was angled just right.

A woman opened the door, wiping her hands on her apron. "Yes? May I help you?"

Burton took off his hat and held it to his chest. "Hello, ma'am. I'm Coach Moore and this is Miss Schultz from Fulton High School. Are you Mrs. Stephens?"

Her face blanched. "I am. Has something happened to Helen?"

"No, I'm sorry, she's fine, ma'am," he stammered, flustered. This wasn't how he wanted their meeting to start. "There are no problems with her at all."

Mrs. Stephens looked relieved before frowning in confusion. "So, what's this about? My husband is in town at the moment."

"That's all right. Again, Helen's not in any sort of trouble."

She gestured for them to enter. He followed Mary Lou inside onto a faded Persian carpet, laddered with rents. The house exuded an air of defeat. The ceiling and floor lines slanted—all angles showed signs of settling through long winters, parched summers. A scrim of dust textured the surfaces of the thread-bare upholstered furniture and lumpy horsehair divan. But there were a few surprises. A rickety bookshelf lined the far wall, loaded with leather-bound books and paperbacks, an unusual sight in a rural farmhouse. Across from the bookshelf were an upright piano and a harp, both polished to a buttery shine.

Mary Lou clasped her hands together. "Ohh, who plays the harp?"

"I do."

"And the piano?"

Mrs. Stephens nodded, her expression appearing to slip from guarded to something more neutral as she looked at the instruments.

"That's wonderful. I'm the band director at the school."

"That so?"

"Yes. In fact, the spring concert is approaching. This year's orchestra and band are both quite good. May I give you a few tickets so that you can bring your family to enjoy some live music?"

A faint smile appeared on Mrs. Stephens's face. "Thank you. I tried to get Helen to play the piano, but she couldn't seem to sit still." She waved toward the door leading to the kitchen. "I was in the midst of rolling out some biscuits; why don't you both come on back and have a seat while you tell me about why you're here?"

Mary Lou and Burton did as instructed and took seats at the kitchen table. The smell of flour hovered in the air. A paperback of *The Good Earth* was set facedown on the counter next to the board with the biscuit dough.

"I see where Helen gets her love of reading," Coach Moore said, bobbing his chin toward the book. "She always seems to have a book in her hand. And she reads some pretty impressive literature for a girl her age."

Mrs. Stephens gave a small nod. "May I make you both a cup of coffee or tea?"

Coach Moore cleared his throat. "We're fine, ma'am, but thank you for offering. As you said, Helen may not be one for sitting still, but she's truly a gifted athlete. Actually, that's why we're here to see you."

Mrs. Stephens picked up her rolling pin but paused and looked at Coach Moore, ignoring the lump of biscuit dough lying on the floured cutting board on the counter behind her.

"Helen's a remarkable runner, even without any training," he said. "I saw her play basketball for your church and was astonished by her speed so I set up a time trial for her. She was faster than anything I expected. But see, the problem is that we don't have a girls' track team at Fulton High. So, if I could get your permission to have her run with the boys' track team, I think she could experience all kinds of success." His voice was sounding faster and faster and maybe even a bit desperate, but he didn't know what else to do so he added a feeble, "Yes, ma'am. I really think she could. Really, she could."

Mrs. Stephens stared at him.

Mary Lou leaned forward. "I know what you're thinking, Mrs. Stephens. When Coach Moore came to me about Helen's extraordinary talents, I couldn't believe he'd even consider encouraging a girl to run. I mean, where will such a thing take her? A girl athlete? I can understand why you thought the piano would be a more productive pursuit."

"Exactly," Mrs. Stephens said.

Burton shifted in his seat. *Where was Mary Lou heading with this?* But before he could say anything, she kept going.

"But here's the thing," Mary Lou said. "Helen isn't interested in the piano and something like track could offer her some interesting possibilities. Did you know that running is something that could help her get into college?"

Mrs. Stephens placed her rolling pin back on the counter. "You don't say."

Mary Lou continued. "And if you're worried about what people may think about your daughter training with the boys, I'll avail myself to chaperone her to any meets she may race in."

Burton kept watching Mrs. Stephens. "And I'll be watching her like a hawk. Nothing untoward will happen under my guidance."

Mrs. Stephens blinked and looked back and forth between them. "Do you honestly believe this could help her get into college?"

"Absolutely," Burton and Mary Lou said in unison.

"I'm a graduate of William Woods College," said Mrs. Stephens, joining them to sit at the table. "While there's no doubt my circumstances are modest, I've held on to what I learned in college through thick and thin. I'd love to see Helen enjoy the same opportunity, but money is very tight these days."

"I understand completely. I myself attended Westminster

College," Burton said, and Mrs. Stephens's eyes flashed at the mention of the men's school affiliated with William Woods. "With some instruction and experience, and if she keeps up her grades, of course, Helen could have a good shot at attending William Woods."

Mrs. Stephens tapped her index finger against her lips as she thought. "My husband will be hard to convince. He can barely understand why Helen should even bother with high school. He thinks she should stop her education and divide her time between working here on the farm and in the shoe factory south of town."

"Helen's a good student." Burton sensed he was close to getting Mrs. Stephens to agree with him, but it felt like a delicate balancing act so he picked his words with care. "It would be a shame to let such a promising young woman not complete high school and see what opportunities are available beyond that."

Mrs. Stephens nodded. "Let me work on him."

"Of course. In the meantime, do I have your permission to have Helen train with me?"

She paused and looked down at her chapped hands before returning his gaze, a determined glint in her eye. "Yes. She can start running, but let's not make a big fuss about it. The fewer people that know about this, the better."

Burton wanted to jump out of his seat and cheer, but he kept calm and crossed one leg over the other. "Yes, ma'am."

30.

ALMOST A YEAR HAD PASSED SINCE BETTY'S PLANE crash. Dr. Minke's prediction that one leg would be shorter than the other was right, so she limped. For months, she had told herself that learning to walk again would solve her problems. In reality, it almost brought about more unsettling questions. She could walk, but pain dogged her with every step. Stiffness plagued her left shoulder. She had returned to school for several weeks in the early spring, but abandoned her studies after deciding that her degree in physical education felt futile. She could not reconcile her hopes for the future with her reality of constant pain and frustration.

It wasn't just Betty who felt stuck. Anxiety seemed to have brought the country to a standstill. Mr. Franklin Delano Roosevelt, a New Yorker, had assumed the presidency in March on a wave of hope, but Chicago remained locked in the claws of tough times. Over the last year, many of her Northwestern classmates had quit college as financial difficulties mounted upon more and more families, so Betty's absence from the roster of the university's graduates was one of many, but Bill would still be graduating that weekend.

On the evening before his commencement, Bill arrived at Betty's house minutes after her parents had left to play euchre with the neighbors. A year ago, if Bill and Betty had found themselves alone, they would have made good use of their un-chaperoned time entwined in Betty's bedroom, but now she didn't look up from the book she was reading. Bill entered the parlor, pecked Betty on the cheek. "Ready to go?"

"Let me fetch something, and I'll be back," Betty said, leaving Bill sitting in the parlor. She hurried to the bathroom, plucked a bottle from the medicine cabinet shelf, poured a couple of pain pills into her palm, and took them with a glass of water. Thinking of the graduation festivities ahead, she grimaced and tucked the entire bottle into her purse.

When she returned to the parlor, she found Bill pacing. The air in the room felt charged with something that she couldn't identify, and he wore an expression uncharacteristic of him. Fear? Worry? Guilt?

"What's wrong?" she asked.

His blue eyes appeared tense, but before she could get more of a read on him, he glanced away. "Want to go?"

"Do I ever." She reached for her hat, but snuck a look around the room. Her father's glasses lay atop a stack of papers on the sideboard, and Bill's pacing appeared to skirt that area of the room. She sidled over and saw a pile of bills. The hospital, the doctor, the visiting nurse—each invoice marked with a stamp saying *unpaid*. Her mind raced. Of course, her father's income as a security guard wasn't much, but some of the bills were from nine months ago. Betty swallowed and turned to face Bill.

"Did you see these?"

He opened his mouth and then closed it. Voices from the neighbors' children riding their bicycles outside on the sidewalk echoed off the walls.

"Betty, I—"

"No, Bill, please let me talk." Betty took a deep breath. She had no idea what to say, yet she had also been practicing this speech for months without acknowledging what she was doing. "I know Dr. Minke says I'm healed, but I'm not. You've stuck by my side and I know it hasn't always been easy, but I worry that we've lost our way together. I need to take care of the debt of my medical bills. I need to figure out what's next. And I think I need to do all of this on my own." She paused, expecting him to argue with her, to say that he was committed to her no matter what.

But he didn't say a word. He walked to the window and looked outside. Silence hovered over the house and Betty wondered if Bill could hear the thundering of her heart. Did she want him to fight for her?

He cleared his throat. "Sometimes you say you wish you were still running and going to classes, but on other days, you never seem to want to leave the house. I don't understand you anymore."

"I don't fully understand myself either. I don't know how to move forward."

"You used to be so motivated . . ." His voice trailed off.

So accomplished, she thought with a bitter twinge.

"I wish I knew how to help you," he said.

"Well, I think I need to help myself now."

He frowned, looking dubious, but sighed. "I've been dreading to tell you this, but my father's business is struggling. I suppose it was just a matter of time. We wanted to believe it had deep enough roots, but it's not going to survive. We're broke."

Betty felt as though her lungs weren't working. Two years ago, she would have said money didn't matter, but it did. Her injuries made that painfully clear. "I'm sorry to hear this."

"I know we've been better off than many people, but still, it's sad. It's hard to watch my parents come to terms with this."

Betty thought of her own parents' helplessness as they confronted her health problems. "So what's next for you?"

"Well, since I can't work for my father, I'll find something new."

Of course. If anyone would land on his feet, it would be Bill. His optimism almost made her smile, but it also confirmed why their relationship was over. While she struggled, she wanted to get stronger and feel independent, not scared and angry that she was relying on him for everything.

"I'm sorry it needs to end like this between us," she said.

He turned his back to her to gaze out the window again. "So am I."

The disappointment in his voice made her throat thicken.

This was it. She would be on her own, and though it frightened her, for the first time in a year, she felt free. There would be no more running because it felt too much like she was clinging to something from her past. She needed to find her own way into a new life.

31.

THE FULTON CRIER

May 22, 1933

Fulton—Have you noticed anything unusual about the boys' track team lately? Yes, they're wearing bright new uniforms and training togs thanks to the Callaway Emporium, but that's not what has us looking at the team twice. How about that tall runner leading the pack? If you look closely, you may see that it is none other than Helen Stephens. Yes, you've read that right: *Miss* Helen Stephens. Turns out the girl is as fleet-footed as Nike herself.

According to Sally Mayfield, who attended a 50-yard time trial organized by Coach W. Burton Moore last month, Miss Stephens tied the world record of 5.8 seconds set by Chicago's Betty Robinson, the Olympic gold medalist. "Helen was a blur! I could barely see her," Miss Mayfield gushed.

Now we are unable to get Coach Moore to confirm or deny this report, but we plan to keep our eyes peeled for this rising track star. And in the meantime, those boys better pick up the pace or they are going to find themselves being left in the dust by a girl!

Coach Moore groaned. Wasn't there anything more pressing in Fulton to report? This article about Helen was the last thing he needed. He stood, tossing the paper into the trash bin next to his desk, but before he reached for his jacket and hat, he glanced at the latest interval times for each kid listed on the clipboard lying on his desk.

In the weeks since Helen had started training with the boys, her progress had been nothing short of astounding. He experimented with different distances to determine where her strengths lay, but no matter what format he tried, she excelled. The previous week he had given all the boys a generous 100-yard start ahead of her for a one-mile time trial and she still finished a few strides ahead of the fastest boy.

"Stephens, are you winded at all?" D.W., one of the faster boys, had asked. When she laughed, he shook his head and grinned. "Jeepers, Coach, how about making her carry a sandbag on each shoulder during our next time trial?"

All the boys chuckled. If anything, Helen's speed seemed to have ratcheted up the boys' intensity and concentration. Coach Moore didn't need to tell any of them to stop goofing around anymore, that was for sure. In the couple of meets the boys had raced against other teams, their times were all faster than anything from past years. He had worried the boys might be sore with Helen, but they were good-natured and no signs of trouble from within the team appeared. Unfortunately, outside the team was another story.

After the kids finished running their mile time trial, Coach Moore had stayed behind another hour or so completing paperwork for upcoming meets. When he finally walked out the school's front door toward the parking lot, a man in faded overalls and a sun-bleached cotton work shirt with the sleeves rolled up to his elbows stepped from the shadow of his battered jalopy.

"Evenin', Coach," the man said, leaving his hat on.

"Good evening."

"My boy's Dexter Ginty."

"Ah, Dexter is a fine young man. He did real well in last week's meet."

"He tells me a girl has joined the team. That right?"

"It is."

The father worked a lump of chewing tobacco in his lower lip. "That allowed?"

"There are track and field events open to girls, yes. She's proven to have remarkable talent so I'm giving her a shot."

The man spat a long stream of dark tobacco juice toward the tire of a nearby car. "Nothing good comes out of girls thinking they're something special."

"With all due respect, sir, I'd say the team's going to enjoy a strong season and it might be partly because the boys are very motivated and challenged this season. We have a good shot at State."

"I don't like that the girl is whipping all of them boys in your time trials. It ain't natural."

"Like I said, she's remarkable."

"Well, how about that girl go be remarkable somewhere else?"

"If she continues to improve, she will," Coach Moore said

evenly. "My guess is that the AAU team out of St. Louis will try to steal her from us and groom her for some big races."

"I reckon that might be for the best."

"Sir, if you come out and watch the kids run, you'll see that nothing unnatural is happening out here. They want to run. I'm helping them get better. That's all."

He snorted. "I don't got time to come watch a bunch of kids run. Some of us work. I hope I don't have to come see you again about this."

"You shouldn't have to. Everything's fine."

The encounter with Dexter's father was enough to make Burton's blood pound in his temples. He had taken leave of the man, climbed into his automobile, and sat clenching and unclenching his fists on the steering wheel for a few minutes before driving away.

And now this newspaper article.

Again, he groaned and reached for his clipboard and stopwatch. When he opened his office door, he found himself face-to-face with Mrs. Stephens.

"Why, Mrs. Stephens, what a surprise. It's a pleasure to see you. What can I do for you?"

She clutched her purse in front of her with both hands and turned her head to look over her shoulder before she stepped closer.

"Have you seen today's *Fulton Crier*?" she whispered.

His heart sank. "I have, but everything's fine."

She pursed her lips but said nothing.

"Honestly, our team practices are going very well," he said. "There's nothing to worry about."

She bit her lip and looked at the floor.

"Would you like me to take you upstairs to Miss Schultz's room for those concert tickets she mentioned when we visited? I heard the band playing the other day and those kids sounded top-notch."

"No, thank you. You see, my husband is furious about this article. He's forbidden Helen to train with your team."

Coach Moore went rigid and was about to remind her of the scholarship possibilities, but one look at the despondency of her expression and he knew her disappointment outweighed his. He sucked on his teeth for a moment. "I'm sorry to hear that."

"I need to go fetch her to bring her home for the weekend."

He pointed to the girls' locker room. "She'll be in there. If you and Mr. Stephens change your mind, she's welcome back any time."

Mrs. Stephens turned and hurried down the hallway to retrieve Helen. Once she pushed through the girls' locker room door and disappeared, Coach Moore pulled on his jacket, feeling numb. When he stepped outside, he watched the boys gathered in a knot on the edge of the track. Normally this time of the season, every practice felt promising, but now with Helen gone, everything would change. The sharpness of the grief tightening in his chest surprised him. With a sigh, he walked toward his team.

32.

February 1934
Fulton, Missouri

**ANNOUNCEMENT OF SALE—FULTON SAVINGS
BANK IS OFFERING 115 ACRES OF ARABLE LAND
IN SOUTHWEST FULTON FOR SALE IN PUBLIC
AUCTION SCHEDULED FOR FEBRUARY 28.**

On her way home from school, Helen ripped the auction
sign off the post at the edge of their land and chucked it into
the drainage ditch running alongside the road. If the bankers
wanted to advertise the sale so badly, they could come over and
fish it from the icy water themselves. She pictured a banker
wearing a fancy suit wading around in the stream to salvage
the poster and smirked, wiping her hands on her canvas work
jacket. A cold wind howled across the fields, whipping through
her clothes. Clumps of snow patched the fields. She jammed
her hands into her pockets and trudged toward home, casting a
final glare at the crumpled sign lying in the muck. Similar auction announcements were posted all over town, but that didn't
make her feel any better.

It was a Friday and her parents expected her to spend the

weekend crating her belongings and helping her father clean the tools and equipment being auctioned the following Tuesday. Helen pushed her hair out of her face as she stared at their farmhouse, her eyes watering from the sharp wind. She'd miss this old place, but not as much as she would have expected. For every good memory of some high jinks with Bobbie Lee, she had three of Pa making her feel lousy. Ever since moving into town, she had felt lighter, free of the pressure of Pa's constant criticism and tirades. School was hard, no doubt about it, and some of the kids were mean as badgers, but her grades were good overall. If only she hadn't been forced to quit the track team. Getting a taste of what it felt like to be good at something and then having it taken away still left her feeling crushed when she allowed herself to think about it.

For that month she had trained with the track team, she had been someone. Someone important and valued. When Coach Moore would spot Helen walking toward the track, his handsome face would break into a broad grin every time without fail. She had never forgotten the first article in which Betty Robinson's father described his daughter as the best girl in the world. Helen liked to think that Coach Moore might say something like that about her. In fact, sometimes she lost herself in imagining that Coach Moore was her father and it made her feel like a million dollars.

Before Christmas, all the girls in school had flown into a tizzy with the news that Coach Moore and Miss Schultz would be marrying before the holiday. Apparently they all believed they had had a shot with the handsome coach. Such foolishness. Helen knew better. She had discovered a water fountain just outside the music room's door, and if she leaned over it to take a drink and angled her head just right, she could watch Coach Moore when he stopped in to visit Miss Schultz. The two of them would stand close to each other, talking conspiratorially, both looking pleased as punch. Miss Schultz's green eyes always trailed Coach Moore when he left the room, a happy expression dancing across her features. Watching them always made a wistful sense of longing come over Helen. Would anyone ever make her feel like that?

The final afternoon of school before the Christmas break, Helen had found Coach Moore in his office. He leapt from his chair to come around the desk to greet her, his eyes twinkling. "Helen, please come in. What can I do for you?"

His unabashed enthusiasm to see her made a lump rise in Helen's throat, but she dug the fingernails of her left hand into her palm to keep from getting sappy. "I heard you and Miss Schultz are getting married."

"We are."

"I brought you a wedding gift."

He accepted the small package wrapped in brown paper gently, as if handling an infant. "This is very thoughtful of you, thank you."

"It's nothing fancy," she mumbled. The way his eyes crinkled kindly when he smiled reminded her of Richard Arlen from *The Island of Lost Souls*. "I made a lot of jars of strawberry preserves last summer. Figured you and Miss Schultz might like a jar of it in your new home. It's good on toast."

"I happen to know for a fact that Miss Schultz adores strawberries. Whenever she gets a milkshake, she always picks strawberry. She'll be delighted."

Helen swallowed and spoke quickly before she could change her mind. "I really miss the track team. I know it was just a month, but it was the best thing I've ever done. I'm writing for the school newspaper now, but it's not the same."

A look not easily identified flickered across his face. *Sorrow?* "We all miss you too and would be honored to have you back any time."

That had been several weeks ago, before her father had defaulted on the deed of trust for the farm. Now any hope of returning to the team was long gone.

As she walked toward the farmhouse, her boots crunching against the layer of icy snow crusting the yard, a dark gap showed in the porch stairs where a plank had gotten loose and fallen off. The steps groaned as she stomped the snow off her boots on her way to the front door and let herself inside.

"Helen? Is that you?"

"Yeah." She didn't wait to see her mother but climbed the stairs, not caring that she was still in her boots, trailing mud and snow. They were in this house for only a few more days. Let the bank clean up her messy footsteps. She entered her room and collapsed onto her bed, breathing in the metallic scent of cold air rising from her coat, and she then reached for the small porcelain jewelry box on her dresser, lifting the lid to peer inside. A cluster of Doogie's yellowed puppy teeth lay in one compartment, a locket passed down from her grandmother lay in the other. She put the jewelry box in a wooden crate on the floor. That was it. The last of her stuff. She stared at the dark rectangles tiling the wallpaper from where she had removed her newspaper clippings about Betty Robinson and Babe Didrikson. Now everything was gone.

THE NEXT DAY she worked in the barn alongside her father to clean it out. He grumbled as he tossed a manure-covered rake down next to her to wipe clean. "You have no idea what it feels like to lose something that you've put your blood and sweat into."

"'Cause you didn't give me the chance," she muttered.

"What?"

"Nothing, sir."

He placed his hands on his sides. "Give you the chance to what?"

"I just meant that I was ready to put my blood and sweat into that track team, but you made me quit."

"What's the point of running around a track anyway? It's a waste of time, I tell you." He tugged at his suspenders to hitch up his trousers. "Put all that physical activity into something useful."

"I was good at it. Coach Moore and those other boys on the team looked at me like I was important."

"Who cares what a bunch of pimple-faced roughnecks thought?"

Helen scrubbed at the filthy rake, but then stopped. She had an idea. "You know, they weren't all hicks. I was leaving John Harris in the dust."

"Harris? The banker's boy?"

"That's right. I've been thinking, I'll bet it was Harris who told all that stuff to the newspaper. I think he wanted me off the team because he didn't like being beaten by me, a lowly farmer's daughter."

In truth, John Harris had been perfectly nice to her, but she had a suspicion of how to get her father's attention.

He narrowed his eyes. "You were beating the tar out of the banker's son?"

"Yeah, I had all of those fellas choking on my cinder."

He grunted and headed off to the pegboard to bring her more tools that needed cleaning and oiling. They didn't speak any more about track. That evening, he was preoccupied at supper and barely spoke. When they finished eating, Pa sat back with a pipe and played checkers with Bobbie Lee while watching Helen and Ma washing dishes out of the corner of his eye.

Eventually, he cleared his throat. "This is going to be a busy spring as we get the new farm up and running. Helen, I reckon I'm going to need you to come home a few afternoons a week to help. We'll be closer to town, though, so it won't be a long walk. I've been thinking that once we're settled, maybe next year you could go back to running on that track team, but only if you keep up with your chores."

Ma's hands froze in the sudsy water, and she turned sideways to look at Helen in surprise.

Helen kept her own face blank as she dried off a pan and placed it in the crate of kitchen supplies they'd be taking with them. "I'll keep up with everything."

Her father nodded, stood, and left the kitchen to head out to the living room to read the newspaper.

Helen lifted the crate of kitchen goods and hefted it out the kitchen door to the spot on the porch where her mother had started organizing what needed to be moved to the new farm they'd be leasing. She put the crate down and straightened, smiling into the darkness. Though the air was cold and her breath left vapor trails swirling up into the darkness, she didn't even notice. She was already thinking ahead to the next spring.

33.

May 1934
Riverdale, Illinois

BETTY DECIDED SHE WOULDN'T RELY ON HER FATHER to pay off her medical bills. She would do it herself. Jim, her brother-in-law, helped her find a job as a secretary in an architecture firm. The straightforward nature of the work suited her. The clarity of the daily schedule. The project deadlines. The clean angles and precision of the measurements on the blueprints. She enjoyed watching the projects take shape from schematics on crisp white sheets of paper to photographs of the final structures. Even with the stalled economy, new buildings were sprouting up around the city.

Betty continued to live at home with her parents, so after a year of working, she had nearly paid off her debts. She socialized with a couple of the other secretaries from work, friends from her school days, and, of course, Caroline and Howard, who were expecting their first baby sometime the following fall.

Jim worked near her office as a professor of economics at the University of Chicago, and when the weather obliged, the two would meet for lunch and sit outside in the main quad. On an afternoon in late May, they sat enjoying the balmy sunshine from underneath the lacy leaves of the honey locust trees in Dan Hall Garden. Betty inhaled the sweet fragrance of the clusters of light green flowers on the trees and placed her chicken salad sandwich on its butcher paper wrapping. Her gaze traveled over the gray limestone architecture surrounding them. "I love the Gothic stonework of this place. It reminds me of Amsterdam."

"It does feel like Europe," Jim agreed, his jaw tightening.

Jim never spoke of the time he spent overseas serving in the Great War. He and Jean married shortly after he came back from Europe. Betty remembered little from when he returned home because she had been so young, but she could still summon sober-faced conversations between Jean and her parents in the days before the wedding and the word *shell-shocked* being whispered repeatedly.

"I suppose our experiences in Europe must have been very different," she said.

Jim stared through the park, lost in thought. "Say, what would you think about trying to run again?"

"No."

"You won't even consider it?"

Betty shook her head. Since ending things with Bill, she had tried to push all thoughts of running from her mind. "I don't run anymore."

"But maybe it would be good for you. I'll help. We can go out together in the mornings before we leave for work."

Suddenly Betty felt overwhelmingly tired. "Jim, simply getting to the train every day is a struggle. Everything still hurts. I can't."

"But what if it makes you feel better?"

Betty let out a strangled laugh. She shifted in her seat and her spine made a cracking sound. "Haven't you noticed? I'm trapped in the body of an eighty-year-old."

"I know it might hurt at first, but maybe getting those muscles moving again could help. You've had a tough go of it, but you could run again if you put your mind to it."

Betty was about to snap at him, tell him to mind his own business, but something held her back. About two years ago, Dr. Minke had told her she might never walk again, but he had underestimated her. He'd also told her she'd never run again, but what if he was wrong? She lifted her legs from the ground in front of her, flexed her toes, and then pointed them, feeling the tendons along her calves and shins contract and elongate. What was the worst thing that could happen if she tried?

She looked up at Jim and found him watching her. "Think about it," he said. "I've got to get back to my office, but I'll see you later."

THAT EVENING WHEN she climbed into bed, she couldn't stop thinking about what Jim had suggested. He had planted a seed and its roots were already threading through her, tendrils curling around her insides like pea vines. She could practically feel her mind rewiring to consider the idea, but risking the disappointment of failure scared her. She fell into an uneasy sleep.

A persistent knocking at the door awakened her. It was dark, the house quiet. She lifted her head from the pillow, looking around her bedroom in confusion.

"Mother?" she whispered.

From outside the door, a scuffling sound.

"No, Betty, it's me, Jim."

Jim? Even in the foggy recesses of her mind, this was the last answer she expected. She rolled to her side, wincing at the pain that shot down her hip toward her feet. Inhaling deeply, she swung her legs off the bed to plant her feet on the floor. The first few steps of the morning always challenged her the most. The stiffness and tenderness of her lower back tended to render her speechless at first. She pushed to standing, grimacing with the pops and cracks in her joints as she straightened and then staggered toward the door and opened it to find Jim standing in the hallway wearing a gray sweat suit.

Betty smoothed down her hair. "What happened? What's wrong with Jean? Are the girls all right?"

"Nothing's wrong. I'm here to jog with you."

"To jog with—" Betty shook her head and rested a palm against the wall to steady herself. "I thought I was supposed to think about it."

"Sometimes thinking too much can be . . . come on, let's just try this. Get changed. It's dark outside. No one will see us. We can start slow."

Insistence was etched into her brother-in-law's face. She glanced back into her room, her eyes resting on her closet door. A couple of years ago, her old sweat suit from Amsterdam had been folded in the third drawer of her dresser. Every time she'd reached in to pull out a sweater, she would see the sweatshirt, and it would bring back a flood of memories. Sometimes she'd lift it out and burrow her face into it, seeking out the smell of sweat, a trace of her hard work, but only the scent of Ivory laundry flakes would waft over her. After the accident the sweatshirt had comforted her. It reminded her of all that she had accomplished and inspired her to work harder on her walking, but as the months went by, she wanted to see it less and less, so she had stuffed it into the back of her closet and tried not to think about it, telling herself it was lost.

But she knew exactly where it was.

She could put it on.

She could go outside with Jim.

She could see how it felt to run again.

With a sigh of surrender, she said, "Fine. Wait while I get changed."

She closed the door but didn't turn on the lights. Maybe if she dressed in the dark, she could pretend she was still sleeping and wouldn't realize what she was doing, what she was risking. She opened the closet door and reached for the top shelf, her hand feeling its way along some wool sweaters until it reached a soft, thick cotton. She yanked it down, tugged off her nightgown, and pulled on underwear and the sweatshirt and pants before her mind could register too much and protest.

Betty glanced over her shoulder at her unmade bed. All she wanted to do was to climb back into it, face away from the door, and forget about all of this running nonsense. Instead she removed her old track shoes from inside the closet where they had been hidden in a shoebox. *Don't think, don't think,* she repeated to herself dully as she laced them on to her feet and lurched for the door.

Minutes later, she and Jim stepped onto the sidewalk.

He pointed to a streetlight in the distance. "We can walk this block to warm up, but then we'll try a light jog on the next one. We can take it block by block and see how you feel."

Betty murmured in agreement and they started moving, a slow walk at first. Each step ricocheted barbs of pain up and down her legs so she focused on the sensation of breathing.

In and out. In and out. One step. Another. How about one more?

When they reached the next block, Jim broke into a jog and turned to urge her along. "Come on, give it a try."

She increased her pace to a slow jog. Pain flared in her hips, but by the end of the block it was more of a steady burn. Did that mean progress? Jim slowed to a walk, but momentum kept Betty jogging. If she stopped now, she wouldn't start again. After several more blocks, her lungs and heart felt dangerously close to combusting, but she kept going. Jim led her on a twenty-minute loop around the neighborhood and soon they were back at the house.

Jim stopped jogging and picked up his foot behind him to stretch one of his quadriceps, but Betty simply stood, watching the vapor of her breath rise and spread into the air. A blush of morning light gave a faint glow to the yard. In between heaving breaths, she said, "It's pretty at this hour."

Jim stretched into a lunge.

Betty bit her lip. "Why are you out here with me?"

"I'm not getting any younger. I could stand to lose a few pounds," he said, bending over to stretch his hamstrings, his gaze downward.

Betty considered this. Jim, tall and lean, had never been at risk for being overweight. Even his fingers stretching toward the flagstone walk were long and thin.

She tried again. "Why does this matter to you?"

He unfolded and looked at her, his expression serious. "When I came back from the war, I wondered what the hell I was doing. Nothing here had changed, but I felt like a completely different person. Everything seemed pointless. How could I just settle back into normal life after what I'd seen? After what I'd done?" He paused for a moment, gazing down the street before turning back toward her. "But slowly, I came back to remembering the man I had been. I gave up thinking I'd ever be him again, but I just wanted to feel a connection to him again and move ahead in a new way that felt meaningful, that honored the old me and the new me. Being a husband to your sister was the thread that brought me back." He chuckled. "This probably sounds pretty crazy, huh?"

Betty stared at him. She understood completely.

"Since your accident, I've watched you go through a lot of the same sense of dislocation and figured I could help. Maybe running could be the thread that connects your new life to your old . . ." His voice trailed off and he studied her closely, looking for a sign of agreement.

Tears flooded Betty's eyes.

"Aww, geez, Betty, I didn't mean to upset you. I'm sorry," he said. "You've done a swell job at coming back from everything. Forget what I'm saying."

She shook her head. "No, no, that's exactly it." Now she

was crying and she sniffled. "I'm sorry, I never knew you went through all of that."

"You were just a kid when I got back. How would you have known?"

"Still . . . thank you." The inadequacy of her words horrified her. "I don't even know what to say."

"You don't need to say anything. We can just run."

She wiped at her eyes with the back of her hand. Someone had understood her all along.

34.

March 1935
Fulton, Missouri

THE ICY AIR STUNG HELEN'S LUNGS AS SHE RAN DOWN the track's straightaway at Westminster College. Coach Moore had decided to train her here, away from the scrutiny of the high school, since the college men didn't give a whit that Helen was a girl. They were just pleased to have their level of competition intensified by her arrival and treated her as they would a younger sister, except she was a younger sister who could run fast. In fact, she beat the men at every distance.

And she wasn't just fast.

She proved to be phenomenal at field events too. At Westminster, she tried the discus and javelin and discovered she could throw them stunning distances. She tried the broad jump and high jump and proved to be a natural in both of those events too.

But as she huffed her way along the track, she wasn't thinking about field events. She wanted to race in the National AAU Championships being held in Missouri at the end of the month. Coach had brought it up with her and then the topic languished. Did he think she wasn't good enough? With that worry gnawing at her, she increased her pace and ran the last half of the final lap at a faster clip. A cool northern breeze buffeted her as she sprinted the final stretch to where Coach Moore waited with his clipboard, stopwatch in hand.

"How'd I look?" she asked, sailing past him. She slowed herself to a jog and circled back to him.

"Why did you take that last two hundred so quickly?"

"To see if I could."

"Huh." Coach Moore turned his attention back to his clipboard and stopwatch as the rest of the runners glided over the finish, talking among themselves. The young men remained in a pack and drifted over to their head coach, who walked with them to the field house.

"So, Coach," Helen said as the other runners moved out of earshot. "What about the National AAU Champs? You gonna send me to it?"

"I haven't forgotten. I've had several meetings with the superintendent about it."

"Several?" Helen groaned. "What? He doesn't want me to race?"

"Let's just say that he hasn't been the biggest fan of the idea, but he's finally agreed. And so have your parents. You can go and represent Fulton."

"Holy smokes." Helen put her hands on her hips and breathed in and out heavily, still recovering from her run. "How about the entry fee? Is the district paying?"

"Don't worry about those details. Focus on running."

"You're paying it, aren't you?"

"Don't think about that stuff."

She balanced on one foot, stretching her quadriceps. If the district wasn't paying—and she was pretty sure her parents weren't paying—there was only one other option. She glanced toward Coach's old rattling Model A parked by the side of the track. He could hardly afford the two-dollar entry fee, but who else would be paying it? "Hey, thanks for sticking your neck out for me." Her voice sounded thick with emotion, but she dug in for the last part. "I promise I'll make you proud," she croaked.

"You already have. Now let's get you back to your boarding-house because I know you have homework. What's happening with *Macbeth*?"

"Lady Macbeth is the one running the show. Macbeth would never have killed Duncan if not for her urging. She's blood-thirsty."

"And power hungry too, right?"

"Yep. Once you murder someone, you're on a slippery slope."

Coach Moore laughed. "That's an understatement." At the field house, they parted ways. "I'm going to take care of a couple of things in the office, but go get changed and I'll meet you out here in a few minutes. You can tell me more about Macbeth's nefarious plans on our ride back to town."

A COUPLE OF weeks later, Helen met Coach Moore outside the high school's front door beside John and D.W., two boys from the high school track team.

"You ready?" Coach Moore called as Helen trotted up the walkway. "Don't use up all your energy."

"Don't worry, I've got plenty," Helen said, laughing, as she shouldered the strap of a canvas sack filled with a change of clothes, and they all walked toward Coach Moore's old Ford. Mrs. Moore leaned out the car's window and waved.

D.W. pointed at Helen's navy-blue sweat suit. "Huh, you look like a real athlete."

"I even have track shoes too, courtesy of the fellas over at Westminster. They loaned me today's whole kit," said Helen as they loaded into the car. "I can't show up looking like a hayseed, isn't that right?"

"You could dress up like the Queen of England and everyone will know you're still a hayseed," John said, giving Helen a light punch to the arm.

Helen leaned forward toward the front seat. "Miss Schultz, I mean, Mrs. Moore—I still can't get used to calling you that— anyway, you sure are a sight. Fulton High isn't the same without you. Rumor has it that the new music teacher is a real crumb." She'd seen the new teacher, a thin young man with glasses that appeared to be about an inch thick.

"Don't believe all the gossip you hear. I'm sure he's doing a fine job," said Mrs. Moore in a stern tone, but from the twinkle in her green eyes, Helen had the feeling she enjoyed hearing how everyone missed her. The district's rule that women had to resign their teaching positions once they married seemed like an awful waste.

While they spent the next few hours motoring east toward St. Louis and talking about school, Helen tried to keep her mind off the upcoming races. She had no idea what to expect. When they pulled up to the St. Louis Arena, she couldn't ignore the thoughts any longer, and her nerves started up. It felt as though a bunch of grasshoppers were let loose in her belly.

"How many people are here?" gasped John, his face pushed up against the glass.

"More than you're capable of counting," Helen said.

All three of them in the back seat cackled with laughter as Coach Moore guided the automobile into a parking spot. They exited the car to join the throngs of people swarming the entrance to the stadium. Inside, rows of bleachers appeared to go all the way up to the high ceiling. Voices boomed over the loudspeakers, a frenetic energy pulsed through the crowd, and a sense of vertigo overcame Helen.

"How about I take the boys off to find some refreshments?" Mrs. Moore suggested.

"Good idea. Helen and I will head over to the athletes' area and get organized," Coach Moore said.

"Helen, do you want anything?" Mrs. Moore asked.

Helen shook her head. The grasshoppers were back in her stomach. She had never seen so many people in one place before. The idea of eating anything made her feel ill.

John said, "If you're feeling too chicken, I can always stick on a wig and race for you."

"I'm fine," Helen said, feeling far from fine.

Mrs. Moore wrapped an arm around her shoulders and held her close for a moment. "You know what I used to tell my music students before shows? Breathe in and out slowly. Try to count to five on both your inhalations and exhalations to steady your nerves. Focus on the counting to distract yourself. And here's the other thing: Being a little nervous is good. It keeps you sharp. You'll be great, got it?"

Helen bit her lip.

"Good luck," D.W. called as he started snaking his way through the crowd behind John and Mrs. Moore.

Helen swallowed and stuck close to Coach Moore as he found the check-in booth for the competitors and talked with an official. A small dark-haired woman sauntered past. Her brown eyes, ringed with dark circles, bored into Helen.

Coach Moore hastened over to Helen, holding a numbered bib made of paper. "You're going to need to wear this while you compete."

Helen bobbed her chin toward the glaring woman who now bounced on the balls of her feet, stretching her thin, muscle-bound arms overhead. "Who's that?"

Coach Moore's gaze followed Helen's. "Stella Walsh. She's from Cleveland, races for Poland."

"She won the gold medal in Los Angeles?"

"She did."

"So, she's the fastest woman in the world?"

"Yes," he said, his face solemn. Her fingers trembled as she tried pinning her bib onto her flat chest. When she finally attached it, Coach Moore was studying her. "Helen, don't let all of this stuff—the crowds, the size of this place—don't let it distract you. You've been running well lately. Remember that."

She faced the crowd and let the yelling and cheering from the bleachers wash over her. "You know what? I think I like it. This feels pretty good."

He clapped her on the shoulder. "Well then, soak it in. This is just the beginning."

35.

THE FULTON CRIER

March 26, 1935

"Monday Will Be Helen Stephens Day in Fulton"

St. Louis—On Friday, March 25, seventeen-year-old phenom Helen Stephens blew away the competition at the National AAU Championships in front of 4,000 spectators at the St. Louis Arena. The newcomer won the shot put and broad jump, but her biggest coup of the day came with winning the 50-yard dash in 6.6 seconds. Helen made her victory look easy, flying across the finish tape about four feet ahead of the Polish champion, Olympic gold medalist Stanislawa Walasiewicz, better known as Stella Walsh.

When asked about her reaction to beating Stella Walasiewicz, Helen gave reporters a sly grin and asked, "Stella who?" And with that mocking response, the Fulton Flash has thrown down the gauntlet to the fastest woman in the world. This rivalry will be the one to watch in upcoming months.

Superintendent of Fulton Public Schools Mr. Waddington announced that Monday will be Helen Stephens Day to honor the city's luminary. "I'm proud to say that I encouraged Coach Moore to cultivate the talent of this young woman before anyone believed she had what it took to be a champion," he explained to a group of reporters who gathered at the high school on Saturday morning. An assembly will be held at Fulton High School at 11 A.M. on Monday. Afternoon classes will be canceled so that all faculty, staff, and students can participate in a parade that will travel to Court and Fifth Streets before returning to Fulton High School.

Helen's medals will be on display inside Fulton Savings Bank through the week.

According to AAU officials in St. Louis, it's not too early to start picturing Helen representing the United States in the 1936 Olympics. All parties interested in supporting this promising young woman are invited to drop off monetary donations addressed to the Helen Stephens Booster Club, located at the Fulton Methodist Church.

Helen sat under the hair dryer, tapping her foot. It felt like hours had passed since Ma and Mrs. Moore had roused her out of bed that morning and rushed her to Mrs. Georgia Richardson's beauty salon to prepare her for Helen Stephens Day on Monday. Mrs. Richardson herself had spent ages snipping at Helen's hair and wrapping it around curlers, and Helen wanted to see the results.

As soon as she had stepped inside the salon, she felt as though she was entering a secret world, one that had been hidden from her for all of her life. So, this was how women managed to look beautiful. Professional help!

Helen looked up to find Mrs. Richardson and Mrs. Moore gliding toward her, both holding several shopping bags. Mrs. Richardson flipped off the power on the hair dryer and pulled the shiny silver dome away from Helen's head. While she leaned close to inspect Helen's hair, Mrs. Moore dropped the bags and pulled out a shoebox, opening it with a flourish.

Helen admired the pair of shiny black high-heeled shoes, but shook her head. "Those will never fit."

"Oh yes, they will. They're size twelves, just as your mother instructed."

Helen's face reddened. "But . . ."

"Don't say another word. Did you know that a group of Fulton citizens gathered this morning to create the Helen Stephens Booster Club? They've raised money to prepare you for some public appearances. Why, you're making a speech on Monday! We've got to get you ready for it! I've used a portion of the proceeds to purchase shoes and some other fundamentals for you."

"Fundamentals?"

Mrs. Moore looked at Mrs. Richardson, and they nodded at each other before pulling Helen out of her seat to lead her behind the salon's privacy screen. Mrs. Moore pulled another box from a shopping bag, scrabbled through layers of white tissue paper, and removed two garments of flesh-colored fabric with clips and strings—Helen had never seen anything like them. Mrs. Moore chuckled. "It's a girdle and garter belt. Now Lord knows you don't have an ounce of anything that needs to be sucked in, but still, it's only proper. Your mother is making some lovely new dresses, but in the meantime, I picked this up for you too so you can walk out of here looking like a new woman."

Mrs. Richardson held up a light blue tea-length dress and nodded. "Well done, Mary Lou. This will do nicely on her."

The women handed over the new clothes and turned their backs so Helen could dress, but after only a minute Helen mumbled, "Um, Mrs. Moore, how does this thing go on?"

Mrs. Moore spun around to see Helen holding the girdle, confounded. "Oh heavens, I envy the fact that you've made it this far without knowing how to wear one of these." She helped her into it while Mrs. Richardson unrolled a pair of silk stockings before offering them the light blue dress. When they were done, the women tugged Helen out from behind the privacy screen and pointed to the full-length mirror.

"Well, what do you think?" Mrs. Moore asked.

Mrs. Richardson held her hand to her heart. "Mercy me, it's a miracle."

Helen hardly recognized the young woman reflected back at her. Her dreaded birthmark? Covered up. New bangs and a dash of pancake makeup had done the trick. Frizzy hair? Gone, tamed and styled into graceful shiny waves. Even the color had improved with shimmery golden streaks running through it. Her gaze traveled down the mirror to the dress. Elegant pearl buttons ran down its bodice. She swayed from side to side, holding out the A-line skirt, admiring how the filmy fabric swished and swirled. Even her nails looked shiny, trimmed, buffed, and polished.

And her feet. Lord, her feet. Her vision blurred with tears as she took in the pumps. She'd given up any dreams of wearing stylish shoes long ago.

She straightened, for the first time proud of her height. She'd never imagined she could look like this. Not after all of Pa's hurtful comments over the years. Even after yesterday's victory, he couldn't bring himself to say he was proud of her. When she'd arrived downstairs that morning, he'd been standing in the doorway to the kitchen, arms folded across his chest.

"Heard you had a lucky race yesterday," he said.

Lucky? She almost laughed. She was tempted to describe how reporters had crowded her after the race, wanting to know how it felt to beat a renowned champion, and how the town was preparing a parade in her honor, but she took in his sour expression, weatherworn skin, and stooped shoulders. How diminished he was. She almost felt sorry for him. Almost. Instead, she kept her face neutral. Her success on the track was because of her hard work. Luck hadn't played a part of it and neither had he. Why give him a piece of her accomplishment? Or the opportunity to cut her down again? She was tired of how he took out his life's disappointments on her.

"I'm the fastest woman in the world," she said. And before he had time to react, she turned to Ma's and Mrs. Moore's beaming expressions and walked out the front door to go to the beauty salon.

As she took in her physical transformation in Mrs. Richardson's mirror, she realized she had a choice with how she dealt with Pa. From now on, she would engage with him as little as possible. Frank Stephens would no longer hold any power over her.

"Oh, honey, I'm so glad you're happy," Mrs. Moore said. "You look like a film star. I'll drive you home. We'll be able to knock your mother over with a feather when she sees you."

Mrs. Richardson blinked away tears. "You are my finest work yet, dear. But before you go anywhere, let me put on the final touch."

She hurried away, rummaged through a cabinet in the back of the shop, and returned holding out a small gold tube. "You must wear lipstick. This cherry red will be perfect. Now pout for me."

Helen raised her eyebrows at Mrs. Moore, who nodded, urging her on. Helen pouted her lips as Mrs. Richardson traced the lipstick over them.

"Now look," she said, handing Helen a blotting paper and miming how to use it. "Doesn't that shade look marvelous?"

Two other women having their hair done had wandered over to take in the spectacle. "She's a vision," one cooed.

Mrs. Richardson stepped back, crossed her arms, tilted her head, and appraised her handiwork. "Good," she announced, nodding. "But if you ever want to do something about your brows, stop by and I can help."

"My eyebrows?" Helen asked, frowning at herself in the mirror.

"I think she's had enough change for one day," Mrs. Moore said, helping Helen shuffle out of the shop in her new pumps. "See you ladies at the parade on Monday."

On the drive back to the Stephens farm, Mrs. Moore told Helen all about the reporters who had swarmed their house that morning, even trampling the tulips lining the sides of the walk. Helen half listened, running her fingers along the soft fabric of her dress. She'd never owned something so silky before. She then twisted her ankles this way and that, so she could admire the heels and the sophistication they gave her long legs. It had barely been twenty-four hours since she had run the race and already her life felt transformed.

Once home, Helen found Ma perched on a chair in the front parlor talking to a man. At the sight of Helen, both sprang to their feet. Helen took a few unsteady steps forward, conscious of the smart click of her heels on the floor.

"This here is Dwayne Goodwin from *The St. Louis Register*," Ma said.

The man shoved his hand out and took Helen's. "Your mama was gracious enough to offer an appointment with you later today, but I said, 'No, ma'am, no chance my editor is going to let that fly,' so I've been sitting here waiting for you."

As he spoke, Helen couldn't lift her gaze from the sight of her own hand in his. She couldn't quite believe those glamorous fingernails clasped in his ink-stained hand were hers. "Well, here I am. What can I do for you?"

"I caught up with Stella Walsh last night to ask her for her reaction and she said your win was a fluke and she doesn't think you can beat her again. Now, what do you make of that?"

"I think she better use a dictionary to look up what *fluke* means. Can you take a picture of my face so she can get a good long look at it in your newspaper? 'Cause she's not going to see it again in a long time. When we're on the track, all she'll see is my backside." Helen watched the reporter's face split open with delight as he scribbled down her remarks in his notebook.

Seeing that he was getting a kick out of her, she added, "I also hope she likes the taste of cinder because she's going to be eating it for breakfast, lunch, and dinner if she chases after me."

"Woo-whee, our readers are going to love this. When do you two plan to face off again?"

"I'm ready any time. She can name the day."

"Terrific," said the reporter, tipping the brim of his cap at her and making his way to the door.

"You know where to find me for more," Helen said, watching as the man pushed his way out the door.

After he had left, Ma wagged her finger at Helen. "No more of that, you hear? I won't have my daughter sounding so boastful."

Helen gave a sheepish glance at Mrs. Moore. The night before, when she had said, "Stella who?" to the reporters, Coach Moore had whisked her away from the crowd.

"Helen, if we're to continue working together, you must be an honorable sportswoman at all times. I will not tolerate any incivilities," he'd said.

"To be fair, they threw me off with her real name. You know, the Polish version?"

He had folded his arms and given her a long look.

"Sorry, Coach," she had mumbled, chastened, but apparently it hadn't been enough because here she was getting a rise out of a reporter again. She couldn't help herself!

Helen took in the scandalized expressions of Ma and Mrs. Moore. "Everyone likes a little gamesmanship. And anyway, Stella started it by calling my win a fluke, so what was I supposed to say?"

Mrs. Moore appeared to be hiding a smile behind her hand, but Ma harrumphed, then pointed to two dresses hanging over a kitchen chair. "I've made progress. You should try them on, but be careful because the bodice seams are only basted so I could be sure they fit you before I sewed them in earnest."

Helen lifted the dresses from the chair.

"And Mr. Draper stopped by earlier with this beautiful coat. He wants you to know that Draper's Dry Goods would love you to stop by and visit," Ma said in an amazed voice. She lifted the fawn-colored wool coat from a shopping bag and handed it to Helen.

"I've never had a store-bought coat," Helen said, holding it out in front of her as though it were something breakable.

"Try it on," Mrs. Moore urged.

Helen slid her arm into one of the sleeves, sighing as her hand brushed along the satin lining. Easing it along her shoulders, she slid her other arm into it and pulled its edges close together, nuzzling her cheek along the soft collar as she rubbed her palm down the front of it, pausing at one of the pockets to pull out an envelope and open it. "Holy cats, there's a gift voucher here for two dresses."

"If you're not careful, you're going to be the best-dressed girl in Fulton," Mrs. Moore said.

Helen shook her head in amazement at the riches being bestowed upon her all because of one good run. Her hand shook as she stroked the collar of the coat. It felt too good to be true.

"This'll look fetching with my rabbit rifle slung across my shoulder, don't you think?" she asked with a wink.

36.

May 1935
Chicago

HAVE YOU READ ABOUT THIS GIRL, THE FULTON FLASH?" Jim asked as he and Betty enjoyed lunch at their favorite spot in the main quad at the University of Chicago.

"No, I haven't read the sports pages in a while."

"There's a young girl out of Missouri, a high-schooler, who beat Stella Walsh and is winning races left and right. She's being hailed as the next big thing."

"Since Babe's turned professional, I suppose reporters must be excited for someone new to keep everyone on their toes."

Jim packed the remains of his lunch away into his sack. "Have you thought about trying out for Berlin?"

Betty snorted. "The next Olympics? No. Our morning runs are plenty, thanks."

Jim dropped the subject, but over the next few weeks, Betty couldn't stop thinking about his offhand remark. She was running well. Certainly not as smoothly and easily as she once did, but she often finished her runs well ahead of Jim now.

She decided to visit Caroline and see how her friend was faring with her new baby, a daughter named Joan. Maybe she would float the idea of training for Berlin to Caroline and check her reaction.

When Betty arrived at Caroline's doorstep and knocked, her friend threw open the door and practically smothered Betty with the strength of her embrace. "You came!" Caroline shrieked.

"Watch out, I brought some of my mother's delicious molasses cookies and I'm going to spill them all over the floor." Betty laughed.

Caroline cocked her head toward inside the house as she accepted the plate. "I hope I didn't just wake the baby."

They waited a moment, listening, but no sounds could be detected, so Caroline led the way into her small kitchen to put the kettle on for tea and then the two tiptoed into Caroline and Howard's bedroom to peek at little Joan lying swaddled in a Moses basket at the foot of their bed. Pink cheeks, a perfect swirl of dark hair, and a pert nose were the only parts of her visible above the folds of a pink crocheted blanket. The women backed out of the room and Caroline closed the door behind her.

"She's a doll," Betty said, embracing her friend.

"Thank you. It's amazing how much time this tiny creature consumes. Do I look exhausted? I feel like I've aged twenty years in the last few months."

"You look wonderful." Since Joan's birth, Betty had seen Caroline a couple of times. Each time her friend seemed a bit paler, her cheeks thinner, but she appeared happy. "And Joan's filling out. She's going to be tall like her mama."

"You should see how quickly she pedals her legs in the air when she's free. I keep telling Howard that we've got another runner on our hands," Caroline said, leading them back to the kitchen.

"What about getting back into it? Running, I mean. I told you how I started training with Jim. Well, he brought up the idea of training for Berlin. At first I thought he was crazy, but now it's all I can think about. What do you say? Would you want to train together? Any interest in giving the Olympics one more try?"

Caroline pulled the kettle off the stovetop before it whistled and poured water into a teapot. She sat, lost in thought as the tea steeped. "All things considered, Joan's a dear little thing and a good sleeper, and I daresay I could use some exercise. What did you have in mind?"

"The IWAC's folded because of the economy, but there's the Catholic Women's team. We could join and see how it goes."

Caroline poured the tea into the teacups. "Howard misses running too. What if he coaches us in the evenings after you're both done with work? Then I can bring the baby and she could nap in the pram while we run."

"Do you think Howard would really want to do this?"

Caroline winked. "I can be very convincing when I put my mind to it."

THE FOLLOWING WEEK, Betty met Howard and Caroline at a park down the street from where they lived. Caroline parked Joan, who was asleep in her pram, in the shade of an elm tree. "I got a good feeding into her before we left, so we'll both be happy." She took a final peek at the baby. "I also rang one of my teammates from Los Angeles. She lives here on the South

Side too so I invited her to train with us. Before she gets here, I want to tell you something so you won't be surprised: Tidye's colored."

Betty nodded, though she was surprised. She had never encountered black women runners, not during her tenure running for the IWAC and not in Amsterdam. "And she ran with you in the Olympics in Los Angeles?"

"Well, no. She and another colored woman, Louise Stokes, qualified for the relay and they both traveled to Los Angeles as part of the team, but they were pulled at the last minute. As the Olympics got closer and closer, things got strange. I don't think the coaches were pleased to have them there, and not all of the other girls were very happy with their presence either. There were some black men who raced well in Los Angeles—Ralph Metcalfe, Eddie Tolan—but Tidye and Louise didn't stand a chance. Bad enough they were women, right? Then pile on the race issue. It ended up being pretty ugly for them."

"I can imagine."

"Training with Tidye isn't going to be a problem for you, is it?"

"No, of course not," Betty said quickly. And she meant it. She didn't have any experience with black people. Her family had never hired any domestic help and she couldn't picture a single black family living in her neighborhood. If there had been any black students at her high school or Northwestern, she couldn't remember them. Now that she thought about it, her classmates and friends had mostly been just like her—white.

Howard spread his hands impatiently. "Enough dillydallying, you two. How about taking a warm-up lap while we await Tidye?"

"Good idea," Caroline agreed. "No reason to stand around here gabbing while the baby sleeps. There's no telling how long I'll get."

So off they went, running along the outside of the park on a worn path. Betty focused on starting slowly, allowing her legs to stretch out with every passing step. The first few always felt the tightest, but after a couple of hundred yards, she had settled into a comfortable gait. When they arrived back to Howard, Tidye was waiting. Betty studied her closely. She was petite and light-skinned with alert, penetrating eyes.

"Tidye, glad you made it," Caroline called out, smiling.

"You think I'd miss a reunion with you and Howard? I just took a peek at Joan, and she's the sweetest little thing I've ever seen," Tidye replied.

"Aww, thanks. Here, let me introduce you to Betty," Caroline said, pulling Betty close.

"It's nice to meet you, Betty," Tidye said, extending her hand. Though she was smiling, her expression was cool and watchful.

Betty's shoulders tightened. She felt a surprising pressure to come off as immune to the potential awkwardness of the moment. It seemed like everyone was studying how she'd behave and she wanted to pass this test. She took Tidye's hand in her own. "It's a pleasure to meet you. Glad to have another sprinter here."

Tidye nodded, turning to Caroline. "I'm actually thinking about giving the hurdles a try this time. My legs are nowhere near as long as yours, but I'm a good jumper, so why not?"

Howard looked pleased and held up his watch. "Good idea, but before we get to thinking about hurdles, let's focus on conditioning and getting the three of you back into fighting shape. Tidye, are you warmed up?"

"Sure am. I ran here from the bus stop."

"Perfect. I want you all to take a lap at three-quarter effort. Sound good?"

Betty nodded. If there was one way to work past any uncertainty, it was to start running.

37.

May 1935
Fulton, Missouri

HELEN'S LAST COUPLE OF MONTHS OF HIGH SCHOOL couldn't have been more different from her first few years. Now no one could get enough of her. People didn't just wave when they saw her; they cheered. She was popular, and no longer as a punch line to a joke, but as a figure of interest, even respect.

One weekend when she was home with her family, Bobbie Lee announced himself to be the official keeper of Helen's scrapbook. He pulled Helen down to the floor of the parlor, a black leather-bound book spread in front of him. "Look here, Hellie," he said. "I've got the *Fulton Crier* article about you winning the meet sponsored by Wright City High. I've also got this column all about how you won that Leacock Trophy. There's even a swell picture of you and Coach Moore standing with it." Bobbie Lee continued to inventory the other races she had won, pointing out pictures and articles, race programs, and racing bibs for each one.

After the National AAU Championships in March, Coach Moore had said they needed to enter her in as many exhibition races as possible so she could set records and establish herself as a serious competitor to attract eventual sponsorship. He had his practical reasons for wanting to race Helen as much as possible, but she had her reasons too. She wanted to show Stella Walsh that she could beat her any time, anywhere, but no matter how many challenges were issued, the woman never took the bait. "Helen Stephens is a nobody," Stella was quoted as saying. "Why should I waste my time racing her at little podunk high schools in Missouri when I can stay here in Cleveland and train seriously?" Stella's public dismissal of her rankled, but Helen knew the Polish Flyer was right. Helen needed to set official records and continue to beat significant competitors.

One afternoon, when Helen went out to the track in back of the high school, a tall, rangy-looking woman waited for her next to Coach Moore, her dark eyes serious, chin sharp.

"Helen, remember Miss Boeckmann from St. Louis? You've raced against her girls in several races recently," said Coach Moore.

"Sure I do," Helen said. Dee Boeckmann, an Olympian from 1928, was the first woman to head the AAU's Ozark District Committee. "Your girls are fast."

Miss Boeckmann fixed her gaze on Helen, looking as if she had discovered a shiny gold coin in her path that she wanted to tuck into her pocket. "But none of them are as fast as you. Listen, I'm here to talk with your coach about you coming to St. Louis to join my squad and train with me at Loretto Academy. I hear you're serious about wanting to go to the next Olympics. There's no better way to prepare than coming to race with the fastest girls in the region." And as if she knew exactly what was in Helen's heart, she added, "We'll be able to show Stella Walsh that your performance in March was no fluke."

Helen considered the offer and let her gaze drop to her track shoes. Miss Boeckmann was missing one thing. Shortly after her race in St. Louis, Coach Moore had shown up one day for practice and handed her the track shoes. They were brand-new, shiny black leather. All this time Coach Moore had been paying for everything without asking for anything in return. And it wasn't like he was swimming in cash. He probably made next to nothing as the high school track coach and assistant coach at Westminster, yet he stuck with her, so while she might not have the fancy tracksuits and facilities that the girls in St. Louis enjoyed, she had something more important: someone who had seen something in her when no one else did. All the money in the world couldn't buy someone like that.

"I appreciate you coming all this way, but I'm going to stay here and continue to train with Coach Moore." She glanced at her coach and though his face remained expressionless, she was quite sure he squared his shoulders.

"Sure, I understand why sticking with Coach Moore is appealing, but I promise you that we have everything you need in St. Louis."

But she didn't have everything. Coach Moore wouldn't be there. Also, none of Miss Boeckmann's girls struck Helen as particularly friendly. In particular, that redheaded one, Harriet Bland, the one who always looked like she had taken a big chomp out of a lemon, rubbed Helen the wrong way. Why give herself over to a bunch of strangers when she could stay close to her family and friends?

Sensing Helen's reluctance, Miss Boeckmann added, "Look, we can help you out in every way you may need it. Clothes, equipment—why, we'll even send you to a dentist if you want."

"Again, Coach Boeckmann, I'm grateful for your offer. Really, I am. But I'm going to stick with Coach Moore."

The tall woman pursed her lips. "I understand. No hard feelings. I'm looking forward to watching your career and am certain our paths will cross again. If you change your mind, you know where to find me. There's no expiration date on my offer."

The woman said goodbye and sauntered back toward the rear entry of the high school.

Coach Moore turned to Helen. "Sure you want to give all of that up?"

"Yep," she said. "My heart's set on William Woods College so I can keep my ma happy by training nearby and going to college. What do you say? Can you make that happen?"

He winked. "I'll try."

38.

May 1936
Malden, Massachusetts

THANK YOU, THESE ARE SO PRETTY," LOUISE SAID, ACcepting a handful of dandelions from her young charge, Ann Clark. The five-year-old darted away on sturdy legs still pale from long winter months spent indoors and plunked herself down in the grass next to her three-year-old sister. Both girls busied themselves with building towers of pebbles. Louise held the dandelions up to her nose to smell them and inhaled the bitter tang of grass and damp earth. Springtime. With the girls immersed in play, Louise dropped the flowers into her pocket and then rubbed her hands, now sticky from the stems, along the sides of her skirt.

From across the park, Miss Francine, another domestic who minded a pair of children from the Clarks' street, waved. Louise returned the greeting, sighing in contentment as she settled into her spot on the bench. She closed her eyes briefly to savor the steady cheerful babble of the little girls and stretch her arms overhead as she soaked in the long-awaited sunshine pouring over her. This was a precious moment of peace amid the anxiety that had been building as the Berlin Olympics neared. It was late May and Louise was still waiting for her invitation from the AAU to compete in the Olympic trials and starting to worry she wouldn't be invited back. After the slight in Los Angeles, it seemed anything was possible.

She cracked an eye open and watched Ann and Barbara stack the pebbles carefully into a tower and then shriek in delight as the tower toppled and they began the process of rebuilding it. It never failed to amaze her that she had been working for Mrs. Clark for four years now.

When she had first arrived as a housemaid, the oldest daughter, Beatrice, was still too young to attend school, but Louise barely saw the eight-year-old anymore, so busy was the girl's school life. And now there were two more little girls: Barbara and Constance. Though still considered a housemaid, Louise oversaw Ann and Barbara for a few hours each afternoon while Mrs. Clark rested as her youngest napped. This baby, Constance, had been colicky since her birth, and still, eight months later, she often fussed and didn't sleep through the night. Louise always looked forward to days when the weather obliged with sunshine so she could escape Mrs. Clark's frayed nerves and leave the house with Ann and Barbara.

The years since Louise had traveled to Los Angeles had passed in a flash. When she had returned from California, embarrassed and crushed by her failure to compete, family and neighbors had been kind with their congratulations, seemingly unfazed by the fact that she had been dropped from the relay. It had been easy to slip back into her life, working and running, with little mention made of returning to school to complete her final year. For one thing, Mama and Papa counted on Louise's wages, but there was also the unspoken acknowledgment that Uncle Freddie's death had unmoored the family, made them concentrate on getting through each day one at a time and not ask too many hard requests of each other.

Once the shock of losing Uncle Freddie loosened its hold on Louise, she had realized what she needed to do to move ahead with a sense of purpose and hope. His death had given her the focus she needed to persist with running despite the disappointment she felt after Los Angeles. She often took out the photo he had given her and studied it before each race to remind herself that some sacrifices were bigger than her own hurt feelings.

As her parents regained their balance in the months following Uncle Freddie's death, it was clear they weren't going to tolerate any lapses in schooling with their younger children. Emily's deft fingers and clever eye for design had produced good income for the family over the years since she had begun taking in piecework, but she never slacked on her schoolwork. Two years after Louise should have graduated, Emily received her high school diploma, and her sartorial capabilities led to a job offer that any girl in town would have coveted: an apprenticeship in a milliner's studio. Emily made the most of the opportunity. As her skills increased, so did her income, not to mention her prospects. One night at a dance hall, she had caught the attention of a young man who worked as a waiter at a fancy hotel in Boston, and they had been going steady ever since. Louise couldn't quite suppress a pang of envy over the fact that it wouldn't be long until her sister announced an engagement, married, and moved out of their home.

Louise knew she shouldn't feel envious. She was twenty-two

and had a decent-paying job, and these days, any job was a prize. Moreover Mrs. Clark permitted her to leave work every afternoon to continue her training with Coach Quain and the Onteora Track Club. Since Los Angeles, she had continued to place well in races, even twice becoming the national champion in the 50-meter dash. After 1932, Mary Carew retired, but Louise continued to race against Olive Hasenfus. And much to the delight of Coach Quain, Louise's younger sister Julia also joined the Onteora Track Club to run and compete, but she never appeared fixated on racing, certainly not in the way that Louise had.

Julia was clever and had a good head for numbers, but with graduation less than two months away, her future remained unclear. College was unlikely for a girl without means, especially a black girl, and without a college degree, a job as a teacher or nurse was equally unlikely.

"Lou-ise," a familiar voice sang, interrupting Louise's thoughts.

From the shadows of a copse of trees at the other end of the park, Julia appeared, waving as she skipped toward them. "Yoo-hoo, girls, I have some lollys for you two sweeties."

Ann and Barbara clapped in delight at Julia's appearance, and she handed each girl a lollipop while making a show of admiring the piles of pebbles. "My goodness, you've both been busy. Look at all of this," she said, but the girls barely even registered their earlier occupation as they popped the sweets into their mouths.

"Thanks for providing distraction. Things were too peaceful here, and I was just waiting for an argument to break out," Louise said.

"Between those two angels? I don't believe it." Julia laughed as she patted both girls on their little blond heads before joining Louise on the bench, a smug look on her face. "So, guess what's happened?"

"What?"

"You know how Mrs. Jackson told me to come by for tea when I saw her at church on Sunday? I just stopped in to see her, and she's found a job for me this summer. I'm going to leave town."

"Really?" Louise hoped her expression looked enthusiastic, but a twinge of dread took form within her. Sometimes it felt as though everyone was moving on with their lives without her.

"Apparently her cousin owns an inn in Oak Bluffs on Martha's Vineyard and Mrs. Jackson put in a good word for me. They've offered me a spot as a chambermaid until Labor Day. Usually jobs start on Memorial Day, but they're making an exception for me, and I can come after graduation."

"My, that's wonderful," said Louise, tenting her hand over her eyes, ostensibly to watch the girls, but really to hide her disappointment from Julia. Oak Bluffs. Every black girl in Massachusetts knew its significance. The small beach town had become a summer haven for well-heeled black families. Judges, physicians, entertainers, even politicians, anyone who was anyone went to Oak Bluffs. After spending a summer there, Julia would return with connections and possibilities. Who knew what doors would open for her?

Louise swallowed, trying to push past her jealousy. Why should she envy Julia when Coach Quain had all but promised her a trip to the Olympic trials in Providence? For the last four years she had been readying herself to compete in Berlin. And not just compete, but win. So why did Julia's job in Oak Bluffs leave Louise with a sting of regret?

At that moment, Ann clapped her hand to her face and howled. Within seconds, her howl intensified into a scream as she tottered to her feet and stepped toward Louise and Julia, but as she moved forward, her toe caught on something, and the girl went down flat onto her face.

Louise leapt toward her. "Annie, you're fine. Let's take a look." She peeled the child from the grass and was met with a constellation of red welts rising on Ann's face, but more alarming was the blood pouring from the girl's chin. Blinking against her tears and blubbering, Ann stared from giant blue eyes filled with panic. Through the gash on her chin, Louise could see the white of bone.

Louise froze.

Her only movement was frantic swallowing against the rising bitter taste of fear in her throat.

It was as if she had been thrust underwater and lost all oxygen for a moment, but then, overtaken with a sense of resolve, she scrabbled for the surface. She yanked off the handkerchief she wore tied around her head and pressed it against the wound to stanch the bleeding.

"Bees! Bees! They got me!" Ann screeched as Louise pushed on the girl's chin. Immediately the dark blue handkerchief turned a dark plum color with Ann's blood.

"Julia." Louise kept her voice even. "Please go to Dr. Conway and tell him to meet me at Mrs. Clark's."

Julia, pale and stunned, nodded.

"Run," Louise commanded to her sister before leaning over Ann. "There, there, little one, you're fine."

Ann slackened in her arms, though whimpers made her chest tremble.

Louise raised her gaze to see Barbara wide-eyed and open-mouthed at the sudden ruinous state of her older sister. The little girl's face crumpled, but Miss Francine appeared at Barbara's side and she waved Louise on. "You go ahead and I'll follow with this one," she said.

Louise gripped Ann tightly and then broke into a jog across the park with the little girl draped across her arms. Suddenly Ann's hands began to claw at where Louise had the handkerchief pressed to her chin. The whimpers transformed to wheezing and she stared at Louise, her eyes desperate as she struggled to breathe.

What was happening?

Louise summoned every ounce of strength and speed and fled across the park and along the sidewalk, running the three blocks to the Clarks' house as if she were being chased by the devil himself. When the Clarks' mailbox became visible, Mrs. Clark and Dr. Conway appeared next to it. Both darted toward Louise.

"She can't breathe," Louise shouted raggedly.

"Annie, darling!" Mrs. Clark called, reaching her arms out for her daughter, but Dr. Conway put a hand on the woman's shoulder.

"Wait, Louise has a good grip on her," he said, his voice calm and authoritative. The three of them sprinted across the lawn toward Miss Mabel, who stood at the front door. "Clear the kitchen table and fetch some towels and pillows, please."

The housekeeper vanished inside. Dr. Conway, Mrs. Clark, and Louise followed.

"Keep the pressure on her chin, but avoid pressure on her throat," Dr. Conway said, ripping open the girl's dress to reveal her bare chest, which was clearly straining with exertion to breathe. "Ice, I need ice."

Miss Mabel spun to the icebox, pulled out a block of ice, and used a pick to chisel off several large pieces that she handed to the doctor. He began rubbing them along the girl's face and chest. Miss Mabel then tucked some pillows under the girl's legs to elevate them and handed Louise a fresh towel. Next Miss Mabel pulled an orange box of Arm & Hammer baking soda from a cupboard and mixed a paste for the stings.

All the while, Mrs. Clark fluttered behind them repeating, "What's happening? What's happening?" Her voice broke higher and higher each time she spoke.

"Sit," the doctor urged the woman without stepping away from Ann. "Catch your breath."

"But what happened?" Mrs. Clark asked frantically as Miss Mabel firmly pressed her into one of the kitchen chairs. "And where's Barbara?" she asked in a voice edged with hysteria as her eyes darted around the kitchen.

Louise gulped. The blood appeared to be staining the towel more slowly. "She's following behind with Miss Francine, the Fergusons' girl. She's fine. I wanted to move quickly—"

The distant sound of Constance's squalling cut through the house and Mrs. Clark's shoulders collapsed.

"Go to your baby," Dr. Conway said.

Mrs. Clark bit her lip, looking back and forth from Ann

to an indeterminate spot on the ceiling in the direction of the upstairs nursery. "I'll go, but only once that girl is away from my daughter."

Confused, Louise looked up to see Mrs. Clark glaring at her, fury mottling her face.

"This is all because of *you*." Mrs. Clark wept.

Never taking his eyes off Ann, Dr. Conway said, "Miss Mabel, take over so Louise can go home."

Miss Mabel moved beside Louise and her hands covered Louise's for a moment with a squeeze, before she nudged her aside.

Stunned, Louise backed away from the table. Suddenly she was also fighting for breath and she reached for her chest, her own hands slick with blood.

"I never want to see you again," Mrs. Clark spat at Louise.

Louise cast a helpless look at Ann, who lay on the table, seemingly lifeless, and fled out the back door. She raced toward home, ignoring the stares of people she passed. Her chest burned and tears streamed down her face. *Was Ann going to die?* When she returned home, Julia and Junior were sitting on the steps, waiting for her.

Julia sprang to her feet. "What's happened?"

Louise collapsed into Julia, burying her wet face into her sister's shoulder. "Everything's ruined."

39.

May 1936
Chicago

JIM DROVE BETTY TO THE 132ND INFANTRY ARMORY FOR the Central AAU Women's Track and Field Indoor Meet. Her breath fogged the window beside her, but she rubbed the condensation away and peeked outside, looking for Caroline and Tidye. Even after barely sleeping the night before, she felt wide awake and alert, as if electricity coursed through her veins instead of blood. She had developed a secret plan that would make her relay team win and increase their odds of receiving invitations to the Olympic trials, but now she needed to execute it.

This relay was her only chance.

A couple of weeks earlier, Coach Sheppard, her coach from the 1928 Olympics, had stopped by her home, the navy-blue blazer he wore with its AAU crest emblazoned on the chest looking crisp and a little intimidating.

"I've been hearing you want to give Berlin a try," he had said, sitting in the parlor with one of her mother's delicate teacups in his large hands.

"That's true. I've been training with Caroline Woodson,

though you probably knew her as Caroline Hale, and also Tidye Pickett."

He raised his eyebrows, confused. "Didn't Caroline have a baby?"

Betty pictured Joan's gummy grin and the way she waved her chubby arms overhead as the women ran past her on each lap. During the track practices, Joan either dozed in her pram or sat on a blanket watching her mother run while her father coached. "She has indeed, but it hasn't slowed her down in the least."

"But can you actually do it? You've fully recovered from your injuries?"

Betty stiffened. Yes, her back and knees ached, and her left shoulder felt tight no matter how much she stretched it, but she had come too far to lose heart now. "I'm stronger than ever. I'm ready." And as she spoke, she knew it was true. She *was* stronger, if not physically, certainly mentally.

"There are a lot of new fast girls running since you last competed in 1932. If you were to decide you'd still like to be involved in the AAU, but not race, I'm sure we could find something for you. Public speaking, maybe some assistant coaching."

"I want to try for one more Olympics."

"Betty, you're an important figure in track and field. I know you have a lot of fans, but do you think there might be something to be said for retiring at the top of your game? Leave everyone remembering your important run in Amsterdam? After all you've been through, getting to Berlin will be tough."

"Coach, after my crash, I was told I might never walk again, forget running. But here I am, ready to race." Her heart thudded in her chest as she spoke, but she pushed on. "You and I both know that winning at the Olympics is about more than physical superiority and conditioning. Only athletes who have the mental ability to tune out the distractions and noise will be successful in Berlin. I did that in Amsterdam and was one of the few Americans to win gold. I can do it again. If anything, my recovery should show you how strong I really am. I didn't get to where I am without focus and tenacity. I'm telling you, you need me there."

He studied her and cleared his throat. "Well, we'll see. There's the Central AAU meet coming up later this month. How about we give you a shot at it to see how you look? What do you say?"

"I want to do the relay. Caroline, Tidye, and I've been running well, and I think we'll win." She gazed at him with what she hoped was a steely glint. What she didn't mention was her inability to lower into a starting crouch without hurting her legs, but as long as she wasn't the first leg of the team, she could take advantage of the standing start positioning. No one would know of her limitation.

He placed his teacup down and crossed his arms. "Really? I admire your confidence. Who's going to be your fourth runner?"

His skepticism made her jaw tighten, but she had no intention of giving away her plan, so she demurred with a lighthearted laugh and wave of her hand. "Oh, we have a few ideas. When do I need to name the final runner?"

"I suppose you can wait until the evening of the event as long as you fill out an application and pay the event fee to hold a spot for your team."

Betty remained expressionless, but a wash of energy traveled through her as she considered her plan to win the relay. "I can do that. I'm in."

So here she was, sitting in the back seat of Jim's car next to her sister, Jean, outside the armory, the car's engine idling with its comforting hum. Jean exhaled from her Chesterfield and Betty inhaled the acrid smoke enviously. Maybe a cigarette would be just the thing to take the edge off her nerves, but before she could ask her sister for one, Jim clapped his hands together. "So, are we going to get this show on the road or sit here all night?"

Jean let out a hoot and nudged Betty. "Let's go!"

Betty reached for the door handle. How lucky she was to have them with her. Her legs trembled as she reached for her bag, but that didn't worry her. Nerves signaled excitement, and as long as they didn't get the better of her, all the sparks and jitters were good. Under the darkening gunmetal sky threatening rain, the three of them climbed from the car. This was it.

They hurried toward the entrance marked by the banners of the race's sponsors, the *Chicago Daily News* and the AAU Polish-American Union. Once inside, Betty exchanged quick embraces with her family and then pushed her way toward the locker room to dress.

BETTY, CAROLINE, AND Tidye stood on the side of the track, watching a tall woman practicing her starts.

"So, that's her?" Caroline asked.

The woman towered over the other runners near her. When

she turned in Betty's direction, the William Woods College lettering on her sweatshirt became visible.

"Yes," Betty said. "I'm going to talk with her."

"What if she says no?" Tidye asked.

"She won't," Betty said, hoping it was true.

"Good luck," Caroline shouted over the noise of the crowd as Betty wended her way toward Helen.

Up close, the Missourian appeared to be a giant. When she caught sight of Betty, she stopped practicing. "Hey, you're Betty Robinson, aren't you? You're here! I've been hoping to meet you."

Betty felt her face redden. "Yes, I'm Betty."

"I left my autograph book in my track bag, but would you mind signing it later?" Helen's voice was surprisingly deep, but friendly.

"Of course."

"Holy cats, this is exciting!"

For all the hype surrounding her, Helen appeared a little awkward, but genuine. Her big-toothed grin was unselfconscious, and Betty couldn't help feeling tender toward the younger woman. Her enthusiasm loosened a little part of Betty, the final piece of her that had remained locked, protecting her against disappointment, and she found herself smiling back.

"Do you know if Stella Walsh is here?" Helen asked. "With the Polish-American Club sponsoring this, I hoped she'd come. She's been saying all kinds of stuff about me to the newspapers and I'd sure like to beat her again tonight." Helen suddenly looked stricken. "I mean, I'm not trying to boast, but I'd sure like to show that lady what happened a year ago in St. Louis wasn't a fluke."

"It looks like you'll have to wait, but from everything I've read, you're a shoo-in for Berlin."

"Oh, I hope so. So what events are you in today?"

"Only the 4-x-100-meter relay."

"You're not doing the individual hundred-meter?"

"No." Betty licked her lips and took the plunge on the plan she had been hatching for months. "Listen, we could use a fourth on our relay team and I wondered if you'd be willing to anchor for us?"

Helen studied her up and down and was about to say something, but the announcer's voice crackled over the PA system: "Calling all runners in the special invitational fifty-yard dash to the starting area for check-in."

Hearing the call for her race, Helen began unbuttoning her sweatshirt and yanking it off. "That's me, I've got to go. My coach will kill me if I miss my start," she said, dropping to a bench to pull off her navy-blue sweatpants before hopping to her feet again. She held her warm-ups in her hands, her expression frantic as she glanced around the starting area for a place to put her things.

"Here, hand those to me. I'll stow everything under that bench." Betty pointed to a spot next to them.

"Thanks." Helen handed her the wad of clothing. "This is my first meet without my coach and I guess I'm a bit on the ragged edge."

"You'll be fine. Good luck," Betty called.

Helen ran toward her start, but called to Betty. "And yes, I'll run the relay with you. I've never been on a team before." She grinned and leapt over a hurdle on the side of the track, revealing a long and easy stride that could have easily measured seven or eight feet long.

Betty shook her head in admiration. She pitied Helen's opponents.

BETTY FOUND A spot on the sideline where she could sit and stretch but still have a good view of the races on the track. Tidye and Caroline left periodically for their races, but Betty's only race was the last one of the evening, so she had several hours to think about the relay.

She kept an eye on the results of Helen's preliminary heats. Sure enough, the girl from Missouri won everything and earned herself a spot in the finals in the 50-yard dash and the 100-yard and 200-yard sprints. Betty liked their chances for the relay. Helen appeared, pushing through the crowd, and found Betty sitting with her friends.

"Here she is, our anchor! You made easy work of all of your races tonight. Well done," Betty cheered before introducing Helen to Tidye and Caroline.

"Thanks. So I've never run a relay before. What do I need to know?" Helen asked.

"We don't have much time, but let's go outside to the sidewalk, so we can show you how the transitions work," Betty said, leading her teammates through the spectators and the front door of the armory. "Caroline, do you have the baton and chalk?"

"I do." Caroline handed Betty the baton while she took several long paces to measure the relay's transition distance and marked the starting and finishing lines with chalk on the sidewalk. When she finished, Betty explained the strict rules surrounding baton hand-offs.

"The first thing to know is that you have to stay calm and trust your teammates. It's when runners allow pressure and anxiety to get to them that there are problems, but with some practice, you'll be fine. Look, Caroline and I will demonstrate. I'll be you, Helen. Start here and take a few steps to get momentum. As Caroline approaches, she'll call 'Up!' and you will reach back with your left hand, palm open. Like this," Betty said, going through all the motions with Caroline.

"You don't look backward to see where the baton is? You just look ahead?" Helen asked, frowning.

"Yes, trust Caroline," said Betty. "You have nice big hands so it shouldn't be a problem. Just open your palm wide and be ready to feel the baton. When you've got it, seize it and run. You're our last runner so you won't have to hand it to anyone. All you need to practice is receiving it. How about you two give it a try?"

Betty and Tidye stepped aside and let the two other women practice. On their first run, Helen fumbled the baton and dropped it.

"Sorry," she said, lifting it from the sidewalk with an embarrassed grin on her face.

"We can try it again, don't worry," said Caroline. "It's dark out here so that makes it difficult."

It took the women several more tries to pass it off smoothly, but Betty noticed Helen was struggling to stay within the regulation zone when taking the baton.

"Helen, you've got long strides so you're going to have to be careful. Do it quickly," Betty urged.

"I'm having trouble not looking back to see where it is," Helen confessed. "And it feels awkward to hold it in my left hand."

"That's understandable, but you'll get used to it," Betty called out as they took position to try again.

After several more unsuccessful hand-offs, Caroline shot a frustrated look at Betty. "Isn't it time to head back for the individual finals?" she asked.

Betty feigned a glance at her watch. No matter what time it said, she knew they were done. "Yes, we should go inside."

"These relays always look a lot easier than they actually are." Helen wiped her hand across her forehead. "What if I can't do this?"

"Don't worry, even if you have to start running from a standstill, you're fast enough to make it up and we'll be fine. Just try not to drop it," Caroline answered.

Helen bit her lip. "I'm going inside to get ready for my finals."

"Good luck," Betty and the others called as Helen hurried away.

Tidye tapped on Betty's arm. "Why's this proving so hard? Hand-offs are always tricky, but maybe we've made the wrong choice with her. Maybe she's better on her own."

Betty smiled, hoping she didn't look as anxious as she felt. "She'll be fine. It'll be easier inside, where the lighting is better." She forced a laugh. "And I've worked too hard to be denied advancement now. We'll do it."

Tidye turned to head to the locker room, but she hesitated. "It's never too late for them to deny us advancement. You understand that, right?"

Betty fought the urge to sigh and tried to sound upbeat. She knew what had happened in Los Angeles with the relay. "We'll be fine. Really. Helen can do this."

Tidye's expression remained dubious, but she nodded and walked away.

Betty settled on a bench next to the track and twisted her wristwatch up and down her forearm as she watched Caroline meet with the other hurdlers in preparation for their upcoming heat. She needed the relay to go well. It was her only event, and AAU officials would be watching the results closely.

HELEN REGRETTED HER agreement to run the relay. After she left Betty and the other girls outside, she assembled with the finalists of the 50-yard dash and tried to push her thoughts of the disastrous outdoor practice runs from her mind so she could focus on the races ahead.

During the first few steps of her 50-yard-dash final, she nearly tripped but still managed to win, though it was closer than it should have been.

Her 100-yard and 200-yard races went better and she won both, but she couldn't shake the sense of feeling jittery and off-pace.

Normally she would have been delighted with her victories, but with the relay approaching, all she felt was dread. When she was racing by herself, she knew she could win, but why was she so bad at the relay? Maybe it was the pesky baton's fault;

it felt odd to carry anything extra when she ran. She liked the freedom of feeling light and unencumbered, but she had told the girls she would do it so she had no other choice.

By the side of the track, Helen spotted Betty stretching and her stomach twisted with anxiety. She had admired Betty for so long and had been so excited to meet her. What if she disappointed her?

Betty was even prettier in real life than she looked in the newspapers, but it certainly wasn't a classic type of beauty that made her attractive. Her chin was pointy and her smile was even a bit crooked, yet her blue eyes sparkled and her smile had an unexpected power, a way of making you feel like you were the best of friends after only seconds of meeting. Betty had a field of gravity wholly unto herself, and Helen was being pulled into her orbit. And it wasn't a bad feeling. Truth be told, Helen felt a little shaky upon meeting Betty; yes, part of that came from being intimidated, but mostly it was the type of shaky that came over her when she was thrilled.

For the final event of the evening, the judges brought the six relay teams together and reminded everyone of the rules. The other women appeared to know what they were doing and a familiar feeling crept over Helen. She tried to concentrate on what the man was saying, but she felt like she wasn't fitting in and was out of her element. Why was she doing this?

When the official dismissed the women, Betty gathered Helen and the two others. "Ladies, this is our race. If you have to sacrifice a little speed during transitions to get the baton, do it. How about we change up our race order? I'll switch with Caroline, so I'll do the hand-off to you, Helen. Sound good?"

Helen's mouth felt dry. "But I didn't practice with you. I was having enough trouble getting it right with Caroline; do you think it's a good idea to change things even more?"

Betty's cheerful expression hardened into something more serious. "Helen, I have complete faith in you. Listen for my command and then run like the wind when I hand the baton to you. You can do this."

Suddenly Helen's legs felt waterlogged.

"Good luck, girls!" Betty called to Caroline and Tidye as she took Helen's arm and marched her down the track toward their starting areas.

"Doesn't the captain usually run the first leg? Why aren't you starting us off?" Helen asked.

"Since my crash, I can't do the starter's crouch comfortably anymore. It hurts my back and legs, so I'm avoiding it. That's why I'm not running any individual races tonight. This is it for me. I'm trying out how it feels to race again tonight."

Helen glanced to the men lining the edge of the track, writing in notebooks. Seeing the AAU officials made something click into place in Helen's head. These women needed her. This race was important for their chances to be invited to the Olympic trials, and it was especially critical to Betty. Helen felt her shoulder being squeezed and looked down to see Betty studying her.

"Let's show everyone what you can do tonight. All I've been hearing is that my chances of running again are over, but we're going to win this, don't you think?"

"Yes, we are," Helen said, jogging away to take her place around the curve. Her legs still trembled, but she felt resolved now. She would not disappoint Betty.

Minutes later, the starting gun fired. Tidye's legs wheeled around the first curve in a blur and Helen couldn't even make out the baton transition to Caroline because they did it so seamlessly. Helen's muscles tightened with the recollection of how she had failed the transition practice outside, but at the same time, Betty had the baton and was barreling toward her with a look of startling determination. Helen needed to loosen and face down the track, away from the women coming in, but she took one final glance over her shoulder. If Betty could run like that after all she had been through, Helen couldn't fail her. She turned and stared at the finish ribbon. The noise of the crowd felt like it was bouncing off every surface of the building. What if she couldn't hear Betty's command? She squeezed her eyes shut for a moment and then Betty's voice pierced through everything.

"UP!"

Helen smiled, took a step forward, and pushed her hand back, but didn't dare start running. A stampede of runners crashed upon her, and when the baton slammed into her hand Helen lurched into running, looking for the regulation relay lines. She couldn't find them, but with the air thick with the swarm of bodies converging on her, there was no time to spare. It was a rocky beginning but she leapt into her stride and took off. Once she was moving, her unsteadiness vanished. She ran toward the finish line, and as the tape stretched across her chest, she raised her arms. *They had done it!* Lungs heaving, Helen slowed. When she stopped, Tidye, Caroline, and Betty were surrounding her, laughing and cheering and hugging.

"Better check to see if you left scorch marks along that final lane," Caroline shouted.

"Good thing I didn't knock you over when I ran into you." Betty laughed.

"Ha, if anything, I'm worried that I might have hurt you during that crash," Helen said, soaking in the exuberance of the victory. "Are you all right?"

"I'm fine. I'm better than fine! I feel wonderful!"

The minutes after the relay were a whirlwind of congratulations and backslapping. The women were ushered into the locker room, where they cleaned off and changed, all giddy with the thrill of winning. Helen buttoned herself into her dove-gray serge dress, feeling nearly limp with relief that the relay was over with no mishaps.

Betty appeared at her side, straightening her skirt. "So, do you have any plans now? What do you say we go out and celebrate?"

Helen couldn't believe her luck. "That would be swell. My coach ended up having to go back to Missouri because his wife went into labor with their first baby so I'm on my own, staying in a boardinghouse down by the university."

"We can go somewhere nearby."

"Count me in."

Moments later, Helen gathered outside on the sidewalk with Betty, Caroline, and a tall man introduced as Howard, Caroline's husband. The rain had held off and the wind that buffeted them felt chilly yet refreshing. "I'll bet we can find a place to eat if we head toward the city," Betty said, pointing toward lights down the street. Tidye had needed to go home, but the rest of the group set off in that direction.

"Goodness, I think I need to take four steps to every one of yours," said Betty, skipping to keep pace with Helen.

"Sorry." Helen slowed, her face reddening. She took a look at Betty, marveling that the woman whose face had graced her childhood bedroom's wall in Fulton for years was now beside her—in the flesh!

"Don't be sorry. Your long stride is"—Betty shook her head—"amazing."

"Thanks." Helen was searching her mind for what she could say, something interesting and witty, when they passed a little joint with a sign lit up in the window saying *BAR*.

"What do you think? How about we head in here?" Betty asked.

"That's certainly *not* where my coach and his wife take me after races." Helen laughed and then pointed to a placard in the window: *No unescorted ladies will be served*. "But what about that?"

"You forget, we've got Howard with us," Betty said.

Caroline and Howard lagged behind, walking arm in arm, so close their heads practically touched, and Helen studied them with a dart of longing. To be a competitive athlete and have found love—what a lucky life Caroline led.

"If this is what you city folks do, then count me in," Helen said as they entered the low-ceilinged dim interior. Only a few men sat at stools around the bar and the handful of tables were open. Along with a haze of cigarette smoke, a scratchy recording of "Blue Moon" drifted over the place from a gramophone.

Howard left the women as he went off to find the men's restroom, and Betty plunked her pocketbook onto a table and began to pull off her coat.

"Think they serve food here? I'm famished," Helen said.

"If they do, I'm not sure you'll want to eat it," Caroline answered, pulling a lipstick from her handbag and quickly tracing it over her lips.

Helen chuckled. "You'd be surprised. I'll eat anything."

"We'll just have one drink and then go find food."

A bartender arrived at their table wiping his hands on the small apron he wore around his thick waist. "Well, well, what are the three of you doing in a place like this?"

Betty said, "We just won races up the street at the armory. We're here to celebrate."

The man cocked an eyebrow. "What kinda races?"

"Running. You can read all about it in tomorrow's papers," Helen said.

"We don't serve unescorted dames here. I could lose my license," the bartender growled.

"Well, we're in luck then, because here comes my husband." Caroline pointed to Howard as he reappeared.

"You're with these ladies?" the bartender asked Howard, making it clear by his unamused expression that he considered Caroline, Betty, and Helen to be anything but ladies.

"I am." Howard smirked at the women, removing his fedora with a flourish.

"Fine. What'll it be?"

"We'll have three extra-dry martinis," Betty said without looking at a menu. "I'll take extra olives in mine, please."

"You got it," the man said, glaring at Betty before turning to Howard. "You?"

"A Manhattan, please."

The bartender gave them all a final contemptuous look and lumbered to the bar. Caroline wrinkled her nose. "I almost wish Howard wasn't with us, just so we could have picked more of a fight with him."

"I'd rather not have to bail you out of jail, my dear," Howard said.

"What's in a martini, anyway?" Helen asked.

"Don't worry, you'll like it." Betty lit a cigarette.

Helen looked around at the dark walls of the bar and the scuffed floor and shrugged. She pulled a cocktail napkin closer and began to tear little pieces off its corner. "You should have seen the list of things my coach left me to think about before my race. A lot of it is stuff he usually does for me, like asking about the schedule, how many qualify from each heat to advance, all those details. And then there are strategy suggestions like making sure I pay attention to my early throws because those count and trying to avoid the outside lanes on the track." By now she had torn the napkin to shreds, and she knew she was talking too much, but she couldn't stop. "He also wrote, 'The best always get beat—prolong it as long as possible.'"

Betty swept the destroyed napkin into her palm before dumping it into her pocket. "Don't worry. At some point, everyone loses. That's what competition is all about."

Helen chewed on her lower lip, grateful that she hadn't caused them to lose the relay. Running races by herself was easier. It felt great to be surrounded by teammates, but worrying that she'd let people down caused too much stress. And honestly, she didn't want to rely on anyone else either. It felt much safer to go it alone. "I guess so, but I really don't want to lose to Stella Walsh. She's the worst."

"Clearly you've never met Babe Didrikson," Caroline grumbled.

"But Stella's such a loner," Betty said. "She never seems to have anyone at races with her and she always vanishes afterward, never talks to anyone. She doesn't seem to have any friends. Now that I think about it, I've never seen her so much as laugh."

Caroline considered this. "You're right. She's certainly different."

At her mention of *different,* Helen became wary. "What do you mean?"

"When I think back to Los Angeles, she had a room to herself at the Chapman Park, where all of us gals were staying, but we never saw her. Even when she won the gold in the hundred-meter, she didn't celebrate. She just left the stadium immediately and disappeared, even wearing her track clothes out onto the street afterward. She's aloof, a loner."

"Do you think it's by choice?" Helen asked.

"Well, she doesn't make things easy for herself. I mean, her choice to race for Poland hasn't endeared her to anyone."

"Why did she do that?" Helen asked.

"They offered her money." Caroline shrugged. "She needs to make a living and it's hard to do that as an athlete, especially a woman athlete."

"But I think it was more than that," Betty mused. "She doesn't seem to belong anywhere. She's lived in Cleveland for ages but doesn't embrace this country, and yet she doesn't really seem to be Polish either. Helen, think about it: Didn't it feel strange to be on your own today?"

"It wasn't as much fun as when Coach Moore's around, that's for sure."

"Exactly. Racing unattached from a team, not having a coach, all of that can feel isolating, so we avoid doing it, but that's how Stella races all the time. It must be hard."

The bartender returned with four glasses balanced on his tray and placed them on the table, sloshing each one slightly, but he made no move to clean up the mess. "This is it. No more drinks this evening. These three ladies shouldn't be here, mister. I don't care how well they did tonight in a race."

Howard stirred his drink. "Got it. I appreciate your enlightenment."

The bartender frowned, but shuffled away.

"I'll bet he's in the back room now looking up the word *enlightenment* in the dictionary," Howard said. The women giggled.

"To tonight's win," said Betty, lifting her drink toward Caroline, Helen, and Howard.

Helen's eyes widened as she drank from her glass, and she could see Caroline and Betty exchange amused glances. The drink spilled down her throat and burned and it may have even taken the roof of her mouth off, but she liked it. She wasn't afraid of its heat. Before she knew it, she had downed the whole thing, and a warm sense of relaxation spread through her. She could get used to this.

After a few minutes and more contemptuous looks from the barkeep, the group finished their drinks and went outside to the sidewalk. Helen looked at Caroline's and Betty's faces reflecting the lights within the bar and a sense of expansive affection came over her. She had meant to have Betty sign her autograph book, but she didn't feel like digging around in her bag to get it out. And she wasn't worried. After tonight's success, she suspected she'd be seeing Betty in Providence.

40.

June 1936
Malden, Massachusetts

LOUISE TOOK A JOB IN THE LAUNDRY. THE WORK LEFT her hands chafed with lye and seared with angry burns, but it was a job. A job without responsibility for anyone else but herself. Now she understood what Mama meant when she had said it was a relief to not become entangled in another family's affairs. Deep in the dark humid recesses of the laundry rooms, Louise told herself she couldn't hurt or disappoint anyone.

The night after that terrible day in the park, Dr. Conway had arrived at the Stokes home. His skin appeared sallow and bags hung under his eyes. He found Louise in the kitchen, sitting at the table with Mama and Julia, listless. He greeted Mama with a respectful nod and cleared his throat. "Ann Clark is fine now. Her throat opened back up so her breathing stabilized, I stitched up her chin, and she's exhausted, but she'll be back to herself in no time."

Louise would have thought she didn't have more tears to shed, but somehow, she did. Her head dropped to her arms and she sobbed.

The doctor rested his hand on Louise's back. "That little girl is lucky she was with you. It was an accident, not your fault. Your calm reaction and speed saved her life, and I've made that clear to the Clarks in no uncertain terms."

"Yet you sent me away when I was helping."

"I was trying to protect you."

"But Mrs. Clark fired me."

Dr. Conway rubbed his hand over his face. "I know. Maybe once she's had some time to collect herself, she'll rethink that choice."

But Dr. Conway's words meant nothing to Louise. She knew it had been an accident. Rationally, she understood this, but it didn't matter. She *felt* guilty. It was as if Ann's accident slit open all of her emotional scars from Grace's death and left the wound gaping, raw and bleeding.

Since that day in the park with Ann Clark, Louise had moved through her days as if in a trance. It had been several years since Louise had replayed the memory of finding Grace, but the routine returned to her that night and she slept poorly. Exhausted, she stopped attending track practices. Mrs. Brown, the woman who owned the laundry, went to the same church as the Stokeses, and as word got around about what had happened with the accident, she had been quick to offer Louise a job. It was fortunate that Mrs. Brown took a sympathetic view of the situation, because Louise was hardly a model worker. She was distracted and directions became jumbled in her mind. Batches of laundry got mixed together and customers complained of missing items. She spilled water on the floor, making it easy for the other laundresses to slip.

"Girl, you're going to hurt yourself if you don't start paying attention to what you're doing," Mrs. Brown had scolded after Louise dumped a load of sheets into a vat of boiling water with a large splash.

Louise didn't even care. She deserved to be hurt. She could see concerned expressions on the other women's faces and wished she were invisible.

After two weeks or so—Louise couldn't be sure how much time had passed—Mrs. Clark arrived in the entrance of the laundry, fanning herself against the heat. "May I please speak to Louise Stokes?" she asked.

Mrs. Brown waved her hand toward the door in approval and Louise wiped her apron across her face. Walking toward Mrs. Clark to step outside and stand in the fresh air, her knees felt as though they had turned to jelly.

Mrs. Clark wore a well-tailored walking suit and her hair, face, hands—everything about her—looked as impeccably groomed as always, but her eyes appeared dull. She pulled a soft linen handkerchief embroidered with delicate flowers from her pocketbook and handed it to Louise.

Louise hesitated before taking it from her and dabbing it to the back of her neck.

"Louise, I've come here to say that we need you back. The girls miss you terribly."

"The girls miss me?" Louise echoed numbly.

Mrs. Clark bit her lip. "What I mean to say is that we all miss you. What happened with Ann was an accident. It wasn't your fault, and I regret some of the detestable things that I said. I wish you'd come back. You've been a great help to me over the years, and I'm very grateful for that."

"Did you know I lost a little sister? She died." As soon as the words left her mouth, Louise wanted to take them back. Why was she telling Mrs. Clark, a woman who had never shown any genuine interest in her, about the most painful moment of her life? Mrs. Clark flinched and somehow this calmed Louise. It gave her a sense of hurting the woman a little and, though she wasn't proud of this, it bolstered her.

"I didn't know that. I'm sorry."

"She had just turned three and was playing with matches. I was supposed to be watching her, but I'd gone outside for a moment. When I came back in, I found her on the kitchen floor, burning, and tried to put out the flames, but I wasn't fast enough." Tears welled in Mrs. Clark's eyes, and Louise kept talking, describing what she saw before she fell asleep each night. "She was wearing her favorite dress, a pretty light blue dress, the color of the sky, but it was on fire. When I finally got the flames out, I left my younger sisters and brother with her while I ran to get Dr. Conway. But Grace died a couple of days later."

"I'm so sorry. How old were you?"

"Eight."

Mrs. Clark gave a small sob. "But it was an accident. You were so young."

"Knowing something was an accident doesn't make it any easier."

"I'm sorry, Louise. I'm sorry for all of it." Mrs. Clark put her arms around Louise and the two hung together. Louise wept for Grace, and for Ann, and for herself, and it made her feel better that Mrs. Clark was weeping too because she wanted the woman to see her, to know her, and to understand what Ann's accident had meant to her.

A knot inside of Louise's chest released, and she took a deep breath, the first one in ages. "I'd like to come back," she said hesitantly, but her agreement did not quite feel right and she thought for a moment. "I'll work for you until the first of July, but then I need to find something new. A fresh start."

NORMALLY WHEN LOUISE left the laundry for the day, she dragged herself home, wrung out and wilted, but after Mrs. Clark's visit, she finished her shift and went home with a clear heart and feeling unburdened. She had talked about the most painful moment of her life, one she blamed herself for, and wasn't met with condemnation. Mrs. Clark, a woman who had always been unyielding in bestowing any sign of connection, had been sympathetic. Louise now could understand what had happened through the eyes of someone else. She had been young. Would she have blamed Ann if something had happened to Barbara? Of course not. She saw this now, and while the realization brought her a measure of freedom, she knew her guilt wouldn't vanish overnight. She'd have to be patient, and being patient with herself didn't come naturally, but ambling along the sidewalk, she felt lighter. She tilted her chin toward the sun and savored the warm breeze that blew down the street. She was eager to see the Clark girls again, but it was time to find a new job. A new opportunity. She didn't know what it would be yet, but she needed a change. The prospect of possibility rippled through her, gave her a lift.

When she arrived at the house, the front door flew open and

Junior tore out of it and down the steps waving a letter in his hands. Mama appeared behind him and stood in the doorway, a broad smile splitting her face.

"Look what's arrived! Look!" Junior yelled. "You've qualified for the Olympic trials!"

Louise took the letter and read through it. As she had known they should have, her racing results from the winter and spring seasons had qualified her for Providence. Now she actually believed it.

PART 4

July–August 1936

THE PROVIDENCE DAILY SUN

"Missouri Girl Smashes World Record"
July 5, 1936

Providence—Missouri's Helen Stephens kept yesterday's meager crowd of 2,000 spectators at Brown University's stadium
riveted as she won all three of her events as a one-woman
track team from William Woods College. The girl known as
the Fulton Flash set a blistering pace in the 100-meter dash
to finish five yards ahead of the second-place racer, Chicago
native Annette Rogers. Her time clipped a tenth of a second
off Stella Walsh's previous best time of 11.8 seconds and set a
new record. Handling the competition with ease, the eighteen-
year-old also won the discus and shot put.

Dee Boeckmann, the first woman to coach an Olympic track
and field team, narrowed the field of 115 athletes to a mere 20
Olympic team members, but the status of these ladies is not
yet secure because budget shortfalls may force the American
Olympic Committee to limit the number of athletes receiving
sponsorship to Berlin. At this point, the 20 women will travel
to New York City to await the AOC's confirmation on who will
travel to Germany to compete. The group contains many familiar faces, including Betty Robinson, the 1928 Olympic gold
medalist who survived a plane crash. She came in fifth in the
final heat of the individual 100-meter race and is included in

the relay pool. Fellow Chicagoans Tidye Pickett and Annette Rogers competed strongly and are also on Boeckmann's proposed roster for the relay pool.

Also a favored relay racer, Louise Stokes, the Malden Meteor, won both of her preliminary heats in the sprint with exceptional times, but she could not overcome the costly mistake of looking over her shoulder and almost stumbling into the last spot during the finals.

In a surprising development, several mothers performed admirably and could be on their way to the Olympics. After winning the 80-meter hurdles, tall and bespectacled Mrs. Anne Vrana O'Brien shifted her serious demeanor as she gushed, "I've never run so fast since my girl was born, two and a half years ago." Plucky Mrs. Caroline Hale Woodson, a team favorite and silver medalist from the 1932 Olympics, came in fourth in the 80-meter hurdles. When asked how she maintains her training with motherhood, she said, "I run while my daughter naps in her pram parked next to the track."

In a touching scene of maternal joy, Mrs. O'Brien, Mrs. Woodson, and Mrs. Gertrude Wilhelmsen of Puyallup, WA, who placed second in the discus and third in the javelin, compared photographs of their daughters. "I've already taught my girl to swim," Mrs. Wilhelmsen boasted. If they advance to Berlin, only time will tell if these women are capable of focusing on the competition at hand without becoming distracted or distraught by the absence of their children.

41.

July 6, 1936
New York City

A FLEET OF TAXICABS CROSSED MIDTOWN HEADING toward Times Square and screeched to a halt in front of the Lincoln Hotel. Betty stepped from one and Dee Boeckmann, Annette Rogers, and Olive Hasenfus spilled out behind her. Item by item, the cabbie disgorged suitcases, dropped them on the sidewalk, and turned toward Dee, his hand outstretched impatiently awaiting payment.

At the same instant, a dented black Ford coughed its way into the melee of idling vehicles and Helen leaned out the window, her eyes round and glittering. "Hey, fancy meeting you here. So this is the big leagues now, huh?" Without awaiting an answer, she threw her door open, oblivious to the crush of people and luggage on the sidewalk, and looked upward, squinting. "Whoa, I've never been inside such a tall building."

"Even when you've gone to Chicago or Toronto for races?" asked Betty.

"Nope. This is a first."

A handsome man rounded the front bumper, his light blue eyes glittering with mischief. "So what do you think, Helen?

Can I be sure that you're actually going to make it onto that boat next week? There are a lot of distractions around here."

"I'll say, but I'll do better on the track than in a dance hall. Don't worry, Coach, I'll stay on the straight and narrow. Now let me introduce you to my friend Miss Robinson." She turned to Betty. "This is my coach, Mr. Burton Moore."

"The honor is all mine," he said, tipping his hat.

Betty shook his hand. "So this is the end of the line for you?"

"Afraid so."

Betty shaded her eyes with her hand and was able to see a pretty woman sitting in the front seat of the Ford with a baby in her arms. Through the dusty windshield, she waved.

All of a sudden, Helen appeared to bite the inside of her mouth and looked surprisingly uncertain. "Coach, thanks for everything. Be sure that no one forgets about me while I'm gone."

"First thing I'll do when we get home is to go talk to the mayor and get the boosters to send you more money. You're going to need it."

"Thanks." Helen hefted a battered valise from the back seat of the car. She leaned into the window to kiss Mrs. Moore. Betty watched, pulling her pocketbook closer to her chest and envying the ease with which they discussed securing more funds. She had only three measly dollars left. How on earth would she afford traveling back to Chicago if she didn't make it to Berlin?

Pushing her money worries to the furthest recesses of her mind, Betty allowed herself to be swept into the hotel by her teammates and porters in burgundy uniforms. The high-ceilinged lobby gleamed with marble floors and mirrors with beveled edges lining its walls. Ficus trees poked out of large ceramic chinoiserie-patterned planters, and a crystal chandelier hung from the center of the ceiling.

At the elevator, Betty paused and turned to see Helen stopped, gaping at the grand decor of the lobby. "Helen? You coming?"

Helen turned in a full circle, taking it all in one more time before bounding toward where the women waited for her. Then they pressed themselves into the confines of the elevator and headed skyward with a jolt. At the seventh floor, they flooded into the hallway, stopping in front of room 704. Annette unlocked the door and Betty, Helen, and Olive followed her inside to find two double-size beds covered in claret-colored damask bedcovers, a walnut-colored wardrobe and dresser, and a small washroom with a claw-footed tub.

"It's tight, but we can make do," Betty said.

Helen crossed the room, pulled open the curtains, and arched her neck to look below. "Wonder what it would be like to stay all the way up on the twenty-seventh floor."

"Expensive," Olive answered, dropping her suitcase on the floor next to one of the beds. "What's this?" she asked, lifting a paper from off the bed's pillow and reading it.

"What do you have there?" asked Betty.

Olive held up a typewritten letter and a colorful flyer. "It's a letter from the American Jewish Labor Committee urging us to boycott the Olympics and a flyer about an event called the Counter-Olympics being held here in August." She handed the documents to Helen, who took them and dropped to one of the beds.

Helen spent a few minutes reading through the letter. "They certainly have a point. Have any of you read *Mein Kampf*?"

"Mine what?" Annette asked.

"It's Adolf Hitler's political manifesto." At the mystified expressions on the other women's faces, she frowned. "It's full of hatred toward anyone who's not what he considers to be pure-blooded German and outlines his ideas about how this Aryan so-called master race must rise up and exterminate all lesser people, especially Jews."

The other women gave one another uneasy sideways glances. Even in the stuffy confines of the small room, a chill passed over Betty. "Since when has running had anything to do with politics?" she asked.

Helen gave Betty an incredulous look. "The Olympics have *everything* to do with politics. Haven't you been reading the newspapers?"

Betty shook her head slowly. Sometimes she read the sports pages, but beyond that? No. She tried to affect a playful tone in an attempt to downplay the nagging sense of having overlooked something important. "The news is always depressing, and it makes me feel dreadfully helpless so I've been focusing on what I'm good at: running. I'll leave the big decisions to the people in charge." She stole a look at Olive and Annette. They were both nodding along with her, their faces red with embarrassment.

"And anyway, why would we boycott?" Annette asked. "We've worked so hard to compete. It seems like this boycott would be punishing us more than anyone."

"Chancellor Hitler, the man who's leading Germany, has instituted all kinds of policies that discriminate against Jews and other groups in the country. There was a lot of debate about this boycott last December and the issue came to a vote. Avery

Brundage, the head of the AOC, argued that the U.S. should participate because amateur sports should be used to bond us all together globally."

"That seems reasonable," Annette said.

"But our participation in these games gives Hitler legitimacy. At least, that's what the president of the AAU argued. His side lost the boycott vote by only a couple of votes. It was close."

Annette grimaced. "It does sound like this Hitler fellow is trouble."

"Yes, he most certainly is," Helen said.

"But why should we get involved in what another country's doing? It doesn't feel like any of our business," Olive said. "And we've got plenty of problems of our own to focus on. I practically had to call everyone in my town to raise the money for this. All my neighbors are broke."

Helen placed the letter and the flyer on the bed beside her and looked at her teammates. "Well, what this letter is telling us is that we're being given a choice about competing in Berlin and with that choice comes a little bit of power. We should all be thinking about what we're going to do with it."

An awkward silence descended over the group.

There was a knock at the door and Annette opened it. Caroline stood in the doorway, a worried look on her face. "Dee has just called for a team meeting in the hotel's dining room."

"Did she say what it's about?" asked Betty.

"Be downstairs in ten minutes. The AOC has decided not to take all of us to Berlin. She's going to announce the new, smaller team."

42.

July 6, 1936
New York City

HELEN LEANED AGAINST THE WALL OF THE HOTEL'S dining room, trying to be inconspicuous. She felt confident that she would be traveling to Berlin, but who else would be joining her?

She watched the women filing in and thought of the boycott letter upstairs in their room, cringing. Why had she bothered to explain Hitler's manifesto? Everyone had been so excited to make the team. Why did she have to be serious and bookish and make everyone nervous? Her teammates were already nervous enough about this budget shortfall business. Even Betty, who tried so hard to be kind to Helen, even *she* had looked mortified on Helen's behalf.

Dee entered the room and sat. With barely a glance at the collection of women gathered around her, she started reading from a piece of paper. "Ladies, I have news from the AOC. It's with great regret that I'm here to inform you that the committee has insufficient funds to pay for a full team to travel to Germany. The committee reviewed the results from Providence and has decided to focus on individual events. Full travel funding will be provided for the following athletes: Helen Stephens, Tidye Pickett, Kathlyn Kelley, Annette Rogers, and Anne O'Brien, all of whom had outstanding finishes at the Olympic trials and represent our country's best shot at medals." She stopped reading and cautiously raised her gaze to sweep over the athletes to gauge their reaction.

Astonishment rendered the group silent. Helen swallowed and kept her gaze trained on Dee. *Only five of the women would be going to Berlin?*

Dee cleared her throat and continued reading her speech. "But athletes who can raise five hundred dollars of their own funds to underwrite their travel will be permitted to come and compete."

At this, indignation buzzed through the room.

"Who has five hundred dollars to spare?"

"Why did they get our hopes up?"

Dee's hand that held her speech dropped to her side and anguish crumpled her face. "Ladies, I'm so sorry. I didn't expect this either. I know the disappointment many of you must feel. Back in 1924, I qualified to go to the Olympics in Paris, but the U.S. decided not to field a women's team and I was stuck at home. Because of that, I wanted to bring as many of you as possible. But I want to make it clear that the AOC is taking its budget shortfall seriously and it extends to all of us. It's covering my travel expenses, but I won't be paid any coaching salary."

The outbursts quieted as the women considered this.

"Do other teams have to do this fund-raising too?" Olive asked.

"Not all of them, no. Some are able to pay for themselves

because they raise enough money on their own. Since everyone's eager to see Jesse Owens compete, the men's team expects to cover their budget through charging admission at their trials this weekend, but as I'm sure many of you know, the women's teams have trouble generating enough audience at our events to make much money. I understand your frustration, but we have almost a week until we leave. Make phone calls, send telegrams. Try to secure outside sponsorship. I urge you not to give up."

Dee hurried from the room. Helen remained against the wall, alone.

What about Betty?

She was not one of the five women on Dee's list.

Helen inhaled sharply. *How could they not include Betty?* She was the first woman to show them what could be accomplished! How many of them were standing in this room because of her? Because they had read about her in their newspapers and wanted to emulate her?

Helen searched the room, but there was no sign of Betty so she darted for the door. Outside, a few women lingered in the lobby, but still, no Betty. Seeing a line for the elevator, Helen hurried to the stairs, taking the steps two at a time, sometimes three. Initially the air was cooler in the stairwell, but soon Helen was sweating, her heart pounding as she leapt up the stairs. At the seventh floor, she hurried to their room. She burst through the door and found Annette sitting next to Betty, who lay on the bed, a look of utter dejection stamped across her face.

"Goodness, Helen, what's wrong?" Betty asked, propping herself up on her elbow.

"I'm fine. Sorry I lost you back there," she panted. "But what are we going to do about you?"

Annette clutched a notepad with the hotel's letterhead at the top and held a pen over it, ready to write. "How are we going to get you to Berlin?"

"I have no idea," Betty said.

Helen started pacing. "That's not an answer. *Think*."

Only the sound of street traffic from seven floors below filled the room. Betty leaned against the headboard and raised her hand to brush her hair away from her face. In the low light, her diamond ring, one of her beloved prizes from Amsterdam, glittered. Betty studied it for a moment, swung her feet off the bed, and rose. "Wait, I have an idea. Where's the closest phone?"

43.

July 6, 1936
New York City

LOUISE PLACED THE PHONE BACK IN THE CRADLE AND leaned her forehead into her palm to stop the aching behind her eyes. How was she supposed to wait to find out if she had the money to go to Germany?

"I don't know if I can make it," she had protested to Mama, trying to keep her voice down. "I'm getting low on cash."

"I'll have an answer for you within the week. It's the best we can do," Mama said. "Sit tight, pray, and be careful with your spending."

Louise pictured Mama putting on her Sunday best and going to see Reverend Thompson at his home. She squeezed her eyes shut. "Please, God, please help me. Please help the good people of Malden find it in their hearts to help me again."

"Excuse me, are you all right?"

Louise opened her eyes to find Betty Robinson gazing at her from where she stood outside the telephone kiosk.

A sheepish expression crossed Betty's face. "I'm sorry, I'm not trying to rush you. I just saw you lower your head . . ."

"No, no, it's fine." Louise slid out of the telephone kiosk and stood. The two women looked at each other uncertainly.

"I'm Betty." She held out her hand.

"I know who you are. I'm Louise," she said, taking Betty's small hand in hers.

"Were you calling home?"

Louise nodded.

"Any luck?"

Louise shook her head. "I won't know until next weekend. My church will try to raise the money. They paid for me to get here, so I don't know if there will be more. It's a lot to ask. Especially because I haven't qualified for an individual event and am only being considered for the relay."

"But you did well in the individual hundred-meter. Didn't you win all your heats?"

"Not the final one. I almost fell and came in last, so I'm nervous. Back in 'thirty-two when I went to Los Angeles as a member of the relay pool, I never raced. What if that happens again? I hate to ask my neighbors to pay all of this money and not even race."

"I know." Betty bit her lip and whispered, "I'm being considered for only the relay too, but I can't ask my family for anything more. They've been supporting me in so many ways for too long."

"So what will you do?"

"It might be a long shot, but after Amsterdam, I was given many lovely gifts." She raised her hand and a diamond set on a gold band sparkled on her finger. Louise inhaled sharply, admiring it. "Yep, this ring, a diamond watch, some gold charms, and a few other really beautiful expensive pieces of jewelry, and of course, my gold and silver medals. I'm going to ask my brother-in-law to sell it all for me. Maybe it will be enough to get me to Berlin."

"Your medals? You're going to sell them too?"

Betty grimaced. "I've worked too hard to give up now. I'm not sure if it will be enough, but . . ." She cleared her throat. "I've got to try."

"I hope your plan works."

"Thank you. I hope you get good news too."

Louise said goodbye and walked across the shiny marble floor, but slowed as she neared the elevators. She couldn't bring herself to go upstairs and see Tidye. Not yet. She envied her friend's guaranteed spot with an intensity that frightened her. Why was this system so unfair? Why did everything always become so difficult? She had done what she was supposed to do; in Providence, she had made it to the finals of the 100-meter sprint. That was supposed to guarantee her a spot to Berlin, so why did the AOC constantly rewrite the rules?

She dropped to a chair and stared at the worn toes of her black pumps. Beside her feet lay a postcard of the Statue of Liberty that someone must have dropped. She picked it up and fanned herself with it. On top of everything else that was going wrong, why did it have to be so dreadfully hot?

"Louise?" Caroline appeared in front of her.

Surprised, Louise clutched at her chest as she took in Caroline's tear-streaked face. "Oh no, you're having trouble finding the money to go too?"

Caroline bit her lip and lowered the suitcase in her right hand to the ground. "I'm going home to Chicago. Dee just told me that even if I raise my own funds, the AOC isn't inviting me to Berlin. My fourth-place finish in the hurdles wasn't good enough. They're betting on Tidye and Anne instead."

Louise's hand rose to her mouth in shock. "I'm so sorry."

"I am too." Caroline's blue eyes grew shiny with tears. "But now it's your chance. When you get to Berlin, give 'em hell, you hear?"

Louise's throat tightened, and she felt her own tears starting down her cheeks as she rose to embrace Caroline. "This is so unfair. We will miss you terribly."

"The good news is that I'll get a big happy welcome from Howard and Joan. If nothing else, I've shown my daughter that girls can train hard too."

When Louise and Tidye had been stuck in that awful attic room in Denver, it had been Caroline who climbed all of those flights of stairs to bring them dessert. This woman who had once leapt out of a plane to earn the money to sponsor her Olympic dreams, this woman who had set a world record alongside Babe Didrikson in Los Angeles, who *should* have won a gold medal in the hurdles in 1932—she was being sent home. What a fickle business this was! They worked so hard, but everything could be lost in an instant; if there was one person who understood this, it was Louise.

"Joan's lucky to have you." Despite the heat and humidity,

she squeezed Caroline tightly, breathing in her lavender-scented powder.

When Louise returned to her room, Tidye was there, lying across one of the double beds reading a newspaper, wearing only her slip. Pearls of perspiration balanced on her upper lip. Despite the open window, the damask curtains didn't budge and the air felt stagnant. She looked up at Louise. "How'd your call go?"

"I'll know more by the weekend." Louise sat on the edge of the bed and kicked off her shoes. She sighed. "I guess you saw Caroline pack her things?"

"Isn't it awful that she can't come? I tell you, this whole business brings so much heartbreak. Why do we do this to ourselves?"

Louise shook her head and unbuttoned her damp blouse to pull it off. "I've been wondering the same thing. When we didn't end up racing in Los Angeles, did you ever wonder if it was all worth it?"

"Sure, I've thought about that a lot, but even though I felt shattered, I wasn't ready to give up. This has become about more than running for me. I want people to see us out there, competing for our country. I don't want to quit until I've been seen for what I'm worth."

"Yeah, but you're lucky. You'll get to show them what you're worth in Berlin." The words were out of her mouth before she knew it. Calling Tidye lucky wasn't fair. It dismissed all of her perseverance and effort.

Tidye's lips pressed together but she said nothing. Instead, she moved to her suitcase, rifling through its contents while a long silence yawned between them. Louise felt short of breath. Why couldn't she apologize and correct what she had just said?

Tidye straightened and held out a yellow dress. "I've gotten a note from Ralph Metcalfe, a friend of mine from Chicago who'll be racing in the men's trials this weekend. He's invited us to meet up with some of those fellas who've gotten into town. Come on, put on a dress, something for a night out on the town. We need to get out of here."

Louise sighed, torn between the temptation to confess she could barely afford to rub two pennies together and wasn't in the mood to go out, and wanting to make amends. "You're right, we could use a good caper. It would be a shame to let this beautiful dress that Emily made me languish in my valise."

"Exactly," Tidye said, nodding at the rose-colored cotton-voile dress that Louise pulled from her bag, but not meeting Louise's gaze.

The women crowded in front of the mirror to smooth their hair and put on lipstick, though neither looked at each other. Louise half-heartedly daubed some powder across her shiny face. All that was left unsaid felt worse than anything the heat could do to her.

BY THE TIME they made it downstairs and out onto the sidewalk, the setting sun no longer beat down, but heat blasted from every surface—the metallic automobiles, the pavement of the streets, the brick buildings. The thin soles of Tidye's pumps warmed from the hot concrete sidewalk underfoot. By the time they had walked a block, a sheen of perspiration glossed both women.

"So where are we going?" Louise asked.

"Swing Street, girl."

Swing Street. Louise had heard of it—the blocks famous for clubs and live music. A shiver of anticipation skipped up her spine. She needed to forget about money, Dee Boeckmann, Malden, even her family. Just for a night. She needed to live in the moment because New York could be the end of the line. In a few days, she could be back at home, working for Mrs. Clark and reading about the team heading to Berlin in the newspapers.

They headed along Seventh Avenue until they reached Fifty-Second Street. Here, neon signs created halos of red, yellow, and bright green, bathing the clusters of brownstones lining the narrow street. The croon of saxophones and piano melodies seeped out from open basement doors and windows. Tidye adjusted their pace to match the saunter of others as they trawled the block, but it wasn't the glorious sense of escape that brought Louise up short—it was the people! Clusters of black and white people mingled along sidewalks. Louise had never seen such a thing. She was used to being the only black woman in school, at track meets, or at work, so this was a whole new world.

And then there was the fact that everyone was wearing such beautiful clothing. Back in the hotel room, Louise's new frock had made her feel attractive and daring with its low neckline and trim silhouette, but now, surrounded by the other clubgoers, she realized she looked plain and conservative. Gauzy sweeping flared hems, elegant T-strap heels, gowns of metallic lamé and crepe de chine—everyone looked so confident, *so* sophisticated. The heat lent the city an intimacy that unsettled Louise, but it also contained a certain allure. So much slick bare skin everywhere. Some of the women's gowns revealed long, smooth bare backs. Men with their shirtsleeves rolled up past their elbows leaned against the brick walls, chatting and smoking with one another. These folks were definitely not on their way to Sunday-morning church services!

Laughter and the clink of glasses floated past them. An easy-going sense of joy suffused the air. Louise never traveled into Boston at night, so the close press of club-goers, the music, the sense of festivity—it was all new to her. Tonight, she could be whoever she wanted.

"HERE WE ARE," Tidye said, steering them underneath a flashing sign and into a dark doorway. "Get ready to meet some of the best athletes in the country. And they're college men," she added in an excited whisper.

Inside, music, heat, and cigarette smoke left Louise dizzy and overwhelmed.

"Tidye," a deep voice called, and a tall black man with wavy dark hair and a thin mustache stood and waved.

"Hey, Ralph, hey, fellas," Tidye cooed. Four other black men rose, all tipping their hats, and Tidye beamed. "This here's Louise, but she's the Malden Meteor to all of you."

The group chuckled appreciatively and Louise shook hands, squinting to see each face in the candlelight from the votive in the center of the table. Surrounding them sat white and black men with double-breasted striped suits and broad shoulders, and women with perfectly coiffed hairdos and evening gowns trimmed with beads that caught the light enticingly. It all felt forbidden and risky, and the fact that no one else seemed to notice the novelty made Louise feel like she was in a strange world, but the racket of worries and sense of disconnect in her head dissolved as one of the men leaned forward, smiling, the bright white of his teeth leaving Louise dazzled. "I'm Mack. How about some champagne to celebrate your races last weekend?" he said.

She nodded and he raised his arm to get a nearby waitress's attention. As Louise watched Mack, she glimpsed Tidye on the other side of him, gazing at him hungrily. The waitress strolled over to their table and stood with a hand on her hip.

"I'll take a glass of champagne for the lady, please," he said, grinning at Louise. In the blaze of Mack's attention, Louise's whole body warmed by several degrees, and when he didn't turn to ask Tidye about a drink, she felt a small flicker of satisfaction.

"Louise, you've probably never had champagne before, have you?" Tidye asked loudly, a sharp edge in her voice, as the waitress sashayed back toward the bar.

Louise smiled, immune to Tidye's barb. Mack was interested in *her* and the realization felt like the best prize in the world.

"New York City is as fine a place to try it as any other," Mack said, and everyone laughed good-naturedly.

Ralph leaned back in his seat, crossing one foot over the other. "Tidye, you want some champagne too?" When she nodded, he signaled to the waitress for one more before turning back to the table. "We've been all over Midtown today drumming up funds with some suits from the AOC. Thanks to having Mr. Golden Boy with us, I think we got plenty."

"I thought your team didn't need to do any fund-raising," Tidye said.

"They have us out there hustling for the General Fund. When you've got a fella like this, someone who everyone wants to meet, you make sure you use him." Ralph slapped the shoulder of the man sitting next to him, a man whom Louise recognized from the newspapers. Jesse Owens.

Louise would have known his wide toothy grin anywhere. The men clinked their glasses of beer against his. Jesse winked at her over the rim of his beer and her face heated. In his lightweight gray suit and fedora, he looked like any other good-looking young man, but ever since his remarkable performance the prior year at the Big Ten track meet in Michigan, at which he had set several world records all within the course of one hour, he was whom everyone talked about. Even back home, Junior talked less about his beloved Red Sox and more about Jesse. The Ohio State student had the gold medal hopes of the country riding on him for Berlin.

"Not sure if some of those old-timers knew what to do when we all marched in," Jesse said. "Probably the first time a colored man ever set foot in some of those places."

Again, the men laughed and clinked glasses.

"So, you all ready for Saturday?" Tidye asked, fanning herself with her hand. "Big couple of days for you boys on Randall Island."

"You know it," Ralph said. "We're taking it easy, but it's too blessed hot to stay in that hotel."

"Sure is," Mack said. He turned to Louise. "Is this your first Olympics?"

"Mack, I know you've heard of what happened in Los Angeles," Ralph said, shaking his head. "Tidye and Louise went to California, but were pulled from the relay at the last minute."

All the men raised their eyebrows and shook their heads.

"Now that's just a shame," mumbled one of them, whom Louise recognized as Dave Albritton, Jesse's teammate from Ohio State who often appeared beside him in newspaper pictures.

The waitress reappeared to set two sweating glasses of champagne on the table, and Dave handed them to the women.

Louise cleared her throat. "I'm actually not even sure I'm going to Berlin. Our coach just announced that the AOC is only paying for five women to compete. Tidye's one of them. She raced so well in Providence that she won herself a guaranteed trip."

"That so?" Mack asked. "Well, Tidye, congratulations, but I sure hope things work out for you too, Louise." She had hoped to make amends to Tidye, but from the way Mack had angled his body to turn into hers, she doubted her success.

"Here's to *all* of us going to Berlin and winning," Jesse said, lifting his beer. Everyone cheered and then quieted as they drank. The cold champagne danced along Louise's tongue and tickled her throat as it slipped down. She had never tasted anything quite like it and she took another, longer sip, eager for more of the fizzy feeling that it brought her. She didn't want to think about fund-raising, or home, or how Tidye seemed to be ignoring her.

After everyone lowered their glasses, Jesse's expression turned sober. "I'm serious, we have to win. If we're going to Germany, we need to show Hitler that all his theories on a master race are a load of bunk." The men grunted in agreement, but Jesse looked at Louise. "What do you make of all this boy-cott talk?"

Louise placed her champagne reluctantly on the table and licked her lips. How had her mouth gone dry so quickly? Mal-den's newspaper had run the occasional stories outlining the debate on whether the U.S. should send a team to compete in the Berlin Games, but she hadn't heeded them much. Back in December, she had been relieved to see the AOC had voted—by a very slim majority—for the U.S. to compete. She hadn't real-ized that talk of a boycott still persisted. Her focus had been solely on qualifying for the Olympics, not boycotting them. She hadn't spent the last eight years training only to decide that the crazy talk of one little man in a country on the other side of the world was going to make her stop. But here, surrounded by these handsome college men, she had a feeling she was supposed to be thinking about more than her own success.

Tidye cleared her throat and chimed in. "We don't support the idea of boycotting. By racing over there, we won't just be showing Hitler that his ideas are wrong, we'll be showing our own country too."

"Exactly," Dave said. "You know, back at school, Jesse and I can't even live on campus. Ohio State is only interested in having us around in ways that serve its interests."

Jesse nodded. "Look, the NAACP was after us for a while, sending letters and writing to the papers telling us not to race, to show 'em we're to strike a blow at bigotry, but that's just letting a powerful opportunity go. Those Nazis aren't the only ones with dangerous ideas about race. We'd be fools if we ignore what's happening over here. We need to show our own country what we can do too."

Tidye drained her glass. "All eyes are on you, Jesse. On all of you fellas, really. Staying home does nothing. After watching the last Olympics from the sidelines, I can definitely say it's important to be on the track holding everyone's attention. Nothing changes if you don't put yourself out there."

Ralph laughed and cocked his head at Tidye as he spoke to the group. "See what I mean? This girl's a firecracker, writing for the *Defender* and all."

Tidye brightened at the compliment and winked at Louise.

"It's great. You're both a part of this too," Jesse said to Tidye and Louise. "We're going to show everyone what we can do."

Louise found herself nodding along with the rest of the group. She wanted to believe what Jesse was saying, but for one night she didn't want to think too far ahead. What she really wanted to believe was that her friendship with Tidye could withstand envy and that a handsome college man could be interested in her, because even simple things like these could get complicated.

44.

OVER THE WEEKEND BETTY ATTENDED THE MEN'S qualifying races on Randall Island, and judging by the packed stands, it seemed everyone else in New York City was there too. But nothing could distract her from the persistent worries circling her mind. Was Jim having any luck selling her prizes from 1928? She tried to focus on the men's results, but instead dollar amounts ran through her mind at all hours of the day and night. *How much would that diamond watch sell for? How about the medals? Even if it all sold, would it be enough?*

She sweltered in the stands above the men's races along with the other track and field women, who squirmed in their seats and fanned themselves impatiently. The stress of waiting for the final verdict on their status was wearing on all of them.

On Monday morning, Betty arrived in the hotel lobby to telephone Jim so early that the valets were running soapy blades along the glass on the front doors and a chambermaid was dusting the furniture. She glanced at the clock above the check-in desk. It was even earlier in Chicago, but Betty knew Jim and Jean would be awake, feeding Laura and Frances breakfast. Betty slid into one of the telephone kiosks and took a deep inhalation as she lifted the receiver to call. Jim answered on the first ring.

"Any luck?" Betty asked.

The line was silent for a moment and her heart stopped.

"Jim? Jim? Are you there?"

"Yes, yes, I'm here." His voice sounded distant and she pressed the earpiece against her head as if that would help the connection. "Betty, we've got it. I'll be wiring the money to a Western Union office near your hotel on my way in to work. I'll leave in about ten minutes."

Betty's eyes clouded with relieved tears. "Really? Did it all sell? It was enough?"

"Every single piece sold. You're going to Berlin. Do you have a pen and paper to write down the address where you'll need to go to receive the funds?"

Her entire body began to vibrate so violently that she could barely breathe as she grasped a pen from her purse and pulled a notepad with the hotel's letterhead toward her. With trembling hands, she wrote down everything Jim told her. When she had all the details, she exhaled with relief. "Thank you so much. Thank you for everything you've done."

His laugh sounded tinny over the line. "You did all the hard work, Betty. We're mighty proud of you and will be following your adventures in the newspaper."

The pale blond hairs on her arms rose with his words. She thanked him again before placing the receiver back on its hook and dancing across the hotel lobby, too euphoric to think. At the far end of the room, the elevator doors opened and Helen appeared. Tousled and puffy from sleep, she studied Betty with a pensive expression.

Betty raised her arms victoriously, and the exuberant look that spread across Helen's face made it all real. After all of this, Betty was going to the Olympics *again*.

Helen exited the elevator and let out a loud whoop as she ran toward Betty to catch her in a hug that lifted her off her feet.

"I knew you could do it," Helen cheered, spinning Betty around. The two ignored the surprised expressions of the hotel staff and laughed and laughed.

Finally, Helen lowered Betty to the ground. As she stepped away, Betty could have sworn Helen lingered and breathed in the smell of her hair, but it happened so quickly she couldn't be sure. Before Betty could get a good look at her face, Helen spun away.

"Betty?"

Betty turned to find Louise staring back and forth between Helen and her, a look of wariness on her face.

"Louise," she said breathlessly. Why did she feel guilty of something? She straightened the belt around her dress. "My brother-in-law was able to sell everything! I have enough money to go to Berlin."

"That's wonderful." Louise gave a rare smile that was wide enough to reveal the gap between her two front teeth. "I received a telegram from home last night with good news too. I'm walking to Western Union now. Want to come?"

"Yes." Betty slid an arm through Louise's. "Helen, want to join us?"

Helen turned toward them, her face flushed. She blinked

and shook her head, dropping her gaze to her feet. "Um, no. I'll stay here. See you both later." Before she had even finished talking, she was heading toward the elevator.

"See you soon." Betty kept her voice cheery even though Louise was looking at her strangely. "We'll be back to start packing for Berlin."

When one of the valets opened the front door for them, Betty stepped aside and glanced back over her shoulder as Louise passed. Behind them, Helen was standing in the elevator, staring at her. Betty paused briefly at the intensity of Helen's gaze before hurrying ahead to catch Louise.

45.

AT SEA, NEW YORK CITY'S HEAT DISSIPATED, REPLACED by cool breezes and mild sunshine. Perfect training conditions. The only problem was that the track's hard wooden planks began to hurt Helen's legs. They offered no give, and each day that she ran on them, her legs hurt more and more. By her third morning at sea, when she awoke and stepped from her bunk, the soft skin of her inner shins felt tender. Each step across the small space of their cabin sent a stab of pain searing up her legs.

Betty yawned, rolling over in her bunk. The edge of her pillowcase had left an indented ridge along the smooth skin of her cheek, and the intimacy of the imperfection brought Helen up short. It was all she could do not to sink to her knees next to Betty and trace her finger along the ridge to her hairline.

"Are you heading up to the track already?" Betty asked.

"Yep. There's always a good crew up there and I can hear the latest of what's going on. Want to join me?" Helen pulled on her track shoes, wincing from the pain in her legs.

"Hmm, eventually," Betty said with a languorous sigh, and

Helen hid her disappointment by tying her laces. Since boarding the *Manhattan,* instead of running, Betty would find a chair on the Promenade Deck and hold court as if she were minor royalty, and in a way, she was, at least as far as the athletes were concerned. The rowers, the equestrians, the swimmers, they couldn't get enough of her. Yes, the weather had been perfect so far, but even without the sun, Betty appeared to glow in the attention of her admirers. Her long, smooth legs, the graceful turn of her wrist as she held a cigarette, and the sparkle in her eyes as she joked—all of it left Helen feeling awed and even a little intimidated. How did Betty manage to hold everyone in her thrall?

Betty stretched her bare arms overhead. "If you swing by here to change before breakfast, I'll join you."

"You sure you don't want to practice now?"

"No, thanks. I'll go later."

"See you in a bit." Helen stood and left, gingerly easing her weight onto each foot as she climbed the stairs to where the track was located. After a few laps around the track, the pain had vanished, and she loosened, waving hello to the familiar faces who, like her, enjoyed the early morning beauty of their surroundings.

Since New York City had faded into the distance, Helen had found herself mesmerized by the wide expanse of the Atlantic. The intensity of its blue. The way light sparkled off its surface. The power of the wind. The play of clouds overhead. Unlike the never-ending stretches of fields at home, the ocean was always changing. When Helen stood on deck, she became transfixed by its power and energy. Here, she had a keen sense of being one small piece within something larger, something alive.

The way the sea moved and the wind blew, she felt as though she were surrounded by an unpredictable wild creature, and it thrilled her.

Unfortunately, the thrill had worn off by the time she sat in the dining hall having breakfast with Betty. The pain had returned, sharper and more insistent than before.

"What's wrong?" Betty asked, looking at Helen's plate of untouched scrambled eggs and toast.

"Nothing."

"Are you sure? Do you miss home?"

"No, not at all. It's just that my legs hurt."

"Shin splints. You need to rest, take it easy. That's what I'm doing. Stop training several times a day. The track is awful hard. My joints start hurting even more when I just think about it. It would absolutely be killing my legs and back if I were to run more than a few laps on it. If you want to socialize, sit in the chairs. You don't have to always be running."

"I'm not like you. I always feel like a beached whale when I drape myself along those deck chairs. You know me, I need action."

"Do I need to point out that action seems to be giving you shin splints? What you need is rest." As she spoke, Betty's gaze trailed one of the male swimmers as he passed their table.

Helen watched Betty's distraction with a pang of disappointment that quickly turned to annoyance. Why did she allow herself to moon over Betty? It was clear that her friend viewed her merely as a younger sister. "Rest? Fine, but please don't say anything to anyone. The last thing I want is for Dee to catch wind of this."

Harriet Bland, a sprinter in the relay pool, sat down across from them with only a single hard-boiled egg and a slice of honeydew melon on her plate. "What don't you want Dee to catch wind of?"

Helen sighed. Leave it to Harriet to appear exactly when she wasn't wanted. "Nothing."

"Oh," Harriet said, disappointed. She laid her napkin across her lap. "I thought maybe you weren't feeling well, and I'd have to find a new table. I'm doing my best to stay in peak shape."

"Then you might want to actually eat something substantial." Helen took a big bite of her scrambled eggs.

Harriet rolled her eyes and tapped her hard-boiled egg against her plate to crack its shell while Betty flagged a server down for more coffee. After Helen's mug was refilled, she took a big gulp, savoring how the warmth spread through her chest. A sense of resolution spread through her as well. She'd go find her jacket and then maybe sit on the deck in a lounge chair and write a letter home. Her legs would feel better in no time.

Helen left the dining room. As she climbed the stairs, she turned at the sound of heels clacking rapidly behind her and found Dee. "Good morning, Helen. I was hoping to see you. Do you have a moment for a word in private?"

Helen willed her face to not give anything away. Could Dee tell that Helen's legs hurt? "Um, sure. Now?"

"Yes, come with me to my cabin?"

Dread filled Helen. They said nothing as she followed Dee to her room. Was Dee about to scold her for not saying anything about her legs? Were shin splints considered a serious injury?

They entered Dee's small cabin and Helen took a seat at the edge of her bunk, swallowing and looking around for a distraction, anything to keep from meeting Dee's gaze.

"It's come to my attention that you may be keeping something from me. As a member of this team, your loyalty is to your country, and since I'm your coach, I expect complete honesty from you."

Dee leaned over toward her, making it impossible for Helen to look anywhere other than at her coach's face. "Have you received any information about a team boycott of the Games?"

Helen straightened. *A team boycott?* Her mind raced back to the letters she and her roommates had discovered in their hotel room in New York and then a second boycott manifesto that had been waiting for Helen and Betty in their cabin. Shortly after boarding, Helen had discovered it and read excerpts aloud to Betty:

> Hundreds of Germans are political prisoners and are confined to concentration camps for two or three years because they are pacifists or against National Socialism.

"So people are being imprisoned because they believe in peace?" Betty had asked.

Helen continued to read before pausing to look up at Betty. "Apparently this man, Carl Mierendorf, was imprisoned three years ago for supporting peaceful relations with France, and no one knows what's happened to him. It says we should refuse to set foot in the stadium until Hitler releases these prisoners, and we should organize and coordinate our efforts to send a message."

Betty leaned in and read, "'We appeal to all women participating in the Games. What would the Olympic Games be if the women athletes were to refuse to take part?'" She stared out their cabin's porthole for a moment. "This group believes that we have a voice, that we have some power?"

Helen didn't know how to respond to Betty's distress. All the anxiety of fund-raising had diverted their attention from the boycott, but now aboard the ship, on their way to Berlin, they had time to think. And worry.

Dee said, "I heard something about letters back in the New York hotel rooms urging you all to boycott."

"Well, we're all here, aren't we? It sure looks like everyone's decided to compete."

"But have these resistance groups been in touch with you? Does anyone seem to be wavering on their commitment to this team? Has anyone said anything about it?"

"Have you asked some of the girls? You're pretty tight with all of your runners from St. Louis. Surely Harriet will tell you anything you want to know."

"How about Eleanor Holm Jarrett? Is she talking about boycotting?"

Helen pictured the glamorous swimmer. Eleanor and Betty often sat on the deck chairs together, smoking and stretching their lean tanned limbs, reminiscing about Amsterdam. Eleanor was married to a nightclub owner back in Los Angeles and a ring with a diamond the size of a golf ball glittered on the hand in which she held her Lucky Strike. "I don't know. The only thing I've heard her complain about are the frumpy team bathing suits. She hasn't said anything to me about boycotting, but we're not particularly close."

"Good, she's a troublemaker. You'd be wise to keep your distance." Dee folded her arms across her chest. "I thought maybe you could help me keep an eye on the girls."

"Why me?"

"You're our most talented sprinter. Whether you know it or not, this puts you in a position of leadership. The girls look to you."

Helen doubted that. If anything, Betty was the group's leader. Her skepticism must have shown because Dee hurried on to say, "It also means you have the most at stake. If something goes wrong and our team can't compete, what are you going to do then?"

The hairs on the back of Helen's neck rose. "I guess I'd be back at William Woods."

"Stuck back in Fulton. What then?"

Helen blinked. It was true. What would she do? Helen Stephens Day would be forgotten. Once again, she'd simply be too tall, too awkward. Too *different*. She needed things to go well in Berlin, but she certainly had no plans to become a rat to Dee.

"So, you'll tell me?" Dee asked.

Helen shivered and her legs throbbed. "Do you know anything about Hitler? Do you know what he's doing over there?"

"Mr. Brundage says he's simply rebuilding Germany, that he's an ally of ours."

"People are disappearing. He's advocating violence and discrimination. He's dangerous."

"Don't be naive, Helen. No place is perfect. Everyone's getting a fair shot at these Games. We've been promised that. I need you to help me make sure that none of the girls get cold feet. Mr. Brundage is concerned about the boycott rumors. The last thing we want is for this team to arrive in Germany and fall apart. Do you understand?"

Helen considered. If they all went, competed, and did well, Hitler would be taken down a few pegs. Maybe people would stop believing in him. She nodded slowly and rose to leave.

"Good girl," Dee said, but Helen brushed her away.

If Dee wanted to ignore all the bad news coming out of Germany, she was on her own. Helen had her own things to worry about.

"Jewish Athlete Dropped from German Olympic Team"

London—Two weeks before the Olympics are set to open in Berlin, Germany has dropped high-jumping champion Gretel Bergmann from its national team. Miss Bergmann rose to pre-eminence in southern Germany and set several records until being expelled as a member from her athletic club for being Jewish. At that point, the Bergmanns moved to London and Gretel enrolled in London Polytechnic and competed in the high jump for her college. In 1934, she won the British Championships in the high jump.

Under international pressure to show goodwill to its Jewish citizens, the German government invited her back to compete for her native country, so Miss Bergmann returned to Germany to ensure the safety of her remaining family members and to support other Jewish athletic clubs. Although she won the Württembergian Championships, tying the German record of 5 feet 3 inches, she has been notified by German authorities that her inclusion on the German Olympic team has been denied on the grounds of "underperformance."

In response to criticism that the National Socialist Party has received over its discriminatory policies, Germany has been citing Miss Bergmann's participation on the German team as evidence that all athletes are welcomed to compete safely in the upcoming Olympics, but her dismissal from the team only raises more questions about the authenticity of this claim.

Only half-Jewish German-born Helene Mayer, a fencer, will compete for the Reich, though she currently resides in California.

This news of Bergmann's rejection becomes public as the American Olympic team is more than halfway across the Atlantic en route to Berlin. When asked to comment on Miss Bergmann's dismissal, American Olympic Committee President Avery Brundage had no comment. Jeremiah T. Mahoney, former president of the American Athletic Union, said, "Until the Nazi regime has ended, the American people will have no reason to believe that the true spirit of sportsmanship, to which the Olympic Games are devoted, can find expression in Germany."

In December 1935, when the AOC debated supporting an official boycott of the Olympics in Berlin, the resolution failed to pass by only three votes.

46.

July 19, 1936
Aboard the S.S. *Manhattan*

IT WAS LATE AT NIGHT WHEN LOUISE AWOKE TO A POUND-
ing upon her door. At first, the knocking sounded faint, but
as she surfaced from the depths of sleep, it grew louder. From
the lower bunk, Tidye groaned and the bedclothes rustled. The
latch clicked open and light from the hallway silhouetted Tidye's slight figure standing at the door.

"Louise? Tidye?" a woman's voice whispered. "Dee says to
come to Eleanor's cabin immediately."

"Eleanor the swimmer?" Tidye asked.

"Yes, see the open door down there? That's the one."

"Why?" Tidye croaked.

Louise slid out of her bunk as whoever was at the door
mumbled an indistinct reply. What was going on? Below her
feet, after several days of rolling, the floor felt stable. No rain,
no heavy winds. She tilted her head to listen to sounds above
the steady low rumble of the ship's engine. Everything sounded
fine and she didn't smell anything burning.

When Tidye shut the door and switched the cabin light on,
her face appeared yellow and waxy.

"Who was that? What's happening?" Louise asked, her head still thick with sleep.

"Olive. She didn't really say."

"What time is it?"

Tidye held her wristwatch up to the light. "Five o'clock."

Both women grumbled and pulled on dressing gowns before leaving their cabin and making their way down the hall. When they reached Eleanor's cabin, they found Dee leaning against the doorway smoking a cigarette and watching the smoke from her exhalation drift toward the ceiling.

Mrs. Sackett, the women's swim team chaperone, stepped from the doorway and beckoned. The athletes followed her. No one spoke.

There, draped across the bunk, lay Eleanor, still in a plum-colored evening gown dotted with seed pearls. Her dark finger curls appeared frizzy and mascara streaks trickled down her cheeks. Her eyes flashed in indignation as the women filed into the tiny room.

"Can't a girl get a little peace around here first thing in the morning?" she said, her voice hoarse. She waved her hand in dismissal. "Everyone get out."

Mrs. Sackett and Mr. Brundage towered over Eleanor's bed, while the team's physician sat on its edge with a stethoscope poised between his index finger and thumb. He moved it toward her chest, but she pushed him away.

"This is ridiculous. Everyone out!" she repeated, louder than before.

"Now, Mrs. Jarrett," Mr. Brundage said, looking down his

nose at the swimmer. "What happened last night constitutes a serious offense."

"What? Drinking? When we received our uniforms, you said drinking and smoking were up to the discretion of each individual athlete."

"You were hardly partaking in an after-dinner drink. I would describe you as intoxicated. Mrs. Sackett confirms you were seen cavorting on the Promenade Deck with a champagne coupe in your hands well after curfew."

"So was everyone in the first-class cabins. All of your precious men were drinking whiskey and gin by the bucketload and playing poker. Isn't gambling a violation of the Olympic oath?"

"My dear, you're in no condition to pass judgment."

"Listen, this is my third Olympic Games and I have a gold medal already." Even in her bedraggled state, her beautiful wide-set dark eyes glittered sharp and dangerous. "If I want a little champagne, it's my right. I'm of age and married. Don't you dare criticize me."

Mr. Brundage straightened the lapels of his dark suit and gave her a pitying look before turning to the physician. "Well, Dr. Lawson?"

The man crossed his legs, his face dour. "It appears that Mrs. Jarrett is an acute alcoholic."

"Are you kidding?" Eleanor raised herself to sitting. "If that's the case, you better give the same news to the rowers, the boxers, the marksmen . . . hmm, probably every male athlete on this boat. And the reporters too. Why, those first-class cabins filled with all of your cronies are wetter than anything outside that porthole. And let's not forget that the reason you know that I was drinking is because *you* were there too. Didn't I see a martini in your hand, *sir*?" Her mouth, smeary with crimson lipstick, slashed into an angry thin line with the last word.

Mr. Brundage's face darkened. A vein at his temple pulsed. He straightened his tie and turned to the women filling the doorway. "Ladies, let this be an example of what can befall you should you choose to engage in immoral behavior. As of now, Mrs. Eleanor Holm Jarrett is officially off the Olympic team and must disembark immediately when we reach Hamburg."

There was a collective sharp inhalation of breath.

Eleanor's face whitened. "You can't do that to me."

"I can and I have." He wagged his finger. "It's a shame you've failed to take things seriously." He turned away from the swimmer and moved toward the door, but Eleanor lunged forward and pointed an index finger at him. The diamond bracelet around her wrist caught the light from the sconce on the wall and flashed like the eyes of an animal in the night.

"Don't walk away from me like that. The newspapers call me the greatest backstroke swimmer in the world. You must hate the fact that I'm a talented woman with money and a career. My independence represents everything you fear, doesn't it? You're a small man, Mr. Brundage, a small man indeed."

He turned back to her but said nothing, though the tightening of his jaw was evident to all. He glanced at Eleanor, his expression icy, before facing the rest of the women. "Show's over, ladies. I recommend that you return to your rooms to prepare for the day. Follow the curfew for the remainder of this trip. I will not tolerate any unladylike behavior from any of you. Am I clear?"

Only the rustling of silk dressing gowns could be heard as the athletes shifted uneasily before drifting back to their cabins as if sleepwalking. Louise laced her fingers through Tidye's and found them cold. Not until the door was shut behind them in their cabin did they face each other.

"Oh Lord, that Brundage man frightens me," Louise whispered.

Tidye switched off the light and sank onto her bunk, pulling her knees to her chest. "We need to try to catch another hour or so of sleep. This feels like a bad dream."

"Maybe someone can talk some sense into him," Louise said, her voice small as she climbed onto her bunk and wriggled under the covers.

"If he's willing to do that to her, imagine what he would do with us if we cross him."

Louise shuddered, burying herself deeper under the covers. "Just focus on racing. Things will get better once we arrive in Berlin." She hoped her voice sounded more confident than she felt.

47.

ON THE MORNING THEY WERE EXPECTING TO SEE THE Irish coast, Betty rose before dawn. One glance toward Helen's bunk revealed her to be fast asleep. Finally. The pain in Helen's shins had been getting increasingly worse, and her nighttime tossing and turning had been preventing either of them from sleeping soundly. Helen's wool blanket draped over the edge of the mattress precariously as if it might fall off and drop to the ground. Betty considered tucking it back around Helen, but held back, not wanting to risk waking her.

Betty was still trying to figure out her new friend. Helen never spoke of the men on the team in a way that indicated any bit of attraction. Even when surrounded by their handsome teammates at Casino Night or while training on the track, she gave no indication of anything beyond friendly interest. There was no flirtation, only talk of news, training, the ship, and what to do once they arrived in Berlin. Her attitude provided a stark contrast to almost everyone else's aboard the *Manhattan*. Bored with the amount of idle time at sea, almost all the athletes—Betty included—were consumed with finding romance at all times of the day and evening. Meals, training sessions, evening card games and cocktails—everything was an opportunity to assess interest in the opposite sex. It was great fun! Betty never found herself sitting beside an empty deck chair, and someone was always willing to offer her a cigarette or fill her wineglass. All of this made Helen's disinterest in the opposite sex a curious thing. Of course, Betty enjoyed Helen's company and she knew that the younger woman admired her, but—the way Helen watched her, followed her—sometimes the intensity of that admiration gave Betty pause. She didn't know what to make of Helen's behavior, and it felt safer not to encourage anything she didn't fully understand.

Gently, she folded the edge of the blanket over the foot of the bunk and crept from the room.

When she reached the Promenade Deck, she faced east, toward the sunrise, where the sky glowed pale peach and a small ship approached the *Manhattan* to exchange passengers, mail, and supplies.

Three more days and they would be arriving in Germany.

Betty unfolded herself on a deck lounger and pulled her coat tightly around herself against the chill of the early hour. Two sailors scrubbed at the track with wire brushes, and at a spot farther down the deck, another woman perched on a deck chair watching the sunrise, a plaid blanket folded over her legs. Even with a scarf tied over her head, Betty knew it was Eleanor. According to all the whispers in the dining room, the swimmer had not left her cabin since the humiliating encounter with Brundage. Along with many of their teammates, Betty had signed a petition protesting Eleanor's dismissal, but it appeared Mr. Brundage had no plans to reverse his harsh punishment.

Gulls wheeled overhead. More and more of them had been appearing as the coast approached. Betty rose and slid into the open deck chair next to Eleanor, coughing so as not to startle her. Eleanor turned and saw Betty. "Can't sleep?"

Betty pulled her knees toward her chest. "I'm sorry the petition didn't work."

"Oh, darling, you tried and I appreciate it. Two hundred signatures! Didn't know I had so many friends." Eleanor kept smiling, but she looked drained. "Don't worry about me. I've got a plan. This isn't the last you'll see of me."

"Oh?"

"Well, let's just say I've got a few tricks up my sleeve. I'm going to call in a few favors."

"Good. If only MacArthur was still the AOC president. Remember how much he liked us?"

Eleanor batted her lashes. "Do I ever. Sorry to break it to you, but I think I was his favorite."

"Of course you were."

"It's hard not to love a girl in a bathing suit."

"I'll say."

Eleanor fixed her hazel eyes on Betty. She wore no makeup, and with her hair awry, she appeared less the glamorous showgirl, more the young swimmer Betty had met eight years earlier. "Everything seemed less complicated when we traveled to Amsterdam, didn't it?"

Betty's stomach tightened as she gazed at the sea. Since finding the second boycott letter in her room, she hadn't been able to stop thinking about it. When she brought up the topic with other athletes, everyone seemed conflicted. Of course, no one approved of what Hitler was doing, but few of the athletes seemed knowledgeable about what was happening in Germany and they expressed reluctance to get involved in the doings of a foreign country. All except for Marty Glickman, one of the few Jewish athletes on the team. When he'd sat down next to her in a deck chair the previous day, she'd asked him what he thought about boycotting and he hadn't missed a beat. "We need to defeat Herr Hitler's appalling bigotry. We have the opportunity to show the world that his ideas about Aryan superiority are not only despicable, but *wrong*," he had said, banging his fist against the armrest of his seat for emphasis. She felt grateful for someone with a strong opinion on the subject, and if she was honest, he'd said what she wanted to hear.

Eleanor stretched her arms overhead. "I suppose I should be heading down to my cabin. I like to avoid crowds these days."

"I know. Good luck."

"You too, darling. We're all going to need it." And with that Eleanor stood, straightening her long coat. She waved goodbye and strolled away, her head ducked down so as not to draw attention to herself.

WHEN THEY ARRIVED in Hamburg three days later, Betty settled into the back seat of a black sedan next to Helen and Annette for the short ride to city hall, where a brief welcome ceremony was planned. The three women stared at the long flags, bloodred with black spidery swastikas, covering all the major city buildings. Merry spectators lined the streets, saluting and waving smaller versions of the ugly flag. Brass bands appeared on every street corner and Sousa marches filled the air. Countless guards lined the travel route. It all felt excessive, staged, too insistent.

After the pageantry of the brief stop at city hall, the athletes were shepherded to Lehrte Railway Station and boarded elegant passenger cars that, like everything else, were draped with swastika-covered flags. Betty dropped to her seat across from Helen as Olive and Annette slid into the red velvet seats next to them.

"Look," Olive said, pulling her team blazer away from her chest and giving Betty a glimpse of something shiny. "We each took our wineglasses from city hall. A bunch of the men did too. Great souvenirs, don't you think?"

"If only we had some of the red wine that went in them," Annette said, giggling.

"I swiped a teacup with the *Manhattan*'s insignia on it and wrapped it in my underclothes," Betty said.

"Once we get to Berlin, I'm going for something with that awful swastika on it," Helen said, pulling out an old newspaper to read.

Outside the window, fields, green and verdant, streaked past, but the sky was gloomy. Thick clouds hung low over the horizon. After about thirty minutes, the train slowed as it traveled through a village station. The station's platform appeared empty, yet the train lumbered to a stop.

Helen looked up from her newspaper. "I thought we were going directly to Berlin."

Everyone arched their necks, trying to catch a glimpse of

what was happening outside. A line of soldiers clad in brown Nazi uniforms, their black jackboots polished to a high shine, suddenly marched onto the platform to assume positions as if guarding each train car. After several minutes, a group of Nazi officials appeared on the platform, behind the soldiers. They boarded each train car in pairs. Wide-eyed, Betty and her teammates watched as two men appeared at one end of their compartment and appraised the athletes, their faces grim.

One official lifted a gloved hand holding a riding crop and smacked it against his other palm. He spoke in a clipped, heavily accented English. "It has come to our attention that many glasses have gone missing from Hamburg's city hall. While this may have been seen as a prank, it is property theft. Surrender the items in question immediately and no further action will be taken over this incident."

When he finished speaking, a soldier stepped forward holding a crate. Under the penetrating gazes of the officials, the Americans shifted in their seats uneasily. Annette's face drained of color and Olive's breath caught and her knuckles whitened on her seat's armrest as the soldier with the crate began to walk down the aisle slowly, his gaze fastened on a spot straight ahead of him. The official who had spoken muttered something in rapid-fire German to the man with the crate before switching back to English, repeating, "Now is the time to return the items. If you do not comply, things will become more serious."

Even though Betty hadn't nicked a goblet, fear bloomed inside her. Dry-mouthed, she stared straight ahead. Each thud of the heels of the soldier's boots along the railcar aisle beat an ominous sound. Several athletes handed goblets to the man as he progressed along the aisle. Olive pulled hers out and handed it to the soldier, and Annette followed suit. When he reached the far end of the train car, the Nazi official marched after him, and they exited without saying anything more.

It was as if a thunderstorm had passed through. The air cleared and lightened. The athletes looked at each other with tight but relieved faces. A low hum of chatter filled the railcar.

As the Nazis reconvened on the platform, gathering the crates of stolen goblets, Helen whistled. "Close call. These people don't fool around."

"That was terrifying," Olive said.

Helen held out a newspaper. "Someone gave this to me before we landed. It's a few days old, but there's a story about how Germany has dropped one of its only Jewish athletes from its team. She's a high jumper and has set records, but suddenly she's being told she's not good enough. Sounds pretty fishy, don't you think?"

Betty took the newspaper and started reading about Gretel Bergmann. What exactly were they getting into?

48.

July 24, 1936
Berlin

THE WEATHER REMAINED UNUSUALLY COLD AND dreary upon the Americans' arrival in Berlin. The men would be staying at the Olympic Village constructed on the western fringe of Berlin about a half hour by bus to the Olympic Stadium, almost twenty miles from the center of Berlin, but the women's housing lay inside the Reichssportfeld, adjacent to the Olympic Stadium, in a large building named Friesenhaus. Helen's first impression of the bedroom she would share with Betty was its unwelcoming temperature. She shivered in the chilly, damp air. "It's das Freezing Haus, huh?"

Betty dropped her bag on the concrete floor. "At least it's clean."

"I'm starving. Can we go find something to eat?"

"Of course, let's put down our luggage and . . ." At the sound of Betty's voice trailing off, Helen turned to see what had distracted her. A sheet of white paper appeared to be tucked under the thin pillow at the other end of her bed, and Helen pulled out the typewritten note and began reading:

Adolf Hitler's Germany has treated many of her best sons in a manner that's unworthy of a civilized state.

The temperature in the already cold room seemed to plummet by thirty more degrees as Helen continued to read another appeal to boycott the Games.

German authorities will start by being very displeased, but they cannot punish anybody. The worst thing they can do is send home those athletes . . .

Displeased? After witnessing how Nazi officials had not displayed the slightest hesitation in threatening the athletes over a few missing goblets on the train ride from Hamburg, Helen doubted the German authorities would limit themselves to only being displeased.

"Is it another boycott letter?" asked Betty.

Helen handed it to her. Betty's eyes darted down the note and then she lowered it to her side.

"Are you going to show it to Dee?"

"No. I saved the boycott manifesto that met us aboard the *Manhattan.* I'll add this one to my growing collection. These resistance groups mean business, but at this point, it's not really as simple as just backing out, is it? We've come all this way. Now we need to show the world that we can win over these Fascists."

"Of course I want to beat them, but that's a tall order. When I went to Amsterdam, nothing went as the coaches planned.

People got sick, the facilities were unfamiliar, weird things happened. I wasn't a favorite at all, but got lucky and won. You can't take anything for granted here. There's a lot of pressure."

Helen lay down on the bed, massaging her temples. Because of the pain in her legs, she had scarcely run in the last week. What if she didn't do well when it was time to race? She'd return home a nobody. After all the fanfare Fulton had showered upon her, the idea of going back to William Woods College as a failure was enough to make her feel ill. She'd told everyone she was the fastest woman in the world and she fully intended to live up to that promise. She simply couldn't go home without a victory.

"What's wrong? Are your legs hurting?"

"No, I mean, yes, they are, but that's not what's worrying me at the moment. Do you think I can't win here?"

"Of course you can. I didn't mean to doubt you. All I'm saying is that we need to be careful. I wish I'd been paying more attention to the news."

"Do you feel guilty about participating?" Helen asked quietly.

Betty placed a sweater on her bed. "Yes. I keep telling myself that I shouldn't, that I'm an athlete whose job is to race, but I can't help it. I don't know what the right thing is anymore. And then I wonder if I'm crazy because there's a good chance that I may not even be selected for the relay."

"I'm sure you'll be selected."

"What makes you so sure?"

"You and Dee go way back. You've already won a silver medal in it. There's a good group of you who could run it and do well."

Betty sat on the edge of her bed. "Do you not want to run it?"

Helen batted at the air. "At this point, I'm just trying to get my shins better."

"So you're not going to try it?"

Something brittle in Betty's tone made Helen roll herself onto her elbow. "I really need to win individual gold. That's what I've been training for. That's what everyone back in Fulton is gunning for."

"But if we're going to win the relay, we need you. *I'll* need you."

Helen pursed her lips and chose her words carefully. "Dee and I have both agreed that we will see how my legs are doing and assess the relay after I've raced in the individual." All relay talk brought about a dull ache behind Helen's eyes. The precision of the transitions, the worrying about the other girls, the pressure not to let anyone down—it was more than she wanted to think about. The expectations seemed stifling.

At that moment, a woman appeared in their doorway. "Ladies, I welcome you to Berlin and am honored to serve such esteemed guests of the Reich. My name is Ruth Haslie. I've been assigned to serve as your translator and guide and am here to help you discover the best experiences and most helpful services that our fine city has to offer."

"Hello," Betty said.

Helen opened her mouth but was unable to form words. The sparkle of the woman's cobalt-blue eyes, the pink glow on the apples of her cheeks, and the pale yellow of her hair, the color of January sunshine—Helen was mesmerized. Even the most rudimentary greeting failed her.

Betty took one look at Helen and shook her head, giggling. "Please forgive our friend Helen. She's hungry and a bit out of sorts. We were on our way to go find something to eat. Perhaps you could help us with that?"

"I'd be honored to join you," Ruth said. "Are you looking for anything in particular?"

Helen coughed, clearing her throat. "Whatever you recommend."

"In that case, there is a delicious café nearby. Please, come with me."

"Is it a long walk?" asked Betty with an almost imperceptible glance toward Helen's legs.

"No, no, it is just this way." Ruth held out a pale hand and directed them out of the dormitory. When they reached the dormitory's courtyard, Ruth began a running commentary explaining all the features of the Reichssportfeld. Helen marveled at the well-tended green lawns as Ruth pointed to the tennis courts and the distant hockey field while talking the whole time. "During the Opening Ceremonies, you will be treated to a view of the *Hindenburg,* the largest commercial passenger-carrying airship in the world. Created by the Zeppelin Company, it is a miraculous feat of German engineering and is named for Paul von Hindenburg, former president of Germany. It has already traveled to Rio de Janeiro and made several trips to North America. Also, you will have the pleasure of viewing the final leg of the torch relay that began in Greece. This is the first time in modern history such a journey has been made, and it symbolizes—"

By this point, Ruth had led them out a gate onto a street

thrumming with activity. Busy cafés filled the sidewalks and Ruth selected one with a cheerful yellow awning. A fair-haired waiter ushered the women to a table.

Helen took a seat, eyeing the distance between herself and Ruth. She lifted her chair and moved it closer so their forearms were practically touching. "Fräulein, what do you recommend on the menu?" she asked.

"Eat a large meal now, for you will find that our evening meals are much lighter than the customary American dinner." Ruth's brow furrowed. "I do not think I answered your question properly."

"Sounds like you're reading from a manual, *How to Impress Your American Athletes*," Helen said.

"I enjoy the schnitzel." The German woman's smile revealed perfectly straight white teeth and her eyes darted around the café before she leaned in toward Helen and spoke quietly. "We were trained on our duties and I received a great deal of written instruction. Am I doing anything wrong?"

"Not at all," Helen said, holding her gaze. "You're perfect. I can't get over how much I've learned about these Olympic Games since meeting you."

Ruth nodded shyly before swiveling to the waiter at her side.

"I'll have whatever you're having," Helen said.

Ruth ordered in German for the three of them. Though Helen had always believed German to be an unattractive language, it sounded much better when spoken by Ruth.

"So how did you end up with this job?" Helen asked. "Are you from Berlin?"

"My father works as an administrator for the city. He's an engineer by training. I've been studying English for many years and passed an exam that allowed me to apply for this job."

"I'm impressed. You speak English beautifully," Helen marveled. "How lucky we are to have you as our guide."

Their waiter reappeared to place three tall glasses in the center of the table.

"Ah, our beers. You will enjoy these. *Prost!* I hope your upcoming races are a success, but more importantly, may I be so bold as to wish for the blossoming of new friendships?" Ruth smiled, lifting her glass in a toast.

"Meeting you offers promising possibilities, that's for sure." Helen lifted the beer closest to her and took a long swig, savoring the cool nip and fizz of the lager. Over the rim of her glass, she and Ruth locked gazes, and it felt as if everything and everyone else dropped away and they were sitting at the café by themselves.

Betty cleared her throat. "So, Ruth, where do you live?"

Ruth turned to Betty, and as she pushed one of her blond braids over her shoulder, Helen felt a sudden desire to reach out and gently wrap one of the silky long plaits around her wrist.

"Charlottenburg, not far from the zoo. Are you familiar with Berlin?" Ruth asked.

"No, not at all," Betty admitted.

"Over the next few days, when your presence isn't required at training, I can take you on excursions and show you the best of Berlin. Of course, I mean both of you." She glanced back at Helen shyly. "Do you have any special requests?"

Helen blinked. As long as they spent time together, she didn't care where Ruth took them. "I just need to be careful not to do a lot of walking."

On the final evening aboard the *Manhattan*, Helen had finally gone to Dee to tell her about her shin splints. Dee had surprised her by taking the news without making a fuss. "Go to the infirmary each day for massage, use ice, and don't let any of the press catch wind of this. Keep it a secret from everyone. We don't want anyone detecting any weakness in you," Dee had said.

At the reference to her leg pain, Helen felt Betty's gaze land on her. She knew she was supposed to stay quiet on the subject, but what was wrong with saying something to Ruth? After all, she was their guide. Helen looked from side to side to see if any of the surrounding café patrons appeared to be paying them any attention, but everyone seemed consumed in their drinks and conversation. "I'm having some trouble with shin splints," she confessed.

Ruth's expression grew serious. "I see. Have you booked appointments for every morning at your team's infirmary? I can save you the trip and do it for you."

"Helen—" Betty's voice held a note of caution, but Helen cut Betty off by raising her hand slightly.

"That would be wonderful, Ruth, thank you." And she lowered her hand onto the back of Ruth's chair.

Ruth didn't miss a beat. "I will do everything to help you perform at your finest."

For the rest of the meal, Helen set out to charm Ruth with stories of shenanigans aboard the *Manhattan*. Betty remained quiet.

It wasn't until the two of them were back in their room alone that Betty said, "I know you were quite taken with Ruth, but Dee told you not to mention your shin splints to anyone. Aside from Stella Walsh, the Germans are our biggest competitors."

"What? Do you think she's a spy or something?"

"I don't know what to think, but don't tell me that everything seems normal here."

"Ruth's fine," Helen snapped, turning away from Betty to busy herself with setting out her practice clothes for the following morning. She couldn't believe her good luck in discovering Ruth, but was it too good to be true?

49.

July 26, 1936
Berlin

LOUISE AND HER TEAMMATES SAT AT A SMALL TABLE amid the whirling and twirling masses filling the dance floor of the Resi, one of Berlin's most talked-about nightclubs.

Annette giggled. "Send one to Jesse."

"He probably gets the most messages of anyone in here. I'll send it to Mack instead." A mischievous grin spread across Tidye's features as she grabbed a pencil and bent over the small piece of paper before sealing it into the capsule, dropping it into the pneumatic tube, and yanking the handle. The women all watched as the paper disappeared, whisked off through the hidden network of tubes running throughout the grand dance hall. The place's glitz and excitement were beyond any the women had ever seen. The dance floor alone was rumored to hold one thousand dancers. And the ingenious method for sending messages between tables? Unbelievable. The women could have spent hours sending messages around the room to the numbered tables.

"I heard that the switchboard operators censor them for anything indecent," Louise said. "What did you write?"

"My little secret." Tidye tilted her head flirtatiously. "But I *may* have signed your name, not mine."

Louise laughed and took a sip of her champagne, twisting in her seat to face the water-jet ballet, where plumes of water shooting higher and higher into the air synchronized to the beat of automated orchestral music. Beside her, Betty bobbed her chin along to the tune while occasionally glancing at Helen and their guide, Ruth. The two women sat in the corner, deep in conversation, their heads so close that Helen's curls spilled over Ruth's smooth fair hair.

Betty, Louise, Tidye, and Annette turned their attention to the dance floor as Harriet stumbled toward them. Upon her arrival, the phone at the center of the table rang and Harriet grabbed it. "Hallo?" she trilled into the receiver. She squinted, trying to make sense of whatever the speaker at the other end of the line was saying. "Ja, ja," she answered before hanging up.

"Another invitation to dance?" asked Annette.

"Yes. This time from table thirty-two," Harriet answered, heading back toward the dance floor.

"Be careful," Betty said, plucking a cigarette from her pocketbook.

Harriet turned to look back at Betty over her shoulder. "Don't be such a stick in the mud. I'm fine. Wouldn't kill you to have a little fun too."

"Just don't forget what we're here for."

Harriet pouted. "Like I could forget."

No one else filled her dance card the way Harriet did. One German man after another lined up to keep her occupied, most of them in military uniform.

Louise glanced away from Harriet's retreating figure as a note arrived in their table's pneumatic mail tube and the women shrieked in delight. Tidye whisked it from the tube's opening. "I think this will be for you," she said, handing it to Louise.

Louise felt her face heat as she opened the folded note.

I'll walk you to your dorm whenever you're ready. —M

She looked up at them. "I think it's time for me to head back."

The women all hooted. "With Mack?"

Louise smiled and gathered her bag and evening wrap. Across the ballroom, she saw Mack rise and say goodbye to his friends.

"We'll be along soon," Tidye said. "But don't worry, we'll stroll back slowly and give you two plenty of time to talk." With her emphasis on *talk,* all the women burst into laughter and Louise looked down, hiding her delight.

Mack was waiting for her outside the dance hall's entrance, his usual wide grin stretching across his handsome face. He offered his arm to her and the two drifted along the boulevard. As soon as Louise had found her sea legs aboard the *Manhattan,* they had made taking a stroll about the deck each evening a habit. Since landing in Germany, they continued to meet for meals and walks together.

Louise pointed at the window of an art gallery, and from outside, they stopped to admire the paintings.

A German woman approached Louise holding a small book. "Good evening, Fräulein Stokes, may I please have your autograph?"

Louise signed her name and exchanged an *auf wiedersehen* with the Berliner.

"Did you ever imagine it would be like this here?" she asked Mack as they continued along the street.

"It's confusing, isn't it? We were told how much Hitler hated us, but no one said how much Berliners would love us. You should see it; whenever we're out on the streets with Jesse, he's swarmed by German girls, screaming his name and pushing their way toward him." He shook his head. "Did I tell you that a couple invited Dave and Jesse to have coffee in their apartment yesterday?"

"Really?"

"And they went," Mack added. "Said the people couldn't have been friendlier."

They passed a newsstand and Jesse's face gazed out at them from the front pages of several different Berlin papers. "Everyone loves him, but you know, the word is that you're the most photographed woman in Berlin," Mack said, tugging Louise closer.

"Who told you that?"

"Our guide read it in one of the Berlin papers."

Louise laughed and rested her head on Mack's shoulder.

"I love your big, beautiful smile," he said. "You should show it off more."

If melting from happiness was a possibility, Louise would have been a puddle on the sidewalk.

BACK IN THEIR room in Friesenhaus, Louise and Tidye changed into their nightgowns and prepared for bed. "You sure look like the cat who ate the canary," Tidye said, giving Louise a smug look before switching off the lamp between their beds. "Good for you. Mack is a dish."

Louise was happy the room was dark so Tidye couldn't tease her more about the elation she knew to be written across her face. Mack *was* a dish. When he had kissed her good night in the Friesen-Garten, Louise could have stayed there all night in his arms. If Tidye and the others hadn't shown up, she just might have, curfew be damned.

"Did you hear that Helen received an invitation to a special party on Friday night?" asked Tidye. Only thin curtains hung over the windows and moonlight spilled through the gauzy fabric, bathing the room in a silvery glow.

"Betty thinks that the German officials are doing everything they can to tire us out. The cold rooms, the parties. They want to see us at our events looking exhausted," Louise said.

Tidye snorted. "They're certainly doing everything they can to intimidate us at every turn."

"True," Louise said, pulling her covers to her chin. The Reichssportfeld alone defied comparison with anything she had ever seen. It had every sporting facility imaginable. Their guide had explained that the stadium could accommodate more than seventy-five thousand spectators. When Louise had entered into it with her teammates for a quick Opening Ceremonies rehearsal, she had not been the only one rendered speechless. Rows and rows of seating towered above them and the seating closest to the track was actually sunken, giving the track and field a stagelike setting. At the top of one of the entrance gate's pillars, two gigantic clocks kept exact time, and inside the stadium was a large cauldron-like structure where a fire would burn throughout the days of competition.

But if Louise was to arrive at events tired, it wasn't going to be because of their cold room and attending too many parties. Every night, she had trouble settling down because her mind was filled with images of Mack. She would replay their conversations and remember what it had been like to wrap her arms around his broad back and kiss him. How was a girl supposed to fall asleep with visions like that filling her head? After a few minutes in the dark, Tidye's breath became soft and steady, but Louise rolled over to her other side restlessly.

A commotion in the garden under their window made her stop moving and tilt her head to hear better. Muffled giggling and whispering floated into their room. Louise crawled across her bed to the window, pushed the curtain aside, and peered out. Below in the courtyard, underneath the boughs of a linden tree, two figures merged into one. Louise concentrated on their shadows. After several moments, they separated. Judging by the taller one's height and husky voice, it was Helen, while the other's gleam of blond hair could only belong to Ruth. The women leaned toward each other again and then eventually parted. Ruth vanished from the courtyard as the door to Friesenhaus creaked open and then closed behind Helen.

Louise remained staring into the courtyard. She had assumed the connection between Helen and Ruth to be platonic, but now she wasn't so sure. She lacked the vocabulary to describe such a relationship, however of one thing she was certain: if Mr. Brundage was willing to throw Eleanor Holm Jarrett off the team for carousing, he would be horrified by whatever Helen was doing with Ruth. Louise felt a pang of sympathy that surprised her. Yes, Helen tended to be loud and too eager to take the spotlight, but without her remarkable athletic abilities, she would simply be an awkward, homely woman unlikely to find satisfaction in a conventional life. What did the future hold for someone like her?

From her crouch, Louise's legs began to cramp so she shifted to slide back into bed, but as she did, dark figures appeared visible in the wooded space beyond the garden below her window. Clouds scuttled across the full moon overhead, but as she leaned closer to the crack in the curtains and looked toward the woods, movement flashed through the darkness. For a moment she held her breath, but then exhaled, watching the moon, waiting for a spell when the clouds would clear and provide an unobstructed view of the woods.

And then she got what she had been waiting for. The clouds cleared. Silver moonlight flooded the garden and the edges of the woods, illuminating a weird tableau. Through the trees, rows and rows of figures became visible. They marched in lockstep to a rhythm that Louise couldn't hear but could feel in her chest as they moved. *One, two, three. One two, three.* Soldiers. The woods were full of them.

As if they could feel Louise watching them, they halted, dropped, and raised rifles to their shoulders for a beat before standing. Shocked, she leaned away from the window, a cold fear gripping her. Had anyone seen her?

A minute passed. She couldn't resist looking again. The soldiers were back on the move. Marching and then dropping to their knees. They did it over and over again, and Louise realized they were practicing. But for what?

She shrank back into bed and curled into a ball, almost expecting the soldiers to explode into the room at any moment. Yet Friesenhaus remained peaceful. Eventually she fell into a fitful sleep, and when she awoke to another unseasonably cold gray dawn, she peered out the window again to an empty garden and woods. No soldiers. In the light of day, the previous evening's military exercises felt unlikely. Had she dreamed them?

And then she saw smudged fingerprints on the glass of the window. Her fingerprints. The soldiers weren't a dream. She had seen them.

50.

July 31, 1936
Berlin

SEVERAL NIGHTS LATER, BETTY STOOD BEFORE THE open door of a shiny black Mercedes-Benz and paused before climbing inside and settling into the deep leather seats next to Helen and Ruth. Though Betty tried to ignore it, she had a funny feeling about the evening ahead of them. Because of the high hopes pinned upon her, Helen had been issued the invitation to a party on Pfaueninsel Island thrown by Reichstag president Göring and Herr Goebbels, the minister of public enlightenment and propaganda. After securing Mrs. Brown, the wife of one of the team doctors, to chaperone, she had elected to bring Betty and Ruth too.

"Don't forget that you're representatives of the United States," Mrs. Brown reminded them as the car maneuvered southwest through the evening traffic clogging the city's streets. "Be sure you act accordingly."

"According to what?" Ruth asked.

"It's an idiom." Helen laughed. "Apparently we're supposed to comport ourselves in a virtuous manner and represent our country with pride."

"I see." Ruth fidgeted with the buttons running up her cream-colored silk frock.

"Fräulein Haslie, it's delightful that you've struck up such a strong friendship with Helen and Betty," Mrs. Brown said, but her narrowed eyes belied the compliment.

"She sure has," Helen said, taking Ruth's hand, immune to Mrs. Brown's chilly tone. "And boy, have her translation and guide services come in handy."

"Mrs. Brown, that's the most becoming color on you," Betty said quickly, gesturing at their chaperone's seafoam-green taffeta gown. "Where did you find such a fetching dress?"

As Mrs. Brown launched into a full description of the shopping she had done in Paris the previous spring, Betty elbowed Helen, hoping to caution her. Helen was getting careless and seemed to be taking unnecessary chances and drawing attention to her infatuation with Ruth, and this worried Betty. Since their arrival in Berlin, Helen's star had been on the rise. Reporters, coaches, teammates, everyone wanted a piece of her. Scores of fans arrived to watch her practice and newspapermen peppered her with questions. Helen reveled in the attention and always had a snappy rejoinder to any question, a broad smile for the crowds. Everyone loved her.

Betty's earrings were pinching her so she unsnapped them as she watched Helen whisper something to Ruth. *Was she jealous of Helen's success?* And if she really poked the tender feeling deep inside her, was she even a little jealous of Helen's affection for Ruth? Since qualifying for the team in Providence, Betty had been trying not to stir up her doubts about her own running abilities, and Helen's idolization of her had provided a comforting tonic while aboard the S.S. *Manhattan*. Did she miss being the center of Helen's attention?

Their car slid to a stop and Betty peered out the window to see swarms of partygoers swarming the dock at the River Havel.

When Helen had first brought up the idea of attending the party, she had been souvenir shopping with Betty and Ruth in a boutique on Kurfürstendamm. At the mention of Pfaueninsel Island and Herr Goebbels, Ruth had appeared uncomfortable. "Are all of your teammates going?" she asked, riffling through a rack of colorful postcards. "I have not heard the other guides speak of it."

"No, I've gotten a special invitation and can bring a few friends," Helen said, winking at Ruth. "Hey, when we're done with racing, what do you say we try for a little day trip here?" She held a postcard of a grand palace. "Sanssouci Palace. It looks so beautiful and romantic and the name means 'without worries'—isn't that perfect?"

Betty barely glanced at the postcard and instead focused on Ruth's tense expression. It was unlike Ruth, who was normally so cheerful, to balk at anything Helen proposed. Since Ruth had mentioned that her family lived in Charlottenburg, Betty had been making inquiries of the other guides about the city and pieced together that the Haslies lived in an upscale neighborhood. The guides had been selected from Berlin's finest families, which begged the question: Did Ruth's parents serve in the Reich?

"Ruth, why do you ask who else is going?" Betty asked.

"It's a party for some of the highest members of the party.

Many important politicians will be there and . . ." Ruth's voice trailed off. She gestured that they should leave the shop and led them a ways down the sidewalk to stand under a plane tree.

Ruth shook her head and studied the people wandering past before whispering, "Betty, pull out your cigarettes and light one so we can talk a moment without drawing attention."

Betty lit one and raised her eyebrows at Ruth, awaiting explanation.

"There are spies for the Reich everywhere. You both must be careful. Helen is a figure of interest and people are watching her."

Betty had taken a deep inhalation. "To be honest, Ruth, I've wondered where your loyalties lie."

"Betty, come on now—" Helen began, but Ruth stopped her.

"No, it is fine. You are smart to be paying attention. Many of the guides probably are informers, but I am not. Because of my language studies and my father's administrative position with the city, I was a good candidate for this program, but I have no real affiliation with the Nationalist Socialist Party."

Betty had figured out that most of the guides were proud members of the party. When she had spoken with Annette's guide, the young German woman had plucked what she called a Nationalist Socialist friendship pin from her chest and handed it to Betty. The smooth, colorful enamel pin with its bold black swastika on its center had felt surprisingly heavy and Betty had tried to appear delighted, even as she pocketed the loathsome memento swiftly.

Betty looked into Ruth's vivid blue eyes. "But that still doesn't really tell us why we should trust you."

When Ruth raised her hand to push back a loose strand of

blond hair from her face, her hand was trembling. "My maternal grandmother was raised Jewish, but converted and married a Protestant," she whispered. "My father has always identified as a Christian. This technically gives me the status of a *mischling*, but since my grandmother spent the majority of her life on the register in a Christian church, her origins have not been discovered. My family must hide this aspect of our ancestry. It is a secret. My father could lose his job. We are merely trying to fit in and not raise any questions in anyone's mind. Please believe me when I say you can trust me."

"But surely they don't keep track of everyone's religion for generation upon generation. That sounds impossible," Betty said.

"If they can locate the information, they track it," Ruth insisted.

Helen inhaled sharply and took Ruth's hand. "Your secret's safe with us."

Betty nodded, although the truth was that she still didn't really understand the full implications of what Jewish ancestry meant. Helen had spoken of the Führer's speeches about creating a master race and eliminating the Jews, but the idea sounded far-fetched, impossible to carry out.

"I'm very fond of both of you," Ruth said, looking back and forth at Betty and Helen, but she allowed her gaze to linger on Helen.

"I'm one of the most visible athletes here. Nothing can go wrong," Helen said. "I'll accept the invitation to keep our hosts happy, right? Let's just go and see what all of the hullabaloo is about. It'll make for an interesting story to take back home." She folded Ruth's arm under her own as if that sealed the deal.

They had returned to shopping for small gifts to bring home, but the seriousness of that conversation had stuck with Betty. Helen was very knowledgeable about newsworthy people and events and their import, but with the breathless news coverage of her athleticism increasing every day, she seemed to believe she was invincible.

Their car had been idling in a line of party guests unloading, and when a liveried servant opened the car door to help the women out, Betty startled.

"Goodness, dear, what's wrong?" Mrs. Brown asked. "Come now, let's have some fun."

The older woman led the way and stood beside the car, smoothing her taffeta evening gown, appraising the scene.

Helen groaned as she stepped from the car. "These heels are going to be the death of me."

"Then why on earth did you wear them? You should be resting your legs," Betty said.

"No dancing," Ruth scolded.

"Aye, aye, no dancing!" Helen gave a mock salute. "Thank you both for worrying about me, but you know the saying, beauty over death!" Helen shimmied and gestured at her full-length gown, a hand-me-down from a friend's mother back in Fulton. "You don't end up as glamorous as this without a few sacrifices. But come on now, admit it, aren't you curious about this party?"

"Berliners have been talking about it for months now. The most elite and fashionable people of the world will be here. And now, so are we!" Mrs. Brown said as the women crossed a pontoon bridge and let out a collective sigh as thousands of butterfly-shaped lanterns glowed overhead in leafy oaks, creating soft pockets of light in the darkness.

A fair-haired, golden-skinned young man wrapped in a gauzy toga offered them a tray of coupes filled with icy-cold champagne. Betty took one and brought it to her lips, but paused to admire the fizzing bubbles racing toward the surface and the reflection of overhead lanterns before taking a sip. A twelve-piece band played jazz on a raised platform over a dance floor and beyond it stood a small white castle illuminated by torches. "It looks just like a fairy tale," she said, sighing with contentment as the champagne danced along her tongue.

"Yes, there's a lovely English garden on the other side of the castle," Ruth said. "There was also a beautiful building filled with flowers and plants, but it burned down many years ago."

"Aren't you something?" Helen looped her arm through Ruth's. "What else do you know about this place?"

"Pfaueninsel means 'peacock.' At one point, a king kept quite the menagerie of exotic animals here, but he eventually donated them to the Berlin Zoo. All that's left are the peacocks. If we were here during the daytime, we would see them strutting around."

"Wouldn't that be something?" Mrs. Brown murmured, her gaze roving the revelers. She raised a hand in greeting to a cluster of matrons and turned to Ruth, Betty, and Helen. "Ladies, excuse me while I chat with some friends. Don't go far." And with that, she swept off.

"It appears there are all kinds of other creatures here strutting their stuff," Betty said, watching a group of young blond women cavorting through the party in togas, tossing carnations into the air. Once the dancing women moved on, Betty caught sight of a familiar head of dark glossy hair. "Eleanor?"

Their former teammate turned. "Darlings! Fancy bumping into you here." Eleanor swept Betty into her arms and then turned to give Helen a once-over. She whistled in admiration. "My, my, Miss Stephens, you've come a long way from Oklahoma, haven't you?"

"Missouri," Helen said.

"What?" Eleanor cupped a gloved hand to her ear and leaned toward Helen.

"I'm from Missouri."

"Missouri, Oklahoma, Timbuktu, does it really matter? We're here"—she spread her slender arms wide—"at the most gorgeous party in the world. Now *that's* what's important, right?"

Betty shook her head in delight. "You're the last person I expected to see."

"Now, now, give me some credit. A girl like me doesn't run home with her tail between her legs." She wrapped an arm around Helen and Betty and pulled them close. "I landed a job as a reporter. Isn't that a gas? Plan to see me all over town for the next few weeks. Wherever there's action, I'll be there." She spotted Ruth. "My, my, who's this beautiful creature?"

After Helen introduced Ruth, Betty raised her glass to the group. "Here's to all of us landing on our feet."

The women clinked their glasses together and champagne spilled over the edges and ran down their arms. Seeing Eleanor, the silkiness of her evening gown against her skin, the scent of gardenias in the air—something released in Betty. She lifted her wrist to her mouth and licked the champagne off, giggling.

"Attagirl. Don't let a single drop go to waste," Eleanor said, hiccupping. Then she let out a small shriek and pointed toward the crowd. "Look."

Betty arched her head to follow Eleanor's gaze. At the moment she spotted Mr. Brundage, his eyes met Eleanor's. He stiffened, his face froze.

Eleanor pursed her lips into a pout and blew him a kiss. "Yoo-hoo, you can't escape me, you old toad!"

He turned on his heel and walked in the other direction, disappearing into the crowd, one more man in a black tuxedo.

"Isn't this rich?" Eleanor howled with laughter and grabbed the sleeve of a passing waiter to take another glass. Betty also exchanged her empty coupe for a full one.

"To Berlin," they all cried, raising their drinks for another toast.

Eleanor stepped back and dabbed at the tears of laughter gathering in the corners of her eyes. "Darlings, I'm off to explore," she said. "See you soon."

As she pirouetted away, Betty, Helen, and Ruth sipped at their champagne, watching the crowd. Suddenly a man in a crisp military uniform appeared next to Helen and tapped on her shoulder.

"Excuse me, Fräulein Stephens and Fräulein Robinson, Herr Göring has expressed that he would be honored to meet you. Please follow me."

Helen shrugged and took a step after him as Betty and Ruth exchanged concerned looks before hurrying to follow.

The never-ending champagne had begun to take its toll and voices had gotten louder, the dancing looser and more daring. Betty passed a woman whose evening gown was hiked up around her thighs, gyrating as her dance partner looked on with a glassy, rapt expression. Torches cast elongated shadows of men and women pressed together into embraces. Betty passed the debauchery and followed the soldier into the castle. Down a long dark paneled hallway they went until reaching a heavy door. The soldier rapped on it, and the door swung open to reveal a long rough-hewn wooden table, its legs carved with elaborate designs. He gestured for the women to enter and then stepped back, his heels clicking together. The door closed with a heavy clank and he was gone.

The room was warm and smelled of melting candle wax and roasting meat, something gamey. Classical music played on a large radio console behind them, its beat low and heavy. Betty looked to Helen and saw her friend's expression, both fascinated and repulsed, so she turned and looked farther down the table to where a corpulent man sat, splayed in a heavy wooden chair resembling a throne. He wore a black silk robe that gaped at his chest, revealing rolls of pale flesh sprouting occasional tufts of graying hair. His thinning oiled dark hair was combed back, though several strands had sprung loose and hung lank across his forehead. Surrounding the second-most-powerful man in the Reich, several women in skimpy peignoirs lounged, glassy-eyed and slack-jawed. Göring squinted at his glass and grunted, and one of the women stumbled to a table to fetch a magnum to pour more wine. Another tottered to her feet and stood behind him, massaging his neck, as he surveyed Helen, Betty, and Ruth. Slapping the masseuse's hands away, he stood.

He snapped his fingers and the wine server thrust heavy

glasses of Burgundy into the hands of Helen, Betty, and Ruth. Up close, the woman's pupils were so dilated that her empty eyes appeared black. Betty looked into her glass of wine. It was dark and thick, almost syrupy. Could something other than wine be in it? She glanced over at Ruth and Helen, who were also peering into their glasses, their expressions similarly troubled.

Betty backed away at the same time Herr Göring approached with one slablike hand extended toward Helen. She remained motionless, but this didn't stop him from taking her hand to lift it to his lips. Behind him, the wine server, masseuse, and other women slunk toward the back of the room, disappearing behind a red velvet wall hanging.

Betty ran her hand over her forehead. Her earlier giddiness from the champagne and the dancing evaporated, and she tried to breathe in the suffocating heat of the room.

He turned to Betty. As his lips landed on the top of Betty's hand, she suppressed the urge to grimace at the beads of sweat collecting on his forehead. When he released her hand, she unobtrusively wiped it down the back of her dress.

"*Willkommen*. Sit. Drink," he growled before reaching for Ruth's hand, but rather than letting him paw her, she stepped back into Helen, who reflexively wrapped her arm around Ruth's shoulders possessively. It took only a split second for Helen to realize what she'd done and drop her arm from Ruth, but it was too late.

A slow, oily expression of delight quirked at the corners of Göring's mouth. "This is interesting. What do we have here?"

Helen pushed her glass to him. "*Bitte,* Herr President Göring, but I'm afraid we have a team curfew. We must leave."

"*Nein.* We only have two chairs, but perhaps you"—he pointed at Ruth—"can sit on Fräulein Stephens's lap? I would like to see that."

Betty peeked over her shoulder toward the closed door. *Could they leave?* The empty mahogany chairs in front of them appeared heavy, impossible to move. Once they were seated, there would be no quick escape.

At that moment, the door clicked open behind them and the soldier reappeared. He murmured something to Herr Göring, who promptly grunted.

The attaché turned to the women. "Fräuleins, Herr President has an important phone call. Please excuse him."

"*Nein,* they wait."

"But we have team curfew," Helen repeated.

Her protests made Göring's leer turn menacing. "Ach, you disgust me. I can cause many problems for anyone. Even a champion," he spat, before turning and storming away, his back as broad as a boulder.

Betty, Ruth, and Helen hesitated, shocked, but then they spun and raced for the door without bothering to wait for the attaché. They continued down the hallway toward the main entrance and dashed outside to the terrace, where Betty searched the crowd for a familiar face. "Thank goodness for that phone call," she said, her lungs heaving with the cool air and the skunky smell of river water. "That was about to get ugly."

"But we could have outrun him," Helen said in a shaky voice that undermined the bravado of her words.

"No. These things cannot be outrun. This is very bad," Ruth said. Her face appeared bloodless, her eyes wide with terror.

"Let's go," Betty said, pointing and moving ahead to weave through the crowd. When she looked over her shoulder to make certain they were following her, Helen was practically dragging a stunned-looking Ruth.

A redheaded woman lurched into her path, a bottle of champagne in her hand. Betty took in the familiar snub-nosed profile. "Harriet?"

Their teammate turned. Her lipstick had smeared, leaving her face blurry, her expression hard to decipher. "Well, if it isn't everyone's beloved Olympians?" she slurred, raising the bottle to drink out of it directly. Foam sloshed from its opening and bubbled down the dark green glass.

"Harriet, we're leaving. You should come with us. It's getting late." Helen reached for her pale freckled arm, but Harriet shook her off.

"I'm staying."

"But we have a busy schedule tomorrow. It's Opening Ceremonies. Come on," Helen urged.

"No!" Harriet's voice rose in indignation. "I'm having fun."

"Are you sure?" Betty said, lowering her voice as people turned to check the commotion.

Harriet leaned in and hissed, "You don't get it, do you? Both of you will race. Helen's the star of the show and you're the one everyone loves. And you?" She looked at Ruth, her lips twisting in an ugly sneer. "I don't know who you are, but you're too beautiful for your own good."

"We dance!" A young blond man in a military uniform appeared at Harriet's side and looped his arm around her waist. He pulled her close roughly, tearing a ruffle from her dress, but neither noticed. Harriet giggled, her arms dangled by her sides as if boneless, and he tugged her away; they vanished into a cloud of laughter and cigarette smoke.

Betty and Helen shook their heads but continued pressing through the crowd in search of Mrs. Brown.

"She's over there," Helen cried, pointing to their chaperone standing alongside a table laden with small plates of sliced Frankfurter Kranz, Kaiserschmarrn, and other desserts.

Betty dashed up to her. "We're ready to go."

"Isn't it a bit early?" Mrs. Brown asked, grasping her dessert plate tightly.

"We need to be home before curfew," Helen said, taking her plate. "You can have this in the car."

"My, you three are such responsible girls," Mrs. Brown said, her gaze lingering on her slice of cake longingly. "Fine, fine, off we go."

Once they were settled in the back seat of their black sedan, a deep rumbling shook the automobile. Red, orange, and bright green flashes of light bathed the air overhead. All four women whipped their heads around in alarm to look out the rear window. Fireworks lit the sky, blooming in sprays of tinted stars. Each boom reverberated in Betty's chest.

"Helen—" Betty started, but Helen waved her off, her gaze resting on Ruth, who sat rigid, her back toward them as she faced the window, her shoulders trembling as if she was weeping.

51.

August 4, 1936
Berlin

WHENEVER HELEN HAD IMAGINED RUNNING THE 100-meter in the Olympics, she'd pictured a glorious summer day and a crowd booming with adulation as she roared down the straightaway to capture her title as fastest woman in the world. In reality, it was nothing like that. For most of the morning of her race, a light drizzle had fallen, but when Helen arrived at the stadium for her first competition, the discus throw, the drizzle thickened to a lashing rain. Multiple events were under way in the stadium, and the whole place felt disorganized, chaotic, and cold.

Helen knew she needed to focus on competing, but since the party on Pfaueninsel Island, Ruth had been a nervous wreck and threatening to leave Berlin. Helen felt sick with how she had put Ruth at risk. She should have known better. Now here she was—alone, drenched, and standing in soggy wet grass awaiting her turn in the discus, an event she had little chance of winning. Her navy-blue sweatshirt and pants hung off her, waterlogged and heavy, and hanks of her hair stuck plastered to her forehead.

Over on the track, the racers began to gather for the 100-meter finals.

Helen strained to see if her running competitors had taken their places, but saw only the three German women who had qualified for the finals circling the starting area. Could officials start the finals of the 100-meter without her? Was that even possible? She shifted from side to side with impatience as Gisela Mauermayer, a German woman in first place in the discus, began bobbing up and down to prepare for her final throw. If Helen missed her race because of the discus, she would be beside herself. She had been waiting far too long for this rematch with Stella and could scarcely wait to beat the Polish runner again!

Helen squinted into the rain toward the starting area for the 100-meter. Five women—everyone but her—stood listening to instructions from the officials. Annette, tall and narrow, towered over dark-haired Stella. Even from her spot across the wide expanse of field, Helen could sense Stella's taut focus and anxiety. Since they had met in St. Louis, Helen had been eager to prove her mettle against the other woman, and when reporters goaded her for a snappy bit of copy on their rivalry for their newspapers, she was always happy to oblige. But watching Stella huddled against the cold wind, Helen shivered. Maybe she had it all wrong. She could get invited to fancy parties and kiss beautiful women, but the truth was that she had more in common with Stella than she did with most other people. Running defined them.

"Fräulein Stephens!" a judge shouted, and Helen sprang forward, rolling up the sodden sleeve on her right arm before reaching for the discus. She wrapped her pruned fingers around the edge of it, slippery and cold in her hands. She stepped into the throwing area, trying to still her mind, but it was impossible not to strain her ears, listening for the announcer to mention final call for the 100-meter. She needed to be done with her field event so she could get to running, so she bobbed, began her spin, and let the cold wind rip the discus from her. As soon as it left her hand, she felt the imbalance, the uncertainty. The discus wobbled and spun through the rain until it landed with a thud nowhere near Gisela's distance marker, far from what she needed to get out of the middle of the pack.

Helen didn't even wait for her official result on the throw, but instead turned and jogged toward the track. When she reached the starting area, she sought out Dee, peeling off her wet tracksuit as she approached her.

"How did it go over there?"

"I'm in eighth place at the moment, but there are still more throws."

Dee sighed. "Well, this is your best event. We know Stella didn't run her fastest yesterday, so don't take anything for granted."

Helen nodded, cupped her hands, and blew on them, trying to regain some feeling in her fingertips.

Annette jogged over and hopped up and down, attempting to stay warm. Goose pimples dotted her skin.

Dee dashed a towel over Annette's shoulders. "What about you? Ready?"

"Ready as I'll ever be."

Dee nodded and the women turned and headed for their

lanes on the track. Helen tried to steady her breathing, but her white satin tank top felt tight across her broad chest. The wet red cinder clumped underfoot, sticking to her black leather track shoes. The last few days jumbled through her mind. The crowds and pageantry of the Opening Ceremonies, her massage sessions at the infirmary, watching Jesse Owens win both the 100-meter and the long jump. She wanted to win too.

She wanted a gold medal.

No, she *needed* a gold medal.

Without one, she was nothing.

With numb fingers, she dug her starting position into the cinder. Small pools of water immediately appeared in the divots where she needed to place her feet. Stella lowered into her crouch. The people in the stands, yelling and screaming, appeared immune to the weather.

The starting official took his position and signaled for the women to take their places. She crouched and rocked back and forth, stretching her shoulders. Her fingers dug into the clumps of wet cinder. Helen followed the starter's commands and let everything and everyone drop away, her mind clear and ready. She inhaled and felt the breath travel easily as if reaching every corner of her body. Her shins no longer hurt. Everything seemed to quiet as the rain eased into a drizzle and the wind died.

The gun fired.

Helen sprang from her starting crouch and leapt into the lead. Her body moved as if in a dream, effortlessly, as if her feet barely skimmed the red cinder. She was alone on the track and all she could hear was the steadiness of her own breathing in and out of her lungs, her heart pounding in her ears. And before she knew it, the ribbon snapped across her chest and she raised her hands. She had done it. No one else was even close.

Her final time: 11.5 seconds.

Though Annette and the officials were congratulating her, Helen turned to find Stella standing several feet away, bewildered and small, her shoulders hunched against the drizzle. Helen reached out and took the other runner's hand in her own. Though disappointment pooled in Stella's eyes, her face relaxed into a shy smile.

Helen allowed herself to be guided by several young girls in white dresses adorned with flowers in their hair to the medalists' podium, but kept Stella close to her side. Together they climbed onto the steps and joined Germany's Käthe Krauss, the third-place finisher. An official took his position with the medals. Once the laurel wreath was placed on her head and her gold medal looped around her neck, Helen smiled at the sea of flags waving in the distance, all different colors, a blurred rainbow in the gray landscape. Music played, but it was hard to hear over the yelling. There was little time to savor anything. As soon as the anthem finished, the officials and her teammates pulled her apart from Stella and towed her toward the sidelines. Dee pushed through the runners and officials and pulled Helen into a tight embrace.

"Well done! Now we need to get you to the telegraph office for a radio interview," she said, thrusting Helen's track bag at her.

A young aide clad in a khaki-colored army uniform moved into their path. "*Sieg Heil!* Fräulein Stephens, the Führer would like to meet you."

"The Führer?" She gazed up to the Führer's special viewing box and there he was, looking straight at her, the little familiar dark-haired man in his double-breasted trench coat, his hand outstretched in that awkward Nazi salute. All the heat that had suffused her since winning vanished and she felt every drop of the cold drizzle pelting her shoulders.

"*Kommen Sie.*" The aide gestured for her to follow him.

"No!" Dee took Helen's arm and tugged her away. "She has a radio interview with CBS now." She leaned into Helen and whispered, "Start walking."

Helen did exactly that. She stretched out her famously long stride and marched alongside Dee to the press office. The attendant hurried along beside them, shaking his head in disbelief.

"I tell *mein* Führer no? You must *kommen. Kommen Sie mit!*"

He reminded Helen of a small dog yipping and leaping along at her heels, an ankle biter. Her vision shrank into a pinhole as she bored her way through the throng, trying to ignore the entreaties of the Nazi official and the calls for attention from the crowd. Dee wrapped one arm around Helen and used the other to push through the people in front of them. They made it to the press office and the young man followed them, watching as Helen was perched in front of a large microphone and earphones were placed on her head.

She forced herself to smile widely, laughed and accepted congratulations, but felt as though she was watching herself from a distance. Her chest seized into a rock of anxiety and she could barely force air into her lungs. *Where was Ruth?* Although she answered the interviewer's questions and even made a few jokes, she had no idea what she was saying, but it didn't seem to matter—everyone looked delighted. She pulled her autograph book from her bag and handed it around for signatures. All the while, her stomach clenched into a tight fist, equal parts anticipation and fear. She knew the Nazi attendant was watching her every move. There was no way she could sneak out of this invitation.

Someone handed her autograph book back, and when the interviewer bade her farewell, she glanced at Dee. The two women locked gazes, resignation in both of their expressions.

They followed the attendant from the press office and down a flight of stairs to a small room. A group of black-shirted men entered, each one circling the space, blocking off the doorways, staring through Helen and Dee, their gazes cold and calculating.

The man at the center of it all, Adolf Hitler, marched into the room and stopped in front of Helen so close she could see the smooth skin of his cheeks, the gray hairs bristling his temples and strange little mustache, and the deep furrows between his clear pale blue eyes. He had taken off his trench coat and now sported a military dress uniform, huge swastikas blazing on each sleeve. He smiled at Helen, eyes bulging with delight, and she looked down at him, trying to suppress the nervous laugh that bubbled in her throat.

Before she knew what she was doing, she thrust out her hand for him to shake and pushed her autograph book at him. She watched in fascination as his translator explained that she wanted his autograph. The Führer took a pen from the man and scribbled his signature on a blank page.

At the exact moment he finished signing, a camera flashed.

Hitler startled and his expression transformed from a broad grin into a murderous grimace. He spun around, searching for the source of the flash and bellowing a stream of guttural commands, his face turning a deep shade of violent purple as he shrieked at the photographer standing beside them. Immediately, four black-shirted bodyguards threw themselves onto the photographer and pinned the man by his arms and waist in front of Herr Hitler.

The Führer, still screaming, leered at the photographer, slapping him across the face with a pair of black leather gloves he held in his hand, and then he started kicking the man in the belly.

Thunk. Thunk. Thunk.

With each thud of impact, the photographer let out a desperate sound, a mixture of groan and cry.

The Führer paused, his teeth bared, and lowered his aim to drive his leather boot into the man's shins. With each strike to the bone, the photographer's face turned gray with shock and terror. After several strikes, his camera clattered to the ground and Hitler drove it into the wall with the toe of his boot. The sound of glass shattering rang out. A bodyguard opened a door and the other guards tossed the photographer through it. His camera followed. The door slammed behind him.

It all happened so quickly that Helen and Dee froze, only startling back to attention as the black-shirted guards encircled them again. Screams still seemed to echo off the concrete walls of the room. Helen stared at the autograph book in her hand. She didn't remember anyone handing it back.

The Führer sniffed and rubbed a hand under his nose before turning back to Helen and Dee. He spoke calmly to his translator, gesturing toward Helen, a look of admiration spreading across his face.

The translator swallowed and cleared his throat before speaking carefully in English. "Welcome, Fräulein Stephens. You must consider running for Germany. Fair hair. You are a big, strong woman. The chancellor says you are pure Aryan, no?"

What was she supposed to say? Helen's insides felt as though they had turned to water and her legs quaked. *"Danke?"*

Hitler spoke quickly to his translator.

"And how do you like Germany?" the man asked.

"Berlin is beautiful. Even in the rain."

"Would you care to spend the weekend with the chancellor at his villa at Berchtesgaden?"

Helen blinked, stunned. *What?*

Before she could react, Dee stepped forward and spoke firmly. "Tell your Führer that Fräulein Stephens is training for Monday's relay. Please thank him on her behalf, but *nein,* she's not available."

Hitler watched the exchange with interest, and when it became clear that Dee was saying no, he gave Helen a long, icy stare and spoke again to the translator.

"Ah, yes," the man said. "He says it's a shame the American women will lose to our team and urges Helen to take care of herself."

Hitler gave a small shrug, still smiling, and then leaned toward Helen to embrace her. She recoiled, but he moved quickly, reaching his hands around her waist and rubbing them up and down her buttocks several times. She inhaled in horror. Was no one going to stop him? He finished his explorations with a sharp pinch, stood back, saluted her, and then marched from the room without a backward glance.

Helen and Dee remained rooted in the center of the small room, stunned.

The aide cleared his throat and gestured toward the door that would take them outside.

With a shaking arm, Helen grabbed Dee's elbow, and they followed him.

In the harsh overhead lighting of the concrete hallway, the aide gave them a wolfish smile. "Fräuleins, be careful."

52.

August 4, 1936
Berlin

BETTY PULLED A SILVER FLASK FROM HER TRACK BAG and poured some whiskey into Helen's coffee. "Drink this," she said.

After taking a long swig, Helen lowered the mug. It was empty and her hand had finally stopped shaking.

From where she sat across from Helen and Betty, Ruth glanced around the team's dining hall. "I must leave today. The Führer has taken a special interest in you and you denied him. It's all too much attention. This can only lead to trouble for me."

"I know, I'm sorry, but—" Helen started to say.

"Ruth's right," Betty said, cutting her off. "You just said that the Führer's aide even repeated the warning to be careful."

Helen cradled her head in her hands. "I've really made a hash of this, haven't I? The last thing I wanted to do was put you at risk. What about your family?"

A wisp of sympathy passed over Ruth's face as she leaned across the table, taking both of Helen's hands in hers. She opened her mouth to say something, but suddenly Harriet appeared beside them, raising a newspaper over the table to get their attention. "Oh my goodness, Helen, I'm so sorry."

The three women stared at Harriet.

"For what?" Helen asked, her annoyance plain.

A smirk curled at the corners of Harriet's mouth. Athletes from other tables were now watching them. Harriet stuck out her chest, dropped the newspaper onto the table, and squealed loudly, "Why, haven't you heard? The Polish team is accusing you of being a man!"

If Harriet had tossed a grenade onto the table, she couldn't have achieved more of an explosive reaction.

From a neighboring table, Annette stood. "What in the world? That's ridiculous!"

"Did she just say *a man*? Sounds like sour grapes to me. Helen, don't read that garbage," Olive said.

"How desperate! It's such poor sportsmanship." Gertrude shook her head.

Everyone else burst into expressions of outrage and amazement, but Helen froze. Betty grabbed for the paper and held her breath, forcing herself to read the headline of the evening edition of one of Berlin's English-language newspapers:

HELEN STEPHENS: WOMAN, MAN, OR FREAK?

Betty gasped, but before she could see more of the story Helen snatched the paper to hold it closer to her face, effectively blocking everyone else from seeing it. "I beat Stella, so they have to spread lies? Those Poles sure are a desperate lot, aren't they?" A tight grin was fixed on her face, but Betty could detect a sharp edge in her voice. Helen rose from her seat, folding the newspaper and tucking it under her arm. "I'm going back to my room to get some rest. See you all tomorrow."

"Don't even think about that baloney tonight. Sleep well," Gertrude called. The other athletes nodded and settled back into their meals, but Betty grabbed Ruth's hand and they followed Helen outside.

"Helen? Wait," Betty called after her.

Helen turned, her face taut with terror.

"What does it say?" Betty demanded, running to Helen's side.

"It says I'm a freak. That I'm lying and really a man."

"But that's nonsense."

"Is it? Betty, I'm not like you. I'm not pretty. I'm tall, ugly, and awkward and I've never been able to picture myself getting married and having a bunch of kids like everyone else. I'm different."

"None of that makes you a freak . . . or a man, for that matter. This is all part of a smear campaign to discredit your victory today. Maybe Ruth's been right. Maybe *this* is how the Nazis will hurt you."

Helen thrashed her finger on the word *Freak* in the headline. "Well, this hurts. This is exactly what I am. I've always been different. Since I've started running, I've become more acceptable, but I'm still a freak. Apparently I've fooled no one."

"Stop saying things like that." Betty turned to enlist Ruth's support in comforting Helen, but their guide had wrapped her arms around her chest and was shivering.

"Girls?" Dee approached the three of them. "I take it you've heard the Polish team's accusations?"

Helen's face reddened and while her gaze dropped to her feet, Betty pictured Helen holding Stella's hand on the medals podium and wanted to scream in fury. Without another word, she tore the newspaper from Helen's hand and ripped it in half. "Of all the betrayals! Why, that Stella Walsh can—"

"She had nothing to do with it," Helen whispered.

"How do you know?" Betty asked, crumpling the newspaper remnants into a ball. "Since St. Louis, she's said all kinds of dreadful things about you."

"Not this. I got a good look at her today up close. It wasn't her."

Dee nodded. "It seems the Germans have become more threatened by you. I'm sure they're behind this."

"But what's she supposed to do now?" Betty asked.

Dee sighed. "Officials are saying she has to have a medical exam to prove she's a woman. A group of doctors at the infirmary can do it."

Betty couldn't breathe. The idea of Helen stripping naked in front of a bunch of strange men and letting them poke and prod her? It was unthinkable. She glanced at Helen and saw the horror of the same realization stamped across her face.

"But once I do it, they'll stand by me?"

"Yes, they'll certify the results and disprove all of this nonsense." Dee rubbed a circle on Helen's shoulder blades awkwardly. "I'm sorry. I know it's not an ideal solution."

For once, Helen appeared defeated. "No, it's not."

"I told Mr. Brundage you would go to the infirmary at seven o'clock in the morning, when it opens. Get it over with. They'll be ready for you. And, Miss Haslie, I'm afraid it's time for you to go."

53.

August 5, 1936
Berlin

A NURSE LED HELEN INTO AN EXAM ROOM AND IN-
structed her to take off her clothing and don the thin cotton gown that lay folded in a square on a wooden chair beside
her. The woman left and Helen changed quickly and sat at the
edge of the exam table. She blinked back tears and started to
tremble. All night long the article had run through Helen's
mind, over and over, and by this point, she could practically
recite it word for word.

The fragile bit of strength she had cultivated ever since winning the race against Stella Walsh back in St. Louis disinte-
grated with every typed word of the story. It had summed up
every doubt that she had ever had about herself. The store-
bought clothes, the permanent wave, the lipstick, the fancy
high heels—none of it could disguise what she truly was: an
imposter. Now the whole world knew what she had known all
along.

And she had lost Ruth.

A sickening sense of vertigo overcame her and she reached for
the metal trash can beside the exam table and retched into it.

When she was done, she stood and wiped her mouth just as the door clanged open. Five doctors marched in, all wearing white medical coats and grim expressions.

"Fräulein Stephens," said one of the doctors, speaking in a heavy French accent. He stepped forward, brandishing a clipboard, and started to thumb through some papers. "We have the report your team doctor conducted before you boarded the S.S. *Manhattan*. This document is official and confirms your sex, so we do not need to conduct an exam."

Relief flooded Helen, but something inside her sparked. A realization. Her relief morphed into something jagged and angry. "Why didn't this information get reported yesterday? Why were the newspapers allowed to perpetuate lies about me without the IOC coming to my defense sooner?"

Five impassive faces glared back at her. The French doctor gave a gesture of dismissal. "Today the newspapers will report that you're a woman. Or maybe tomorrow."

She tried to keep her voice measured, calm. "But again, why didn't anyone come to my defense sooner?"

The man licked his lips, seemingly enjoying himself as he took his time with his verdict. "That is not our job. Nevertheless, I will write up a report and make it available to the public later."

All the humiliations she had suffered over the years flooded through her in a torrent. Pa's cruelties, her cousin's abuse, Ish's taunts of Popeye. Though she realized the doctors could probably see through her near-transparent gown, she stood, steeling herself against their callous inspection of her, their nonchalance toward her pain and indignation. This was no time to back down. *Let them look.* After all, wasn't that what they were really here for? She straightened her shoulders and loomed several inches taller than the men, and this brought a measure of satisfaction.

She gritted her teeth. "The fact that lies have been spread about me is unacceptable. I insist that the IOC issue an immediate statement confirming the truth about my sex. Write your report *now*."

The doctor removed his glasses and polished both lenses with the lapel of his white coat as he glanced around at his colleagues. "Ah, if nothing else, the mademoiselle confirms her sex with her impatience and lack of reason, *oui*?"

A German doctor chuckled. "Fräulein, what is the rush? All attention is on the German women now and their victory in the relay is imminent. While you have proven to be a force on the track, there is only one of you and your teammates are"—he pursed his lips—"lacking. You will not be news anymore. No one is interested in hearing more about the distasteful subject of your sex."

The other doctors sneered in agreement, and Helen was filled with a rage so hot and all-consuming, she could have sworn the dank room heated several degrees. She raised her finger and pointed it at the German doctor, stepping toward the men menacingly. They shuffled away slightly.

"I will do everything in my power to see that my teammates and I beat your team and win gold in that relay. I'm tired of you *little* men in your *little* white coats thinking that you're so superior to me. At this point, I have many friends who are reporters and I can assure you that I will have them dig around in your *little* lives to find things that would be greatly embarrassing if they were to make it into the press. Perhaps some financial malfeasance that could jeopardize your business standing. Or maybe the discovery of private associations that could bring instability to your family life. Or possibly revelations that you have a taste for something distasteful, shocking, maybe even deviant. Because with all of your smug expressions and the advantages endowed by your powerful positions, I'm sure there are things you hide. Whatever your secrets, let's put *your* lives up to public scrutiny and test *your* reputations and see how it feels, shall we? It could be an interesting experiment, don't you think? So, before we have to discuss this any further, go and write up that report that clears my name *now*. If your report is not included in this afternoon's newspapers, expect some uncomfortable consequences. Are we clear?"

Without another word, the doctors scurried for the door.

54.

August 5, 1936
Berlin

I HAVE NO IDEA HOW I WILL BACK UP MY THREAT IF THEY don't come through with their report, but it sure was satisfying to tell those doctors off," Helen said, her blood still throbbing hot and angry through her veins.

Dee, sitting on Betty's bed, folded her arms across her chest. "Your name will be cleared. I'm sure none of those fellows wants to test your resolve. Plus, Mr. Brundage doesn't want any gold medals in question."

Betty paced the floor of the small dorm room. "Maybe Mr. Brundage should be more concerned about the welfare of his athletes than the medals count."

Dee shifted and crossed her legs. "Ladies, it's time we start talking about the relay team. Helen, if you want to race in it and your legs feel strong enough, I see no reason to hold you back."

Helen wasn't going to let aching legs stop her now. Thinking back to her encounter with Hitler, how he had abused the photographer and then mistreated her, made her resolve to win even stronger. She also blamed her German hosts for her loss of Ruth, her first love. She could summon the memory of how

Ruth would shiver with delight as Helen kissed the soft patch of skin on her neck with such clarity that it made her chest ache. "I'm ready to give the relay everything I've got and then some. We've got to win it and beat these Germans."

Dee picked at the satin trim at the edge of the wool blanket beneath her. She didn't look at either woman as she spoke. "The Germans have a very strong team. They're the favorites. Even with you out there, I'm not sure we have enough speed to beat them."

"Who else will race?" Betty asked.

"Helen is a given. Beyond her, I'm thinking of you and Annette. You both have relay experience and have been running well."

"And the fourth?" Helen asked.

"I don't know yet. We'll see how Tidye does in the hurdles over the next couple of days. Harriet's been racing well too."

At the mention of Harriet, Helen couldn't stop herself from leaping out of the bed to tower over Dee. "That's not true. Harriet's sick with a cold that she's gotten from not taking care of herself. I know you've been coaching her for years in St. Louis, but she's distracted and not running well. She couldn't even make it out of the preliminary heat of the individual hundred-meter."

Dee's face reddened. "I know Harriet's not your favorite person, Helen, but let's try to be fair here."

"What about Louise?" Betty asked.

Dee's face clouded. "She's a possibility."

Betty persisted. "She's been training hard, and as you know, she went to Los Angeles and didn't get to race there. Olive went to Amsterdam but never competed, but she's been running well too. And they also worked hard to raise their money."

"Betty, feel free to step aside to give one of them the opportunity to race. After all, you've already won two medals." Dee jutted out her chin in challenge. When Betty winced and kept silent, Dee went on. "These women have gotten the opportunity to come. Not everyone will end up racing, but being here is the experience of a lifetime. Do you really think most of these women would have ever traveled to Europe if it wasn't for this? I'm giving them a chance for broadening their horizons, certainly more of a chance than most women will ever get. You two have no idea of the pressure that's on me about these decisions." Dee's voice started to rise. "There's a lot that goes into deciding these relay teams, issues you two know nothing about. For one thing, our German hosts aren't thrilled about how well the Negro men are doing."

"What does that have to do with us?" Helen asked.

"Mr. Brundage is worried about antagonizing our hosts with more successes from colored women, and as you've pointed out, we have a bunch of women who could run in the relay without offending Herr Hitler."

"But why Harriet? How about Olive or Josephine?" Helen grumbled.

"Harriet enlisted some influential sponsors to her cause. I may have to race her to keep everyone happy."

"Well, I can think of at least a couple of people who won't be happy," Helen said. "Listen, running's all I've got. We have to win this. Harriet shouldn't be our fourth."

"I have a long history with Harriet and she's a friend," Dee snapped. "Helen, running *isn't* all you have. Look around. You need to think about what's really important." And with that, she stormed from the room.

Helen blinked. She reached to her bedpost and lifted her gold medal from where she had hung it the previous afternoon. Lying on her palm, it felt heavy and cold, but it glimmered. Wasn't her life supposed to be amazing now that she had won? Instead it felt like she had lost everything.

But had she?

Helen startled as Betty plunked down on the bed to lean against her shoulder. She looked down on the straight part in Betty's golden hair, inhaled her scent of lemon shampoo and damp wool sweater, and felt a knot inside her loosen. Since Harriet had handed her that newspaper article in the dining hall, Helen's mind had barely stopped spinning, but with a start, she realized she had overlooked something important.

None of her teammates had believed the lies. People believed in her.

55.

August 7, 1936
Berlin

C AN YOU TAPE IT INTO MY SHOE?" TIDYE ASKED, HER
face contorted in pain.

Louise stared at Tidye's bare foot. Since the previous day's accident, purple bruising had darkened and the foot had swelled.
Louise lowered to her knees in front of where Tidye sat on her
bed. How was she going to slide a sock over it, much less get her
shoe on?

How had things gone so wrong?

The previous day had started gray with rain forecast for
later in the afternoon, and the women felt fortunate that the
weather was cooperating for the morning's competitions. In
the stadium, Louise awaited Tidye's race while seated next to
Mack in the front row, sunken below the track. He smiled and
his big brown eyes gleamed.

"Winning medals agrees with you, doesn't it?" Louise said,
tucking herself in close to him, not so close that anyone else
would notice, but close enough to feel warm, feel the solidity
of him beside her.

The starting gun fired, and on the track, the women headed
toward the first hurdle and sailed over it.

"I won't deny that I'm enjoying some of the perks that come along with winning." Mack ran a finger along Louise's bare forearm, sending a shiver up her spine. She gave him a wink but her delight was short-lived.

Because she was distracted by Mack, Louise almost missed it: the split second when Tidye's toe didn't quite clear the top of the bar on the third hurdle. In the air, Tidye fought to right herself, to fix the imbalance that catching her toe had caused. Louise held her breath as Tidye raised her arms to the sky as if reaching for something to steady herself, but nothing came to her rescue. Instead she crashed to the cinder. Louise felt her breath catch as Dee and several officials scuttled to where Tidye lay crumpled into a ball.

After Tidye had been carried off the field, she downplayed her injuries and sent away the medical staff that had descended upon her, before waving Louise over. "Help me get out of here without anyone noticing," Tidye gasped.

Without asking questions, Louise and Mack smuggled Tidye out of the stadium and returned her to Friesenhaus.

A day had passed, and judging by the worsened state of her foot, there was no doubt about it: Tidye could not be considered for the relay. Louise lowered the roll of medical tape to the floor. "Do you really want to try this?"

Tidye winced. "I'm out, aren't I?"

"I'm sorry, but I don't see how you can race. You can't even walk."

Tidye covered her face with her hands. "But this was my chance," she wept.

Something in Louise snapped. "You got your chance. It

didn't end the way you wanted, but you had your moment to run and compete. I would give anything for a shot like that. I've come all this way and wanted to race so badly that I can barely stand it. I know your foot is hurting, and you can cry because of the pain, but don't cry because you didn't get a chance. You got it and you should be proud."

Tidye inhaled sharply, but before she could say anything, a knock at the door made them both jump. A voice called out, "Come on out to the lounge. Dee's holding a meeting about the relay."

The sound of feet shuffling away from their door made Tidye sigh. "True, but this sure isn't how I wanted my chance to go."

"Somewhere back in New York, an old AOC bigwig paid money to send you here to represent the United States. They only paid for you and four other women. Don't forget that. And today, thousands of people watched you line up to race wearing a United States team uniform. They all saw you on that track, Tidye."

Tidye sniffled and gave a sheepish smile. "You mean they watched me fall."

"At least you got a chance. That's still something."

"But I felt like if we could win medals, we would really show everyone what we can do."

"I know, but Mack, Jesse, Ralph, and all of the other fellas are showing exactly what Negroes are capable of, but us girls, we've got to stop worrying about the finish line and focus on the starting line. If we can get more of us competing, we'll have more chances to win. Don't you see? We need more of us in the game!"

"I'm sorry. You're right. I know you are." She leaned forward and kissed Louise on the forehead. "Now let's go get you on that starting line."

Louise lifted Tidye from the bed and helped her hobble to the lounge, to one of the few chairs scattered in the room. Once Louise settled her friend, she leaned against the cold white plaster wall, waiting for everyone to convene. She couldn't sit, not with her mind turning over and over with a mess of thoughts. Dee would pick Helen, of that Louise had no doubt. Helen's winning time during the Olympic trial finals in Providence had been 11.7 seconds. None of the other women had broken twelve seconds in any of their runs and most of their times were bunched pretty close together. For the last month, Louise had mentally reviewed all of their results countless times in her head, but she couldn't shake the suspicion that Dee wouldn't rely on past times alone.

Dee entered, last to arrive, and cleared her throat. "Ladies, thank you for all of your hard work over the last few weeks as we've trained and prepared for these Games. I know everyone is hopeful about this relay team. The German women have a strong foursome and they're going to be tough to beat. We need to put out a team with the most experience and speed. Like all of you, I've spent a lot of time thinking about the right racers for this challenge. After a great deal of consideration, I've decided that the team will consist of Helen, Betty, Annette, and Harriet. We don't have much time left, but we'll spend it practicing hand-offs and then I'll decide on racing order."

Murmurs from the women broke out. Louise lowered her face, afraid to see the looks of exuberance on the four who had been selected and anguish on those who hadn't, but Tidye's voice rang out clear and angry. "Why did you bring all of us here, if you were going to stick with a group you've known the longest?"

A low mumble of agreement spread among the eight women and everyone looked at Dee expectantly.

"I'm doing the best I can. I'm sorry."

Harriet pulled a handkerchief from the pocket of her dress and blew her nose. "I know all of you are thinking that I shouldn't be the fourth racer, but the truth is I've been working my tail off. I've earned my spot."

At this, the room erupted into chaos. From her seat, Tidye wagged her finger at Harriet while Helen implored everyone to calm down and Betty and Annette looked like they wanted to disappear. As Dee tried to talk over the shouting, Louise felt her face grow hot. She slipped from the room.

Twice. Twice she had made it this far only to be denied competition. Why had she done this to herself again? If the AOC was willing to let Helen Stephens, its fastest racer, suffer the indignity of being branded a fraud by the Poles, what made her think she would have anyone fighting for her? She marched outdoors into the Friesenhaus's garden. Maybe she would leave, keep walking, go find Mack, and never return to her team-mates, but as she stepped outside onto the warm paving stones of the courtyard, she heard someone calling her name.

"Louise? Wait!"

She turned to see Olive hurrying toward her.

"This is the worst, huh?" Olive asked. She pulled a silver flask from the cardigan of her navy-blue sweater and held it out. "Want to take the edge off?"

Louise waved it away. She didn't want to take the edge off. She wanted to feel every ounce of her anger because she'd have to push it all down and go out before the public to support her team. "I'm mad at myself for believing there was a chance it would work out differently. When I started running as a girl, I loved the feeling of being fast and powerful, but over the years it became about . . . about so many other things." She had run because of guilt, because of promises she made, because it felt like the only opportunity available to her.

"We've been at this for a long time. Remember when that girl cheated us out of a first-place finish during a time trial? Was that in Malden or Medford? That was a long time ago."

Louise felt her throat thicken, her chest heat in anger. "And here we are, eight years later, being disappointed again."

"Dee's never been one of my favorites. I was only fifteen when we went to Amsterdam, and she was never very friendly. Poor Betty actually had to room with her the whole time. Still, I was glad when a woman was given the job to coach us. And it's not like she's getting a fair shake, working and dealing with all of this pressure without even getting paid." Olive gave Louise a knowing look. "There's controversy on the men's relay team too. Marty Glickman and Sam Stoller have been bumped off the roster to make room for Ralph and Jesse, but everyone is saying it's politically motivated because Marty and Sam are Jewish." She gave a weary shake of her head. "This whole thing can be heartbreaking, but it's all I know. Do you think you'll keep doing it?"

It's all I know.

Louise peered past the walls of the courtyard. Was running all she knew?

56.

August 9, 1936
Berlin

SUNDAY, THE DAY OF THE RELAY FINAL, BEGAN WITH the air heavy with the metallic smell of rain. The dampness made Betty's back ache and her knees stiff. In her bed, she waited for dawn, staring at the ceiling. When Dee had announced the relay team, Betty felt sure that every woman in that room knew she wasn't the best pick. Everyone had piled on Harriet, but didn't they remember that in Providence, Betty had barely made the cut? The other women accused Dee of playing favorites with Harriet, but wasn't that impulse behind her selection of Betty too?

What if everyone pitied her too much to criticize her?

Or worse, what if she was put on the team out of pity?

A sickening sense of fear descended upon her. What if she caused them to lose?

"What's wrong?"

Betty rolled to her side to see Helen watching her. "I shouldn't be running today," Betty confessed. "I wish Dee had picked someone else, one of the girls who doesn't have any health problems like mine. We're going to need every tenth of a second we can get. Why, those German women set a new world record yesterday during preliminaries! Who knows what they'll pull off today?"

"Maybe they'll be overconfident. Come on, get up. All we can do is run the best race we can." Helen clambered out of her bed and started dressing in her team tracksuit.

Betty sat and tugged at the curlers in her hair. If only she had Helen's unshakable confidence in her ability to win. "You don't even want to do this race."

"True, I haven't wanted to run this one." Helen pulled on her sweatshirt and then sat down on the edge of her bed across from Betty. "The relay's always felt stressful. The idea of relying on others or being responsible for anyone else frightens me. I've been on my own for so long. It's easier to just focus on my running, not have to worry about anyone else. I don't want to disappoint anyone."

Betty stared at Helen. She'd always assumed Helen's reluctance to embrace the relay lay more in her lack of confidence in her teammates. "What do you mean? How would you disappoint anyone? You've been winning everything easily."

"I've always been a disappointment to everyone. For as long as I can remember, things with my own family have been difficult, and I've never really had good friends. It wasn't until Coach Moore came along that I had someone who believed in me. But even with all of the success I've had since I started running, I've felt like a phony, like it was just a matter of time before everyone saw me as the awkward, disappointing person I've always been."

"But that's horrible. Surely you don't really mean that?"

"Betty, when you've spent most of your life being told that you're not wanted, that you're ugly and a freak, you start to believe it, and believing those things can be a hard habit to break. So the other evening, when Harriet showed up in the dining hall waving that horrid newspaper around, I felt like the jig was up. Everyone would finally see the truth about me."

"But those were all lies."

"Yeah, but the accusations of me being an imposter felt all too true."

"All of our teammates knew those were lies."

"I know, that was the most amazing thing. I didn't expect everyone to react that way. People have been treating me poorly for most of my life. It wasn't until I started running that people began to pay attention to me. I mean, pay attention in a good way. I went from being an outcast at school to having Fulton throw a holiday in my honor, and it's felt too good to be true, like it's just a matter of time before my life takes a turn for the worse again. I've been so afraid to lose because it's felt like if I keep winning, people will continue to like me. But I don't think that's the case now." Helen smiled. "Do you remember back when we met in Chicago and you asked me to run the relay with you?"

"Of course."

"Well, when I couldn't carry that baton to save my life, you told me I could do it. Your confidence in me meant a lot and it worked. Now I want to do the same for you. I want to run this relay today. We can do this."

Betty blinked back tears, tossed her curlers on the bedspread, and rose to embrace her friend. Enveloped in Helen's strong arms, Betty felt safe, ready to try anything. "Thank you."

Helen pulled back and looked down into Betty's face. "You're feeling better?"

"I am." And she was.

"I'm off for my final massage on my shins. The doc used some cream yesterday that felt wonderful, and I'm hoping they use it again on me."

"Today is the day to break out the best stuff."

Helen nodded and laughed and—again—embraced Betty tightly. Nestled into Helen's thick sweatshirt, Betty sighed a little and blinked back unbidden tears. She knew what Helen meant about feeling like an imposter. She could relate. Despite her past successes, she feared she would be the slowest woman on the track during the relay. But even more worrisome, what would she do *after* this race? The last eight years of her life had been focused on running and then recovering her health. What would happen when all the pageantry and special treatment of Berlin was over? Would she return to her quiet life of living with her parents, being a secretary in the architecture firm? Without the Olympics in her future, what lay ahead?

"Are you crying? I thought you were feeling better!" Helen said, rubbing Betty's back.

"Oh, I'm just being sentimental." Betty stepped back and wiped at her eyes. "This is my last Olympics. I'm sad that it's almost over."

"Me too. I'm surprised by how attached I feel to our sister-hood of athletes," Helen said, shaking her head. "But it's not over yet. We have one final thing to do! What do you say? Are you ready?"

"Of course," Betty said firmly. "You go. I'll dress and get something to eat. Meet you in the dining hall in an hour or so?"

"I'll head there as soon as I'm done," Helen called as she opened the door and left.

Alone, Betty crossed her arms over her thin nightgown and surveyed their little room. The smell of fresh paint still clung to the walls, but also there was the earthy scent of damp clothes. Helen's medal gleamed where it hung from her bedpost. Betty bent over, groaning as her back cracked, but she lifted it and put the medal around her neck. Did she regret selling her own medals? Was all this effort and sacrifice going to be worth it?

With shaking hands, she removed the medal from her neck and returned it to Helen's bed before slowly dressing in her white team skirt and navy-blue blazer. She glanced at her wristwatch. Only a couple of minutes had passed. She couldn't imagine going to the noisy dining hall and making small talk for the next hour. And anyway, she wasn't hungry.

After fixing her hair, she laid out a game of solitaire on her bed to keep herself occupied. She'd play a hand or two, collect her thoughts, and then go get something to eat. But after several minutes of staring at her cards, she swept them into a pile and leaned back against the bed's wooden headboard. She closed her eyes and tried to summon her memory of Amsterdam, the sensation of crossing the finish line in first place. She needed to calm down.

Instead, she was taken back to Wilson's plane, the moment

when the engine stopped. She had known something terrible had gone wrong, but for a second, she had been overwhelmed by the beauty of her surroundings. The quiet. How the lake had shimmered in the distance, blue and clear. How the world below them—the buildings, cars, streets—had all been miniaturized and the land reduced to its most basic shapes. It had been peaceful and perfect—before terror had set in. Or maybe it had been terror that provided the sharp contrast in perspective, that beautiful tipping point between moving forward and falling, between daringly risky and fatal. She pulled herself off the headboard and sat, her face in her hands. Why was she thinking about this now? How was this supposed to help her?

She swung her feet off the bed and stood to look outside the window. The sky was growing darker with impending rain.

"Betty?"

She turned to see Annette in the doorway, holding a telegram out to her. "I'm on my way back from the mailroom, but I wanted to drop this off for you."

"Thank you," Betty said. She unfolded it.

The Western Union Telegraph Company

Received at Berlin, Germany   1936 Aug 9   8:09 AM

GOOD LUCK IN TODAY'S BIG RACE. ALL OF YOUR NORTH-WESTERN TRACK TEAMMATES ARE CHEERING YOU ON. I HAVE YOUR 1928 GOLD AND SILVER MEDALS SAFE AND SOUND FOR WHEN YOU RETURN. BEST WISHES, BILL RIEL.

She read the telegram several times, her eyes blurring with tears.

Bill bought her medals from Jim?

"Is everything all right?" Annette asked, still standing in the doorway, watching her.

"Yes, I've received surprising news from an old friend."

"Good news?"

"Great news, actually." Betty couldn't stop staring at the telegram.

"I'm so glad. Do you need anything?"

"No, no, you should go get ready for our race."

Annette left, and Betty packed her uniform and shoes into her track bag, double-checking that she had included the correct shoes. She had survived a plane crash and overcome the odds to return to the Olympics. What was she so worried about? Before she left for the dining hall, she tucked the telegram into her bag with a steady hand. She had everything and didn't need any good luck charms, but she'd bring it anyway.

57.

August 9, 1936
Berlin

HELEN TOOK HER PLACE AT THE FINAL LEG OF THE RE-lay and hopped up and down, shaking out her arms and legs, trying to stay loose. Red flags marred with swastikas filled the air and the cheers of the crowd were deafening.

When Helen had run the individual 100-meter, she'd felt antsy and preoccupied. She had wanted to absorb the significance of the moment and couldn't, but this time on the track felt different. Helen tented her hand over her brow, looking toward the other end of the track. There stood Annette, looking serious but calm. Even Harriet, across the track at the start, seemed immune to the crowd. She gave Helen a small wave and then went about the business of checking her starting position.

Helen glanced across the curve in the track and found Betty smiling at her. It felt right that she'd be the one passing off the baton to Helen. They'd proven to be a good pairing. This time, Helen wouldn't wait for Betty to collide with her. She knew to start gently, put her hand out, and trust that the baton would be there.

An unexpected sense of love and of solidarity with these

women and all that they had gone through to get there filled Helen.

No matter what happened next, this was their team.

At the starting area, the official took his spot and raised his gun to the sky. The women dropped to crouches. The starting commands echoed throughout the stadium. The gun fired.

The racers moved so quickly. Despite her irresponsible behavior over the last few weeks, Harriet ran effortlessly and passed the baton to Annette, who moved down her straightaway with ease. When the pack clustered around the second hand-off, the Germans took the lead and a sense of urgency buzzed through the stadium. Marie Dollinger surged ahead. Betty's face strained with effort and concentration as she chased the German, but she wasn't going to be able to close the distance. Every fiber of Helen's body came alive with the electricity of the challenge that was becoming more real with every split second. This would be the race of her life!

Beside her, Helen sensed Ilse Dörffeldt tighten. The German woman pranced in place like an impatient Thoroughbred. Despite the frenetic energy surrounding her, Helen took a deep inhalation and let out a slow exhalation. Though her heart was banging against her rib cage, she felt eerily calm.

It contradicted her every instinct, but Helen turned away from Betty to focus on the finish line. She couldn't look back, only forward. She needed to trust Betty. Feeling the air around her hum with the power of the crowd's anticipation, she waited. *Please come, please come now,* she thought. Her knees trembled.

"Up!"

Betty's voice rang out above the chaos clearly and there was no time for relief, just action. Helen reached backward, felt the smooth wood of the baton against her palm, and grasped it.

Behind her, a commotion filled the air, a wail of agony.

Helen resisted the urge to look behind her, to see what had happened.

Instead she ran.

LOUISE HELD HER breath as Tidye's hand clamped around her forearm. On her other side, Mack let out a low whistle of amazement.

They all watched as Helen ran along the final straightaway as if the baton in her hand were a lit stick of dynamite.

She crossed the finish in first place. *First place!*

But instead of cheering, the stadium fell silent, all attention affixed to the spectacle unfolding in the spot where Marie had handed the baton to Ilse and she had dropped it.

Ilse Dörffeldt had fallen to the track and was now crawling after the baton, still rolling along the cinder. It reached the rim of the outmost lane and stopped. Ilse grasped it, but it was too late. The race was over. The British, Canadians, Italians, and Dutch had all followed Helen over the finish line.

In a stadium filled with tens of thousands of people, it felt like everyone was holding their breath.

But then, like a conductor, Helen raised her hands in victory, and it was as if everyone let out a collective exhalation. Yelling and screaming resumed.

Betty, Annette, and Harriet arrived from their different corners of the track and collapsed upon Helen.

Mack nudged Louise and she glanced over to Hitler's special

viewing box. The man had leapt to his feet and stared at the track, his expression aghast. Ilse raised her gaze to look at him and he shook his head, irritated, and smacked his black gloves against his thigh before turning to disappear from his box.

The next few minutes of arranging the top three teams on the medals podium happened quickly. Against a stormy sky, the American flag rose while the opening notes of the national anthem soared over the stands, drowning out the feverish conversations surrounding Louise. Even after all that had happened, the anthem still made her vision swim with tears. Though this country had betrayed her in so many ways, she couldn't bring herself to reject it. Its promise still had the power to stir something powerful in her.

Betty raised her gold medal to the crowd, her eyes shining with joy and relief. Annette sang and Harriet smiled widely for a photographer crouched in front of them. But out of everyone, it was Helen who mesmerized Louise. For once, Helen was oblivious to the raucous cheering and the cameras and appeared satisfied to simply be surrounded by her teammates, as if that was all she had ever needed.

Over the loudspeaker, the announcer reeled off the standings and final times for each team. The crowd boomed with excitement, but the numbers meant nothing to Louise. It wasn't the finish line that interested her.

She looked toward the sky where the Olympic flag flapped in the brisk wind. Mack, Jesse, and the men had been setting records and winning medals, and though she was proud of them, a flash of impatience filled her. Beyond the stadium was a whole world filled with girls who had no idea how fast they could run if given the chance. Louise nudged Tidye and bent toward her friend's ear, yelling to be heard over the din. "Someday they won't be able to stop us girls."

Tidye nodded, giving a rueful smile, and wrapped her arm around Louise's waist.

Afterword

BECAUSE OF WORLD WAR II AND ITS AFTERMATH, AN-other Olympics would not be held until 1948.

What became of these fast girls . . .

Betty Robinson

Settling back into a regular life after the excitement of the Olympics proved to be a little bumpy for Betty. She returned from Chicago and found herself in a whirlwind romance that resulted in a brief marriage, but it was annulled. Soon after, she married a man who had first spotted her in 1931, when she had arrived at a Northwestern football game in a wheelchair while convalescing from her plane crash. From a distance, he had fallen in love with Betty, and he sought her out when she returned home in 1936. Eventually she became a mother of two. She kept her Olympic medals in a Russell Stover candy box, only to break them out to give motivational lectures throughout the Chicago area. Occasionally she would meet for lunch with Jesse Owens and his family.

Betty and her husband moved around the country several times before settling in Colorado. At the age of eighty-four, approximately three years before her death, Betty celebrated the upcoming 1996 Atlanta Olympics by running in the official torch relay through Denver with her family.

She remained close friends with Helen for the rest of her life.

There are historical events that I moved or compressed for the sake of a smooth narrative, and the most significant change that I made was to set Betty's plane crash in 1932, though it actually occurred a year earlier, in June 1931. Betty's fiancé, Bill Riel, is a fictional character based on her college boyfriend who was a university football, basketball, and tennis star. Though Betty sold many of her Olympic prizes to pay her way to Berlin, she held on to her medals.

Helen Stephens

Helen's 1936 Olympic record in the 100-meter sprint remained in place until Wilma Rudolph beat it in the 1960 Olympics in Rome.

Despite Helen's undeniable athletic success, there was no clear path for her to follow when she returned from the Berlin Olympics and tried to make a living as an athlete. Severe AAU rules regulated retaining amateur athlete status and limited the options for many young Olympians to capitalize on their skills and experience, and for a woman, the possibilities for turning professional and snagging endorsement deals were practically nonexistent. Although it made for a rocky existence, Helen forged her own way working odd jobs, playing basketball and softball, and bowling. She even owned and managed a semiprofessional basketball team, making her the first woman to do so.

During the last few months of World War II, Helen enlisted

in the Women's Reserve of the U.S. Marine Corps, but was never deployed, and later worked as a reference librarian for many years. She also fell in love and spent her life with a long-term partner, but fearing discrimination, she never made her homosexuality public.

Helen dedicated herself to promoting women's athletics. Over the decades, she remained in touch with many of her friends from the Olympics, including Betty, Harriet, Stella, and Dee, and she ran in exhibition and masters races. An early member of the National Track and Field Hall of Fame, she worked tirelessly to have many of her teammates inducted as well, and served as an activist and coach working on behalf of women athletes until her death in 1994.

In Helen's obituary, *The New York Times* described her as "one of the great female athletes of her day," a feat made that much more remarkable for the challenges she had to overcome. Frank Stephens did little to support Helen's educational and athletic successes; while not as blatantly cruel as I portrayed him, he was distant and made his dissatisfaction with his lot in life plain for all to see. It's true that she was assaulted by a sixteen-year-old cousin when she was in fourth grade and later experienced a sexual encounter with a visiting teacher.

Louise Stokes

Upon her return from Berlin, Malden honored Louise with a parade. Soon after, she married a professional cricket player and had a son. Though she stopped running, she continued to pursue her love of athletics and took up bowling. She founded the Colored Women's Bowling League, thereby creating an opportunity for more black women to compete, and over the next several decades, she won many awards. After Louise died in 1978, a statue was erected in the courtyard of Malden High School to commemorate her athletic accomplishments.

Of all the main characters in this novel, I knew the least about the real-life Louise Stokes. Aside from a few newspaper articles and mentions in books, there was very little historical data about her, so I filled in the gaps of the lives of Louise, her mother, and her sisters through researching the lives of black women in Massachusetts during this period. Uncle Freddie is a character of my own creation.

Tidye Pickett

Tidye returned home to Chicago and worked her way through college and graduate school. She married and raised three children. She became an educator and then served as a principal at an elementary school for over twenty years. Upon her retirement, the school honored the former Olympian by naming itself after her. She passed away in 1986.

Louise and Tidye have gone largely unrecognized for many decades, but their perseverance in the face of racial and gender discrimination in the 1932 and 1936 Olympics paved the way for Audrey Patterson, a black woman from Louisiana, to win an Olympic medal when she finished third in the 200-meter sprint in London in 1948. A day later, Alice Coachman, a high jumper, became the first black American woman to win an Olympic gold medal.

Stella Walsh

Despite Stella's adoption of Polish citizenship, she never settled into European society and she spent the rest of her life living in Ohio, though the American press consistently belittled her athletic accomplishments despite the fact that she went on to set records and win races for many more years.

On the eve of the Melbourne Olympics, at the age of forty-five, she married in Las Vegas, but with her American citizenship finally complete through marriage, she fell short of qualifying at the Olympic trials and announced her retirement.

In 1980, seventy-nine-year-old Stella was shot in the chest during a random mugging in the parking lot of a convenience store in Cleveland. She died immediately. Later, her autopsy revealed that she was intersex. This finding confirmed what her closest friends had long suspected, but it was a bombshell to the rest of the world. The discovery led some officials and athletes to demand that her medals and records be rescinded, but there was never a decisive ruling on the case.

Caroline Hale Woodson

This character is based on several Olympians from this era: Evelyne Hall, Evelyn Furtsch, Kay Maguire, Simone Schaller, Jean Shiley, Anne Vrana O'Brien, and Maybelle Reichardt.

Dee Boeckmann

For Dee, the Berlin Olympics marked the beginning of a long trailblazing career in coaching, teaching, and athletic administration that took her all over the world. During World War II, she worked in China with the American Red Cross. She became coach to Japan's national women's track and field team and served as a director for the 1964 Olympics. She was inducted into the National Track and Field Hall of Fame in 1976. When she passed away in 1989, she was spending her final days in Creve Coeur, Missouri.

Olive Hasenfus

Though Olive traveled to the Olympics in 1928 and 1936 but never raced, she returned home with a medal she won during an exhibition race in Germany after the Berlin Games. Her talent and persistence also inspired her two brothers to be her teammates and compete in canoeing at the Berlin Olympics.

After 1936, she married, started a family, and continued to support women's athletics by serving as an official and referee of sporting events. Whenever anyone argued that athletics could harm a woman's fertility, Olive would refute the point by cheerfully listing all of her titles and records from over the years and then pointing to her three healthy children.

Babe Didrikson

Babe led a long, storied career as both an amateur and professional athlete and competed in everything from billiards to tennis to basketball to swimming. Her competitive spirit wasn't limited to only athletics. She gave exhibitions in needlepoint and often boasted that she could type eighty-six words a minute.

In 1934, she even pitched several innings in three different Major League Baseball professional exhibition games, but golf became her passion. After only three years of playing it, Babe competed against a field of all men in the 1938 Los Angeles Open, a PGA event. She went on to dominate the world of golf, setting many records that still stand, both as an amateur and a professional, and became a founding member of the Ladies Professional Golf Association (LPGA).

Babe married one of her early golfing partners, George Zaharias, but after a dozen years, she began a relationship with Betty Dodd, another professional golfer. Dodd moved in with Babe and George and lived with them for the last six years of Babe's life.

In 1956, competing and winning significant golf tournaments and working to raise cancer awareness right up to the end of her life, Babe succumbed to colon cancer at the age of forty-two.

In her *New York Times* obituary, it was noted that though she had once greeted opponents with taunts about beating them, as she aged, she began encouraging and supporting other young women on the golfing circuit.

Acknowledgments

THIS BOOK WOULD NEVER HAVE REACHED THE FINISH line without a fantastic group of teammates, coaches, and fans. Librarians and archivists played a critical role in helping me locate information about the women in this story. Thank you to Marge Loitz of the Village of Thornton Historical Society, Lily Mysona of the Malden Public Library, Kevin Leonard at Northwestern University Library, Kristi Sievert at William Woods University, and Tatyana Shinn, Laura Jolley, Heather Richmond, and Elizabeth Engel at the Columbia Research Center of the State Historical Society of Missouri in Columbia.

I'm sure it's strange to see a familiar beloved figure fictionalized, and I appreciate the goodwill the families and friends of these women have extended toward me. A heartfelt thank-you to Sharon Kinney Hanson, Brook Doire, and Amy Hicks for their passion and firsthand knowledge about these pioneering women track stars. I'm also grateful to Glenn Stout for championing Louise Stokes and generously sharing his research with me.

This story's success relied upon the trusty counsel of early readers. Kerri Maher, S. J. Sindu, Jenni L. Walsh, Nyamekye Waliyaya, and Kelleen Cummings—thank you very much for your time, insight, and encouragement. I'm also thankful for

Keely Platte, Madison Ostrander, and Crystal Patriarche at Booksparks.

My agent, Barbara Braun, read many early drafts of this novel, and her thoughtful feedback and support have been invaluable. My brilliant editor, Lucia Macro, saw the potential in Betty, Helen, and Louise from the first moment I mentioned them, and her wise advice and guidance has made all the difference. I'm forever indebted to the amazing team at William Morrow—Liate Stehlik, Molly Waxman, Asanté Simons, Jessica Lyons, Jennifer Hart, Rachel Meyers, Owen Corrigan, Lainey Mays, and Virginia Stanley.

My friends and family have been the best cheering squad, and I feel fortunate every day for their love. Dave, Kate, and Cookie, you are my gold medals—thank you.

About the author

2 Meet Elise Hooper

About the book

3 A Conversation with Elise Hooper

12 A Note on Sources

Insights,
Interviews
& More . . .

Meet Elise Hooper

Chris Landry Photography

A native New Englander, Elise spent several years writing for television and online news outlets before getting an M.A. and teaching high school literature and history. She now lives in Seattle with her husband and two daughters. Previous novels include *The Other Alcott* and *Learning to See.* ✒

A Conversation
with Elise Hooper

**Q: *How did you discover this story about
Betty, Helen, and Louise?***

A: When my younger daughter, an avid
swimmer, was in fourth grade, she chose
Gertrude Ederle for a biography report.
Do you know who Ederle is? I didn't.
She was a teenager from Manhattan
who won several Olympic medals in
1924 and became the first woman to
swim the English Channel. Ederle's
story intrigued me and led me to wonder
about the stories of pioneering women
athletes.

I should back up here and explain
something else. When I was seven years
old, I went to the Ice Capades at the
Boston Garden and became captivated
by Peggy Fleming. My family and
I hadn't even made it to the parking
lot before I was begging to take ice-
skating lessons and setting my sights
on becoming an Olympic figure skater.
It took me several years and many hours
of practice in a nearby rink to figure
out a heartbreaking truth: I was too
tall to be an ice skater. (There were
other reasons I wasn't destined to
become an Olympian, but let's just go
with the height issue.) Though I hung ▶

3

A Conversation with Elise Hooper
(continued)

up my ice skates, I never quite let go of my Olympic ambitions. I started running, skiing, and playing field hockey and tennis. Each time I picked up a new sport, I fantasized about going to the Olympics, but the hope became a little more distant. During my midtwenties, I set myself to fulfilling another longtime dream, qualifying for the Boston Marathon, and I ran it in 2001. Over a decade later, I played on tennis teams that made it to the finals of the USTA League National Championships—twice. Still, none of these accomplishments was anything close to the Olympics.

It was at this point, sitting on my living room couch and reading about women Olympians, that my forty-year-old self decided that my best shot at going to the Olympics would be through writing a novel about athletes. Through my research, I came across the story of Betty Robinson and couldn't believe I'd never heard of this woman. Running was a world I understood. Soon I found Helen, Louise, Tidye, and all of these other early Olympians and knew in my gut that I'd found the subject of my new novel. I would get to the Olympics after all—three of them, in fact—just not the way I'd imagined as a kid. But that was okay. Life is full of surprises.

Q: Why did you choose to write this book as a novel instead of a history?

A: Let me be clear about something: I'm a novelist, not a historian. Historical figures and events inspire my imagination to go to work creating and developing characters and putting them into action. For me, real life is a jumping-off point for creativity. When I started telling people that I was working on a book about women Olympians from 1936, I tended to be met with looks of confusion. "I didn't realize women were even in the Olympics back then," friends would say. That was all the confirmation I needed that this book was a good idea, so I decided to make it my mission to introduce readers to these women Olympians and their amazing stories, but the historical record contains many gaps and inconsistencies because their experiences and accomplishments weren't taken very seriously and documented. I used old newspapers to piece together what happened, along with several biographies and documentaries on these athletes. All the unknowns made for a fertile landscape to craft a novel.

For example, aside from general biographical information, little can be found about Louise's life. When I first ▶

A Conversation with Elise Hooper
(*continued*)

started reading about her hometown of Malden, Massachusetts, I discovered that the town has a World War I monument, erected in 1920, but in 2017, historians determined that the list of names on the commemorative plaque was incomplete, and a movement got under way to create a new monument to recognize all the veterans who had been left off—African Americans, women, and others. Reading about this monument led me to create the Uncle Freddie character and imagine the challenges that a young Louise would face.

Q: So what changes did you make from the real history of these women?

A: Aside from the timing of Betty's plane crash and the very little I could find about Louise's life, I followed the biographical milestones of these real women's lives and used them to create scenes, imagining the dialogue and the inner lives of these characters. People from this generation didn't tend to talk about their feelings, so I had to imagine what they felt about most of their victories and disappointments.

One of the most complicated sections of this story to figure out was how the women's relay team was selected for the 1932 Olympics. The accounts of what happened at the Brown Palace Hotel, the encounter with Babe Didrikson on the train, and the existence of the NAACP's telegram to the women's track and field coaching staff were confirmed by numerous sources, and all of these incidents led me to believe that racism played a forceful role in deciding which four women would run in the relay. The fact that many of the team portraits in Los Angeles did not include Louise and Tidye supported this view. By studying old reports, newspaper accounts, and photos and employing common sense, I was able to assemble a theory about how the Olympic Committee approached selecting the women's relay team. In short, its process was inconsistent, subject to political influence, and beset by racism and gender discrimination.

Without twenty-four-hour television news and social media, people in the 1920s and 1930s were not always as aware of what was happening beyond their local community, so my portrayal of Betty as an advocate for women athletes following the 1928 Olympics is exaggerated, but I wanted to depict the debate that was happening firsthand through a character. Similarly, news of the potential boycott of the Berlin Olympics was widespread, but unlike Jesse Owens, none of these women went on the record to describe their position on the topic, so I did my best to show ▶

A Conversation with Elise Hooper
(continued)

the range of feelings the athletes might have felt about the prospect of not competing. Of all the women, Helen was the most knowledgeable about the topic and had read *Mein Kampf* prior to visiting Germany. The language of the boycott letters included in this novel is quoted from the original one she collected during her travels in 1936.

Unfortunately, historical events don't always happen in the order that best suits a novelist's desire for a perfect story arc, so I altered the timing of some events to fit within a tighter narrative of braiding three characters' journeys together. As mentioned earlier, I moved Betty's plane crash up a year to escalate the drama leading to the 1932 Olympics. Additionally, the 1936 party on Pfaueninsel Island happened at the close of the Olympics, but I moved it to the opening to build dramatic tension about the risks these women faced and to end the story with the excitement of the final relay race. To the best of my knowledge, Ruth Haslie had no Jewish heritage, but I wanted to bring the issue of the threat Nazis posed to German Jewry closer to the American athletes. The scene during which Helen met Hitler is based on their real encounter, detailed in Helen's Olympic diary and described to her biographer, but his parting warning to Helen to be careful is fictional.

Adolf Hitler requested to meet with Helen Stephens after she won the 100-meter sprint at the 1936 Olympics. (*William Woods University Records [CA6180], The State Historical Society of Missouri, Manuscript Collection*)

Q: *Can you describe your research process?*

A: I always start off by reading everything I can find on a topic: books, academic and journalistic articles, newspapers—all of it. I take notes and start imagining my characters and their journeys. Librarians, historical society archivists, and journalists emailed me scanned yearbook pages and hard-to-find old ▸

A Conversation with Elise Hooper
(continued)

newspaper stories, the primary
sources that helped me flesh out these
characters. I also traveled to the places
that shaped these women. Reading
Helen's handwritten diary and holding
her old track shoes, finding the
train tracks that Louise first ran on
(now almost completely paved over
in a strip mall's parking lot!)—all of
these things provided details and
sensory experiences that felt critical
to writing this story.

Old newspapers helped me understand
the people and events of the times, both
big and small, and also to get an ear
for the language and gossipy tone of
the 1920s and '30s so I could write the
newspaper articles, letters, and telegrams
in this novel.

The 1936 women's track and field team aboard
the S.S. *Manhattan*, en route to Berlin, July 1936.
Standing (*left to right*): Fred Steers (manager),
Martha Worst, Annette Rogers, Kathlyn Kelley,
Gertrude Wilhelmsen, Louise Stokes, Elizabeth
Robinson, Dee Boeckmann (coach). Kneeling:
Evelyn Ferrara, Helen Stephens, Harriet Bland,
Alice Arden. Sitting: Tidye Pickett, Simone
Schaller, Josephine Warren, Olive Hasenfus,
Betty Burch. Missing: Anne Vrana O'Brien,
Katherine Dunnette (chaperone). (*Helen
Stephens Collection [C3552], The State Historical
Society of Missouri, Manuscript Collection*) ❧

A Note on Sources

I must have read through hundreds of articles on Newspapers.com to help me flesh out this novel. This website allowed me to access stories from all over the country dating back to the 1920s and '30s and read about everything from FDR's political rallies in Chicago to the women competing in rolling pin throwing contests outside of Boston.

The oral histories at LA84.org should be read by anyone with an interest in Olympic history. I paid special attention to those by Evelyne Hall Adams, Maybelle Reichardt Hopkins, Simone Schaller Kirin, Jean Shiley Newhouse, Anne Vrana O'Brien, and Evelyn Furtsch Ojeda to help me build my imagined world of Olympians. The official Olympic reports of 1928, 1932, and 1936 offer photos, maps, engineering plans, and very detailed accounts of everything related to these Olympics.

I also read the following books and highly recommend all of these to better understand the women who inspired *Fast Girls* and the times in which they lived:

Berlin 1936: Sixteen Days in August, by
    Oliver Hilmes
*Black American Women in Olympic Track
    and Field,* by Michael D. Davis

Fire on the Track: Betty Robinson and the Triumph of the Early Olympic Women, by Roseanne Montillo

The First Lady of Olympic Track: The Life and Times of Betty Robinson, by Joe Gergen

The Forgotten Legacy of Stella Walsh: The Greatest Female Athlete of Her Time, by Sheldon Anderson

The Life of Helen Stephens: The Fulton Flash, by Sharon Kinney Hanson

Nazi Games: The Olympics of 1936, by David Clay Large

A Proper Spectacle: Women Olympians, 1900–1936, by Stephanie Daniels and Anita Tedder

Their Day in the Sun: Women of the 1932 Olympics, by Doris H. Pieroth

Yes, She Can! Women's Sports Pioneers, by Glenn Stout

And last but certainly not least, there are several amazing documentaries on this subject, including *Olympic Pride, American Prejudice.* This film can be easily accessed through multiple video streaming sites and covers the contributions of African American athletes during the 1936 Olympics. I also recommend PBS's *The Nazi Games: Berlin 1936,* and of course, *Olympia,* by Nazi propagandist Leni Riefenstahl, serves as a haunting visual primary source on the Berlin Olympics. ∾